Peyton's
PLAYLIST

JESSICA L. RUSSELL

PEYTON'S PLAYLIST

Copyright © 2021 Jessica L. Russell

Cover Design & Formatting: Dark Water Covers

TRIGGER WARNING

This book contains scenes that include sexual assault, trauma, PTSD, panic attacks, alcohol abuse, short descriptions of domestic violence, minor discussions of child abuse, and parents not accepting their daughter because she is a lesbian. Please ***do not*** read this book if you don't think it's right for you.

READER DISCRETION IS ADVISED.

This book is dedicated to everyone out there who has ever taken care of a loved one who was, or still is, struggling with an addiction and/or alcoholism.
You are not alone.

PROLOGUE

"Memories" // Maroon 5

August 2019 – Paris, France

As I stand in the Musee d'Orsay staring up at Vincent Van Gogh's famous *Starry Night Over the Rhone,* I can't help but think of how much my mother would have loved it here. How she'd have reveled in all the paintings and drawings and sculptures. How much she would have loved being here with me, showing me every piece.

I didn't get to come here with my mother. But I am here now.

I look back on how much my life has changed over the past few months, at just how far I've come.

From the time I saw my mother standing in that blue dress I loved so much, looking happier than I've ever seen her.

The days I'd spent sitting with my father as he lay in the hospital bed with nothing but the sound of the heart monitor keeping me company.

From that night when I felt the icy sting of the cork screw pierce my thighs, slicing them open, and the overwhelming fear I'd felt afterwards not knowing what was going to happen next.

I blink hard as a single tear rolls down my cheek, remembering how lost and alone I was. How detached and broken I'd felt. How isolated and incomplete I'd become.

My scars became the thing that defined me. Two ugly, jagged lines that ran across my thighs that no one could touch, and therefore, no one could touch me.

I was so distant from everyone. I'd become a ghost of the person I used to be. I'd built a wall around myself so high I never thought I'd let anyone in.

But never in a million years did I expect what happened to me four months ago. I never knew one person could split open everything I ever knew about myself, and change my world so completely that now, I am in Paris, crying in front of a Van Gogh painting.

1

"Manic Monday" // The Bangles

April 2019 – New York, USA

"**P**eyton, *to the pharmacy for customer assistance! Peyton, to the pharmacy for customer assistance!*"

My name rings out through the speaker system as I sit on the toilet, rolling my eyes. "Fuck me."

I told you I had to pee. I can't get three minutes to empty my bladder?

I hurry to get through my bathroom break and make my way to the register at the pharmacy, where a line of people now wait before me.

I glance back at Emily who is standing behind the pharmacy counter, carefully filling an orange plastic prescription bottle with round yellow pills. "Where's Sydney? Why isn't she covering for me?" I ask.

Emily doesn't meet my gaze as she guides each pill into the bottle, mindful not to drop any. "She said there was some

3

mistake with the truck shipment. She had to take care of it right away."

I roll my eyes even harder. "It couldn't wait two freaking minutes so I could pee?" I whisper. Emily chuckles and dumps the pills back into the automatic pill counter to make sure she has the right number of tablets.

I love my boss, I really do, but sometimes, Sydney can be so melodramatic.

I scan the store around me, putting on my best customer service smile, and call the first person in line. "How can I help you?"

The customer tells me their name, and I turn behind me to the hanging bags—hung alphabetically, by last name—each one filled with bottles or boxes or tubes of medications and the paperwork that goes with them, and search under B for Becker. I do this repeatedly for the next twenty minutes because Mondays are the worst.

Most people had done all their grocery shopping and errands over the weekend, so working at a store on a Monday morning is quite possibly the most boring job ever.

Unless that store is also a pharmacy.

People who'd waited all weekend to get through to their doctors about needing a refill or new prescription, now wait for the people working in the pharmacy to fill it. And most people are nice enough about it. The people who need something simple—like antibiotics for an ear infection—wait patiently enough.

But every now and then, we'll get one asshole who'll try to get his painkillers, or anxiety medication filled on a Friday— even though it's not due to be filled until the following Monday.

As a person with personal experience with anxiety medicine, I don't get why it's so hard for some people to understand: the pharmacy cannot legally fill a controlled substance early. Unless given specific permission by the patients' doctor, and even then, New York state can red flag it and tell us not to fill it until a specific date. It's not the pharmacist's fault, or the technician's fault, or my fault. But people sure as shit do like to yell at me for it.

So, one of the pharmacy technicians—usually Ben because Emily is too nice and non-confrontational—will kindly explain that we will fill the prescription when the state and insurance company allow us to, or else we'd all be arrested for drug dealing. Most people are decent about it, and others, well, aren't.

There was even one time we had to call the police.

It's a rare event though, in our small town of Genesee Falls, located in Upstate New York, somewhere between Buffalo and Rochester. We're the only pharmacy in a ten-mile radius. But some people prefer driving into Octavia—the closest city to us —to get their prescriptions filled because *they* have an "Express Scripts" which means *they* have more than two pharmacists working there, and can get their medications filled "in fifteen minutes or less!"

Worst slogan ever.

While we are in the middle of changing owners.

I do just about everything at the newly owned and named *'Kingston's Pharmacy'*—formerly known as *'Deckert's Drugs'*— from checking out customers, to stocking shelves, cleaning floors, and anything else Sydney asks of me.

After the twenty-minute line of pharmacy customers, the store dies down, and I stand behind the register, tapping my nails against the counter. I watch Emily and Lisa—the head pharmacist and pharmacy manager—count pills and fill the orange bottles with tablets of all different shapes and sizes and colors.

I lean against the corner of the small wall that divides the actual pharmacy between me, the register, and the wall full of hanging prescriptions. "Do you guys need any help?" I ask, bouncing on the balls of my feet.

Lisa glares at me. "You know you're not allowed behind that door," she nods toward the waist-high double swinging door. "Until you have your pharmacy technician certificate."

I groan. "I know, but I am so close. I only have two classes left after this semester, and I'm taking both of them this summer, so by the time Ben leaves in August, I'm all yours," I say with a smile.

Ben Jones is the other pharmacy technician, but he's leaving for college out of state in August on a basketball scholarship. "I've already talked to Sydney about it. As long as I pass the test and get my certificate, she says the job is mine."

A small smile forms on Lisa's thin lips. "Good. It'll be nice to have someone back here I already know. We won't have to train a total newbie."

Emily caps a bottle and prints out the label to stick on the front. "Will you still be in school on Tuesdays and Thursdays?"

"Yeah, as long as I'm able to. I'm getting all my classes in two days a week. I might have to take a night or online class, though," I admit with a shrug. "It's not too bad. I can still work the rest of the week."

Emily hands me a bunch of pharmacy bags with prescriptions in them. "Here. Hang these up. You know how to do that."

I smile and take the bags.

AFTER I EAT MY HOMEMADE LUNCH OF A HAM AND CHEESE sandwich, a fruit cup, some carrot sticks, and a tiny bag of salt and vinegar chips, I go to the bathroom and wash my hands. As I open the door, a loud, "Hey!" makes me jump, my hand landing on my chest.

"Sammy! Don't do that!" I say, giving her a gentle push on the arm as we both laugh.

Sammy and I have been best friends ever since I started working at *Deckert's* almost a year ago. We both work the pharmacy register and take turns stocking and ringing out customers' prescriptions. She's a few inches shorter than me, with hair that's shaved in the back and on the sides, but longer on top. It's always dyed a color that isn't natural, and I love it.

Today, it's turquoise.

"Sorry. I just wanted to say hi before I start my shift. It's getting busy out there," she says with a groan.

Our store is located in the middle of town, in the small business district, and every day from noon until two, people come in to buy drinks and snacks and allergy medicine and ibuprofen and every other knickknack you can think of.

And they all talk.

Every single customer will tell me their whole goddamn life story about how their cat has allergies, and can only eat one brand of cat food, and *Deckert's*—no, wait, *Kingston's*—is the only pharmacy that carries the right probiotic powder they have to sprinkle on top of their cat's food every morning so little Muffins won't have the sniffles.

Don't get me wrong, I enjoy talking to people, but some people just don't know when to stop.

I smile at Sammy. "Go clock in and get on register. Sydney has me stocking until my shift is over."

"You're so lucky! Can we switch?"

"Not a chance in the world."

I'M IN THE MIDDLE OF STACKING THE BENADRYL WHEN A handsome younger man walks into the store, wearing a fancy black suit, and I do a double-take. He's tall, at least six feet, with tousled dark brown hair that's falling in all directions, and blue-gray eyes that are so distinct, I can see them from across the store. He stops in the middle of aisle two and glances around as if unimpressed with his surroundings, and he lets out an exasperated breath.

Then his eyes meet mine, and his lips curl up into a smile. I dart my eyes away and go back to stacking the boxes. He approaches me and crosses his arms. "Just the person I was looking for," he says.

I glance up at him, and my eyes widen.

Holy shit. He's even prettier than I thought.

His eyes narrow, and he puts a hand on his abdomen. "Can you please tell me where to find the Imodium?"

I fight back a snort. "Sure. It's in the next aisle over, 3B."

"Thank you, and while I have you here," he crosses his arms again, leaning slightly to one side. "Can you tell me where to find the snacks, like chips and soda?"

My eyes narrows slightly as I place a box of Benadryl on the shelf, balancing the shipping container on my leg. "Of course. That's down this aisle," I say as I point with my other hand. "And over there, in 5A."

"All right, and just one more thing. Where can I find condoms?"

I clear my throat as I set down the empty container, trying hard not to laugh at this guy. Imodium, food, and now condoms?

He's got to be fucking with me.

"Over there in 4B, against the wall by the pharmacy. But you'll need someone from the pharmacy to unlock the case for you."

"You keep the condoms locked up?"

"Yeah, they were one of the most stolen items in the store. Not sure if it's because it embarrasses people to buy them, or if it's because they're expensive, but we have to keep them locked in the prophylactics case. Right up there," I say as I point toward the pharmacy.

"Okay, well, thank you for your help," he pauses and looks at my name tag. "Peyton. Lovely name, Peyton." The way he says my name makes it sound almost dirty, and a chill runs down my spine. "How long have you worked here?"

I bend over to pick up another box of allergy medicine and continue to stock the shelf. "About a year now."

He rests an arm against the shelf I'm stocking and watches me stack the boxes. "That's a long time to work at a drugstore."

"I'm also a college student."

He quirks an eyebrow. "You go to university?"

I fight back the urge to scowl. "No. Community college. Private college is a bit too expensive for me."

He glances down at my inventory, avoiding my gaze. "I get that. What's your major?"

I look at this guy's designer black suit, his silk tie, his shoes that shine so bright in the fluorescent lights it almost makes me blink. *He so does not get it.* "Nursing, but I'm also getting my pharmacy technician certificate so I can make more money until I become a nurse."

He cocks his head to the side and smiles. "That's ambitious."

"Thanks," I say and turn back to the allergy medicine.

"This store used to be called something different, right?"

I sigh, wondering when the hell this guy is going to let me get back to work, but I can't be rude to a customer. "Yeah, it's under new ownership now."

"I noticed on my way in you don't have a sign up yet."

My cheeks turn red for some reason as if it's somehow my fault that we don't have an official *'Kingston's'* sign. It's only been a few days. We just took the old sign down on Friday. "Well, it's brand new. I'm not even sure when the new sign gets here. I'd have to ask my boss, but the new store is called *'Kingston's Pharmacy.'* We used to be *'Deckert's Drugs.'"*

9

"I'm aware. There was an article in the local paper," he says as if remembering a humorous anecdote.

I chuckle. "Yeah, not much exciting happens in this town." This guy actually read the *Genesee Falls Gazette*?

He turns and looks at the different allergy medicines I'm stocking, picks up two different generic ones, and eyes me. "Tell me, Peyton. In your professional opinion, which one of these would work best for my itchy eyes and runny nose?"

I stare at him blankly for a moment. *Who the fuck is this dude?*

Behind me, I hear Sydney running toward me, and can tell she's out of breath. "Peyton! Oh, my god, Peyton!" Sydney calls, and when she reaches me, she puts a hand on my shoulder. I turn to look at her, and she's clutching her waist. Her long, manicured nails make me nervous being so close to my face, but she doesn't press them into my skin. Her thin braids are pinned back in a bun, and her eyelashes have purple tips today. I wonder why she's so flustered.

Sydney looks at the man before me. The man with the million questions. The man who won't leave me alone and let me do my job. The beautiful man with the sexy dark hair and stunning eyes, and she holds out her hand. "Hello! I'm Sydney Anderson, the store manager. I see you've met Peyton Katz. She's one of my best employees!"

My eyes narrow as I watch the man take her hand and shake it. "It's nice to finally meet you, Sydney. I'm Alexander Kingston. But please, call me Lex."

2

"I like it" // We The Kings

I lose the ability to form words.

Alexander Kingston. This guy is Alexander Fucking Kingston.

As in *Kingston's Pharmacy*.

He holds out his hand for me to shake. "It's a pleasure to meet you, Peyton Katz." His smile is cunning, like messing with me before had been some kind of challenge he'd just won.

I bite my tongue and take his hand. "The pleasure is mine, Mr. Kingston."

"I insist that you call me Lex." He gives me a quick wink before turning back to Sydney.

Sydney's bright blue eye shadow and dark pink lipstick match well with her brown skin tone, and even the new sapphire employee shirts we all wear now.

Our old *Deckert's* shirts used to be orange—bright, pumpkin orange.

At least Kingston's has made some improvements.

"Lex, let me show you around," Sydney says with a smile as she leads him toward the other end of the store, and I stare at the two of them, holding an empty container that was once allergy medicine.

Behind me, Sammy is trying not to laugh, but I hear it anyway.

I turn and glare at her.

That arrogant prick.

OUR HOUSE IS A MODEST LIGHT YELLOW COLONIAL ON YOUR basic suburban road, but it stands out from everyone else on Peach Tree Lane. The open front porch is white with faded, chipped paint. The wood on the fourth step is warped so badly, I'm always afraid my foot is going to go right through it, and the railing on the left side is loose and missing two balusters.

In the beginning, the house was beautiful and kept neat and clean, my parents working as a team to make the house a home for me—for us. But after Mom passed, my Dad stopped caring. Uncle Jack and Aunt Michelle, my Dad's best friends, would come over and help him with things like washing the dishes and mopping the floors and doing laundry. For a long time, Michelle made us food that he kept in the freezer and my Dad would reheat in the microwave. Once I got older, I started watching YouTube videos on how to cook simple things, but I was only twelve. I made a lot of pasta and grilled cheese.

We can never keep up with the town regulations of what they consider to be an acceptable grass height, and our lawn mower barely works.

I can never get the damn thing started.

When they first bought the house, my mother planted a

garden in the front yard with a brick border and filled it with tulips, lilies, hyacinths, zinnias and cosmos. Now it's just weeds and grass, but every once in a while, I'll see a sprig of red or pink or orange in May, and I remember that twenty years ago, my mother planted that seed and somehow, after all these years of harsh winters and spring droughts and a hostile living environment, the flowers continue to bloom.

As soon as I walk inside, the scent of must and wet dog hit me faster than it should with just a hint of Old Spice. The stairs are on my right, straight back is the kitchen and laundry room, and to my left is the living room. I hang my keys on the old brass hooks on the wall to my left, and find my Dad sitting in his recliner watching fishing shows on TV, and our ten-year-old black lab, Cosmo, sleeping next to him.

Yes, my Dad still has regular TV, with regular cable.

It's weird.

It took me until two years ago to finally get rid of his old box television and upgrade to an HDTV just so he could watch half the channels. My father is a stubborn old man, and has been that way since before I was born.

He was thirty-five when I came into the world, and I'm his first and only child. My Mom was a lot younger, only twenty-two, and her family didn't like my father for getting her pregnant, even though they were madly in love and married. Then she died when I was five, and it was just him and me. He was forty years old and all by himself with a five-year-old daughter.

He tried his best, but he didn't have a clue what to do with me.

"Hey," I say as I kick off my shoes, and Cosmo looks at me, whining. "What's up, Buddy?" I ask Cosmo as I bend down and scratch his head.

My Dad looks down at both of us and smiles. His blue eyes

are as bright as the sky. His short, dirty blonde and gray hair is overdue for a haircut. And the stubble on his chin and cheeks tells me he hasn't bothered to shave for a while now. I'll probably have to remind him if he doesn't do it soon. "How was work?"

"Met the new boss today." My Dad looks confused. "The new owner, Lex Kingston, came into the store. I was stocking allergy medicine, and he walks up to me, pretending to be a customer. He started asking me where everything was. I thought he was just some random guy messing with me."

"He was testing you," he says.

"Testing me?"

"Yeah. He wanted to make sure his employees know the store. And you do, so you've got nothing to worry about."

"I guess." I straighten and toss my purse on the ancient red microfiber couch that's been there since my grandparents gave it to us when my Mom was pregnant with me.

"You hungry?"

"I could eat," he says.

I make my way through the dining room that we never use, except for storing stacks of boxes against the wall and a cheap wood table scattered with bills and documents, and into the kitchen to scour the fridge for something easy to make. I pull out some ham, turkey, cheese, and mustard and make us both some sandwiches. I add some lettuce and tomato to make them somewhat healthy.

We eat together in the living room. I sit on the couch that smells like an attic and watch a man on television wrestle with a bass on a fishing line.

It's not my favorite thing in the world, but it's kind of funny to watch.

I glance over at my Dad as he finishes his sandwiches. I always make him two because I know he hasn't fed himself. I can't help but glance down at his brown recliner, strings of the tweed fabric pulling out in random places, more duct tape on the corner of the arm than I'd like to admit, and the red checkered fleece blanket that hangs over the back of the chair to cover the rip on the top where even more stuffing is popping out. The chair is almost as old as me, but my father refuses to get a new one.

Stubborn, stubborn, stubborn.

When I finish, I excuse myself. "I have some homework I have to finish before class tomorrow. Do you need anything else before I go upstairs?"

My father eyes me sidelong. "I do not need you to wait on me hand and foot, Peyton. Go, do your homework."

I put my hands up defensively. "Hey, I was just trying to be nice." I kiss my Dad on the cheek and scratch Cosmo behind his ears and head up the old oak staircase, mindful to skip the sixth step as the tread has been broken for over a year now and my Dad keeps forgetting to fix it.

When I turned sixteen, my Dad switched bedrooms with me. He gave me the master bedroom and a queen-size bed that had sat unused in a guest room at his best friend's house that he and his wife no longer needed because they were turning the room into a nursery.

It's probably the best birthday present I've ever gotten.

The closet is triple in size, and there are built-in bookshelves on the wall next to my desk. Besides that, it's a pretty simple room, but I keep it neat and decorated. My bookshelves are overflowing with my favorite fantasy and science fiction and adventure novels, most of them being gifts from birthdays and holidays passed. Being a full-time college student, the only books I can afford now are textbooks.

And even those are a bit out of my price range.

I change out of my work clothes and take a quick shower

before I sit down at my desk and open up my laptop to the paper I started working on last night. I've got two pages left to write and a test to study for tomorrow.

On Tuesdays and Thursdays, I'm in class from 9:45 am until 5:15 pm without more than a ten-minute break, unless a class gets canceled. Or I decide to skip.

I've done that before, but only when I'm completely drained. I can justify skipping one day of school. I cannot justify skipping a whole day of paid work.

It takes me an hour to finish my paper, then I'm on my bed with my Biology book on my lap, reading until my eyes can no longer see clearly.

~

MY BIOLOGY EXAM WASN'T AS BAD AS I THOUGHT IT WAS GOING to be, and I walk out of the classroom with a weight lifted from my chest.

When I get home from school, it's quarter to six o'clock at night, and my Dad has already left for work at the factory. He's been a security guard at ACore Electric my entire life, usually working second or third shift because the pay is more per hour.

I let out a long breath and fight the knot forming in the pit of my stomach.

This is my least favorite part of the day.

Now that my Dad is at work, it's time to check the house.

Ever since my Mom died, my Dad's been drinking. And I don't just mean beer—even though he drinks that too—but bourbon is his poison.

And *a lot* of it.

So much that sixteen months ago, he was diagnosed with liver disease caused by alcoholism—more specifically alcoholic cirrhosis—and it's been a long and bumpy road ever since.

So, now, every night after he goes to work, I search the house from top to bottom for a bottle of bourbon because I know all of his hiding places.

I haven't found anything in a few months, and for that I am grateful. If my Dad starts drinking again, he could end up in the hospital, or worse.

He could die.

So, I search the linen closet, under the kitchen sink, inside his toolbox, behind the books on the living room shelf, and under his dirty clothes in his laundry basket. I breathe a sigh of relief when I don't find anything.

I'd asked him once if he'd ever considered going to an AA meeting, even though my father is the most atheist a person can get. He glared at me and gave me a firm *no*, before leaving the room and slamming the door behind him. I've never asked him since.

I PULL MY THIRTEEN-YEAR-OLD HONDA ACCORD INTO THE small parking lot of the pharmacy only to see Sydney and Lex standing outside the store yelling at two men, one on each side of the doors, each one holding a rope. In the middle is something under a white sheet, something I'm assuming is the new sign for the store that says, "*Kingston's Pharmacy.*"

Looks like Lex finally got the sign he wanted.

As I get out of my car and approach everyone, I see James Oliver, the other store pharmacist, standing back and laughing at the two men while smoking a cigarette. Ben Jones, the other pharmacy technician, is next to him whispering something I can't hear and James laughs again. It's only quarter to nine in the morning, and the store isn't open yet, but everyone is usually inside by now.

I walk up to Sydney right as she shouts, "No, higher on the left, the *left!*"

I watch the guy on the right lift it higher and snort. "Hey."

Sydney grunts but doesn't turn around. Lex leans back and turns to me, his eyes graze over me like I'm something dark and mysterious he can't quite figure out.

I like that.

"Hey, missed you yesterday," he says.

"I have class on Tuesdays."

"Right. Community college girl," he says, like it's not as important as any other college. "How's it going for you?"

"Really well, actually," I say with enough confidence as a Kardashian.

He can bite my ass.

He smiles. "Good," he says and walks over to me and leans in close to my ear. "It has to be going better than this joke." He points up at the sign. "They've been here since eight." His eyes go wide for a second, and he shakes his head. I fight back a smile.

"I bet Sydney is loving this," I say sarcastically.

He looks at me with eyes that are begging me to save him, and I smile. *That's what you get, punk-ass Ivy League rich boy.*

"She's driving me crazy."

"She drives everyone crazy."

The men finally align the sign correctly and mount it to the brick wall. Lex blows out a breath. "All right!" He claps, and we all join in. "Let's get this sheet off!"

Sydney counts to three, and the man on the right pulls off the white sheet revealing the brand new, bright blue and white *Kingston's Pharmacy* sign.

It's really boring.

But we all clap and Sydney has never looked more excited.

ALL MORNING, LEX HOVERS OVER US, WATCHING EACH OF US DO our jobs. Luckily for the boys, not even Lex can go into the pharmacy without a pharmacist's degree or a PTC, so he can't bother James or Ben too much. He watches them from the door for a bit, making Ben so nervous, he drops a bottle of blue pills all over the floor, making James huff in frustration.

He watches me for half an hour as I assist customers with their prescriptions, asking me questions, giving me compliments, telling me I have excellent customer service skills.

Lex hovering like this is making me super anxious.

But he smells like mint and cedar, and *oh my stars* he smells so good. I don't even realize I start leaning into him until I'm practically falling on him, and I have to catch myself on the counter and spin before Lex glances over and notices.

"Are you okay?" he asks.

"I'm fine," I say.

Big fat lie. And I hate lying.

No, I am not okay. You need to go back into the office because standing next to you is like being on an episode of *Hot Ones* and you are the last chicken wing.

Your Scoville level is off the fucking charts, Lex Kingston.

I'm relieved when Sydney finally calls him into the office, and I can finally focus on getting my work done.

As soon as Sammy gets there, I'm desperate for my break, so I grab my lunch and run out of the store. I walk across the street to the little town square and sit on a bench to eat. It's a beautiful April afternoon, and I pull out my iced coffee and sandwich. I stick my earbuds in my ears and slide through my phone. I need a break. I need a happy song, and what's possibly the happiest song in the history of the world? *Have it All* by Jason Mraz.

And everything is perfect until someone sits down next to me. "Beautiful day, isn't it?"

Goddamn it, I cannot catch a break.

I look over and see Lex sitting next to me with a fast-food cup in his hand, and french fries in the other. "You want some fries?" He offers me the container.

I pull out my left earbud. "No, thanks." I wipe my face on a napkin and grab all my wrappers and toss them into the garbage bin. I drink my coffee in my reusable mug and eye Lex sidelong, waiting for him to either leave or say something.

"Sydney says you're taking over for Ben when he leaves for school in August? For the pharmacy technician job?"

"That's the plan."

He leans back on the bench and crosses his arms. "How old are you?" he asks.

I narrow my eyes. "Nineteen, why?"

He shrugs. "Just curious."

I look at my phone. I have twelve minutes left of my lunch break, and he is ruining it.

"So, what is there to do for fun in this town, Peyton?"

I sigh. "Well, we have a movie theater, but there are only two screens, and it's closed on Mondays and Tuesdays." I take a sip of my coffee.

"And?"

"And what?"

"A movie theater? That's all you have?"

"There's a bar if you're an old, sad, divorced alcoholic. We've got a dry cleaner if you're really into that stuff," I say and point behind me. "And my favorite place is the used bookstore."

"Wow, a used bookstore. Well, shit, if I'd known there would be a used bookstore in Genesee Falls, I'd have come here sooner." He says as he gets up and tosses his cup and fries in the waste bin. He stands in front of me, blocking the sun from my eyes. "Is that it?"

"I'm afraid that's it."

"Well, maybe I'll see you in that bookstore sometime," he

says as he makes his way back to the store. I watch him go, his hands in his pockets. There's a slight jaunt in the way he walks, and I'm not sure if he's doing it on purpose.

But I like it.

Goddamn it.

3

"One Way or Another" // Blondie

I get a text from Sydney on Thursday that says, '*Mandatory Staff Meeting for all employees of Kingston's Pharmacy in Genesee Falls on Friday, April 26th at 8:15 am, in the break room. Breakfast will be provided by Mr. Kingston!*'

When I arrive Friday morning, the break room has been completely renovated. Before, we had one small table with four plastic chairs. Now there are three tables with cushioned chairs and a brand new refrigerator, a coffee maker with a selection of sugars and creams, and in the middle of the room is a buffet table with all of the breakfast foods; bagels, cereals, breakfast pizza, coffee, tea, milk, cream, flavored creamer, and juice. It's like the breakfast fairy stopped by and left this for everyone.

I look at the wall of lockers and notice even those are new. Each locker now has a numerical keypad with a digital code, instead of the old combination locks.

Wow, Kingston's sure is fancy.

I look down at the floor and see all of our lockers have been cleaned out. Each one of us has a box with our name written on the front, and mine is mostly empty, except for a black zip-up hoodie I keep at the store for when the air conditioning is on full blast. Which is a lot.

I glance over at Sammy's box, that's overflowing with crap, most of which is garbage. I laugh as she runs over to me with her mouth open and her cheeks flushed. "How the fuck did Sydney get my locker open? I switched the locks!"

I can't stop laughing. "She probably broke the lock, dumb ass. It's not hard."

Her lips form a tight line, and she bends down to start throwing all her crap away, while I go get a bagel and some coffee before Sydney starts talking.

I sit in a new cushioned chair and eat my everything bagel with garlic herb cream cheese and watch Sammy clean out her box. "You know, if you threw that paper away a month ago, you wouldn't have to do it now, in front of everyone."

She glares at me and opens her mouth to say something, but Sydney walks in, her voice booms around the room. "All right, everyone! Welcome to our first official staff meeting as 'Kingston's Pharmacy!'" She claps, and we all try to clap with her, but we've got coffee and plates in our hands.

"You've all seen the new break room!" Sydney says and extends her hands around the room with enthusiasm. "And that's just the beginning! Everyone will be assigned a new locker that comes with a four-digit code, one that only you and I will know."

Sammy gives up and sits next to me. I offer her part of my bagel, and she takes it with half a smile.

"Okay, I'm going to give the room to the man of the hour, Mr. Lex Kingston, everybody!"

Sydney claps again, and we try to clap with her, but the sound is sad and lame.

He walks in the room from the office attached, and my breathing hitches. Today he's wearing a light blue button-down shirt with dark gray pants. His dark hair is a tousled mess like it was on Monday. I can't believe it's only been four days since we've met. It feels like a lot longer.

He walks around the break room like he owns the place—and besides the fact that he does—he looks *insanely* hot.

How is it fair that this man gets to be rich, successful, and so fucking beautiful, it physically hurts to look at him? His blue-gray eyes stand out so much against his shirt. I can't stop staring.

Sammy leans into me and whispers, "My God, he is hot."

I eye her. "You're a lesbian."

"So, what? I can still think a guy is hot. Doesn't mean I want to fuck him. *You* think Khaleesi is hot."

"Yeah, but I'd fuck Khaleesi," I admit, honestly.

Sammy laughs, rolling her eyes. "Okay."

I look back at Lex, and my heart breaks again. And that's when I realize he's staring at me.

I dart my eyes away from him, looking down at my bagel and begin to pick it apart.

"Good morning, everyone! It's been a pleasure working with you guys for the past week, and I look forward to spending the next seven weeks with you."

I turn back to Sammy and mouth, '*Seven weeks?*'

He is staying in Genesee Falls to help transition a tiny little pharmacy like this for *seven fucking weeks?*

You've got to be kidding me.

I look up at the ceiling like there's some deity or universal fuckery behind this, and mouth, '*Why?*'

Sammy grabs my arm and whispers, "Shit! I forgot. I have to talk to you when this is over."

I look at her with furrowed brows and mouth, '*What?*'

But she shakes her head as Lex continues to speak.

Everyone who works at *Kingston's* is here this morning, which isn't saying much. We have Sydney, the store manager. Old Dave who works register in the back of the store, Little Dave who mostly stocks and cleans but sometimes works the back register when we get busy. Lisa Wu and James Reid, the two pharmacists. Ben Jones and Emily Martinez, the pharmacy technicians. And there's Sammy and I who work the pharmacy register, and stock aisles near the pharmacy. We're short-staffed and always hiring, but no one wanted to work at *Deckert's*. Maybe now that we're *Kingston's*, we'll be able to hire a few new people.

Lex talks to us for about ten minutes about all of his plans for the store, including some reorganizing and redecorating and upgrading our old computer system with a brand new one. We're getting new registers soon, which means all of us will have to train on the new system. Sammy and I groan at the same time when he says that. But once everything is done, everything with the store should improve overall.

Sammy raises her hand, and I look at her. My eyes asking a silent *what the fuck are you doing?*

"Are we going to be getting any sort of pay increase?"

Lex smiles. "That's a great question, Sammy. And I was just about to answer it. Not right away, unfortunately. But, once we have all the store improvements in place, and we start to see some increase in profit margins, especially now that we're accepting more insurance plans with the pharmacy, we're projecting that in six months from now, we'll be able to give everyone in the store some kind of pay increase. Now I can't tell you how much that will be yet, but it is in the plan."

Sydney claps for Lex, and we all join in as I eye Sammy, secretly clapping for her.

"Any more questions?" Lex asks as he looks around the room, and no one raises their hand. I'm still looking at Sammy, shaking my head. "All right, guys. You enjoy your breakfast, and have a great day."

Everyone breaks away, most people gather around the breakfast pizza, and Sammy pulls on my arm. "I totally forgot to tell you when I got here. My stupid locker stuff distracted me!"

I turn my chair to face her. "What?"

She looks around the room to make sure no one is listening. "Yesterday, when you were at school, I was working the pharmacy register, and Mr. Big Bucks over there came up to me and started asking about you."

My eyes go wide, and my lips form a tight line, fighting the urge to look in Lex's direction. "What?" I whisper.

"Yeah! He was like *'Does Peyton have a boyfriend?'* and *'What kind of movies does Peyton like?'* He asked me what your favorite book was! I was like, *'I don't fucking know! She has a million!'*"

My face is burning, and now I can't control it. My eyes betray me, and I glance to my right and see Lex mingling with the pharmacists, shaking hands and laughing with James. He looks so professional with them, like an actual adult. But the other day when he sat next to me on the bench, he behaved like an immature douche.

But he remembered the bookstore.

I can't figure him out, and it's driving me crazy.

"Well, what else did he say? And what else did *you* say?"

"Well, I told him..." She pauses, looking almost ashamed.

"What, Sammy?" *Oh, god, what did she say?*

"I told him that you don't date."

Oh. *That.*

I slink back in my seat and take a sip of my coffee. "What did he say to that?"

"He asked me why."

I nod, tracing my thumb over the pattern on the disposable coffee cup. Suddenly, all hope of ever being a normal girl, being with a normal boy leaves my body, and shame enters through my skin, slamming into my bones, and etches itself there for all of eternity.

"I didn't tell him. The second I said it, I regretted it. I shouldn't have said anything, Peyton. I'm sorry. It slipped."

I shrug. "You weren't lying, though."

"Yeah, but you'll date again. Eventually. One day. When you're ready," she says and puts a hand on top of mine. "Maybe he'll ignore what I said and find out for himself. I mean, he was asking me a lot of other questions. He wanted to know everything. I *tried* to just tell him how much you *love* Taylor Swift..."

"Oh, god," I say, and hide my face in my hands. "She's my guilty pleasure, Sammy! I can't help it if her songs are so damn catchy!"

"Yes, I know," she puts her hands up defensively. "You can't help that you have shit taste in music."

I playfully punch her in the arm. "What else did you tell him?"

She lets out a deep breath. "He wanted to know about your family. I said to ask you about that one since that's a bit complicated."

"True dat," I joke.

"He asked about food and hobbies, and why you want to be a nurse and a pharmacy technician. I told him the truth about that one. PT's make more money, and you need money for school."

"I can't believe he asked you all of that. Why do you think he's so interested in me?" I ask, and I glance over at him as he's making himself a cup of coffee.

Sammy cocks her head to the side and glares at me. "Peyton, I know you don't see it, or don't believe it, or ignore it, or whatever, but you're hot. I should know, I'm a lesbian."

I snort at her joke and look down at my hands. It's true. Ever since *that night* I haven't been able to truly see myself as beautiful, not like I once did. Now, I see myself as broken and damaged, like an apple that looks fine on the outside, but when you take a bite, it's black and rotten inside.

Sammy takes my hand again. "Peyton, I'm serious. You're beautiful. And I don't know what his intentions are," she says as she eyes him warily. "But I'd be more than happy to find out."

I smile and sip my coffee before heading out to work, leaving Sammy to plan her interrogation.

FRIDAY'S AT THE PHARMACY ARE ALWAYS SLAMMED. IT'S THE LAST day of the week people can get through to their doctors for a new or renewed medication, and our computer system is over-flowing with prescriptions today.

We're non-stop with customers, and Sammy isn't on the clock until noon, even though she had to come in this morning for the staff meeting, she got to go home for a few hours afterward.

She lives in a small apartment in town above the barbershop with her girlfriend, Shane. Her parents are not accepting of her being a lesbian because of their fanatical religious beliefs. I'm not a religious person, and I'm not even sure if I believe in any god or goddess, but I know in my heart if a higher power does exist, they'd never force you to choose them over your own child.

When Sammy's parents first kicked her out, my Dad welcomed her into our home for two months, until Sammy and Shane were able to find an apartment together. And it was by far the best two months of my life. Being able to live with my best friend, having a sister, and having someone help me take care of my Dad.

It was nice having her there, and I miss her sometimes, even though she only lives five blocks away.

I'm ringing out a customer when Sammy walks up to me and winks. I eye her, curiously. "What?"

She shrugs. "Nothing. Busy today!"

"It's Friday, it's always busy," I say dryly.

She bumps me out of the way with her hip. "Go on your lunch break already."

"I'm in the middle of something," I say, motioning to the customer before me.

"But it's noon. Go take your lunch. I got you covered."

I roll my eyes. "Fine."

I go to the new break room, grab my purse out of my new locker, and my lunch out of the new fridge and head outside. I head across the street and sit on the grass this time, setting my hoodie on the ground under me, so I don't get my ass wet. I check my bank app on my phone to see how much my direct deposit was, and I can't help but frown.

It's never truly enough to pay for everything I need, and buy food.

Just as I start to unwrap my sandwich, a shadow falls over me, and someone sits down next to me. "Having a picnic all by yourself?" He asks.

I close out of my bank app so he can't see just how truly pathetic we mortals really are, and I slip my phone back in my purse. I look over at him, and he's holding a paper bag and a smile on his face.

"So, what did you bring for lunch today?"

I look down at my sad, pathetic sandwich, and lift it a little. "Tuna."

"Well, as delicious as that looks, I have Chinese food that I got from the place across the street," he says as he points with his free hand. "And *someone* told me you love General Tso's chicken. And wouldn't you know it, I happen to have some! So, what do you say?"

I eye him and the bag and mentally strangle Sammy.

He pulls out container after container until the bag is empty, placing them on the ground in front of me, waiting for me to decide if I want to eat it. A fork appears on top of the container, as he opens one and begins to eat. I smell the chicken, and my stomach grumbles, begging me to eat it. I look at my sandwich and back at the container and back at Lex.

"It's not poisoned, I promise," he says.

I swear under my breath, toss my sandwich back in my bag and eat the chicken. It's sweet and spicy and delicious, and I can't remember the last time I had General Tso's.

"It's good, right?"

I nod but don't say anything because I'm too busy stuffing my face. Lex chuckles.

"What?" I ask with a giant piece of chicken in my mouth as I glare at him.

He shakes his head. "Nothing."

That's what I thought, punk.

After a few minutes, I slow down my eating and take a sip of water. Lex sets his fork and container down and looks at me. "So, why don't you date?"

I freeze. My whole body goes entirely still. I blink hard and swallow. "What?" I manage.

"Sammy told me you don't date. I was just wondering why."

I scoff. "I date."

His eyes narrow. "Really?"

"Yeah, totally. I date all the time." I'm trying so hard to play this cool, and it's not working, because I *hate* lying, but I feel like I have no other choice.

"Okay. Who do you date?"

"Uh, I date boys."

"Boys," he laughs.

"Yes. I date boys. Sometimes even girls."

"Well, that's very modern of you."

"Hey, don't knock it till you try it."

He shakes his head. "I'd never knock it. Probably wouldn't try it either, but I'd *never* knock it."

I sigh. "I date, okay. Who and what I date is none of your business." I take another sip of water.

"All right. Want to go on a date with me?"

I choke on my water. I start coughing, spitting water everywhere, my eyes burning. I grab a napkin to clean off my face and try to wipe off the water that is now soaking my *Kingston's* shirt.

"Are you okay?" Lex asks, fighting back a chuckle.

I'm fucking mortified, asshole. What do you think?

"I'm fine," I choke out. I cough until my airway is clear. "Is that even allowed? I mean, aren't you technically my boss?" I ask.

He sucks in a breath. "Technically, my Dad is your boss. Well, no. My Dad is Sydney's boss, and Sydney is your boss. I'm..." He laughs, at a loss for words. "I don't think I'm anything to anyone in there. At least, not until my father dies, or signs the company over to me."

I eye him warily. "Then why are you here? If you're not the one in charge? Why are you the one telling Sydney how to change everything, and why we should rearrange the entire store, and giving her a heart attack in the process?"

"Because my Dad decided it was time I finally do something with my life. I needed to stop partying, and stop acting like the typical white privileged male douche bag, and become a full *grown-up* white privileged male douche bag. I just can't seem to grow the mandatory white beard yet."

I roll my eyes and try not to laugh, but I can't help myself. "Well, we do have white hair dye in the store if you need it."

He chuckles. "I'll keep that in mind." He looks at me with

kind eyes, and my whole body grows hot. "So, what do you say Miss I-date-boys-sometimes-even-girls? Have dinner with me?"

I eye him carefully and sigh, defeated. "I've never actually dated a girl."

"You don't say?"

"But, I've considered it."

"That's cool," he says. "But have you considered dating me?" He points to himself and smiles with those perfect white teeth, and blue-gray eyes that look so bright against his shirt I want to melt, and I can't tell if it's because I'm hot, or he is.

I think long and hard before I answer him.

This could complicate things. Then again he is only here for seven weeks. Which means he probably wants to have sex with me.

Yeah, this is definitely going to complicate things.

But maybe not if it's just one little, tiny date?

"You're sure I wouldn't get fired? If we went out?"

"No, I promise. I won't let anyone fire you, or write you up, or get you into any kind of trouble."

I turn and look at him one last time, reminding myself if he mistreats me, I can always report him to Sydney, who would report him to human resources in the corporate office.

I'm sure *Daddy Warbucks* would love that.

My insides are twisting, and my heart is pounding so hard, I'm surprised he can't hear it.

My god, why does he have to be so fucking beautiful? It's unfair. How can I say no to those eyes? To that hair? To that ass?

"Okay."

Oh, my god, did I just say yes to him?

He smiles at me. "When are you off?"

"I work tomorrow until five o'clock, and I'm off on Sunday."

"Would you like to have dinner tomorrow night?"

I smile a little, even though my heart is hammering in my chest. "Okay."

"I'll pick you up at 7:30?"

"Okay."

And I think I might throw up.

4

"Anxiety" // Julia Michaels

I spend most of my Saturday helping Sydney with the new floor plans Lex has created, starting with the main entrance. I keep looking around the store, expecting to see Lex come around a corner, complimenting us on how amazing the new store is starting to look, but he's not here.

"Hey Syd, where's Lex?"

"He's not here today, Sweetheart. He won't be back until Monday," she explains.

"Okay," I say. "Just wondered."

She eyes me. "Sure, you did."

"What?"

"Girl, I see the way you look at him. And I see the way he's been ogling you," she glares at me accusingly like we've done some unspeakable crime together that I refuse to admit.

"I have no idea what you're talking about."

"Mm-hmm," she says, but this time her lips form a smile.

The day drags on. Sammy doesn't get in until one o'clock,

35

and by then, my insides have grown wings and are about to fly away. She's standing behind the pharmacy register playing with a hangnail, not a customer in sight.

"Sammy," I call out in a whisper. She looks up and smiles at me. I managed to get away from Sydney for a minute, peering around the aisles before I make a run for it and hide behind the register. I look up at my friend, my expression grim. "I don't know if I can do this."

Sammy eyes me sympathetically. "Peyton," she starts.

"No, don't. I'm serious. I feel like this is a bad idea."

She takes my hand. "It's been a year."

I glance around the store and back at the pharmacy. Lisa and Emily are working today, and seem too busy counting pills to pay attention to what Sammy and I are talking about. "I know, but what if..."

She knows what I mean, and sees the sheer panic on my face. "Then say no," she whispers.

My stomach does a flip. "What if he doesn't take no for an answer?"

"Then kick him in the nuts. Peyton, do you really think the owner of our store, the one you work in, would do that? He has to see you here almost every day for the next seven weeks. Sweetie, I know this isn't easy for you, but not every guy is a rapist."

I shush her. "I know that," I start, but a customer approaches the counter, and I turn, heading back toward Sydney.

"We can talk more on break, okay?"

I nod, wishing I still had a valid prescription for Xanax.

~

SAMMY AND I SIT IN THE BREAK ROOM AS SHE TRIES TO CALM my nerves. "I understand you're nervous about this," she shrugs. "Shit, I would be, too. But I think Lex is really into you. And he's nice, and he's rich, *and holy hell, he is hot as fuck.*"

"I know that. But how can Lex be '*really into me*' when he's only known me for a few days?"

"He has good taste and clearly wants to get to know you better," she counters.

I glare at her. "What if I have a panic attack right in front of him?"

She lets out a breath. "Well, you've got two options. You can be honest with him and risk scaring him, risk letting a really nice, hot guy who likes you in on the truth, which by the way, you're going to have to tell him eventually, or fake a heart attack?"

I groan. "*Sammy...*"

"Well, I don't know! I've never had a panic attack before. I've only ever seen you have one, and it looks a lot like a heart attack," she shrugs.

"What do I do if he touches me and I don't want him to?"

She smiles at me like I'm a little kid, and cocks her head to the side. "You know what to do. Tell him to stop."

"Yeah, I know what to do, Sammy. The problem is that it didn't work the last time!" I shout. My nerves are making me upset, and I take a deep breath. "Sorry, sorry."

"It's okay. You're overthinking this. It's just a date. This is supposed to be fun and exciting, and a good kind of nervous. Not a scary, anxiety-filled, kind of nervous."

"I know. *Fuck*, I hate him! I hate him so much for making me like this!"

"I hate him, too. Steve is a piece of shit who deserves every single bad thing that's ever happened to him, and ever will. But *you* deserve to be happy. *You* deserve to be loved. Don't give him this power over you. Fight back. Fight for yourself. And fucking win."

God, I love Sammy. I leap out of my chair and hug her so tight, she starts coughing for air. "Can't... breathe..."

I pull back. "I love you."

She smiles. "Love you back, sister." I sit down, feeling the slightest bit better as her smile grows. "You better text me every single detail."

~

IT'S JUST A DATE, I TELL MYSELF. OVER AND OVER AND OVER again.

I get home around five-thirty and shower. I have time to get ready, thank god, but my anxiety is making it difficult.

When finished, I go to my room and blow dry my hair. It's long and brown and falls to my elbows. It's naturally wavy, so I straighten it with my flat iron. Usually, I wear my hair in a bun, braid, or an octopus clip because it always gets in the way. Lex has never seen me with my hair down before, but that's how I prefer it.

I ransack my closet for something nice to wear, but I'm not a wealthy person, and most of my clothes are from thrift shops or clearance sales or gifts over the years from birthdays and holidays. Lex is rich, and I have a feeling he's taking me some-where that doesn't allow jeans or yoga pants.

Fuck!

I push through all my dresses that are hanging up. Most of them are sundresses, and they're cute, but not fancy. I have one black dress that I wore to a funeral in the tenth grade but I'm not even sure it fits me anymore. And it's ugly.

I pause for a moment, and I remember. The next thing I know, I'm running down the hall into my Dad's bedroom—my *parents'* bedroom—and fling open his closet. Inside is mostly flannel shirts and a few dress shirts he owns for rare special occasions. But he never got rid of my mother's clothes. He just couldn't do it. Instead, he had them all vacuumed sealed and saved in zip-up garment bags that are supposed to be "must and dust-proof".

When I was a kid, I remember my Mom wearing a gorgeous sapphire dress that looked so radiant, I begged her to let me wear it. But it was way too big on me and cost more than her monthly car payment. Not that she paid for it. It was the last gift her sister ever gave her. I think it's why my mother loved it so much. It's the last fond memory she had of my aunt —a woman I hardly know.

Well, Mom, don't let me down now.

I push through all the hanging bags until I see a hint of blue. I grab the bag and return to my room, laying it down on my bed and carefully unzipping it. My Dad had tossed a few dryer sheets in before he vacuum sealed the dress, and I cannot believe they *worked*!

I pull out the blue dress, and it's perfect. Not a wrinkle or crease in sight. I hold it up to my nose, and relieved it doesn't smell like an attic, I hold it up to myself in the mirror. It falls passed my knees, and the neckline is low.

Please, let this fit me.

I don't remember what size or how tall my Mom was, but my Dad always tells me how much we look alike. I carefully slip the dress on and zip up the back. I stare at myself in the mirror.

Holy shit.

I look exactly like my Mom. My chocolate brown eyes, peach skin, round face, and full lips all scream Elizabeth Katz.

I blink, and I'm me again.

My boobs are a little too big, I push them down on each side and adjust the dress a bit.

Holy cleavage, Batman.

I grab my black waist high cardigan and slide my arms through, the sleeves cut at the elbows, and it stops at my belly button. I rummage through my jewelry box and find my matching fake sapphire necklace and earrings and put them on.

I stare at myself for a few minutes. It's strange to see myself this way again. It's been almost a year since my senior ball, since the night that changed everything. I haven't dated anyone since.

God, am I crazy? Am I really ready to date someone?

I should have talked to Dr. Young before agreeing to this.

Dr. Young had been my therapist for nine months after my senior ball. She helped me a lot and taught me many coping strategies for dealing with PTSD and trauma. Things like mindfulness meditation and breathing exercises. She gave me a list of free apps to download on my phone that I've used in the past. I mostly use them when I have nightmares and wake up in the middle of the night, unable to go back to sleep.

Physical activity is a big one, but I think between working, going to school full time, and taking care of my Dad, I get enough physical activity.

But distractions are my favorite. It can be anything from journaling and expressive writing to art therapy to music therapy. I'm a fan of all three, and I don't have much time to write or paint, but music... music is life. And finding music that helps you express how you're feeling when you can't find the words, or music that makes you feel happy when your sad, or finding a song that just helps you in general. I have so many songs on my phone, so many playlists, I've lost track. It's the only thing I ever spend money on that I consider extravagant.

Dr. Young was so helpful to me, and even my Dad, during my dark days, and no matter what I said, or did, or how rude I was to her at times, she never took it personally. She told me that, one day, I would date again, and I laughed in her face and told her to go fuck herself. She wasn't mad.

I was so sure I'd never be interested in men again. But over time, I found myself wanting to be kissed, held, even touched —something I *never* thought would happen. But that doesn't mean I'm ready to actually have sex.

See, *this* is where things get complicated.

Because I wasn't raped. I was sexually assaulted by my high school boyfriend on the night of our senior ball, and it was terrifying and violent and horrible, but before he had the chance to rape me, some of our classmates heard my cries for help, and found us in the back of the limo. They pulled me out and got me back to the school, where the chaperon's called an ambulance, and the police.

So, I'm still a virgin.

But the idea of being touched like that again scares me like nothing else in this world. The fear of being overpowered or someone not listening when I say, "*No!*"

I never want that to happen again.

I shake myself out of my memories and grab my make-up bag.

I take a deep breath, reminding myself that I can do this, that Lex is *not* Steve, and start applying my primer.

5

"Wonderful Tonight" // Eric Clapton

Being five feet seven inches tall, I rarely wear high heels. Hell, I only own one pair of basic black ones because they go with pretty much anything. I dig them out of my closet and slide them on, and give myself a few minutes to get used to them again. I haven't worn them in months. I walk around the house, up and down the stairs.

God, I hate wearing heels.

I'm tempted to go and change into my black flats when the doorbell rings.

Cosmo barks as I stop in the middle of the stairway.

Crap. I left my purse upstairs.

I run up to grab it and look in the mirror one last time, making sure everything is on straight, and make my way back down.

I open the door and hold Cosmo by the collar as he barks some more. "Cosmo!" He quiets down. Standing on my porch

43

is Lex in a black suit with no tie, his hair still a tousled mess, just the way I like it, and his eyes rove over me as if he can't decide where to look. I smile and pull Cosmo back so I can open the door.

"Hi," I say and he finally meets my gaze, then glances down at Cosmo nervously. "Don't worry. He's old and looks scarier than he is. Come in."

Lex saunters inside with his hands in his pockets and looks around casually, but keeping an eye on Cosmo.

"Cosmo, go lie down, boy. Go on," I say. He whimpers at me, but he listens and lies down on his bed next to my Dad's recliner.

I stand there for a moment, unsure of what to do or say next when Lex looks at me and smiles. "You look..."

My face burns, and I look away from him, brushing my hair behind my ear.

"I like your hair down. I didn't realize how long it was."

"Yeah," I say as I twirl the end around my finger. "I never wear it down at work. It always gets in the way."

He smiles. "You look beautiful."

"Thanks. You look nice, too," I say.

We stand there awkwardly for a moment before Lex says, "Shall we?"

"Yeah, let me just..." I grab my keys from the hook by the door, and we make our way outside. I lock the door, and he leads the way to his car.

I don't remember seeing this car in the parking lot of the pharmacy. A black Mercedes Benz—probably brand new—sits before me, and I stare at it wide-eyed. Lex opens the passenger side door for me and motions for me to get inside. His smile is sly as he winks at me. "Milady."

I snort. "Thanks." He closes the door.

He gets in on his side. It smells like leather and vanilla and...

cigars? I don't have time to ask before we're off. I have no idea where we're going, but we're going to get there ridiculously fast. My hand reflexively reaches up toward the '*oh shit*' handle, but there isn't one.

Lex glances over at me with a grin. "Sorry. This car goes a lot faster than I mean her to." He slows down and drives the actual speed limit. I put my hands in my lap, and my text alert goes off.

I pull out my phone and see it's a message from Sammy. '*Soooo, how's it going?*'

"Who is it?" Lex asks, curiously.

"It's just Sammy," I admit.

He laughs. "She checking up on you?"

"Always."

He glances over at me as I text her back, '*Just got in the car, on our way to the restaurant. I'll text you later. Please don't keep blowing up my phone all night. Lex will think we're insane.*'

"You and her are pretty close I take it?"

"She's my best friend."

My phone goes off in my hand, '*LOL he definitely already thinks that. Have fun!*' she says, with a wink face emoji. I roll my eyes and toss my phone back in my purse.

"Did you guys go to school together?"

I shake my head. "No, Sammy is from Octavia, and a year older than me. She's been working at the pharmacy for a while. We became friends when I started working there last summer. Last October, she finally came out to her parents about being a lesbian, and they were not okay with it. They wanted her to go to conversion therapy," I start.

Lex makes a face. "Shit. That's fucked up."

"Yeah, so she comes into work one day, a total crying mess, telling me she was going to be homeless, end up living in her car, and I'm like, '*Um, no, you're not!*' So, I brought her home

45

with me, and she lived at my house for two months before her and her girlfriend were able to find an apartment together. And my Dad is so amazing, he told Sammy that if it didn't work out with Shane, she was always welcome to come back to our house." It all came out so quickly, I'm surprised Lex understood it.

"Your Dad seems like a cool guy."

"He's the best." *Minus being an alcoholic.*

"So, is it just you and your Dad?"

"Yeah, and Cosmo. And sometimes Sammy, if her and Shane get into a fight."

"What about your Mom?"

I pause for a moment, playing with the chain on my purse. "My Mom died when I was five. Cancer."

"I'm sorry." Lex is serious. Not a side in him I've seen before. "My Mom passed away, too. I was twelve. She was in a car accident."

A wave of empathy washes over me. "I'm sorry, Lex."

He lets out a breath. "Well, that's one sad thing we have in common."

"True, but not many people understand the loss of a parent. Especially a mother."

He glances at me for a second, and back at the road. "You're very wise for someone so young."

I smile and look at him. "Well, they don't call me 'Community College Girl' for nothing."

WE ARRIVE AT THE RESTAURANT, AND HE PULLS THE CAR UP to the front of the building. I look out my window and see a line of people out the door and wonder how the hell we're ever going to get in. All of a sudden, my door opens, and a man dressed in a blue blazer holds his hand out to me. "Miss?" It takes me a second to realize he's a valet.

A freaking valet.

I take his hand and step out of the car, Lex appearing around my right shoulder. He tosses the guy his keys and takes my hand. I expect to be pulled to the back of the line; instead, Lex leads me to the door, and we walk right in. A young man around my age is standing behind the counter and smiles at Lex. "Mr. Kingston! How are you this evening?"

He knows Lex?

"Doing great, Charlie. How are you?" Lex slips the kid a green bill, but I can't see the amount.

"I'm fantastic. We've got your table waiting."

Lex nods, and this Charlie guy leads the way. I look around this place, and my breath catches in my throat.

There's a Koi pond in the middle of the restaurant with a fountain.

And there's an upstairs because suddenly, I'm walking up them to the second floor. This restaurant went by so fast, I didn't even catch the name of it.

He shows us to a square table by the window that has a 'Reserved' sign and a bottle of champagne in an ice bucket already waiting for us.

Charlie pulls out the chair on the left side for me, and Lex takes the seat across from me. To my left is a floor to ceiling window where you can see the entire city of Octavia and the river beyond. The sun is setting in the distance; the sky is a mixture of pink and orange and blue and purple.

Charlie sets two flutes on the table and pours us each a glass of champagne, and I eye the glass nervously. "Your waiter will be with you in a moment."

"Thanks, Charlie," Lex says, but he's staring at me.

I set my purse down next to my feet and lean in closer to him. "Lex, I'm not old enough to drink. I'm only nineteen."

He watches me as he drinks from his fancy champagne flute. "It's okay. As long as you don't order anything from the bar, they won't ID you."

"But what about the champagne?"

He shrugs. "You don't have to drink it." He takes my glass in his hand and drinks it all in one gulp. "There. Order whatever you want. They have soda and Shirley Temples."

You cheeky bastard.

Our waiter appears at the table and hands us our menus. The name of the restaurant is *Black and Blue*, and I can't help but chuckle. He gives us a few minutes to decide.

Lex asks. "Have you ever been here before?"

"No. I've never even heard of this place. It's beautiful. I've never seen a Koi fountain inside of a restaurant before."

"One of my friends told me about this place when I found out I was going to be living here for a while."

"Do you live in Octavia?"

"Well, I tried to find an apartment in Genesee Falls, but..."

I nod. There is nothing fancy enough for him there. And I knew it. "I see."

I open the menu. My heart stops dead in my chest. They don't even have dollar signs next to the item, just a number casually listed next to it. A side salad is 15. A Caesar salad is 18. If you want to add chicken to a salad, it's 7. Shrimp is 10.

Fucking hell.

"So, you've been here before?" I ask nervously.

"It's my favorite place in the city, so far."

Wow. "What's good?" I ask nervously. *I am so out of place here.*

"Well, I don't know what you like, but they have amazing prime rib, Filet Mignon, any cut of steak is good. Phenomenal lobster tails."

"I've never had Filet Mignon before, or lobster tails," I admit.

Lex looks at me and starts to laugh, only to realize I'm not joking. "Wait, seriously?"

I shrug. "I've had prime rib, before—once. With my grand-parents. My grandpa grilled it himself. It was delicious." I look over the menu and notice that a shrimp salad costs thirty-two dollars.

Thirty. Two. Dollars. For a salad.

What the actual fuck?

My train of thought is cut off by the waiter returning, asking us if we've decided.

Lex looks at me, and I shrug again. I look up at the waiter. "Can I get a Shirley Temple, extra cherries, please?" I ask with a wry smile, as Lex nods at me as if to say *'touche.'*

"Absolutely. What else can I get for you, Darling?"

I glance up at Lex, who smiles at me with a wink, silently telling me to get whatever I want, and, even though I did, I should *not* feel guilty about it. "You know, I think I'll have the Lobster tail with the Filet Mignon. Medium, please."

"That sounds amazing," he says, and I tell him what sides I want, and he moves onto Lex.

"What can I get for you, sir?"

Lex's gaze is locked onto me as I set my menu on the table, and take a sip of water. There's something in his eyes that I can't quite figure out. He hands the waiter his menu and says, "You know, I think I'll have what the lady's having. Everything the same."

"All right, I'll get those right in for you."

The waiter takes our menus and leaves the table, Lex still staring at me. "What?" I ask shyly.

Lex leans forward, resting his arms on the table, cocking his head to the side. "I've dated a lot of women," he starts, and my expression must change because he stops. "No, I don't mean it like that. I just mean I've been on a lot of first dates, a

49

few second dates, and rarely any third—and not once have I ever been with a woman who ordered a steak."

I furrow my brows. "What did they get?"

"Most of them ordered some variation of vodka, like a martini, and *all* of them ordered a salad."

I can't control it. I burst out laughing and cover my mouth to muffle the sound. I lean in toward him, and whisper, "Did you see that one salad cost thirty-two dollars?" I say as I continue to laugh. Lex watches me, and I can see a smile tug at the corner of his mouth. "What could a salad possibly have that makes it thirty-two dollars? It's cut-up vegetables on a plate!"

Lex snorts. He almost spits out his champagne as he covers his mouth with his napkin. "Well, I think they remove the tails from the shrimp here."

"Well, knock me over with a feather."

The waiter appears again, this time with my Shirley Temple and a bowl of rolls. He sets them down in front of me, and my stomach grumbles. I take a roll and break off a piece, popping it into my mouth.

"Hungry?"

I swallow my bite and say, "I haven't eaten anything all day." I'd been way too nervous to eat.

I look around the restaurant for a moment and remember, *this is a date.* Everyone around us is engaged in conversation, and Lex has been doing the fair share of asking questions. He knows about my Mom and school and work.

I set my roll down and steel myself. "So, Lex. Where did you go to school?"

He looks at me, almost surprised I'm finally showing interest in him. *Good.* I know I'm not good at the whole dating thing, but I want Lex to know that I *am* interested in him.

"I graduated last year from Cornell."

"Wow, Ivy League, boy." *So I was right.*

He smiles. "We'd make a great crime-fighting team. Ivy

League Failure and Community College Deans List." He drinks the rest of his champagne and pours himself another glass.

I fight back the urge to ask him if that's a good idea.

"What do you mean failure? And how would you know if I'm on the Dean's list or not?" He glares at me and cocks his head to the side. "Okay, fine, I made it last fall, but I don't know if I'll make it this semester."

"The only difference between you and me is that I come from money. You probably could have gone to Cornell if you had my family's fortune, and I probably *should* have gone to community college because I barely graduated. I never studied, I partied way too much, and I spent my days getting high with my frat brothers."

I hand him a roll. "Eat." He takes the roll from my hand and sets his glass down. "You would be bored at community college. There are no fraternities—hell, we don't even have dorm rooms—so there aren't any parties. Half of the people in my classes are women in their thirties going back to school now that their kids are in school. And the only place to get high is behind the science building, in the parking lot. I think one of the professors sells marijuana out of his car."

He laughs and finishes his roll.

"Okay, so we've covered school," I start. "We already know our work situation. What about family? Besides your Dad? Do you have any siblings? Aunts? Uncles? Cousins? Grandparents?"

"No siblings, that I know of," he rolls his eyes. "But it wouldn't surprise me if one day, some random kid shows up at my father's doorstep claiming to be his, and being right. My father would demand a DNA test, the results would come back positive, and he'd pay the kid off."

"Wow, you don't like your Dad much," I deduce.

"He's not my favorite person."

"Who is?"

Lex is thoughtful for a long time before he answers. "My mother was," he pauses, and my heart sinks.

I instantly regret asking. "I'm sorry, you don't—" But he cuts me off.

"No, it's fine," he reassures me. "My grandmother—my mother's mother. I don't get to see her often because she lives in Florida now, and she never got along with my Dad, but she always smells like cookies, and before my Mom died, she took care of me a lot. I visit her in Florida as much as I can. Not as much as I'd like, but I guess she's my favorite person—well, favorite family member. I don't have any aunts or uncles."

I smile and sip my Shirley Temple. Lex eyes me curiously. "What about you? Who's your favorite person?"

I bite a cherry off the stem and smile. "Well, Sammy would kill me if I didn't say her, so, for the sake of my life, I'm going to say Sammy."

"Well, of course," Lex smiles, and it's the most beautiful thing I've ever seen.

"But besides Sammy," I shrug, looking down at my drink. "My Dad. I have very few memories of my Mom. My Dad's parents died when he was my age, so I never met them, and I haven't seen my Mom's parents since I was twelve. They don't like my Dad much. I do have an aunt and uncle on my Mom's side who live out near the Finger Lakes, but I haven't seen them in years."

"So, your Dad because of lack of choices?"

"No, my Dad because he stayed when no one else did."

Before Lex can respond, the waiter appears with our food.

Lex wasn't lying about the Filet Mignon. Or the lobster tails. Never in my life have I eaten food so delicious before, or so fancy. This place is beautiful, even if I don't fit in here. It feels like a once in a lifetime experience, so I'm going to enjoy it while I can.

Lex watches me eat like I'm a spectacle at a zoo or something new and fascinating to be seen. A woman eating a steak couldn't be that crazy, could it? It's making me more nervous than I already am. "Could you stop staring at me?" I ask quietly.

"I wish I could, I do," he replies. "But you're so captivating."

"Because I'm eating a steak?"

"Partially."

"You watched me devour General Tso's yesterday. How is this any more shocking?"

"Well, that wasn't a date." I raise my eyebrows in question. He smirks. "Not officially."

I set my fork down and swallow my bite. "What's the other part?"

He watches me closely as he drinks more champagne. He sets the flute down on the table and looks around the restaurant and back at me. "You are, by far, the most beautiful woman I have ever seen."

My heart skips a beat, and I can't help but glance around the place. It's filled with rich, beautiful women, and men. People who are probably lawyers and doctors, and successful businessmen like Lex and his father. A woman sitting at the bar wearing a red dress and red high heel shoes tips her head back in laughter, her long blonde hair trailing down her back.

"Like today?"

He laughs. "No, in my entire life."

I pause. "Like who's not famous?"

He laughs harder. "No, out of any woman I've ever seen, dead, alive, famous, anywhere, human, on this planet. You outshine them all."

Whoa. I want to believe this is a line. I want to think he's only saying it because he wants to get me into bed with him.

And yet, out of every other woman in this room, Lex can't take his eyes off me. All week long, Lex hasn't been able to take his eyes off me.

My stomach twists, and my face turns hot. "I—thank you," I whisper.

Even if it is a line, it's a damn good one.

"So, Sammy tells me you love Taylor Swift?"

"Oh, god," I groan and stuff my mouth with another bite of meat. My face growing hotter by the minute. Lex is laughing at me. "Okay, I do not *love* Taylor Swift," I defend myself. "I simply appreciate her ability to write a hit song every single time."

"Right," he says.

"Come on. I can't help that all of her songs are catchy!"

"I wouldn't know. I've never heard her songs before."

My mouth drops. "Come on!" He shakes his head, laughing. "That fancy-schmancy car of yours better have Bluetooth, because you're in for a wild ride home." The look on his face clearly says, *I think I'm going to regret this*, as he takes another bite of steak, and I laugh. "Okay, Ivy League Boy, what kind of music do you like?"

~

WE ORDER THE TIRAMISU FOR DESSERT AND SPLIT IT. IT IS absolutely delicious.

When we're finished, the waiter leaves the check on the table, and I look out the window again, taking in the city before me. I've never seen Octavia like this before; it's stunning with the street lights and nightlife. I've only ever been out here at night for a class.

I look back at Lex as he's signing the bill. "You ready to go?" He asks.

I nod and grab my purse from under the table. Lex takes my hand, and we head downstairs. I touch his shoulder. "Hey, give me a minute? I need the restroom."

He nods, and I make my way through the crowd. I'm surprised there isn't a line. I get to the mirror and set my purse down on the counter next to the sink. I wash my hands and check my teeth for any signs of food. I don't see anything, but pull out a travel size bottle of mouth wash, and swish it around my mouth for a few seconds, and rinse my mouth out with water.

I freshen up my lipstick and check myself in the mirror one more time. Letting out one last breath, I make my way out of the ladies and meet Lex where I left him, and we leave the restaurant.

It's just past ten o'clock at night, and Lex drives me back to my house, during which I play him some music on my phone.

"This is Taylor Swift?"

"Yes."

"And that other song before this one was her, too?"

"Yeah."

"And the one before that?" He asks as he pulls up in front of my house.

"Also, her."

"And they were all *different* songs?"

I glare at him and scoff. "You and Sammy planned this!" I say as he chuckles and gets out of the car. I start to open my door, but Lex is there before I can get out, holding his hand out to me.

I take it.

He walks me to my door, and we stand there awkwardly. I haven't dated much, but I know he has.

Does he expect me to invite him inside?

I find myself staring at my hands, playing with the chain of my purse.

Lex closes the distance between us, and his finger grazes my cheek. I lift my head to face him and find he is dangerously close to me.

My heart races, and my insides twist.

He licks his lips, his eyes locked onto mine. "Can I kiss you?"

My stomach clenches, but I want to kiss him. Everything in me wants to feel his lips on mine, on my neck, leaving a trail down my chest...

Breathe, Peyton. It's just a kiss.

I nod.

I count the seconds, and my breathing hitches and his lips find mine. They're even softer than I imagine.

His kiss is sweet and slow, and I find myself falling into him. He wraps his arms around me and his lips part. Before I know it, my mouth is opening for him, and his tongue finds mine, my arms wrap around his neck. His hands graze slowly down my back and around to my hips.

His hands move up my sides, higher and higher, and I pull away, breaking the kiss before his hands reach somewhere too far.

I take a deep breath, putting my hands on his chest as if to say, *okay now, it's only our first date.*

Lex smiles at me and leans against the storm door. "That was..."

"Yeah. It was..."

"Nice."

"Very nice," I say, still trying to catch my breath.

He stands up straight and takes my hand. "You're off tomorrow?"

I look at him blankly for a second before I gather my thoughts. "Yeah, tomorrow."

"You busy?"

I sigh, disappointed. "I've got a paper to write and two tests to study for."

He smiles. "Ah, community college girl. What's that like, studying?"

I laugh and eye him. "Hard."

"Well, I guess I'll see you at work on Monday?"

"Yeah, definitely."

He brushes a strand of hair behind my ear. "I had a good time with you tonight, Peyton."

I smile. "Me too, Lex."

He turns to leave. "See you Monday." He makes his way down the porch steps to his car.

"See you Monday," I say as he drives away, my head still spinning.

6

"Take On Me" // A-Ha

As soon as I get in the house, I kick off my shoes, pull out my phone, and text Sammy. '*I ate lobster tail and Filet Mignon for the first time in my life tonight. I played Lex Taylor Swift songs on the way home, and he made fun of them. Then he kissed me on my porch. Holy shit. I've never been kissed like that before.*'

I lean back against the door, that stupid grin still plastered on my face. I blink hard as I hold my phone close to my chest and breathe.

Just breathe.

My phone goes off, and I look down at Sammy's reply. It's a string of emoji's that signify squealing, excitement, shock, and happiness. Then a string of exclamation points, '*!!!!!!!!!!!!!!!!!!!*'

I run upstairs and toss my purse on my desk before I fall backward onto my bed, '*Oh my god,*' I start to text. '*What is wrong with me? I'm getting way too excited about this.*'

'*No! You're not!*'

'He's only here for seven weeks.'

'Well, maybe now he'll have a reason to stay.'

'LOL Yeah, right. Millionaire playboy Lex Kingston stay here? In Genesee Falls?'

'If he falls for you, he'll stay. Or maybe he'll take you with him. I can already see it happening.'

I pause. *Take me with him?* I shake my head. 'You know I can't go with him. I can't leave my Dad.'

'Your Dad is a grown-ass man.'

'Who has a life-threatening disease and no other family to take care of him.'

'Do you think your Dad would want you to not live your life because of him?'

'Goddamn it. Will you stop with all the logic and reasonable explanations for everything?'

I toss my phone down on my bed next to me. I know Sammy is right, but I also know that I can't leave my Dad by himself. He'll die! He's a stubborn bastard who refuses to do what he needs to stay healthy, and he needs someone to gently remind him to take his medicine, and eat, and not drink bourbon.

Who is going to do those things if I leave?

I shake the thought out of my head. I guess if Lex likes me, he will have to stay here, or in Octavia, or one of the many smaller cities within a fifty-mile radius he can choose to live in, if he wants to stay close to me.

I'm getting ahead of myself again. It was just a date.

I close my eyes and remember the kiss.

And smile.

∽

WHEN I FALL ASLEEP, I DREAM ABOUT LEX.

We're standing on my front porch, and he's kissing me,

slowly, softly, down my neck, tracing my collar bone, his hands gently squeezing my hips, and I plunge my fingers into his hair. Nothing in my life has ever felt this amazing.

But when he looks at me, it's not Lex.

It's Steve.

I push him away, and my back slams into the screen door. Suddenly, I'm lying down in the back of the limo, and he's on top of me.

"Get off me!" I cry out.

Steve's smile is wicked, as he eyes me like he's won.

"Get off! Get off!" I'm crying, punching and pushing and screaming, and I'm awake.

I sit up, my heart hammering in my chest, my skin covered in a gleam of sweat. I run to the bathroom and splash cold water on my face.

I should have been prepared for the nightmares to come back.

Dr. Young warned me they might. Especially when I started dating again.

Three months ago, I stopped going to therapy once my Dad's medical bills became too much for us. Even when there were times I needed it, I didn't have an extra fifty dollars a week to give her.

I go back into my room and grab my phone. It's half past three in the morning. I open up one of my meditation apps the doctor told me about and listen to it until I fall back to sleep.

I don't dream about either of them again.

I SPEND THE DAY DRINKING COFFEE, WRITING MY PAPER FOR psychology, and studying for my exams. Around one o'clock, my hangry stomach finally wins, and I run downstairs to get something to eat.

My father is sitting in his recliner with Cosmo next to him, flipping the channels on the TV when he says, "You've got a delivery."

I eye him. "Huh?"

"You were busy, so I set it on the kitchen table. Didn't want to disturb '*study Peyton*.'"

I scoff at my Dad and go into the kitchen, where a giant bouquet of red and white roses sit in a clear vase, with a tiny envelope on top.

My jaw drops.

There must be two dozen.

I pick up the envelope and open it. Inside is a note written in slanted cursive. "*Peyton, you are a breath of fresh air. I hope to see you again soon, XX, Lex.*"

I forget myself for a minute, and become a smiling giddy idiot, and start dancing around the kitchen as I pick up a single white rose and inhale its sweet scent.

I stop dead as I turn and see my Dad standing in the door-way. "So, who's the guy?"

My lips form a tight line, and I put the rose back in the vase. Ever since my last boyfriend, my Dad has been wary about the idea of me dating. Not that he'd get in the way, but I can see in his eyes that he's worried.

"He's just a guy from work," I say.

"A guy working at a drugstore can afford to send you two dozen roses?" He asks. "Wait a minute, I know all the guys at your work. Who is it? Ben?"

"No, it's not Ben. He's..." I start, but not exactly sure how to tell him that I'm dating *Lex Kingston*. I sigh and just say it. "Remember how I told you about the new owner coming into the store the other day?"

My father looks at me with furrowed brows. "The guy who was messing around with you?"

"Yeah. Well, it turns out, he was more *flirting* with me? I don't know, that's what Sammy said. But his name is Lex, and he's technically not the owner. His Dad is the owner."

My father doesn't say anything for a long time. He looks at me, at the roses, and back at me. Then he nods and says, "Can't wait to meet him," before he turns back toward the living room.

I stand there, my hands in the air. "That's it?" He doesn't reply.

I shake my head, and put more water in the vase then set it on the windowsill behind the sink.

I reheat some leftovers from the other night and head back upstairs to finish my work, but I need to thank Lex for the flowers.

I can't believe he sent me two dozen roses.

We didn't even have sex.

Shit. Does this mean he's expecting it?

He *is* twenty-four. And loaded. And could probably get it from any woman anywhere...

Of course, he's expecting it. Isn't every red-blooded straight male in the world?

Seriously, fuck you, society. Fuck you, very, very much.

I suddenly realize I am going to have to tell Lex two things.

One—I am a virgin.

Two—I was sexually assaulted by my ex-boyfriend, and I have PTSD. So, having sex with me might be difficult.

Wait, is that four things?

Will he be willing to wait? Will he be patient with me? Will he get upset when I have a panic attack when he touches my thighs?

Fuck, fuck, fuck.

I pick up my phone and see I have a new message.

It's from Lex.

'You've got mail.' Is all it says.

I notice it was sent a while ago, but I'd put my phone on silent to study this morning, and hadn't checked it all day.

I slide open my phone and open up my texts to Lex's number. We hadn't texted much over the past few days, just a few greetings, and on Friday when I sent him my address.

I tap on the text box and start to type, '*The flowers are beautiful. Thank you so much!*' I say with a few added emoji's. But I hesitate to hit send.

Is that enough thanks for two dozen roses?

I delete it all and type, '*No one has ever sent me roses before. They're beautiful. Thank you.*' With a red heart emoji. I hesitate again before pressing send.

I don't think there is anything I can say that will be enough.

I bring my phone with me to my computer and plug it in to charge. I try to focus on my paper, but can't help checking my phone. I leave Lex's text page open, so I can see the read receipt.

After ten minutes of waiting, I click off my screen, turn my phone on silent and flip it over so I can focus on my paper.

It only takes me another hour to finish eating and writing my paper. I read through it one more time before printing it and sticking it in my bag.

With a sigh of relief, I grab my phone and plop down on my bed. I click my phone on and see I have three missed texts from Lex.

My stomach does a flip, and I bite back a smile.

'*You are most welcome. It was my pleasure.*' A string of heart emojis, a kiss, followed by a blushing face. '*How's the paper going?*'

He sent them over thirty minutes ago. I'm so glad I finished my paper and I'm not distracted.

'*All done.*' I reply. '*What are you up to on this lovely Sunday afternoon?*'

It doesn't take long before I see the read receipt, and the three little dots that mean he's typing.

And the butterflies just won't quit.

'*Reading the most boring legal documents for the pharmacy merger I've ever read in my life.*'

'*Well, that's a terrible way to spend a Sunday.*'

'*I agree. You want to go get ice cream with me?*' He asks.

I stare at my phone screen and read his message.

'*I've been craving a hot fudge sundae for like a week now.*'

I still don't reply, but he knows I've read his messages. I have my read receipts turned on.

'*That is if you're done studying.*'

I smile. I think I made him sweat a little.

I like it.

'*I'm finished.*' I reply, grinning wickedly to myself. '*Let's go get ice cream.*'

I PULL THE CLIP OUT OF MY HAIR AND BRUSH IT OUT. AFTER taking a shower early this morning, the natural wave is back, and it's mostly dried, but still a bit frizzy. I spray it with some hair spray and brush it again, and toss on my favorite pair of boot cut jeans and a cute purple top.

Last night's make up got scrubbed down the drain, and I don't have time to do it all again, so I dab on a bit of mascara and lip gloss before I'm running down the stairs, just in time.

Lex doesn't ring the bell. This time he knocks.

Cosmo probably scared him. He doesn't bark as much when someone knocks, or when he's sleeping next to my Dad.

I grab my keys and turn to my Dad. "Hey, we're going to get some ice cream. Want me to bring you something back?"

My Dad leans back in his chair, glancing out the window behind him, and I know he can see Lex standing there. He's quiet at first, before he straightens and says, "No, sweetheart. You go have fun."

I smile. "Thanks, Dad. Love you!"

I open the door and see Lex standing there in dress pants and another button-down shirt, and I wonder if he even owns a pair of jeans. "Hey," I say.

His hands are in his pockets as he looks me over, his lips curling into a crooked smile. "Hi."

I pull the door closed behind me, and we stand there for a few seconds before he reaches out his hand to me, and I take it.

We get into the Mercedes and drive. I have no idea where we're going because the ice cream shop in Genesee Falls doesn't open until Memorial Day. He's heading toward Octavia, and I wonder what ice cream shop is open at the end of April?

"Any more music you want to play for me?"

I smile wickedly and pull out my phone. As I connect to his Bluetooth, I decide today is 80's day.

He laughs when *Take On Me* by Aha starts blaring out of his speakers, and I start dancing to the beat. "I've even got the 80's hair going today!" He's fighting to keep his eyes on the road. "This is one of the best 80's songs of all time! Come on, you have to know it!" I say and start singing along.

"What am I going to do with you, Peyton?" Lex asks.

I shrug and smile and keep on singing.

7

"Lovesong" // The Cure

After I play him some Tears for Fears and Depeche Mode, he pulls into a parking lot of a candy store, and I realize that it's also an ice cream parlor.

"*Ava's Candies*. Wow, I forgot about this place. I haven't been here since I was a kid," I say.

"I've never been here, but I've heard they make amazing hot fudge sundaes."

We head inside and order two sundaes, and take them outside to sit at a green table with an umbrella. I make sure to grab some extra napkins.

We're both silent for a few minutes as we eat, and I look around and notice we're the only ones there. "So, is it as good as you thought?" I finally ask Lex.

He moans, and my stomach does a backflip. "Even better."

I don't know what it is about this man that drives me crazy, but also makes me insanely attracted to him. I believed, in the beginning, I was attracted to Steve before he turned into a giant asshole. But whatever these feelings are that I feel for Lex are far stronger, and seemingly etched into my soul forever.

And it's only been a fucking week.

Shit, maybe I do need to get laid.

I shake away the thought so the ice cream doesn't come hurling back up, and set my spoon down.

I only ate half my sundae, and Lex eyes me. "Full already?"

I blink hard. "Brain freeze."

He nods and looks down at his bowl, contemplative. "I'm guessing that was your Dad in the chair leaning out the window looking at me?"

I laugh. "Yeah, that's Harry Katz."

"Does he approve of me dating his daughter?"

I shrug. "It's not up to him."

He eyes me carefully. "He doesn't care who you date?"

"He cares," I say. "He just trusts my judgment. Especially now," I add before I can stop myself.

Lex's eyes narrow. "What do you mean?"

My heart beats like a heavy weight, almost pulling me down with it. "I just mean now that I'm older and more responsible," I say. It's too soon to tell him the truth, even though I *hate* lying to him.

He smiles. "So, I shouldn't expect the typical father talk from your Dad?"

"No. Not from Harry."

My heart slows down to its normal pace and we finish our ice cream.

"Okay, where to next?" He asks.

"I don't know. Where do you want to go?"

"We could go back to my place." My face clearly says something, because he says, "Or not. That's cool, too."

"Um," I start, not entirely sure what to say.

"I just meant we could watch a movie or something, that's all," He clarifies, clearly nervous by my reaction.

But I stop him before he can start again. "Have you been to the falls?"

~

Genesee Falls has few scenic things to do, but my personal favorite is the hiking trails with all of the waterfalls, hence the name of the town.

We pull into the parking lot and make our way to the trails. There are three different ones you can take; the short one, the longer one, and the really long one. Judging by Lex's shoes, I pick the short one.

"Next time, wear sneakers."

He furrows his brows. "I don't think I own sneakers."

"What shoes do you work out in?"

"You assume I work out?" He says with a sly grin.

"You're a rich white boy who probably has a gym in his house. Of course, I assume you work out."

He shrugs. "If only I had the time."

"Buy sneakers, and next time we can walk the real trail. It's about three miles all the way around, but it's worth it. Halfway there, you get to the big waterfall and it's gorgeous."

"I'll make a mental note," he says and holds his hand out to me.

I take it.

We walk hand in hand in silence for a while as we pass small waterfalls that have formed in the rock wall over time. "How come you didn't mention this place?"

"Hmm?"

"The other day on the bench, I asked you what there was to do in this town. You never mentioned the waterfalls."

"I guess I never pegged you for the waterfall, scenic view type. Or it slipped my mind."

"Fair enough. What else slipped your mind?"

69

I let out a long breath. "There's a vineyard about five miles outside of town that has wine tastings, but you have to be 21," I say, pointing to myself. "Not 21."

"And?"

"Every July we have a small-town festival that has pony rides and cotton candy and kettle corn and a duck derby—"

"A duck derby! What is a duck derby?"

"You really don't want to know," I say as we pass another small waterfall.

"But I do," he says and pulls me closer to him. "I really do." He kisses the back of my hand, and I can feel it move up my arm and into my heart.

I stop walking.

We're alone on the trail, nothing but trees and waterfalls and rocks. Lex wraps his arm around me, resting his hand on the small of my back. "How about I kiss you until you tell me?"

I smile. "You're going to be kissing me for a while."

And his lips are on mine, soft and sweet and eager. His other hand moves to cup my face, and I find my hands entangled in his hair. He's half a foot taller than me, and I can feel him pulling on my lower back, trying to bring me closer.

I could kiss him forever. I could leave my fingers in his hair forever.

I can feel his lips curl into a smile as he breaks the kiss, just for a moment. "Tell me now?"

"No." I kiss him more. I've never done this before. I'd never been into public displays of affection with Steve—not that this trail is very public—but I've never been so *passionate* before.

Then again, Steve was not a good kisser. And he was the only boy I'd ever kissed before.

Until last night.

And now it's like my whole body has finally come alive. Everywhere Lex touches me, a tiny electric pulse surges through my skin, making my stomach turn into butterflies.

He runs his fingers ever so slightly down my left side until his hand lands on my hip, and he gives it a gentle squeeze. "What about now?" He asks through panting breaths.

I shake my head. "Nope."

He moans against my lips and my insides melt along with all the ice cream I just ate.

"Are you sure you don't want to come back to my place?" he asks with a chuckle.

I stop and pull away from him.

I put my hand on his chest and blink hard.

"Peyton?" His tone is genuine concern for my suddenness.

I breathe calmly, just how Dr. Young taught me, and do what Sammy told me to do. "No." My answer is firm, but not mean.

I meet his gaze, his eyes are full of understanding. "Okay. That's fine." He says, taking my hand in his and squeezing. "Are you okay?"

I take another breath. "Yeah," I smile. "I am."

I pull him back on the trail, and we walk together in silence for a moment before he finally asks, "Seriously, what's a duck derby?"

MY PHONE AUTOMATICALLY CONNECTS TO THE BLUETOOTH when we get back in the Mercedes, and *Lovesong* by The Cure starts playing.

I can't help but smile.

We're both silent for the ride back to my house, but he holds my hand the entire time.

As he pulls up to my house, the song ends, and I notice my Dad's already left for work.

Lex walks me to my door and smiles. "What was that song?"

"Just now?"

"Yeah?"

"Seriously?!"

"What?"

"*Lovesong*, by The Cure. You've never heard The Cure before? You poor, sheltered rich boy."

He laughs and wraps his arms around me, planting a kiss on my nose. "I like that song," he says. "Is your Dad home?"

"No, he went to work."

Lex nods, and I can tell how much he wants to stay, but based on my reaction before, I know he won't ask to.

I look up at him and smile. "Thank you."

He brushes his lips lightly against mine. "For what?"

"For the roses. For the ice cream. For the walk in the woods."

"Thank *you*, Peyton."

"For what?"

He kisses me one last time. "For making me feel whole again."

8

"How to Save a Life" // The Fray

"Oh, my *god!*" Sammy says. We're sitting in my car parked in the pharmacy lot. I've just finished telling her about ice cream and waterfalls and The Cure. "You just had the best weekend, *ever!*"

I cover my face with my hands. "What is this feeling? It's too soon, it can't be love. Is it lust? Desire? Am I *in like* with him?"

She laughs. "You're definitely in like with him. It's the whole new relationship energy. You've got the warm and fuzzies! He gives you butterflies in your stomach and makes your toes curl."

"I feel like I'm dropping on a roller coaster and it's a never-ending hill," I admit. "It's so confusing because I want him to kiss me and touch me, but..." I pause for a second, trying to find the right words. "At the same time, my body reflexively pushes him away."

"Just give it time. It's not going to happen overnight. Have you told him anything yet?"

"No, it's too soon. But I think he might suspect something."

"What? How?"

"When I told him 'no' yesterday he had this look on his face like he was concerned, and he asked me if I was okay."

Sammy smiles. "So, when are you guys going out again?"

I shake my head. "I don't know. He hasn't said anything. Shit, am *I* supposed to say something? Sammy, I'm not good at this stuff!"

"Relax, Peyton! He's asked you out on two dates, two days in a row. He will ask you out again."

I let out a breath. "We should get back inside."

Sammy looks at the time on her phone. "Oh, shit!"

We grab our things and head back to the store.

Lex and Sydney are interviewing people for the open customer service associate positions, even though new people won't be starting until we have the new computer system up and running.

Half of the store is a complete disaster, and the other half looks like a shiny new nickel. We've got a crew of guys working on painting the walls and ceiling and replacing the floor tiles. Sammy and I run back to the break room, and I toss my things in my locker, trying to catch a peek of Lex in the office, but the door is closed.

I sigh and head back out to the construction area. Sammy goes back to the pharmacy register, and I go back to stocking cold medicine.

ALL AFTERNOON, SYDNEY KEEPS LEX BUSY BY DRAGGING HIM ALL over the store with plans for the remodel and doing more interviews, but every time he walks by me, his fingers brush the small of my back, and our eyes meet for just a moment.

Sometimes he winks at me, sometimes he smiles, and every time, I wish we had the entire store all to ourselves.

By the time five o'clock rolls around, I know my day is over, but Lex's is far from it. I clock out and get my things from my locker and hear Sydney talking to Lex in the office.

"Hey, Syd, why don't you go take your break? I can handle things around here for a bit."

"Are you sure?" She asks.

"Yeah, go on. Go get your dinner."

I hear her say something else but can't make out the words. I stand in front of my locker, pretending to busy myself with my things. "Hey, Peyton! You have a nice night!"

I smile. "Night, Sydney."

As soon as she's out the door, I shut my locker and head for the office. No one else is in the break room, and I peek my head in the door. Lex is leaning back in an office chair, staring at a computer screen. "Hey," I say.

He straightens and smiles at me. "Is there anyone else out there?"

I shake my head. "No."

He stands up, pulls me into the office, and kisses me. It happens so fast, I wasn't prepared. "Lex! Someone could walk in!"

He shrugs. "What can I say? I'm a rebel." And he kisses me again, wrapping his arms around me. "I've been dying to do that all day," he says as he brushes a stray piece of hair behind my ear.

"How long do you have to stay?" I ask as I slide my arms through his.

"Until the store closes."

I frown. "I guess I won't see you until Wednesday?"

His eyes narrow. "Really?"

"I have school tomorrow," I remind him.

"When do you get home?"

75

"Usually around six."

"You go to school in Octavia, right?"

"Yeah, why?"

He's thoughtful for a second. "Well, I'll be here in the morning, but I have a bunch of meetings tomorrow afternoon in the city, and I'll be out there for the rest of the day. Maybe we could meet up for dinner?"

I smile. "Really?"

"And we don't have to go anywhere fancy this time," he says.

"Where do you want to go?" I ask.

"I don't know. How familiar are you with Octavia?"

I laugh. "Well, I can tell you exactly where the Dunkin', McDonald's, and Tim Horton's are but that's about it."

He scoffs. "No Taco Bell? And you call yourself a college student!"

"We don't have a Taco Bell," I admit.

"What do you kids do for hangover food?"

I ponder for a moment. "We do have a Denny's."

"Ah, the illustrious pancake." He kisses me again. "What if we meet up at my apartment and go from there?"

Lex's apartment.

Man, he really wants to get me in his apartment.

"Did your apartment come with a Zagat guide?"

"It might have, or we could just look on the internet."

I smile, and he kisses me again so deeply that I couldn't think straight if I had a map and a compass.

And before I even have the chance to protest, the doors to the break room open and voices bellow out. We pull away from each other, and Lex sits back down in the office chair.

"I'll text you the address," he whispers, and I nod and walk out of the office, wave politely to the painters in the break room, and make my way out of the store.

≈

TUESDAY GOES BY QUICKER THAN I THINK IT WILL, PROBABLY because I'm fighting with my anxiety all day about going to his apartment.

By the time my last class ends, I have a few missed texts—two from Lex and five from Sammy—and I wait until I'm in my car to read them.

'Three dates in a row? Damn, girl.'

'He's got it bad!'

'He is looking mighty good today. He just left for his 'meetings' in Octavia.'

'And don't panic about being at his apartment. You're only going there to find a place to eat and you're leaving. Just breathe.'

'Ugh, Shane is pissed at me. Can I crash at your place tonight?'

I toss my backpack in the back seat, stick my keys in the ignition, and text her back. *'Of course. I'll call my Dad now.'*

My father still has one of those old flip phones because he's an old man who refuses to change with the times. He also doesn't do texting. I've tried to teach him numerous times, even with T9, but he gets frustrated and grumbles, "I don't need to text people, grumble grumble grumble."

He doesn't answer, so I call again. And again, and again.

Fuck.

I call Sammy.

"Hey," she says.

"Are you at my house yet?"

"Just pulled in the driveway. Why? What's up?"

"My Dad isn't answering his phone. Will you make sure he's okay?"

"Yeah, I'm headed in now." I hear her rustle around with her things and a door close. I'm trying not to freak out, but he knows it makes me crazy when he doesn't answer his phone. He knows I'll start to panic. "He's not answering the door," she says.

"Why are you knocking? Just walk in."

I hear the door open. "Dad? It's Sammy." She pauses. "Hello? Dad? He's not in the living room or kitchen."

"Check upstairs."

"Peyton, what if he's in the shower or something?"

"Then you'll hear water running. Just go check!"

Goddamn it.

"Oh, my god!"

"What is it?"

"Dad? Dad! Peyton, you need to get home. Your Dad! He's unconscious on the floor!"

"Is he bleeding?"

"I don't see any blood."

"Okay, is he breathing?"

I wait for the longest ten seconds of my life for an answer. "Yes, he's breathing."

I let out a breath. "Okay. Call an ambulance. Tell them a man with alcohol-related liver disease has fainted. He might have jaundice or something. I'll be right there."

"Okay, I'm on it."

I hang up and start my car, and call Lex at the same time, even though I know driving while on my cell is illegal. It goes to voicemail.

"*You've reached Alexander Kingston. Please leave a message, and I'll get back to you as soon as I can.*"

"Hey, it's Peyton. I'm sorry, but I can't meet up with you tonight. It's a long story, but my Dad is sick. He has to go to the emergency room again. I'm on my way home now. I'll text you later."

I toss my phone on the passenger seat next to me and take a different way home, avoiding all of the traffic jams on the state route.

By the time I pull up to the house, the ambulance is in the driveway. I run inside, and they're already carrying him downstairs on a gurney.

"Is he okay?" I ask, out of breath.

"We're not sure yet," says a dark-haired male paramedic. "We need to take him to the hospital for more testing, but from what we can tell he probably has a minor head injury from the fall, possible dehydration, and most likely jaundice. There might be more," he continues as they pull the gurney out onto the porch and down the steps. "Are you the other daughter?"

"Yes, I'm Peyton Katz."

"Your sister said he has liver disease, but she wasn't specific."

"He has alcoholic cirrhosis," I say.

The paramedic nods. "Well, I have a feeling he's got more wrong with him. His breath reeks of alcohol." Sammy appears by my side and takes my hand as I blink back the tears.

He's drinking again. Why is he drinking again?

They load my father into the ambulance, and the paramedic comes back. "Do you want to ride with us up to Octavia Memorial?"

"No, I'll follow you guys up there. Thanks," I say. He waves us goodbye, and they turn their sirens on and drive off.

I sink onto the steps of the porch and pull my knees into my chest. Sammy sits next to me and wraps me in her arms as I cry.

After a few minutes, I pull myself together and turn to her. "I have to get up to the hospital. You know how he is with hospitals, especially if he's still drunk."

"Do you want me to come with you?"

"No," I say as I wipe the tears from my face. "You stay here and keep Cosmo company. And can you feed him for me if I'm not back on time?"

"Of course."

We both stand, and I hug her as tight as I can. "Thank you for being here. Shit, if you hadn't come over tonight, I wouldn't have found him until—"

"Well, thank the stars my girlfriends pissed at me, again."

I wipe my face on my shirt. "She'll get over it. She always does."

"I don't know. I tried to clean the apartment for her, you know, as a surprise, and I cleaned it wrong. I moved everything around, and her OCD went into overdrive, and she lost it."

I eye her sympathetically as I head inside the house. "It's not her fault."

"I know. I try so hard to do things the way she needs them done, but I guess I have to let her do them. I just feel guilty that she does all the cleaning."

"Does she get mad that she does all the cleaning?"

"No."

"Well, there you go. You're in everyone's fantasy relationship. The one where they never have to clean because their partner does it all, like Monica and Chandler."

"I guess."

"All right, I'm going to grab my phone charger and a book. I'll probably be at the hospital for a while. I'll keep you posted."

"Yeah, me too."

WHEN I ARRIVE AT OCTAVIA MEMORIAL, MY DAD IS ASLEEP IN A small room alone, *thank the fucking stars*. Having a roommate tends to piss him off even more. A female nurse with blonde hair pulled up into a bun, and wearing pink scrubs with cupcakes on them, is checking his vitals. "Has he woken up at all?" I ask.

She shakes her head. "Not yet. Are you family?"

"I'm his daughter, Peyton."

"Okay, Peyton. I'm going to get you a family bracelet so no one kicks you out."

I smile gratefully as she leaves the room. I look at my father lying in a hospital bed with tubes and wires attached to him.

He's going to be so pissed when he wakes up.

The nurse comes back in with a plastic bracelet for me and snaps it on my right wrist. She finishes taking down his vitals. "Has a doctor been in to see him yet?"

"He's only been here for about fifteen minutes, and we just got the ambulance report. But a doctor will be in to see him soon."

I nod and thank her. She leaves the room, and I sit in the chair beside his bed and pull out my phone. I haven't even checked it since I called Lex. I have four missed calls from him and a bunch of new texts.

All from him. My heart sinks.

The first two are from earlier today, the first being his address, and the second saying, *'Text me when you get here. You need a special key for the elevator, so I'll have to come down to meet you.'*

Well, that didn't happen. I scroll down to read the rest.

'Is everything all right?'

'What's wrong with your Dad?'

'Which hospital are you going to? The one here in Octavia?'

'I'm sorry, I don't mean to bother you. I'm just worried. Let me know if there's anything I can do.'

The cell phone service in this hospital sucks, but I try to reply anyway. *'Hey, I just got to the ER. We're at Octavia Memorial. My Dad is still asleep, but he's not going to be happy when he wakes up. I'm so sorry about tonight. I was looking forward to seeing you.'* I press send and wait. It takes a few seconds, but it goes through. *'Thank you, and you're not bothering me. Please text me. I'm going to be here for a while. I have to let Sydney know I may not be into work tomorrow, depending on what the doctors say.'*

While I'm thinking about it, I go back to my text list and

click on Sydney's name. *'Hey Sydney, my Dad is in the hospital again.'*

I get Lex's reply as soon as Sydney's message sends. *'Don't worry about work. I'll cover for you. I'll talk to Sydney, too. Just take care of your Dad. Do you need me to bring you anything? Is there anything I can do?'*

I smile, wishing he was here just so I had someone to hug. I look over at my father, looking so lifeless, so helpless, and let out a breath. *'No, thank you, though. If I think of anything, I'll let you know.'*

~

AFTER A PHLEBOTOMIST COMES IN AND TAKES SEVEN TUBES OF blood from my father, a transport guy comes in the room. "Is this Harry Katz?"

"Yes," I say.

"All right, I've got to bring him down to imaging for a bit. The doctor ordered an ultrasound of his liver. It shouldn't be too long, probably thirty minutes or so," he says as he unlocks the wheels of the bed and moves the IV bag from the metal pole and attaches it to the side of the bed.

"Okay, thank you," I say as he smiles and leaves me alone in the room. I grab my purse and head for the nurse's station. "Excuse me?" I say to the woman sitting at the front desk. She smiles and looks up at me. "Do you know where a coffee machine is?"

"Yup, there's a lounge down the hall. Follow the blue line and turn at the second left."

"Thanks."

I'm relieved to know it's not far from my Dad's room to coffee and snacks, even if it is vending machine food. It's better than nothing. I get some coffee, a bag of chips, and an almond joy and make my way back down to his room. He's not back yet, so I sit down in the chair and grab the TV remote.

By the time my father returns, I've finished my dinner, for lack of better options, and my Dad is starting to stir in the bed.

"What the hell... get these tubes..." he says, and I set my coffee down and stand. The transport guy puts the bed back in place and locks the wheels, putting his IV bag back on the metal pole, and gives me a look that clearly says, '*Good luck.*'

I grab my Dad's arms and hold him down, so he doesn't pull out his IV. "Dad. Dad!" I say, and he looks up at me.

"Peyton? What the hell am I doing here?"

"Calm down, and I'll tell you, okay?"

"I don't need to be in the goddamn hospital again! Now get me the hell out of here!"

"Listen to me!" I say, loud enough that the nurses in the hall look in the room. I pull the curtain closed, not that it will prevent them from hearing us.

I'm on him again, and he's still struggling against me, so I grab him by the wrists and slam his arms down at his sides. "What the hell, Peyton!"

"Stop fighting me!" I say. He looks me in the eye, and slowly, he stops pushing against me. "Sammy went to the house after work today. She needed a place to crash, and she found you on the bathroom floor. You were passed out because you started drinking again, and now you have a head injury and jaundice, and who knows what else! We had to call an ambulance and bring you in to make sure you're all right."

"Peyton," he starts, but I don't let him finish.

"No, *don't*. You *know* you're not supposed to be drinking! You *know* the rules. And this isn't about being treated like a child. It's about being treated like a person *whose liver is failing,* and can no longer process alcohol!" He doesn't say anything because he knows I'm right. He tips his head back and closes his eyes, a single tear falls down his cheek.

"*Don't you dare start with the waterworks*! I am so fucking pissed off at you right now, I could punch you! But I can't do that, because you're my father, and *I love you*, and you're the only goddamn family I have left. So if you wouldn't mind, I'd like it if you'd continue to *live* so I'm not left alone in this world!"

I let go of him, and he looks at me wide-eyed, his jaw trembling. "Peytie, I'm—"

Before he can say another word, the curtain slides open.

Two doctors appear before me, one older gentleman with brown skin, silver hair, and a faint beard, like he hasn't shaved in a few days. The other man is younger, with dirty blonde hair and green eyes. I stand there with my arms folded across my chest, tears swelling in my eyes as they both smile at us.

"Good evening Mr. Katz, and?"

"Peyton," I say. "His daughter."

"Peyton! Nice to meet you. I'm Dr. Larson, and this is my colleague Dr. Owens," he says, and he reaches out a hand to greet me. I shake it.

The two men take their time explaining that my father has a minor concussion, and his liver needs to detox before he can go home. They will be keeping him in the hospital for forty-eight hours on an all-liquid diet, and any medication he needs so his liver can heal from his relapse.

"Mr. Katz, I know you've been told this many times before, but the only way to heal your liver is lifelong abstinence from alcohol. If you don't stop drinking, there is no medical or surgical treatment that can prevent liver failure, and if your liver fails..."

"I'll die. Yes, I know."

He knows, he just doesn't care.

After they finish their plans and explanations, the doctors leave us alone, and a nurse comes in with a new IV bag and a shot with some form of medication. I don't ask what it is.

Frankly, I'm too exhausted, and I need to get home to sleep so I can work tomorrow. I cannot afford to miss another day of work. I've missed so much in the past few months, and Sydney is always so understanding.

The nurse leaves, and I approach my father. "Dad," I start.

He takes my hand and squeezes it. "I'm sorry, Peytie."

I bend down and kiss him on the forehead. "I know."

"I love you, kiddo," he says, fighting back the tears. And it almost breaks me.

"I love you, too." I stroke his hair back for a minute before I say, "Are you going to be okay if I leave? I have to work tomorrow, but if you need me to stay, I can figure something out."

He shakes his head. "I'll be fine. You go home, get some rest, and go to work."

I eye him. "Are you sure? Because I'll stay if you don't want to be here alone."

He looks at me. "Peyton, I am not a child."

"I never said you were."

"I'll be perfectly fine by myself. I won't even be by myself. I'm sure these nurses will be in here every five minutes to give me something or check my damn vitals!"

I roll my eyes and sigh. "Do I need to call Jerry?"

He shakes his head. "No, I'll call him in the morning from the hospital line, let him know I'm stuck in here for a few days. He'll get someone to cover my shift."

"You're here until Friday morning, the doctors said. Remember that."

"I know. I'll remember." He kisses the back of my hand.

I turn back to the chair and start gathering all my stuff together. "I'll stop by after work tomorrow."

He nods. "Okay. And Peyton?"

"Yeah?"

"Tell Sammy I said thanks."

I give him a half-smile. "I will."

9

"With a Little Help From My Friends" // The Beatles

I wake up the next morning with Sammy bouncing up and down on my bed, saying, "Happy Hump Day!"

I groan.

"It's time to get up for work! If you're going—I figured since you're home, you're going. I mean, you never call in off unless it's life or death. Oh, my god, it's not life or death, is it?"

"No, it's not," I say, my voice hoarse.

"When did you get home last night? I didn't hear you come in."

"After midnight. You were already asleep on the couch."

"So? You could've woken me up."

I give her a half-smile. "Yeah, I know."

"You shower first, and I will make you the famous Samantha Clarke's Five Star Ultimate Breakfast of Champions Feast of the Gods!"

I chuckle and pull a pillow over my face. "What time is it?" It comes out muffled.

"Seven thirty-four," she says.

"Five more minutes?"

"No. You have to get ready and tell me everything that happened at the hospital last night before you leave because I refuse to be left out of the loop, especially since I'm the one who found your Dad yesterday."

"He says, 'thanks.'"

Sammy smiles. "I'd say, '*anytime*,' but I really don't ever want that to happen again."

AFTER I SHOWER AND TOSS MY HAIR INTO A MESSY BUN, I PUT ON my work clothes and make my way downstairs. It's just after eight, and Sammy has made some concoction of scrambled eggs with cheese and vegetables and toast.

"Your breakfast awaits," she says in a horrible British accent.

I chuckle. "Don't ever do that again. They'd kill you across the pond." She pours me a fresh cup of coffee, and I half moan, half sigh in gratitude. "Bless you."

She smiles. "You're welcome. Now, dish."

I grab the creamer out of the fridge and fill her in on everything Dr. Larson said at the hospital last night, and my father's minor flip out when he woke up.

And my absolute takeover of Harry Katz in a hospital bed.

Sammy's jaw almost hits the floor. "You actually said that to your Dad?"

"I was livid. He could have died, and sometimes I think he doesn't even care."

She takes the egg pan off the stove and sets it in the sink. "I don't think he doesn't care. I think he's struggling, and sometimes..."

"I know. It's not easy for him, either," I say. I know my father loves me. For the past fourteen years, I've been the number one person in his life, and he'd do *almost* anything for me.

But alcohol has taken over so much of him for so long, I honestly have no idea how he does it.

But I guess that's why they're called functioning alcoholics.

I finish eating Sammy's breakfast, and it's fucking amazing. "I don't know what Shane's problem is. You can live with me for these eggs alone."

"See? I told you. *Feast of the Gods!*"

I put my plate in the sink and hug her. "Thank you. I don't know what I'd do without you."

"I do. You'd cry a lot. You'd be terribly lonely, have no one to talk to, or get any good advice from," she boasts.

I pull back and shake my head. "You think mighty highly of yourself."

"I can't help that I'm fabulous."

∽

WHEN NOON ROLLS AROUND, LEX PULLS ME ASIDE AND ASKS IF we can have lunch together.

"Wait, you're asking me? Usually, you just make an appearance and sit down."

"I want to know what's going on with your Dad, make sure everything is okay." I grab my lunch from the fridge, and Lex eyes me and shakes his head. "Have you learned nothing?"

I roll my eyes and sigh as he tosses my brown bag lunch back in the fridge, and pulls out two submarine sandwiches and a couple of vitamin waters.

We make our way outside and sit at a picnic table in the town square.

"So, what's going on? I'm surprised you came into work today. I thought you would've stayed at the hospital."

I start at the beginning. I go into all the details, and times he's almost died, been in remission, only to relapse again. Every single time I've almost lost my father, and been left alone, with no family left, and I fight back the tears. "It's the other reason why I want to be a Pharmacy Technician. I can make more money here so I can help pay my Dad's medical bills. We almost lost the house last year." Remembering this triggers a memory of my father on the phone with the bank, begging for another extension. Just one more month for him to get the money together so we didn't end up in foreclosure.

"My Uncle Jack stepped in and gave us a loan, but he knows we can't pay him back." Another memory of my father accepting the check from Uncle Jack. I wasn't even supposed to know about it, but I watched from the top of the stairs as Jack handed my father the check, and the look of absolute defeat on my father's face when he took it.

"That's also why I came into work today. I can't afford not to. My Dad's missing work right now, and he'll be out of work until this weekend. That's three days' pay he's not getting this week. He makes good money working at ACore. It's just a matter of him *going* to work. I guess I'll be making a late payment this month," I say with a shrug because it's not the first time.

"*You're* making the payments?"

"It's only because my Dad doesn't know how to use the computer. I've tried to teach him, but he's so stubborn," I shrug. "I don't mind doing it. That's what family is for."

Lex looks at me with those blue-gray eyes as if he's finally deciphered an ancient text that gave him the answers to everything he's been looking for. "I think I'm starting to understand," he says.

"Understand what?"

"You're not a typical nineteen-year-old college girl. You're *wise*. You had to grow up a lot faster than most people. You had to become a responsible adult when you're still a teenager, and

I admire you for that. There's no way I could have done everything you're doing when I was nineteen. My god, I was horrible at that age."

I snort. "I bet."

Lex eyes me. "I have a video of me on spring break in Cancun that would make you second guess our entire relationship."

"I can't wait to stumble across that video on YouTube," I joke.

Lex chuckles as he plays with the cap of his vitamin water. "So, is your Dad terminal?"

I take a sip of my water. "That depends. If he continues to drink, yes. If he stops drinking, he'll be okay in time. The only thing that can heal his liver is abstinence from alcohol."

"And that's hard for him."

"He's an alcoholic."

"Has he ever gone to rehab or AA?"

I force myself not to laugh. "He's been in treatment centers before because he was legally required to stay for seventy-two hours, but my Dad is not an AA guy. It's a pretty religious program and he's a hardcore atheist."

"That must have been hard for you. Growing up with a Dad like that, especially when he's your only parent."

I blow out a breath, "It wasn't always easy," I say as I remember. "There was this one time when I was thirteen. Back then, when my Dad would work overnights at ACore, I'd stay with Uncle Jack and Aunt Michelle. I'd sleep in the guest room, and Michelle would bring me to school in the morning, and I'd walk home. And this one time, I walked in the house and found him passed out on the living room floor lying in a pool of his own vomit."

Lex stops chewing for a second and sets his sub down.

"Sorry, I just remember seeing him like that, and for the first time in my life, I saw him as a regular person, and not this amazing guy with superpowers. When I was little, I truly believed my Dad was a secret superhero."

Lex laughs. "Really?"

"Yeah, but I guess that's how all kids see their parents. We put them on pedestals until we're old enough to realize they're just people, too."

Lex nods. "I was about four or five when I realized my Dad was an asshole."

"What was it for you?"

He thinks for a second before he answers. "The first time I saw him punch my Mom in the face."

I look at Lex, wide-eyed, shocked. "Oh my, god."

"The second time I saw it, I grabbed one of the fireplace irons and started hitting him with it until my mother stopped me."

I don't know what to say. I take his hand and squeeze. "I'm sorry," I manage.

He smiles at me. "It was a long time ago."

"Did he hurt you?" I whisper.

Lex licks his lips and looks down at his sub, but doesn't answer. I almost regret asking, but he places his hand on top of mine and gives me a half-smile. "Yeah, he did. But I fought back, or tried to, at least."

I blink hard and shake my head. "Lex, I'm sorry."

He lifts my hand to his lips and kisses me. "Peyton, I want you to know my father taught me how *not* to treat people, especially women. I would never hurt you."

"I never thought you would," I say honestly.

He smiles and kisses my hand again. "Good. Good." And I think he looks relieved. "Is there anything I can do?"

"For what?" I ask as I wrap up the rest of my sub.

"For you? For your Dad? Is there any way I can help you guys in your situation?"

I smile kindly. "No, but thank you." I stand and lean over

the table and kiss him, not caring if anyone across the street can see us. He kisses me back, but I can see his eyes darting at the store.

"Peyton, what if someone sees us?" He jokes.

I smirk. "What can I say? I'm a rebel."

He laughs, climbing over the table and kisses me until our break is over.

10

"I Will Wait" // Mumford and Sons

My phone rings right after five o'clock as I'm getting ready to leave work. I'm standing in the break room, staring at a number I know to be the hospital line.

"Hey, Dad. What's up?"

"Hey, sweetheart. I was just thinking you don't have to come visit me tonight."

I pause for a second, thrown by his words. "What do you mean?"

"I didn't get much sleep last night. All these doctors and nurses are driving me crazy, and I don't want to be a grouch to you. I've put you through enough. Why don't you go home and relax and eat pizza and watch TV for a change?"

"You really don't want me to come see you?"

"No, not tonight. Please. I'm too tired for visitors."

He sounds grumpy all right. "Okay. If you change your mind—"

"I won't change my mind. I love you, Peyton. You have a good night. I'll talk to you tomorrow."

"Okay, talk to you tomorrow."

We hang up, and I stand there, stunned. Lex is leaning against the office doorway, arms crossed. "Everything okay?"

I snap out of it and look at him. "Yeah. I guess I'm *not* going to see my Dad tonight."

"Really?"

"He says he's '*too tired and grumpy*' for visitors."

Lex smiles at me. "What about you?"

I narrow my eyes. "What *about* me?"

"Are *you* too tired and grumpy for a visitor?"

A smile forms on my lips. "What are you thinking?"

He saunters over to me, closing the distance between us. "I am leaving here at exactly six o'clock tonight. Maybe I could stop by, bring dinner? Maybe we could watch a movie?"

I smile as I take in his wicked grin, pretending I don't notice his eyes roam over me and my stomach clenches. "That sounds nice," I say. He glances through the windows of the break room doors to make sure no one is coming before sliding his hand around my nape and kisses me. This kiss is deep and hard, and eager, and when he pulls away, I'm left wanting more.

"I'll see you later," he says and walks back into the office.

I CAN'T HELP BUT WORRY ABOUT MY DAD BEING IN THE HOSPITAL all alone. I know he'll probably hang up on me, but screw it.

While I wait for Lex to arrive, I go sit on the wooden swing on the front porch and call the hospital.

"Hello," he says, clearly annoyed.

"Hello, Mr. Grumpy Puss. I was just calling to see if my father felt like chatting for a few minutes."

He huffs into the phone, "Peyton, don't you have a new boyfriend or something?"

I laugh. "No, he's not my boyfriend—well, I don't know. We've only been out on a few dates. But for your information, he's coming over tonight with pizza and a movie. I just wanted to make sure you're doing all right before he gets here."

I can feel my father smiling on the other end of the phone. "Pizza and a movie, huh? Is that old school for Netflix and Chill?"

I roll my eyes, but smile. "Yes, Dad. That's exactly what it is. How are you feeling?"

"Annoyed and irritated, but other than that, fine. The nurses are letting me eat ice chips for dinner. Lucky me. They're sugar-free, gluten-free, and fat-free!"

I laugh, relieved that some of my father's sense of humor is returning. "You're going to come home *so* skinny. All the other Dads will be jealous of your new Dad-bod."

He chuckles. "*I'm too sexy for this hospital gown*," he starts mock singing Right Said Fred, and my insides relax.

"Dad?"

"Yeah, sweetheart?"

"You sound better."

He pauses for a moment. "Well, I can't leave my baby girl all alone on this planet, now can I?"

I blink hard, but I can feel the tears swelling in my eyes. "I'm sorry about last night. I didn't mean to yell at you, I was—"

"You were right," He interrupts me. "Peyton, I know you're upset with me, and I know I hurt you by drinking again, and I'm sorry. I had a bad day, and I slipped. I can't promise it won't ever happen again, but I can promise that I'll try my hardest for it not to. I promise the next time I'm having a bad day, instead of thinking about a bottle, I'll think about you. About how much I love you, and how much we need each other, and how much I can't let my baby girl down."

I wipe a single tear away from my cheek and say. "Okay. I love you."

"I love you, too. Now, I'm going to hang up this phone and go back to watching bad hospital cable, and you go have fun with your *friend*."

Just as he says it, I smile and see Lex walking up the porch steps holding a brown paper bag.

"Okay, I'll talk to you tomorrow. Night."

"Goodnight," he says.

I hang up the phone, setting it on the swing next to me, and try to wipe away any trace that I was crying, but it doesn't work.

Lex stands before me, still in his work clothes, tan dress pants, and a dark blue button-down shirt. He sets the bag down on the wicker table next to the swing and slides his hands in his pockets. "You okay?"

"Yeah, I'm fine," I say and stand up. "Just my Dad." And the next thing I know, my arms are around his waist. I desperately need to feel something other than worry and fear and panic that I don't even think about it. Lex wraps his arms around me, pulling me close to him. We stand there for a long time, and he doesn't ask me why I'm hugging him like this. He simply hugs me because he knows I need it.

When we finally break away, he takes my face in his hands, and he kisses me. His lips soft and sweet.

I pull back, and turn toward the bag on the table. "Is that our food?"

"No," he starts, "that's wine and ginger ale."

My eyes narrow. "Ginger ale?"

"I figured in case you didn't want wine. I wasn't sure if you'd be interested or not."

"Well, I've never had wine before."

He furrows his brows in surprise.

I walk over to the bag and pull out a bottle to read the label.

"I mean, I've had tastes at Christmas and Thanksgiving before, but I don't know if I've ever had Shiraz."

Lex picks up the bag and takes out the other bottle. "I also got a bottle of sweet," he says as he shows me a bottle of Moscato. "The Shiraz is a dry wine, and since I didn't know what you liked, or if you liked either, I got both."

I smile. "I've never had either, so I'll have to try both."

I grab my phone from the swing and motion for him to follow me inside, but can tell Lex is a little unsure. "Don't worry. I put Cosmo out in the back yard. He should be okay for a bit." Lex blows out a breath and we head for the kitchen. I grab two wine glasses from the back of the cupboard and rinse them out. "I don't think anyone has used these glasses in years," I admit.

He's opening up random drawers before he looks at me. "Corkscrew?"

My head suddenly feels like it's been struck, and I think I may spin out of control. I blink hard, steeling myself. "Third drawer," I say and point.

It took me six months before I was able to even look at a corkscrew again without having a panic attack, but I still haven't been able to touch one.

I bring the glasses over to the table and watch as Lex pulls the cork out of each bottle, and puts the corkscrew back in the drawer, and I let out a relieved breath.

He smiles and pours one glass of Moscato and one glass of Shiraz. He hands me the Shiraz first, and I take a sip. "Oh, *god*," I say, as I make the same face I made the time I drank fresh lemonade before I put the sugar in. "That's so bitter."

Lex laughs. "It's an acquired taste."

I grab a bottle of water out of the fridge and drink, desperate to get that awful taste out of my mouth.

"You'll like the Moscato better." He holds out the glass to me, and I take it warily. "Don't worry, this one is a lot sweeter."

I smell it before I lift the glass to my lips. I'm surprised because it's actually fucking delicious. "Okay, that one is good," I say.

"I'm glad you like it." He takes my glass and fills it half full, doing the same for his, but he drinks the Shiraz. "So, I was thinking about ordering pizza if you're interested?"

I smile. "Absolutely.

We make our way into the living room and sit down on the sofa, and the smell of must and dog wafts in the air around us. My stomach clenches as I slowly look around as realize that Lex Kingston is in *my house*, sitting next to me on my couch. On *this* couch. My cheeks redden as I see his eyes dart to my fathers tattered armchair, but Lex doesn't say anything. Instead, he looks at me with a warm smile. "So, where does one order pizza from in Genesee Falls?"

I let out a relieved sigh and pull out my phone to open up the menu for the local pizza place for Lex to scroll through. "What are your favorite pizza toppings?" He asks.

I shake my head. "My favorite pizza toppings are not date friendly," I admit as my face flushes.

Lex looks at me and cocks his head to the side. "Aw, come on. You've got to tell me now. What are they? Anchovies? Feta Cheese?"

I take a sip of wine and set it down on the coffee table. "Garlic and onions."

Lex laughs. "As delicious as that sounds, you're right, that's not date friendly at all."

"Not if we enjoy the kissing part," I say as I lean in and press my lips to his.

He takes another sip of wine and sets it down on the coffee table, along with my phone. He turns his body, so he's facing me and swings my legs around, so I'm facing him. "And I very much enjoy the kissing part."

He wraps his arm under my knees and pulls me close to

him, so my legs are laying across his lap, our bodies touching. He wraps his right arm around my left side, holding me up, our faces inches apart. "Do you enjoy the kissing part?" He whispers.

My insides are twisting and flipping, and a flash of sweat coats my skin, but I nod. "Mm-hmm," I manage. And his lips are on mine.

This is the first time we're alone, in a place where we have the option to do more than kiss, and my mind and body are conflicting.

I want to kiss him, but I'm not sure how much *more* I'm ready for, or how much more Lex wants from me.

Lex pulls his lips from mine, but he doesn't stop. He drags them down my neck sending a jolt down my spine. Shock spreads through my body as he kisses that spot between my neck and shoulder, and a noise escapes my lips that makes him moan against my skin.

His hand is roaming down my back, my arms somehow found their way around his neck, and he looks at me with pleading eyes, like I'm the only person in the entire world who can give him what he truly needs.

"Lex," I whisper, and he comes undone at the sound of his name. His lips are on mine again, but they're not gentle. They are eager and crushing me, and my heart feels like it could explode at any moment.

I feel him pushing me backward like he wants me to lie down on the couch, and I begin to panic. My heart skips a beat as I put my hands behind me, catching myself. I lift my right hand and push it against Lex's chest. "Lex, wait," I say.

"What is it?" But before I can answer, his lips are on mine again.

I push against his chest, but he's no longer pushing me backward. He grabs my right leg with his left hand and uses his right arm to scoop me up. It takes me a second to gather myself and realize what he's trying to do. He's leaning back on the couch, and I'm straddling him now—one leg on each side—and my face is inches from his. My heart is pounding in my chest as his lips meet mine.

A wave of dizziness takes over as I close my eyes. His hands roam over my hips, and I can tell he's fighting the urge to move them against his. He's playing with the hem of my shirt, sliding his fingers ever so slightly underneath to touch my skin. His hands are warm as they slide under, and I try not to panic.

Breathe, Peyton.

"Lex," I say.

He kisses my neck down to my collar bone and back up again, and his hands slide up my sides, higher and higher and then I feel him.

I feel *him.*

And my anxiety wins.

I push his hands down, and pull away. "Stop. Stop!"

He pulls back, and I can tell by the look on his face that he heard the panic in my voice.

He removes his hands from my shirt and sits up straight, and I lean back, giving us space, so I'm no longer sitting on that part of him.

"Hey, are you okay?" He asks.

I take a few deep breaths before I'm able to speak without my voice shaking. "I just need to slow down."

"Okay," he says, totally understandingly. But I can feel his eyes on me, and he takes my hand. "Hey, what's up?"

I let out a breath. "I have to tell you something."

He straightens. When I don't continue right away, he says, "Did I do something wrong?"

I blink hard and shake my head. "No."

"Are you sure?" His tone full of concern.

And guilt consumes me at the sincerity in his voice. "No, you didn't do anything wrong."

"What is it?"

I breathe and get up from his lap. I sit next to him on the couch and pick up my wine glass and take a long drink. "Okay so, you know how you're older than me and you've had more experience and you know... you've... been with women before?" I start, so very badly.

"Um, yeah?" he says, seemingly confused.

I take another drink. "Well it's just that... I've... I've never... "

Realization dawns on his face. "You mean you've never..."

I shake my head. "No."

"You've never—really?"

"Really."

"You're a..."

"A virgin... yeah," I finally admit, sheepishly. "Biggest virgin in the world," I say and point to myself.

He chuckles. "Why 'biggest virgin in the world'?"

I take another sip of wine. "Because I haven't done anything besides kissing."

He slinks back on the couch, his eyes wide. "Okay," he says, and I feel every muscle in my body tense.

I wait for him to say something, *anything* else, but he just sits there. He picks up his wine glass and drinks, so I drink the rest of my wine before I whisper, "Is that okay?"

He finally looks at me with furrowed brows and shakes his head, as if shaking himself out of a trance. "What? Of course. Why wouldn't that be okay?"

"Well, you're not saying anything, and you're twenty-four, and a lot more experienced, and you've been with women before, and I doubt any of them ever told you no."

Lex leans back. "You're right. It's been a long time since I've dated a virgin. I think the last time was when I was seventeen."

My cheeks flush, and I look away, embarrassed.

"Hey, it's okay," He starts, and takes my hand again. "Peyton, there's nothing wrong with it. I'm not upset or anything. It's just new for me again."

I don't meet his gaze. "Okay." My insides feel like they're about to liquefy. "So, can I ask you something?"

"Of course," he says.

I wish I had more wine to drink. "I understand if you're not, but..."

Breathe, Peyton.

Lex squeezes my hand. "If I'm not what?"

I take a deep breath. "I was wondering if you're... if it's okay with you if we wait?"

"Wait?"

I bite my lip. "If we take things slow?"

"Oh," he says, and I can hear the disappointment in his tone. "Are you not interested?"

"No, Lex I am interested," I admit.

I stand up, grabbing my wine glass, and make my way back into the kitchen to pour another glass. I drink, fighting back the tears.

This is it. It hasn't even been two weeks, and I've already fucked it up with my stupid nerves and anxiety and fucking virginity.

He doesn't even know the worst part yet.

Lex is standing in the doorway, holding his glass and watching me. "Peyton, I'm sorry. I didn't mean for it to come out that way. I'd never pressure you into doing something you don't want to do."

I drink and breathe a sigh of relief. "Trust me, it's not that I don't want to, I just I need to take things slow. Just for a little while."

He closes the distance between us and brushes my hair behind my ear. "Okay," he smiles. "If that's what you need."

"And you're not mad?"

"No, I'm not mad. Disappointed? Maybe, a little, but mad? How can I be mad about that?"

I glance up at him. "You promise?"

He kisses me. "I promise. Being a virgin isn't that big of a deal."

I eye him. "Except it means we aren't going to have sex."

He shrugs. "Not right now, and maybe not for a while, but we'll get there eventually, right?"

"I don't know, Lex. I can't give you a date or a time frame," I admit, somewhat frazzled.

He pulls me into him. "Okay. Okay, that's fine. Sex is off the table until you decide to put it back on." He kisses the top of my head. "There's no pressure, no rush. I'll wait until you're ready." I hold him tight, hoping what he says is true, hoping this is enough for him. For now. He pulls back and looks at me with a smile. "Why don't we go and order that pizza?"

I nod, and we head back into the living room.

11

"I Knew You Were Trouble" // Taylor Swift

Friday morning, I go into work late because I have to pick my father up from Octavia Memorial and bring him home.

We stumble in the front door together, me half carrying him, his arm around my shoulder, my arm around his waist.

"Peyton, this is ridiculous! I can walk into my house by myself!"

"Well, you almost fell walking out of the hospital, and they had to get you a wheelchair, so I'm not taking any chances," I say.

He grumbles, "I've been lying in a goddamn hospital bed for the past three days. My legs just need to get used to moving again."

I roll my eyes and get him to his chair. "The doctor says you need to rest today, and if you feel up to it, and *only* if you feel up to it, you can go to work tomorrow."

"I already talked to Jerry. I *am* going to work tomorrow, and I'm working a double to make up some of the hours I lost."

I let out an exasperated sigh. "The doctor sent over some prescriptions to *Kingston's*. I'll pick them up and bring them home when I'm done with my shift."

"Yeah, yeah," he says as he bats me away with his hand, and picks up the remote for the TV.

Once I get him situated, I bring him some bottled water, and Cosmo jumps up to lay by his side. I kiss him on the forehead. "Love you. I'll see you later."

He grumbles something along the lines of 'You, too,' and 'Get out of here.'

SATURDAY IS INSANELY HOT. IT'S ONLY THE BEGINNING OF MAY, and it's already over ninety degrees and humid as fuck.

I wake up around eleven-thirty in the morning, and I'm already sweating through my t-shirt. I pull it off, and grab a tank top out of my drawer, and kick off my sweat pants, that are completely stuck to my legs, and put on a pair of cotton shorts, and head downstairs.

My Dad is at work by now, but he saw the note I'd left for him last night, and he wrote me back.

'I didn't forget to take my pills. I also brought them with me to work, along with the lunch and dinner you made me. Thank you, baby girl. Love you, Dad.'

Relief fills my insides as I think he's finally starting to come around.

I make some coffee and pour a bowl of cereal and play with my phone while I eat. I have one final paper due on Thursday I should work on this weekend, but it's way too hot to spend the day sitting in my room with no air conditioning. My Dad doesn't even put the window units in until June, and even though today is ninety degrees, tomorrow will probably be closer to seventy.

Welcome to spring in upstate NY!

After I finish eating, I take a quick shower and toss on a white tank top and black shorts, put my hair up in a messy bun on the top of my head, and I decide my Honda could use a shower, too.

I grab my little Bluetooth speaker and phone and head out to the garage where my Dad keeps all the cleaning supplies. I set my speaker and phone down on the plastic picnic table we have in the backyard and put my playlist on shuffle.

I attach the nozzle to the hose, and fill the bucket with soap and water.

I pull my car up the driveway into the backyard. Last night, I parked in the street since my Dad had to work in the morning. We never park in the garage. My Dad's stuff is so jam-packed in there, not even a motorcycle could fit.

I spray down my car as I belt out the words to *You Need to Calm Down* by Taylor Swift. I pull the sponge out of the bucket and begin washing my car.

I sing and dance along to the music as I push the orange sponge around my car, noticing new places she is rusting, and frown at the silver paint flaking off in tiny flecks. I make my way all the way around, and apparently, it's Swifty day, because my playlist is set to shuffle, but my iPhone keeps playing Taylor Swift songs. *22* comes on right after *Shake it Off*, and now *I Knew You Were Trouble* starts playing, and I spray my car down with the hose as I sing along, shaking my hips to the beat.

I don't even realize how loud I am being, when I hear someone clear their throat.

I jump back and see Lex standing there with a smirk on his face, watching me in his expensive tan pants, light blue silk button-down shirt, untucked and unbuttoned at the top.

My hand is on my chest—well, the sponge is on my chest—as he approaches me. "Oh, my god. Don't do that!" I say. I'm holding the spray nozzle in my other hand as my cheeks flush, but I laugh at myself. "I thought you were in meetings all day."

"Well, the good thing about being the boss is you can look outside and realize no one wants to be at work on a Saturday as lovely as this. So, I sent everyone home."

"Lucky them."

Lex shakes his head as he eyes me up and down. "Lucky *me*."

He approaches me with that look in his eyes like he wants to eat me alive. I lift up the hose and grin wickedly.

He eyes me carefully. "You wouldn't."

"Wouldn't I? Because I wouldn't want to ruin those fancy clothes of yours?"

"That's one reason." But he walks closer, and I step backward, holding the hose out like a gun, tossing the sponge back in the bucket.

"Freeze, or you're going to get wet."

"I don't believe you."

He takes one more step and I spray him. Shock fills his face, and the next thing I know, Lex is chasing me around my car. He picks up the bucket of freezing soapy water and aims it at me.

"Oh, no. No, no, no!"

"Oh, yeah!" He says as he chases me again until he's close enough to toss the contents of the bucket over my head. I scream when the water hits me, sending a cold chill down my spine. I drop the hose as I stand there frozen. Lex lifts me up into a bear hug and sets me down on the picnic table. He picks up the towel, and wraps it around me while he stands there dripping wet.

I look at him and bite my lip. "Did I really ruin your clothes?" I ask as I pick up my phone and turn off the music.

Lex shrugs. "Guess we'll wait and see."

"I can toss them in the dryer and find you something to wear. I have men's sweat pants and shorts and t-shirts I wear around the house." He quirks an eyebrow. "What? They're comfortable."

Lex looks down at himself. "I'm pretty sure if the water didn't ruin them, the dryer definitely will."

"It's a good thing you're rich and can buy a new outfit," I joke and toss him the towel.

He wipes off his face, sets the towel back down on the table and brushes his lips against mine. "Is your Dad home?"

"Nope. He's at work."

His grin turns mischievous. "We have the whole house all to ourselves? Whatever will we do?"

I bite my lip. "I'm sure we can figure out something."

He kisses me, and I've never been more grateful for stockade fencing in my whole life.

Lex slides his hands under my knees and wraps my legs around his waist, pulling me closer to him. "Is this okay?" He asks.

I smile. "Yeah." My heart is pounding, and I entwine my fingers in his hair, and his hands rest on my back, holding me against him. He kisses me again, gently at first, and my mouth opens for him. Our tongues meet, and he tastes like spearmint and vanilla, and I moan against his lips.

The next thing I know, Lex is lifting me up from the picnic table. "Oh, my god!" I chuckle as I cling to him for dear life. "What are you doing?"

He carries me in the back door that leads to the laundry room and sets me down on top of the dryer, my legs still firmly around his waist. "Giving us a bit more privacy," he says.

My stomach knots at the thought as he kisses me again.

His hands roam from my back, down my sides, and grab hold of my hips. His touch is gentle at first, but the more we kiss, the stronger his grip is, and I find my leg squeezing him tighter.

Oh, god. What am I doing?

I can feel we're both about to lose control if we don't stop soon, and the thought makes my stomach seize up.

I don't know if he does it intentionally or not, but Lex pulls me closer, pushing himself against me, and I feel his hard on.

My breath catches in my throat.

"Lex," I say as he starts kissing my neck.

My stomach turns in knots.

"Lex," I say again. His lips feel so good against my skin, but I need room to *breathe*.

This is too much.

"Lex," I put a hand on his chest, and I can feel his heart beating.

His mouth is on mine before I can say another word. His hands move up my legs, under my shorts, and brush against the top of my thighs...

Suddenly, I'm in the back of a limo, and Steve is on top of me. "Lex! Stop!" I scream, louder than I mean to, and shove him back. The image of Steve and the limo sputters to life. Thrown, I blink hard to push it out of my mind and it quickly fades to nothing.

It was a flash. A flash of a picture of what happened that night. But that's what happens when anyone touches my thighs.

"Peyton..."

I'm afraid to meet his gaze because I know he can see me trembling and trying not to cry, so I breathe a few more times before I put my hands down.

Lex is standing a few paces away, his hands held up defensively. "I'm sorry. I didn't mean... I thought... did I hurt you?"

I blink hard and shake my head. "No," I say and slide down from the dryer and fold my arms across my chest. "You didn't hurt me."

He runs his fingers through his hair. "I'm sorry. I got carried away. Are you okay?"

I rub my hands over my face. "I just... it was too much." I admit.

"I'm sorry."

"Okay," I say, at a loss of words.

I hate this. God, I hate this so much! Why can't I be a *normal* girl in a *normal* relationship? *Why can't I have sex like a normal fucking person?*

I turn toward the kitchen, averting Lex's gaze. "Are you sure you don't want me to dry your clothes?" I ask trying to keep my voice steady.

"It's hot. They'll dry soon."

"All right. I'm going to go change. You can come in. I'll only be a minute."

"Okay," he says, but his tone is uncertain.

I walk in the house without waiting for him to follow.

When I get to my bedroom, I fall onto my bed and scream into my pillow. I scream so loud, I'm sure Lex will run up stairs to find me a hysterical mess, but he doesn't. I stop and wait and listen, but he still doesn't come. So I scream again, and swear, and cry, and wish with every ounce of my being that this stupid pillow was Steve. I begin to squeeze it, pretending it's Steve's neck and I'm choking him until he's blue in the face.

I let it all out for a good five minutes. And when pillow-Steve is finally dead, I clean myself up, change my clothes, and make my way downstairs.

12

_____

"Photograph" // Ed Sheeran

I find Lex standing in the middle of the stairwell, admiring our family pictures my Mom began to hang on the wall before she passed, and I finished once I got older. He's looking at one of my father, my mother, and me, sitting on a red wooden picnic table in front of an ice cream stand that says _Abbott's_ in blue cursive letters, all three of us holding an ice cream cone up to the camera as if we're toasting the world. I'm sitting on my father's leg and my mother is pressed against me, her cheek to mine, our smiles almost touching. I wish I could remember that day. "I think I was three in that picture," I say.

He turns to me as I meet him down there. "You were cute."

"Thanks. Be careful of the step behind you. The tread is broken."

Lex glances down at the sixth step, and slowly nods. He looks back at the pictures on the wall and takes a step back, leaning lightly against the banister. "You look so much like your Mom," he says.

"That's what everyone keeps telling me."

"Who took all of these?" He asks as we walk up a step, looking at pictures of me in Halloween costumes as a toddler: a ladybug, a kitten, an owl, Tinkerbell. Me sitting on Santa's lap with my Dad kneeling next to me because I was crying, me blowing out three birthday candles on a bright pink cake, my father grilling hamburgers on the grill in the backyard, a picture of my father and Uncle Jack with their arms around each other's shoulders smiling, like nothing in life could ever be better than that moment.

"My Mom, mostly," I say. "A few were taken by anyone who happened to be around if she felt like being in the picture. She didn't like having her picture taken though, she was more of a behind the camera person. But she knew once she had me, she needed to have some pictures of herself. Especially after she was diagnosed."

"So, was that her job? A photographer?"

"Yeah. She did weddings, bat and bar mitzvah, birthday parties, baby showers, you name it, she'd capture it on film. Liz Katz Photography was popular, and she gave everyone the friends and family discount. She was so talented. She could have charged double for her work, but she wasn't in it for the money. She just loved her job."

We make our way downstairs, both of us mindful to avoid the broken step, and head back out to the backyard. "I just have to clean this up real quick," I say.

"I'll help," he says as he picks up the bucket and sponge.

"My Mom was always taking pictures," I start. "It's one of the few vivid memories I have of her. She always had a camera around her neck, even in the car. Everywhere we went, she was taking pictures. She had a digital camera, and she liked the convenience of it, but she preferred film. She had a studio in the basement where she developed all her pictures. It's still down there, too. My Dad was never able to get rid of it," I say as I turn off the water and roll up the hose.

"Every weekend, we'd go somewhere as a family: the aquarium, the zoo, a museum, the beach, a baseball game, a park, the hiking trails to see the waterfalls. She wanted to make as many memories with me as she could, even though I was too young to remember most of them. But she took pictures of them all and made scrapbooks. There are shelves of them inside. She also used to have this saying. She told me every night before I went to bed, *'Never forget, never regret, and never go to bed upset.'"*

We finish cleaning everything up, and I close the garage door.

Lex smiles, "That's a good motto to live by."

"I think she just wanted me to remember her," I say. "Her favorite was black and white film. And with the digital camera, she could change the colors to all kinds of different modes, and I think she liked having those options."

We head back inside the house, and I take Lex's hand. "Hey, follow me. I want to show you something."

"Okay," he says, as I lead him back upstairs to my bedroom.

As we get to my door, he drops my hand and stands outside, nervously. I grin, "Don't worry, I won't take advantage of you."

He chuckles and glances down at his feet, his face turning red. "Are you sure this is a good idea?"

"I just want to show you some pictures, Lex." I head over to my closet and pull down an old black hatbox covered in white flowers. I walk over to my bed and set it down. "Are you just going to stand there?"

He's standing in my doorway with his hands in his pockets, and I suddenly feel awful about before. But I don't know what to say.

I sit down on my bed with one leg under me, the other foot

resting on the frame of my bed, and I eye him. "It's okay, Lex. You can come in."

He splays his hands out, looking down at himself. "I don't want to get your bed wet."

I give his clothes a once over, and point to the space in front of me. "It's fine. Please?"

He takes a breath and shuffles over to my bed, taking a seat where I pointed.

I open the hatbox and pull out the pictures hand fulls at a time. I flip through the pictures, searching for one specific photo. "There is a picture in here I want to show you, but it might take me a while to find it."

"That's okay." As I flip through them, I toss the pictures onto the bed, and he looks through the ones I've already discarded. He picks up one from when I was fourteen wearing my *Taylor Swift 1989* shirt and skinny jeans. It was the year I'd dyed my hair blonde. Lex's lips curl into a smile as I glare at him. "Wow, you really are a Swifty *stan*."

I snatch the picture out of his hand and put it behind me. "I am not." My cheeks burning.

I dig down to the bottom of the hatbox until I discover a picture I haven't seen in so long. I can't remember when I saw it last, but I remember how it makes me feel.

The overwhelming memories flood through my mind and heart as I carefully take out the picture of my mother in the sapphire dress I wore on my first date with Lex. She can't be much older than I am now. Behind her is my father, his hands on her hips, my mother is reaching back to touch his face as she smiles at the camera. My father looks so happy and healthy in this picture, so normal, that every time I look at it, I feel like this could've been my life. I could've had two happy, healthy parents, but instead both of my parents got sick.

One made sick by god knows what: genetic factors or some universal fuckery that decided I didn't deserve a mother. And the other by choice because he was so heartbroken, he couldn't face reality anymore.

My eyes burn as I hand Lex the picture. "That is my favorite and least favorite picture of my parents."

Lex takes the picture and his eyes go wide. "Is that the same dress?"

"Yeah."

"Wow, this is a major doppelganger moment," he says as he looks at my Mom, then at me, and back at my Mom.

"Her hair was shorter, though."

"So, why do you both love and hate it?"

"Because it reminds me of what I could have had. And also, of what my parents did have. So, it makes me happy that they were happy once, but sad that I didn't get to be a part of it."

"You were though. For a little while."

"Just not long enough to remember." Lex hands me back the picture and I hold it for a minute, debating whether I should keep it out or put it back in the box. With a sigh, I toss it back inside.

We look through the rest of the pictures for a long time. Some of them I can explain, others are as new to me as they are to him. A few of them I decide to keep out and frame, or add them to one of the memory books I have.

Lex finds a picture of me as a toddler, I'm not sure how old exactly. My hair is a messy bunch of light brown curls that fall to my shoulders, and I'm holding a dandelion. "This one is adorable," he says.

I lean in close to him to get a better look. "I remember that one. My Mom had a bunch of copies of it. She made it in all these different tones; sepia, black and white, and one where the picture is black and white, but the dandelion is yellow. I think it's in one of the memory books downstairs. It was her favorite picture of me."

Lex grins. "I can see why. You were a beautiful baby."

I flush. "What can I say? I've got good genes."

He puts the picture back in a pile and lays down on his side, his elbow digging into my mattress, propping his head on his hand. He watches me as I start putting the rest of the pictures away. "Peyton?"

"Yeah?"

He's quiet for a moment as if he's trying to find the right words. "Are you all right?"

I narrow my eyes. "What do you mean?"

He sucks in a breath. "I was just wondering if there's something you're not telling me?"

I pause for a second as my heart stops, then I slip the top back on the box. I gather the few pictures I want to frame and stack them in a pile and set them on my nightstand.

I don't answer his question.

I stand and put the hatbox back in my closet and turn back to Lex. He's sitting up on my bed now, looking at me concerned. "Look, it's all right. You don't have to tell me. It's none of my business. I'm just worried. The way you've reacted when I touch you sometimes, it made me wonder, and I don't want to do anything to scare you, or upset you, or make you feel uncomfortable—"

"Lex," I start, but the words get stuck in my throat. He's quiet, and I sit back down on my bed and stare at my hands. I close my eyes and say, "I'm not ready to tell you."

I hear him exhale, almost as though he's relieved, and he takes my hand. "That's okay."

I'm fighting back the tears as I say, "I'm afraid to tell you."

I feel him slide closer to me on the mattress. "Why?"

"Because," I start, and the tears begin to fall, and I can't stop them. I bite my lip, trying to stop it from trembling, but I can't. I hide my face in my hands, then brush away the tears. "If I tell you, it could ruin everything, and I don't want to ruin this."

Lex puts his arms around me and pulls me into him, kissing

the top of my head. "Peyton, there is nothing, *nothing*, you could tell me that could ruin this."

"You don't know that."

"I *do* know that."

Lex holds me for a long time as I gather myself together. As embarrassed as I am to be crying in his arms, I love being held by him. I wish we could stay like this forever.

But I've got snot coming out of my nose. *Goddamn it.*

I grab some tissues from my nightstand and wipe my nose. "Sorry," I say.

He brushes a stray hair behind my ear. "You have nothing to be sorry for."

I sit there and shake my head. "Sometimes I wonder why you're dating me."

His brows knit together. "Why would you think that?"

"I'm sorry, that sounded seriously self-deprecating. I didn't mean it like that. I just meant because of the age difference and because I'm complicated."

"No, you're not."

"When it comes to sex, I'm very complicated."

He chuckles. "Because you've never had it?"

"You could be out there with anyone, having all the sex you want. But instead, you're here with me looking at old pictures my dead mother took almost twenty years ago."

Lex puts his hand on mine and squeezes. "Peyton, I think it's time I tell you something about me."

13

"Maneater" // Hall & Oates

Lex and I make our way downstairs and grab two cold bottles of water out of the fridge, then head outside to the front porch to sit on the swing.

"Are you hungry?" he asks.

I look down at my phone and realize it's been hours since I ate breakfast. "I could eat."

"What are you in the mood for?"

"Chinese?"

Lex smirks. "Do they deliver here?"

"They do. I'll go grab the menu."

I run back into the kitchen and grab the menu for the only Chinese food restaurant in Genesee Falls. The very same place Lex bought me General Tso's from the day he asked me out to dinner.

We look over the menu together, and Lex calls and orders a smorgasbord of pints and quarts.

When Lex hangs up the phone, he takes a sip of water. I

observe him, and for the first time since I met him, he seems nervous.

"So, what did you want to tell me?"

He smiles shyly and stares at the bottle in his hands, twisting the cap between his fingers. "A few years ago, I was in a relationship with this woman. We went to Cornell together, and I was sure she was the woman I was going to marry. Victoria Locke. She was the perfect package, too. My father actually approved of her. She came from a wealthy family, she had '*good breeding*' as he liked to say. She was beautiful, smart, funny, and yeah, we had sex."

I slink back in my seat a bit and start fidgeting with my water bottle.

"I loved her, or at least, I *thought* I loved her. But in hindsight, I don't think it was love. It was just lust and desire and power, and who had the most power over the other person. And the truth is, she did. She had so much power over me. We had sex, and she'd take my American Express Black card, and go on a shopping spree, spend ten, fifteen thousand dollars, and then we'd have more sex."

"Fifteen thousand dollars? In one day?" I ask, my mouth gaping.

"Yeah."

"What's an American Express Black card?" I ask, curious.

Lex glances at me and laughs, only to realize I'm not kidding, "Wait, seriously?"

"I'm assuming it's a credit card of some kind?" I say and take a sip of water.

He nods. "It's a credit card with no limit."

I spit out my water.

Lex laughs at me as he points to my chin.

I look at him as I wipe my mouth on my shirt. "No limit? Like none?"

"Nope. None."

"So, you could buy a house?"

"Yup."

"You could buy all the cars at a dealership?"

"If you really wanted to."

I cannot wrap my mind around this concept. "You could charge something that costs a million dollars?"

"I've never tried, but yeah, that's what no limit means."

"Whoa. What's the most you've ever spent at once?" I ask.

Lex eyes me sidelong. "I think we're getting a bit off-topic..."

"Sorry! Go back to your story," I say, and grit my teeth.

Lex sighs. "She had me by the balls. Literally, and figuratively. We were together for two years before I found out she was only with me for my money. She was sleeping with another guy the entire time we were together. She was never planning on marrying me, she never would have signed a prenup. She broke my heart, and it took me a long time to learn how to trust women again. And it's not something I do easily." Lex finally sets his water down and turns to look at me. "Peyton, we've only known each other for a few weeks, but still, not once have you asked me to buy you anything. To take you shopping. To pay off a debt you owe. Not once since the day we met have you even brought up my money—except in a joking manner, which is totally acceptable. You are the first woman I've ever dated in my entire life who has never asked me for money."

I stare at him, shocked. "I... I don't know what to say. I mean I don't care about your money. I never have. God, I'm sorry!"

His brows knit together. "For what?"

"I was asking all that stuff about your Black credit card! I didn't mean it like that! I'd just never heard of a card with no limit before and I didn't mean—"

He laughs. "Peyton, it's fine. You were curious. And just to be clear, it's a no-limit card, but you have to pay the balance in full every month, so I'm careful with how much I spend. The most I've ever spent at once was on my car."

"Wow," is all I can manage to say. Lex presses his lips together, but doesn't say anything else. "Technically, you *do* buy me stuff."

He narrows his brows. "Like what?"

I point to the delivery guy walking up the porch steps. "Like that."

Lex smiles and pulls out his wallet. "Dinner doesn't count." He walks over and pays the delivery boy.

"I think it counts," I say as I stand up and help him with the bags. We set them on the wicker table, and eat out of the containers. "And don't forget the two dozen roses you sent me."

He shakes his head and swallows. "Gifts don't count, either. There's a difference between me wanting to give you something, and you asking me to pay off your credit cards."

I scoff. "Don't worry. I don't have any credit cards."

He eyes me like, *really?*

My eyes widen and I splay my hands out before me, like, *dude, look around you.*

Sometimes, I don't think Lex understands how people without money live, but I don't say anything. It's a little weird dating a multimillionaire, while we're a lower-middle-class family, barely making enough to make ends meet. I have moments when I wonder what my life would be like if we *did* have that kind of income, that kind of financial freedom, but I try not to dwell on it too much.

My father always taught me to be self-sufficient. To never rely on anyone else, especially a man, because you never know how long that will last, or if that person will hold it against you. It's the reason my father never went to my mother's family for help after she died.

We're both quiet for a while as we eat until Lex says in a

hushed tone, "Peyton, the fact that we're not having sex yet doesn't bother me."

I push the garlic chicken around with my plastic fork. "It doesn't?"

He looks into his container and back up at me. "No. There is more to a relationship than sex. We haven't been dating that long. It gives us time to get to know each other. It's not that I don't want to, trust me, I do." He takes a bite of broccoli and pauses for a moment. "But I don't want a repeat of what happened with Victoria. And I want it to be right. I don't want you to feel uncomfortable or scared. And what I feel for you is..." He stops, his eyes contemplative as if he's trying to find the right words.

"Is?" I whisper, biting my lip.

"I've never felt like this about anyone before. Not Victoria. Not any girl I've ever dated, ever slept with, no one. What I feel for you is deeper than all of it. I don't want to lose that."

My stomach turns into butterflies, and I feel like I could fly away. "I know the feeling," I say, and he smiles at me.

"Yeah?"

My cheeks flush. "It's a bit overwhelming."

"In a good way?"

I smile. "Yeah, kind of scary-good."

He takes the container out of my hand and sets both of ours down on the table, sliding closer to me. "It's absolutely terrifying. But it's also a wonderful, exciting, I-never-want-it-to-end sort of feeling."

"Exactly."

Lex kisses me, and I don't even care that I have garlic breath.

14

"School's Out" // Alice Cooper

The following week is long and busy.

I spend the majority of my free time studying for my final exams after work on Sunday.

And on Monday, even though Lex is relentless.

Monday evening, he pulls me into the office and closes the door, pushing me up against it. "I'll take you anywhere you want," he says as he kisses my neck. "Somewhere nice and romantic." He kisses a trail up to my ear, and a chill runs down my spine. "Or somewhere fun and simple. Shit, I'll buy you a happy meal," he nips on my ear lobe, and my fingers fist his shirt. "If it means I get to spend tonight with you."

I steel myself and put my hands on his chest. "I *have* to study. I have one week left. Two days. Just two teeny, tiny days, and then I'm yours," I say.

He smiles. "I like that idea."

"For the whole time you're here," I remind him.

"Well, minus work and your summer classes."

"Yeah, but those are easy. One is an online class I can do anywhere, anytime I want. Three o'clock in the morning if I need to. And the other is Tuesdays from ten to one. It's *so* easy."

I kiss him as his hands roam around my hips. "Okay, okay." He pulls himself back and lets out a breath. "I am a mature adult. I can handle this as such." He looks at me standing there in my work clothes, my hair up in a messy bun, my purse over my shoulder, my keys in my hand, a smile on my face. "Fuck, Peyton. You will be the death of me." And his lips meet mine again. Hard and loving and desperate. He wraps his arms around me and lifts me up, and I think if the office were big enough, he'd spin me around.

I chuckle against his lips. "Lex, I have to go!"

He groans. "Okay, okay." He sets me down and kisses me on the nose. "Have fun studying."

I roll my eyes. "Tons."

I listen before I open the door to the office, and make sure no one is in the break room before I leave. But when I walk out into the store, I see Sammy and Emily standing behind the pharmacy counter, biting back a laugh.

I glare at Sammy, and she motions with her hands for me to text her.

I GET THROUGH MY FIRST TWO FINALS ON TUESDAY BY TWO o'clock, and I'm driving home with my windows down and my music blaring. I'm singing loud and proud to *Like A Girl* by Lizzo, when I pull into my driveway, relieved to be half finished with school for the semester. Dad's home sitting in his recliner, relaxing on his day off with Cosmo when I walk in the door.

"How'd it go?" He asks.

"Amazing," I say, through a smile.

"Glad to hear it," he says with a tiny tug on the corner of his lips.

I spend the rest of the day studying for my final two exams on Thursday, cook my Dad and myself some steaks on the grill, with store-bought potato salad on the side, and binge-watch a few episodes of *Lucifer* on Netflix before passing out with my TV on.

When I arrive at the store Wednesday morning, I see Lex and Sydney standing at the Pharmacy counter playing with our brand new computer system.

Sydney has the biggest smile on her face when I approach the pharmacy. "Peyton! You're going to have so much fun on this today! It's got a touch screen and a new internet search feature! So, if the customer has a question about any medication we have in the store, prescription or not, we can search for information about it, and print it out for them right here!"

My eyes go wide. "Wow! Did Elon Musk deliver these himself?" My tone is way too sarcastic, and Lex glares at me but snorts.

"So, I have my manager work to do in the office, but Lex is going to train you on here today," Sydney's smile widens, and she winks at me.

"Really now? Are you going to train me today, Mr. Kingston?" I ask him seductively.

Lex looks at me, his eyes burning. "Why yes, Ms. Katz. I will be training you today. Is that okay with you?"

"Absolutely," I say, and I head into the break room to clock in.

Training with Lex is absolutely hysterical, and fun, and quite possibly the best day I've ever had at my job.

We're standing dangerously close to each other as he's explaining the new computer screen. It's all the same things, just all different buttons, and a brand new layout.

He leans into me as he says, "And this button here is the

same as the old register, but instead of pressing three buttons, you only have to press one," he breathes into my ear.

"Well, that is much easier."

We wait for another customer to come to the pharmacy so I can actually *use* the register. Behind me, Ben and James are working, counting pills, and filling orange bottles. "So, how are the new pharmacy computers?" I ask.

Ben pushes his glasses up the bridge of his nose. "They're nice. A lot faster than the old ones and way easier to use."

"That's cool."

Lex taps my shoulder when an older woman approaches the counter. I grab her medicine, and Lex walks me through the steps again. The counter is high enough that you can't see what's going on from the opposite side anywhere below the waist. On me, the counter hits me just above my belly button.

So, I press the buttons on my screen, and the woman follows the prompts on the smaller screen before her. And she can't see Lex as he slides his hand over my hip, slowly, carefully moving it, so it lands on my ass.

My face burns as I look up at him, my lips curled up in a tight smile.

"Have a nice day!" I manage to say to the woman as she leaves the store, and I turn around and playfully slap Lex's hand away. "Oh, my god," I whisper. "What—"

But before I can finish, my second favorite person in the whole world enters the store. "Sup, Lovebirds?"

Sammy.

I smile at her. "Sammy! Guess who gets to train you on our new registers today?" I say, just a little bit too excited.

Lex smiles. "That would be me."

Sammy squeals and jumps up and down. "Goody! I get some quality Lex and Sammy time!" she says as she points to him, before heading into the break room to clock in.

I look at Lex, shake my head, and laugh mechanically. "Oh, man. You are so in for it."

His eyes knit together. "What? I like Sammy."

"I know! I do, too! But you're dating her best friend. Her sister from another mister! She is going to grill you so hard!"

"Oh, no..."

"Oh, yeah!"

When Sammy comes back, I head out for my usual lunch break, but when I head for the door, it's raining.

Damn.

I head back into the break room and watch Netflix on my phone while I eat my lunch, Lex free for the first time in two weeks.

I guess I am starting to like him.

I finish eating and as I head back out to the store, I see Sammy and Lex whispering to one another. Sammy is telling him something vehemently in his ear, and Lex is shaking his head and saying something back to her. This goes on for a few minutes until a customer comes up to the pharmacy. He shows her how to use the register, and as soon as the customer is gone, they go right back to their conversation. And I'm instantly regretting everything I said to him before.

Apparently, *I'm* the one getting grilled.

When I walk out of the break room, they pull away from each other faster than lightning. Pretending they weren't just having a very in-depth conversation.

I eye Sammy who avoids my gaze, and make my way to the stationery aisle to begin unloading pens and paper.

I wish I were close enough to the pharmacy to hear what they're saying because for the rest of the day, I'm itching to know what they were just talking about. What could she have possibly told Lex? Or what could he have possibly told her?

Are they keeping secrets from me?

Or am I just being paranoid?

I am definitely being paranoid.

~

MY EXAMS ON THURSDAY ARE A BIT HARDER THAN THE TWO ON Tuesday, but by three o'clock, I am out of school and free at last, and I feel so amazing to be finished with my first year of college.

I sing my way home to a playlist of upbeat songs, including *Mr. Blue Sky* by Electric Light Orchestra, *Home* by Edward Sharpe & The Magnetic Zeros, and *Sucker* by the Jonas Brothers. As I pull in my driveway, I notice there are a bunch of balloons on my porch.

Furrowing my brows, I get out of my car and run up the steps. About a dozen pink, purple, and blue balloons float on my porch, with one Mylar balloon in the middle that says, "Congrats!" across the center, and on the bottom is a small box with an envelope underneath.

My heart skips a beat.

I bend down and pick up the envelope. My name is written on the front, so I turn it over and open it.

"Peyton, Congratulations on finishing your first year of college. This weekend, you and I are going to celebrate, that is, if you want to. Because I'd love to celebrate with you. Inside this box is a small hint at what I have planned. XXXXX, Lex."

That man sure does like to kiss me.

I pick up the box, and a chill runs down my spine. Apparently, three weeks is the balloons and white box anniversary?

I carry the balloons and box over to the swing and sit down, scared, yet curious, to open it. I take a deep breath and pull off the lid.

Inside is a silver necklace with a small *diamond* star? Cubic Zirconia? Swarovski crystal?

Oh, my god, did Lex buy me a *diamond necklace*?

A star. Is that the hint?

I take out the necklace and look at the box. It reads, "Jared, The Galleria of Jewelry."

Oh, my god. *Lex bought me a diamond necklace.*

My stomach twists into a knot.

I never thought I was a jewelry girl, but no one has ever bought me jewelry before. And if this is how it feels, maybe I *am* a jewelry girl.

And I am definitely falling in love with Lex Kingston.

15

"I'm Gonna Be (500 Miles)" // The Proclaimers

On Friday, I'm wearing my new star diamond necklace I'm still in a bit of shock over. The night before, I took a picture and sent it to Sammy, with three giant shocked-face emojis and said, '*It's a real fucking diamond.*'

It didn't take long for her reply of a hundred different emojis to come through expressing what I'd call *all the feels.*

I walk into the store, expecting Lex to be there waiting for me, only to find the office empty. Sydney comes in through the double doors of the break room alone as I walk over to the lockers to toss my purse in. "Hey, Syd. Is Lex in the store?"

Sydney smiles and eyes me suggestively. "You two can't go one day without making out in my office."

My cheeks flush as I smile. "I just have to ask him a question."

"Mm-hmm. Is it about that bling on your neck?" She asks as she walks up to me and takes the little star in her hand. "Honey," she starts. "Do not let that man go!"

I try not to think about the fact that Lex is leaving in a few weeks. "So, is he out there?" I ask as I point toward the double doors.

"No, girl. He's not working this weekend. He'll be back on Monday. But," she says as she heads for the office. "I was asked to give you something." Her smile is sly and full of excitement. I follow her. She turns on the office light and grabs a Manila envelope off her desk and hands it to me. I take it from her, and she claps her hands. "Please open it, please, please, please!"

I laugh and look at it. It's a standard Manila envelope with my name on the front. I feel it, making sure there isn't any more jewelry inside. It feels like more paper.

"Come on, Peyton! Open it!" Sydney presses.

"Okay, okay," I say, and rip the top off. Inside is a note from Lex, an address, and a short list. Sydney and I examine it, and she frowns.

"That's all that's in there?" She takes the envelope from me and checks. "Well, what's it say?"

I read it aloud, "*Dear Peyton, By now, you should've received your gift, and the first clue to our weekend of celebrating Year One Done of Peyton Katz's First Year of College,*" I pause and look at Sydney. "*Weekend* of celebrating?" I repeat.

Oh, boy.

Sydney winks at me. "Sammy and I worked out the schedule. She's covering for you on Saturday."

I smile gratefully and continue reading, "*This envelope isn't nearly as exciting as Sydney thinks it is, so please apologize to her about that,*" I look up. "Sorry, Sydney." She rolls her eyes and motions for me to go on. "*Inside, you will find an address, and a list of supplies you'll need to buy from the pharmacy sometime today. Do not forget to buy these items. Do not forget to bring these items to the address. After you get out of work, your father has a set of instructions waiting for you at home. When you get home, follow those instructions, and then put the address into the GPS on your phone, and drive there. I'll be waiting. XXXXXXXXXXX Lex."*

"Oh, my god, girl! He's got a romantic weekend waiting for you!"

My stomach twists at the thought.

I look down at the list:

- Bug Spray
- Sun Block
- Dry Shampoo
- Aloe Vera
- Ibuprofen
- Benadryl

Well, that's a random list and definitely *not* clue number two. What could Lex possibly have planned for us this weekend? What is waiting for me at this random address?

A thought occurs to me then; maybe this is what Sammy and Lex were talking about on Wednesday? Perhaps he was asking her advice on a gift? A surprise? Some kind of top-secret celebration?

And now I have to work eight hours and drive who knows how long—or how far—before I find out.

∽

THE DAY DRAGS ON, AND AS SOON AS SAMMY GETS THERE AT noon, I grill her for information. But she keeps her mouth shut.

When I come back in after my lunch break, I stay at the pharmacy with her for a bit, pretending I still need help learning the new registers.

"Samantha Clarke, you need to tell me right the fuck now what is going on, because he says he has a whole weekend planned, and that means he thinks we're spending the night together somewhere, and—"

"Oh, my god, relax," she says as she grabs my flailing hands and pins them to my sides. "I know exactly what he has planned," she whispers, "and it's not *that*."

"But I'm spending the weekend with him?"

She takes my face in her hands. "Aw, my poor, innocent, little Peyton."

"Sammy!"

She laughs. "Come on. Do you really think I'd let Lex do anything that would make you uncomfortable or put you in a situation you couldn't get out of? Why do you think you're *meeting him there?*"

I look at her long and hard. "I don't know."

"So you have a way out. If you need to leave, for whatever reason, you can get in your car and go. He won't be mad or anything."

"Really?"

"Really."

I eye her sidelong. "And you won't tell me anything else?"

She shakes her head. "I will not spoil anything for you. But trust me, you're going to love it."

I doubt that but don't say anything.

My nerves are a hot mess for the rest of the day, and by the time I get home, I'm itching to get in the house.

I run up the porch steps and into the house to find my Dad standing in the hallway sipping a cup of coffee, holding out an envelope for me.

"Thank you, thank you, thank you!" I say, as I stumble across the hallway and rip the envelope open.

"Yup. Have fun, kiddo," he says, and heads into the living room.

Inside is another letter from Lex.

"*Dear Peyton, These are your instructions; go upstairs and pack a bag. Bring enough clothes to last until Sunday, hell, pack an extra day's worth, just in case. Bring comfortable and warm sleep pants, warm socks, long layers, but make sure whatever you bring, you will be comfortable. You do not need anything fancy. You don't need 'date' clothes. This weekend is all about comfort. If you want, bring your own pillow—I understand some people are picky about those things. If you have any extra sleeping bags or warm, fuzzy blankets, please bring those as well. The more we have, the better. Don't forget a toothbrush and any other toiletries you may need over the weekend. I don't expect shopping will be much of an option where we'll be. When you're finished packing, plug the address into the GPS on your phone and get your cute little ass up here. I can't wait to see you. XXXXXXXXXXXXX Lex."*

When I finish reading the letter, I have to remember to breathe. "So, I guess I'm going away this weekend," I tell my Dad, wondering if he will be okay with it.

But he doesn't argue. "I know. Lex told me. You still have that pepper spray I gave you?"

I smile. "In my purse, tucked in tight."

"Good girl," he says with a wink.

"Dad, are you going to be okay with me gone?"

He rolls his eyes at me. "Peyton, I am a grown man."

"I know that," I say defensively. "But, if you need me to, I can have Sammy come and check in on you."

He sighs and grumbles, "Lex already took care of it."

I narrow my eyes. "He did?"

"Yeah, when he called me and told me about this *thing* he has planned, he said Sammy would be stopping by a few times to make sure I'm okay. Does that make you feel better?"

I smile so wide, I can feel the love growing in my chest for them. "Yeah, it does." I run up to my Dad and kiss him on the cheek.

"Yeah, yeah, now go on, go do your thing," he says as he bats me away.

I squeal and run upstairs to start packing. But before I do, I text Sammy.

'You are by far the best best friend a girl could ever have. Thank you. I owe you forever.'

~

IT DOESN'T TAKE ME LONG TO PACK EVERYTHING I NEED INTO MY Honda. Just as I start typing the address into my phone, I get a text from Lex.

'You on your way?'

'Leaving now.'

'Good. See you soon.' Wink face, smiley face, kiss face, red heart emoji.

I send him three red hearts back and enter the address into my phone.

Holy shit, two hours?

The address looks to be somewhere in the middle of nowhere because when I zoom out on my phone, there is nothing, and I mean, *nothing* around it for at least twenty miles.

"Where the hell are you bringing me, Kingston?"

I press the start button, turn on my music, and hit the road. I'm jamming out to David Bowie and Queen and The Killers on my *'Road Trip'* playlist. The drive isn't too bad at first, until I get to the mountains and woods and the glorious *I'm-pretty-sure-I've-seen-this-in-a-horror-movie* scenario, when my speakers tell me to turn right.

"You have arrived at your destination."

"Bullshit!" I say to Siri as I drive up a winding pathway through dense trees, and at first, I think I'm lost.

And then I see it.

In the middle of nowhere sits a log cabin with a wrap-around porch that opens into a deck on the right side. The entire place is covered in white fairy lights, and I see a large dark blue pickup truck parked in the driveway. A part of me wonders if I'm in the right place until I see Lex open the front door and step out into the evening light.

I park next to the truck and cut the engine. "Did you get a new truck?" I ask as I get out of my car.

He glances at the truck and back at me. "Maybe. Might have just borrowed it for the weekend," he says as he approaches me. He wraps an arm around my waist and kisses me. "Took you forever to get here. God, what were you doing?"

"Listening to the crazy GPS lady tell me where to go."

"Wait, do you actually drive the speed limit?"

I roll my eyes as we unload all the things I packed, including the bag of items I bought from the pharmacy. "You know those signs aren't just a suggestion. And I have a perfect driving record, thank you very much."

Lex shakes his head at me. "And here I thought you were a rebel."

We bring everything inside the cabin. If I thought the outside looked like Tinkerbell's house, the inside was the home of the fairy godmother herself.

It's a single-story cabin with a slanted ceiling and a circular chandelier in the middle. To my left is a living room with a couch, two chairs on each side, a coffee table in the center, and a massive stone wood-burning fireplace on the wall, with a crackling fire already going. Above the mantle hangs a giant flat screen television.

To my right is a small kitchen with a square wood table and sliding glass doors that lead out to the deck.

And straight ahead is a single bedroom with a giant canopy bed. The cabin is filled with flowers and more fairy lights.

I can smell something cooking in the kitchen as Lex carries my things into the bedroom. I pull out my phone to text Sammy, but there's no service.

Lex stands in the doorway, leaning against it. "Cell service out here is a bit iffy. The WiFi works great, though. There's a landline if you need to make a call," he says as he points to a phone on a table next to the couch.

I smile and nod as I take in the place, but I don't move. I think Lex can sense my nervousness and he approaches me. "Hey," he says.

"Hey," I reply, biting my lip.

He takes one hand in mine, and the other one slides under my new necklace. "Do you like it?"

I sigh. "Are you kidding me?" I ask as I wrap my arms around his neck and kiss him. He kisses me back, gently and sweet. I pull away and say, "I still don't understand the clue, though."

He smiles. "You will soon enough. I hope you didn't eat," he says as he makes his way over to the stove.

I shake my head. "No, I was a bit too distracted."

"Good. Because I cooked."

My jaw drops. "*You* cooked? Lex Kingston! Have you been holding out on me?" I walk into the kitchen and pause next to the sink.

He eyes me sidelong. "I have many surprises in store for you."

"Who taught you how to cook?"

"My grandma."

"Ah, Florida Grandma?"

"That would be the one. Hand me that?" He asks as he points to a ladle.

I grab it off the hook behind the sink and give it to him. "So, what are you making?"

"Well, teaching Sammy the new register on Wednesday came in very handy."

I cross my arms. "I bet it did."

"The secrets she told me about you," he says with a wink.

I take a deep breath and remind myself she's taking care of

my Dad while I'm away. I lean against the sink and turn to Lex. "Anything juicy?"

"She said one of your all-time favorite foods is Fettuccine Alfredo. Which happens to be one of my Grandma's family recipes."

"Okay, Bobby Flay," I joke. "Can I help?"

Lex tosses a towel over his shoulder. "You can grab a bottle of wine and pour some if you'd like." He points to a bucket with ice, and inside are two small bottles. One for me and one for him. On the table are two wine glasses, one already has a bit of wine in it, and I assume that's Lex's Shiraz. I take out the bottle of the Moscato, relieved to see it's already been corked, and pour myself a glass.

I watch him as he stirs the noodles and sauce. That seems to be the only thing to do with this meal, a whole lot of stirring. Lex flips off the burners and dumps the pasta into a strainer in the sink.

"Can I help now?"

He smiles as he tosses the strainer around. "Nope. This is gift number two."

I bite my lip as I watch him spoon the pasta into the Alfredo sauce and stir. "Lex, you really didn't have to do all of this."

"I know. I wanted to."

Anything to spend the night with me. Not that that's where this is heading. I mean, yes, we are literally spending the night together. And we just had a long conversation about this. Oh, god, is this completely innocent? My mind is racing with questions and nerves and doubt and skepticism when finally Lex holds out the saucepan and tongs. "Dinner is served."

I sit down as he scoops a generous amount of pasta onto each of our plates, places a bowl of bread in the center of the table, and sits down in the chair opposite of me. I take a sip of wine and put a cloth napkin on my lap. "This looks delicious."

"Well, try it first. It's been a while since I've cooked anything."

I twirl the fettuccine around my fork and take a bite. "Oh, my god," I say. The Alfredo is creamy and garlicky, with a small pepper kick to it. "This is amazing."

Lex smiles. "High compliment. Thank you."

We eat and watch as the sky darkens from the sliding glass doors. I sip my wine and realize I still have no idea where we are. "So, what is this place?"

"It's a cabin I bought on my eighteenth birthday."

"Really?"

"I'd just graduated high school, and my Dad and I weren't getting along. I needed a place to escape. A place far away where he'd never think to look. One of my friends from school has a place not too far from here so, and I came up here with him and his family for a couple of weeks. One day, he and I were driving around and we saw a for sale sign out on the main road, so we came in to look at it. It needed some work, but it was cheap, so I made the guy an offer and he took it. I was able to get him a check in a few days. He packed all his stuff, and I had a place to live that was completely mine."

"Wow, that's a big step for an eighteen-year-old."

He twirls his pasta around his fork. "Maybe. But to this day, my Dad still doesn't know about it."

"Really?"

"As far as I know. My friend and his parents covered for me when my Dad finally figured out where I was."

I drink more wine, but Lex doesn't refill his glass. When we're finished eating, he clears the table, and I offer to help with the dishes. He rinses them off and puts them in the dishwasher. "Nope. All done."

I scowl at him. "Am I of no use to you at all?"

He approaches me and takes my hand, lifting me to stand. "I never said that." He kisses me. "Okay, part two."

I furrow my brows. "Part two?"

"Did you bring any extra blankets or sleeping bags?"

"Yeah, they're in the back seat of my car."

He smiles. "Okay. I'll get them. You go into the bedroom and put on your warmest, most comfortable pants, socks, shirts, and a hoodie. You did bring a hoodie, right?"

I roll my eyes. "Of course I did. I brought two. You said comfort, and nothing says comfort more than a hoodie."

"Good. Go change."

I head for the bedroom and close the double doors behind me. I change into my dark gray sweat pants, toss on the fuzzy socks I got for Christmas, and my navy blue hoodie. I grab my toothbrush and hairbrush out of my bag and run into the bathroom attached to the bedroom and brush my teeth. The bathroom looks like it's been recently renovated; it even has a Jacuzzi bath and stand-alone shower in the corner. I rinse out my mouth and wipe it on a towel. I drag my brush through my hair real quick then place it on the small shelf above the toilet. I take a deep breath and head back out to Lex.

He's standing in the living room wearing the least Lex outfit I've ever seen him in. He must have had his clothes in the living room already because before me is a man wearing a red Cornell hoodie with black Cornell sweat pants and sneakers. "Oh, my god! You're wearing sneakers!" I say.

His face brightens and he looks down. "What? Is that what these are?"

I smile as I approach him. "Are we going on a midnight run? Because you said *comfort*, and knock-off *UGG* boots aren't exactly running shoes."

He laughs. "No, no running. But we are going somewhere. Come on, it's not far."

16

"Venus" // Sleeping At Last

We get in the giant dark blue pickup truck and drive. It's ten o'clock now and really dark here, like *holy shit, I can't believe we're actually driving out here when it's so dark.* Luckily, we're only in the truck for a few minutes before Lex makes a left hand turn into a field and cuts the engine. "We're here."

I look at him, confused. "We're here? As in, this is where you hide all the bodies?"

He laughs. "No. Come on." He takes out two flashlights and hands one to me. "I have one more surprise for you tonight."

I get out of the truck and follow him to the back when he unfolds the cover of the bed. I shine my flashlight and gasp. The bed of the truck has a memory foam mattress, which is covered in sleeping bags. On top are fuzzy blankets and pillows, and my mouth is open far too wide for the middle of the night. Lex holds out the can of bug spray I brought from the pharmacy.

"That list of things I had you get were the things I forgot," he admits with a shrug.

I spray the air around me, hoping that will be enough, and stick the can in my hoodie pocket. I stare at the bed of the truck and look at Lex. "What... How did you... What?"

"Sammy mentioned that you really love stargazing. I heard a rumor that's why you named your dog 'Cosmo,'" he says as he climbs up and removes his shoes, setting them in the corner of the truck. He holds his hand out to me, and I climb up and sit on the edge to remove my boots. He takes them and sets them next to his sneakers. I hand him the can of bug spray from my hoodie pocket and he tosses it aside. "I also read that there's a meteor shower tonight and tomorrow. Not a big one like Perseid's in August, but big enough that if we're in the middle of nowhere," he says as he motions around us, "we'll get to see some."

He crawls up the bed of the truck, and I follow him. He pulls down some blankets for us to crawl under and brings them up over us. He fluffs a pillow and lays back, his left arm under his head, and he looks at me.

I sit there in complete awe. "This is what you and Sammy were planning on Wednesday?"

"Yeah."

"Oh, my god."

"Do you like it?"

"I..." I can't even find the words. "No one has ever done anything like this for me before," I admit. "The star," I say as I reach for my necklace. "It was the clue for this."

He smiles at me, and nods, and clicks off his flashlight.

I eye him sidelong before I do the same, and look up at the dark sky. There are hundreds, thousands of stars visible from where we are tonight. And as I sit there, a song begins to play in my head, and I smile.

As *Venus* by Sleeping At Last plays in my mind, I lay back

on a pillow next to him, close enough to feel his warmth, my head almost touching his arm. "Are you trying to make me fall in love with you, Lex Kingston?" I can feel his head turn toward me, but he doesn't answer my question. "Because it's working." My chest tightens, and I can feel the tears burning behind my eyes, but before they come, Lex moves quicker than I can grasp.

His arm slides under my back, and he's hovering above me. His other arm is next to my head, holding himself up. And his lips are on mine, crushing me, deep and hard and passionately, and I moan against his lips. My arms wrap around his neck, my fingers find his hair, messy and soft and he smells like mint and cedar and smoke.

At first, I'm afraid. I'm so scared I'll have a flashback of that night a year ago in the limo, and I wait for it to come.

But it doesn't.

Lex keeps kissing me, and I open my eyes and look up at the stars, and I see them.

Three shooting stars zip through the sky as Lex kisses my neck, and my heart sings. I smile as the tears begin to fall.

Lex pulls away. "What's wrong?"

I can't see his face in the dark, but his tone is of genuine concern. "Nothing," I say through a smile. "Nothing, I'm just happy."

"Are you sure?"

"Yes," I say and pull him to me, and kiss him again. But my body betrays me.

"You're trembling," he says.

"I guess I'm cold."

He pulls the blankets up around us more. "Is that better?"

"Yeah." But it's not true, because I'm not cold.

I'm afraid. Not of Lex, but of everything I'm feeling, and everything I'm thinking, and everything I want, but know I'm not ready for. Lex nips my ear lobe and my toes curl, causing my breath to catch.

He pulls away, steeling himself. I can tell he wants to keep kissing me, but instead, he says, "We're missing the stars."

I bite my lip, "The stars aren't going anywhere." My voice is so low, I'm surprised he heard me.

He chuckles, "Well, the shooting stars are. At about twenty-six miles per second."

But I don't care, I kiss him. I kiss him hard and wrap my arms around him and pull him closer to me. I can tell this surprises him because he pulls back and eyes me cautiously, questioningly. I simply smile at him, placing my hand on his cheek.

"Kiss me, Lex." And he does. His lips meet mine, then they make a trail down my neck, as far as he can go, pulling my hoodie to the side. My hands slide under his hoodie meeting his shirt and I wrap-around his waist. When his lips meet mine again, they're hard and eager and wanting and I feel like I'm about to combust.

But Lex pulls back again, out of breath, and looks down at me. "We're going to miss the meteor shower," he finally says.

"Yeah, that is why we're here," I say.

Lex rolls over and lies next to me. I curl into him, resting my head on his chest but turned enough so I can still see the sky. He kisses the top of my head and wraps his arm around me. "Are you warm enough?"

"Yeah," I say.

We watch the sky for a long time, and count the shooting stars until we lose track. We find constellations, and patterns that aren't constellations in the stars, and we wonder if anyone else has ever noticed them before. We stay long into the night, until we can barely keep our eyes open. I'm almost asleep on his chest when he touches my shoulder. "Hey," he says.

"Yeah?"

"We should get back. It's late. We can come back tomorrow night if you want."

I smile. "Okay."

We get our shoes back on and climb down. Lex covers the bed, and we get in the truck and drive back to the cabin.

When we get inside, I'm barely able to get my boots off and make it to the bedroom. I struggle to get my hoodie off and toss it onto the chair by the window as I climb into bed.

Lex removes his hoodie and bites his lip. He stands in front of the bed, unsure of what to do. "What's wrong?" I ask.

He rubs the back of his neck. "I, uh, wasn't sure if you wanted me to sleep on the couch or..."

"Oh."

I'm suddenly wide awake.

He looks at me, questioningly. "It's your decision."

Shit.

I inhale deeply before I speak. "I don't want you to sleep on the couch," I admit, and I can see him relax a bit as he flips the light switch off and approaches the bed. "But, Lex," I start, my heart pounding in my chest.

"Yeah?" he says as I feel him sit down and slide under the blankets.

"I'm still not ready to..."

"I know."

"Okay," I say, and lie back on my pillow.

We're both very still for a long time, too nervous to move. After *a while*, I take a deep breath and turn to my right and scoot closer to him. I can tell he's surprised by my movement, and it takes him a second to realize what I'm doing.

"Sex is off the table, but cuddling is perfectly okay," I say as I squeeze next to him, resting my head on his shoulder. He wraps his arm around and pulls me into him.

"I'm glad you came. I was worried you might decide not to."

"How come?"

"I didn't know if you'd be ready for this, or if any part of it would make you uncomfortable."

I let out a breath. "Well, this is new for me. But it's not like I knew *what* this was with you being all secretive about it."

"I'm surprised Sammy didn't tell you."

"I tried to get it out of her, but she kept her mouth shut. She didn't want to ruin the surprise."

Lex is quiet for a moment, then asks, "So, you've never slept with anyone before?"

I roll my eyes. "Only Sammy."

A laugh bellows out of him.

"I mean, literally, slept with. Whenever she crashes at my place, she sleeps with me since my bed is comfortable, and there's enough room. But, no, I've never slept with a *man* before. In either context."

"And are you okay with this?"

I smile. "Yeah, I'm okay."

He kisses the top of my head. "Good. Because Peyton?"

"Yeah?"

"I'm falling in love with you, too."

17

"Secrets" // One Republic

I fall asleep with a smile on my face, and when I awake on Saturday, I hear thunder rumble and rain patter on the roof. The side next to me is empty, but it's the smell of coffee and bacon that gets me out of bed.

The wood floor is slippery in my fuzzy socks, and I partially walk, partially slide out of the bedroom and lean against the door frame as I watch Lex cooking again.

How does he make that look so good?

I approach him from behind and wrap my arms around his waist. He glances over his shoulder at me with a smile, before dropping the spatula and turning, wrapping his arms around me. "Morning, sleepyhead."

I yawn. "What time is it?" I never even checked my phone.

"Almost ten."

"You should've woken me up."

He kisses the top of my head. "But you looked so cute sleeping in my bed."

I lift my head to face him. "So, what do you have planned for today?"

He lets go of me and turns back to the stove, where I see bacon and eggs cooking on a skillet, and a silver toaster glowing red in the corner. "Well, I *was* planning on doing some hiking and showing you the lake. Maybe taking you out on my boat, but," he says as he points out of the small window behind the sink. "I don't think that's going to happen now." He frowns as the rain comes down hard. I glance out the window, and lightning flashes in the distance.

On the opposite side of the sink is a pot of freshly brewed —and freshly ground—coffee. I pour myself a cup and watch Lex dish the food onto plates. "Do we have a backup plan?"

He sets the plates on the table and smirks at me. "I do, but trust me, you don't want to hear it."

I frown and eye him suspiciously as I sit down at the table, and he hands me a fork. I sip my coffee, and he sits down across from me, drinking his coffee. "Why?"

He looks up from his cup, eyeing me, seductively. "Because it includes all things dirty."

My face flushes as I look down at my plate, setting my cup down and picking up my fork. Even though my stomach twists at the thought, I can't help but smile.

"Did you sleep well?" He asks.

I nod. "Very." He takes a bite of toast and looks at his plate. "Did you?"

He finishes his bite and lets out a breath. "Honestly, not really."

My face falls. "Why?"

He takes a breath. "Last night was difficult. I had to get up to shower. Twice."

I pull my leg onto the chair and rest my chin on my knee. A wave of guilt runs through me, and I'm not sure why. I didn't do anything wrong. I didn't lead him on. I've been as honest with him as I can about everything. He knows I'm not ready. But I still feel guilty.

Thanks a lot, society.

"I'm sorry," I say quietly.

He quirks his head. "I didn't mean it like that."

I push my food around with my fork, wishing I could eat. Lex gets up from the table and kneels next to me, spinning my chair around so fast, I almost fall. "I'm sorry that came out wrong. I'm not upset with you."

"Okay," I say, but it sounds more like a question.

He takes my hand, lacing our fingers together. "It's not a secret that I want you. And I understand you're not ready for that yet, and I'm not trying to pressure you. I'd never do that. But sometimes, it's difficult. And last night when you were sleeping next to me, all I wanted to do was touch you and because of how much I care about you, I just..." he stops and looks down for a minute, as if afraid to finish his thought.

"What?" I whisper.

Instead of finishing, he pushes himself up and kisses me. He moves my leg down and stands on his knees, his hands on the sides of my face. He pulls away. "I meant what I said last night," he whispers.

And I wonder if he's afraid to repeat it.

A tug pulls at the corner of my lips, and I look him straight in the eye, my heart hammering in my chest, my stomach full of butterflies because it's probably too soon, but I don't care, so I say it anyway. "Lex, I love you."

My words make him come undone.

His lips are on mine. He wraps my legs around his waist and lifts me into the air. Before I know it, my back hits a wall, rattling the chandelier. Lex is holding me up as he kisses me, my arms around his neck, my fingers in his hair.

And again, I wait for the memory of Steve pinning me down in the limo to flash in my mind.

But it doesn't come.

And I'm so relieved by this that it takes me a minute to realize Lex's hand is under my shirt, touching my skin.

I'm still waiting for something to happen, waiting for my body to seize up, waiting for Steve to come into my head.

But nothing happens.

I feel Lex's hand move higher and higher until he pauses. "Is this okay?" He asks.

I'm honestly not sure. So, I whisper, "Yes."

I guess I'm about to find out.

I'm not wearing a bra, so when his hand touches my breast for the first time, my breathing hitches. No one has ever touched me before. Lex's hands are soft and gentle as he cups my right breast. His thumb grazes over my nipple, sending a wave of nerves through me, and my stomach tightens. I moan against his lips, and Lex presses himself into me.

Now, I'm *really* waiting for something to happen. A flash-back, a memory, *anything.*

But nothing does.

Lex kisses a trail down my neck, from my ear lobe to my collar bone, but my eyes are open. I'm staring at the opposite wall of the log cabin where a giant deer head is mounted above a window, and all I can think is, *why am I so calm right now?*

Am I better?

Did Lex cure me?

Or did I somehow heal myself?

What is going on? *How am I totally okay with this?*

I put my hands on Lex's shoulders and push back. "Lex, stop."

He gently bites down on my shoulder and groans. He lets go and pulls back, kissing me softly and smiling kindly. He sets me down, but I take his hands in mine and look up at him. "There's something I need to tell you," I say.

~

WE GO BACK TO OUR BREAKFAST, COLD BUT STILL EDIBLE, AND eat in silence. When we're finished, I help Lex clear the table and clean up the mess on the counter.

The rain continues to pour down on us, and Lex checks the weather app on his iPad.

"It looks like it's supposed to rain all day, but it should clear up tonight."

I sit on the couch with a fresh cup of coffee and one of the books I packed in my hand. I don't plan on reading it, it's mostly just something to keep my hands busy. I'm sitting sideways with my feet up on the couch, my knees under my chin. Lex comes around and sits down next to me, pulling my legs over his lap.

We're both quiet for a long time because I can't seem to find the right words.

He finally breaks the silence. "Peyton?"

I take a deep breath and set my coffee and book down on the coffee table, biting my lip. "Do you remember when you asked me if there was something I wasn't telling you, and I said I wasn't ready to tell you?"

"Yes." Lex takes my hand, entwining our fingers together.

"I think I'm ready to tell you now."

He nods but doesn't press me. He waits patiently for me to continue. I breathe, but can't meet his gaze. I think back and remember what Dr. Young told me all those months ago.

Decide if my partner is ready to hear my story.

I'm pretty sure Lex has always been ready to hear it.

Remember, I don't have to share everything all at once.

Well, my story isn't that long, and I've already told him part of it.

Know that there's no "normal" way for either of us to respond.

This is the part that makes me the most nervous; how will he respond?

Keep in mind that trauma can resurface when I share my story.

Save the best for last; will I have a panic attack when I tell him? Will I get flashbacks? How will he react if that happens?

I take a breath and steel myself before I say, "Last year, on the night of my senior ball, my ex-boyfriend sexually assaulted me."

Holy shit. I let out a breath.

I feel like an elephant has just got up from my chest—like I've lost fifty pounds.

Lex doesn't move or speak. He doesn't let go of my hand, either. Instead, he squeezes it even tighter.

"You've trusted me, Lex. You've told me all those things about your father, and your ex-girlfriend, and I've wanted to tell you. I've just been so afraid to say it out loud. The only people who know about it are my Dad, Sammy, and my old therapist."

He's quiet for a while, and then he asks in a low voice, "Did he rape you?"

My fingers twist the hem of my shirt. "No, but he tried. He hurt me, bad. I have scars on my thighs from a corkscrew—"

"What? A corkscrew?" His tone is a combination of shocked and angry.

"My dress was really long and tight, and he couldn't get it passed my knees, and we were in the back of the limo, and it was the only thing he could find to cut my dress. He didn't even realize he'd cut me until he saw all the blood."

"Oh, my god," Lex whispers. He blinks hard. "Oh, my god. That's why Sammy said to hide the corkscrew."

"What?"

"On Wednesday, I mentioned getting wine, and she said something about making sure you don't have to see or use a corkscrew, but she wouldn't tell me why."

I push the memory of it out of my mind. "I still can't hold one."

I stand slowly and start to pull down on my sweat pants, but Lex grabs my wrist. "What are you doing?"

"Showing you," I say. Slowly, he releases my wrist, and I tug on my sweat pants a few inches, revealing the most vulnerable part of myself.

Only three people have ever seen these scars before, not including the doctor and nurses that stitched them up: Sammy, my Dad, and Dr. Young.

And now, Lex.

The scars are thick and ugly and jagged and run across both my thighs. I needed over thirty stitches.

Lex reaches his fingers out, but I stop him. "Don't. Don't touch them."

He pulls his hand back and nods.

I pull my pants up and sit back down. "Do you remember when I was washing my car, and we ended up kissing in the laundry room?"

His eyes widen. "Vividly."

"I don't think you realized it at the time, but your fingers brushed against them and that's when I freaked out."

Realization dawns on his face. "Okay."

"It's a trigger for my PTSD. If anyone touches my thighs, I have a panic attack."

"Oh," he breathes.

"Now you can understand why having sex with me would be difficult if you can't even touch me in some places."

"Is there anywhere else?"

I think for a moment as my finger traces the pattern of the stitching on the back of the couch. "I don't think so."

"Okay." Lex is staring straight ahead into the fire. It's nearly gone out, but he hasn't gotten up to add more firewood. His hands are folded neatly in his lap, and my insides are screaming. I'm desperate to know what he's thinking, how he's feeling, why he isn't saying anything else?

I look back at the stitching, idly tracing the lines and continue my story. "So, um, after he cut me and he saw all the blood, he moved his hand away from my mouth to put pressure on my thighs. I think, maybe for a split second, he'd realized he'd gone too far. But it was at that moment I was able to scream for help. A few kids from my class opened the limo doors and found us. These two girls—Megan and Lacy—helped me. Their boyfriends grabbed Steve and held him back so I could crawl out. Megan and Lacy half carried me back to the ball and called an ambulance and the police."

"Is he in jail?" Lex asks.

I choke out a laugh, "No. Steve was charged with misdemeanor assault because of the stitches I needed. But because it was his first offense, and he was so young, the judge 'didn't want to ruin his life,'" I explain using air quotes. "So, he was sentenced to three months' probation. But I got a restraining order. He was forced to finish the last few weeks of high school at another school. After we graduated, I heard through some friends that he got into Stanford and was living it up in California. I haven't seen or heard from him since the court date."

Lex slumps his shoulders and looks down at his hands. "I can't believe he didn't do any jail time."

I pull my legs under me, resting my chin on my knees, "He didn't rape me. And even if he did, I still don't think he would have gone to jail," I scoff, "Have you seen the news lately? This country isn't exactly pro-women right now, or ever."

He leans forward, resting his elbows on his knees, and rubs his eyes with his palms, "It's fucking bullshit."

I can tell Lex is upset and a part of me wonders if I shouldn't have told him. He doesn't speak for a long time, and I don't either.

But I don't get any flashbacks of Steve. I don't feel any of the panic I used to feel when I'd think or talk about him. The only thing I'm afraid of right now is what Lex is thinking. If he's second-guessing our relationship, and I can feel the tears well up in my eyes. My chest feels so tight, I can barely take a breath.

Lex turns to face me, his expression softens as he brushes my tear away with his thumb, "What's wrong?"

"I'm just wondering what you're thinking?" He furrows a brow. "Do you still want to be with me?"

Lex cocks his head to the side, his lips curling up the slightest bit as he brushes a stray piece of hair behind my ear. "Peyton, I am so sorry that happened to you. But I meant what I said that day in your room, when we were looking at those pictures. There's nothing you could tell me that would make me stop loving you."

Loving you.

He just said *loving you.*

"Oh, my god," I whisper as I hide my face in my hands and let the tears fall. But these aren't tears of fear or pain or trauma, they're tears of relief. Lex pulls me into him, wrapping his arms around me, holding me as long as I need him to, and I cry into his chest until there's nothing left in me.

18

"Kiss Me" // Ed Sheeran

We sit together in front of the fireplace for a while, long after my tears dry. Thunder rumbles outside, and I'm exhausted from crying. Lex shifts in his seat, and I sit up. "Do you need me to move?"

"No," he says, but he's shaking his hand.

"Your hand fell asleep."

He shrugs. "Actually, my whole arm fell asleep, but it's fine."

I slide down from his lap and sit next to him, watching him shake his arm. "Sorry."

He shakes his head. "Please, Peyton. I don't ever want you to be sorry again." I watch him flex his hand open and closed as he eyes me sidelong. I can tell he wants to say something, but he's afraid to.

"What is it?"

He folds his hands in his lap, but doesn't meet my gaze. "Why now?"

"What?"

"What made you decide to tell me now? Why today?"

I hug my knees to my chest. "Before, whenever we would kiss, and it would go too far, I'd get a flashback. A memory of being back in the limo with Steve. But last night in the back of the truck when you were on top of me, I didn't get one. That's why I started crying. I think I was just so relieved that it didn't come. And earlier when you had me pinned against the wall, I was afraid I'd get another flashback, but I didn't. I don't know why or how or what exactly has changed, but I think I'm finally starting to heal. I think I might be ready to try other things. Maybe it's because of how much I trust you? Or how much I care about you? I don't know, I wish I could give you a solid answer, but I can't even explain it to myself. The only thing I'm still nervous about is..."

"Touching your thighs," he finishes my thought.

"Yeah."

"It's weird how that happens, isn't it?"

"What do you mean?" I ask.

"When I was a kid, I was terrified of my father. I was always afraid when he'd get home from work. Sometimes he'd completely ignore me, and other times he'd call me down into his office just to scream and hit me. And I remember one day when I was about fifteen, I just wasn't afraid of him anymore. I couldn't explain it, either. I just walked into his office, and he lifted his fist to me, but I punched him right in the stomach before he had the chance to hit me. And it was like a weight had been lifted,"

"Like an elephant got up from your chest?"

"Exactly," he smiles. "Was that what it was like for you? Just now?"

I smile. "Yeah."

He takes my hand. "Then I guess we both know how it feels." He kisses the back of my hand and eyes me questioningly. "So, you said you wanted to try other things?"

I bite my lip as my face flushes. "I said I *might* be ready. I mean, you touched my boob earlier, and that was nice."

He raises an eyebrow as his lips curl up. "Really?" He tugs on my hand, and I crawl over him, straddling his lap. I wrap my arms around his neck, and he plays with the hem of my shirt. "Did you have anything specific in mind?"

I press my lips together as I advert his gaze. "No," I admit, sheepishly. "I don't really know what I'm doing. All this stuff is new to me."

Lex lifts his hand to my face, his fingers brushing across my cheek. "I don't want to do anything you don't want me to do."

It's so hard for me not to say, *I want you to do everything,* because I know I'm not ready for everything yet.

Baby steps.

I think for a minute and say, "What about the bases?"

He grins. "Like first base, second base?"

I blush. "Yeah, those. Isn't that how people normally start out?"

"Sometimes. Mostly teenagers, but I mean, yeah, we can start there if you want."

And now I feel super self-conscious. "Don't make fun of me."

"I'm not. I swear," he says, but he's totally laughing.

"It's dumb."

He takes a breath and cups my cheek in his hand. "It's not dumb. I'm sorry, I'm an ass." He kisses me. "Let's start there. We've pretty much mastered first base. Kissing is definitely our thing," he says.

"Yeah, we're really good at that," I agree. My lips meet his, and I open for him, letting his tongue meet mine. I bite on his lower lip.

He moans against my mouth as his hands slip under my shirt and slowly slide up to my breasts. He pulls back for just a second. "Is this okay?"

"Yes."

I let my fingers trail down his chest and slide under his shirt. I feel his hands cup my breasts gently, his thumbs graze over my nipples, and I whimper against his lips. I fist his shirt in my hands and pull. He lets go of me so I can get his shirt over his head, and I toss it onto the floor.

Heat floods through me. *My stars, he is beautiful.* "I thought you said you didn't work out?"

There's no way this body is natural.

He smiles seductively but doesn't answer me. His lips meet mine again, but this time, they're full of passion and eagerness. I explore his chest with my hands, and I can feel Lex's moan rumble throughout.

He tugs at the hem of my shirt and eyes me questioningly.

I look down and realize what he wants to do.

I don't say anything at first, and he stops. "It's okay if you don't want to."

I slide my hand around the back of his neck and kiss him, hard and wanting. I pull away slowly, biting my lip. My stomach twists, and my hands shake, but I take the hem of my shirt and slowly lift it up and over my head. Lex's hands are on my waist as he takes me in, and I fight the urge to cover myself up.

His eyes are ravenous as he says, "You are so fucking beautiful."

His hands slide up my back as his lips meet my neck. A trail of kisses run down my neck, over my chest, until his lips meet my breast. My back arches when his tongue grazes my nipple and my breath hitches.

He gazes up at me. "Is that okay?"

I look down at him and nod. "Mm-hmm," is all I can manage.

He takes my breast in his mouth again, and my hips begin

to move against him, and I don't even realize it. That groan escapes him again, and he looks up at me. "Be careful."

I scoff. "You, too," I say, and he chuckles.

His lips meet mine, and he pulls my body into him, our chests touching. This is the most intimate I've ever been with a man before, and I've never felt so incredibly amazing. Every nerve in my body is on fire, my stomach is filled with butterflies. Every time his hands move to touch another part of me, my toes curl.

And all I can think is that I want *more*.

I pull away for a moment. "So, what's second base?"

He eyes me for a second before he says, "Dangerous."

I frown and run my fingers through his hair. "Please?"

He blinks hard. "Touching you," he says as he slides his hand down my abdomen, below my belly button, my stomach clenching at the touch. He plays with the hem of my pants. "Down here."

I bite my lip, and my hips absentmindedly grind into him again. "Peyton," he growls.

"I'm sorry, I'm not doing it on purpose. My body is kind of taking over here."

"Mine might, too, if we don't stop soon."

I cup his cheek in my hand. "What if I touch you, too?" I slowly slide my hand down his chest, down his gorgeous abdomen, below his belly button, and just when I'm about to reach inside his pants, he grabs my wrist.

"Don't."

I slink back slightly, confused. "Why not?"

He frowns, a wrinkle forming on his forehead. "You don't have to do that."

"But I want to. Isn't that what second base is?" He looks down at my hands, letting out a long breath. "Lex, I don't understand."

He leans back to meet my gaze. "I don't want you to feel like you have to do something you're not ready for."

"I know," I say.

He puts my hand on his chest above his heart, and I can feel how fast it's beating, and I smile. "Are you okay?"

"I think it might explode," he admits. He kisses me gently, his hands moving lightly down my sides. "Are you sure you're ready for second base?"

I swallow hard and exhale. "Yes."

Nope. Don't have a fucking clue if I'm ready. This is all trial and error.

He slides his right hand around to the front of my pants and slowly slips under. His fingers graze over my underwear. I jolt back the tiniest bit, and Lex looks at me. "If you want me to stop, just tell me."

I nod. My entire body tenses up, waiting for him to touch me again. My stomach is in knots.

I don't know if I'm ready for this...

His left hand slides to the small of my back just as his fingers tug at the waistline of my underwear.

I close my eyes and breathe.

My heart is racing, and my whole body is trembling, and Lex gently kisses my neck as I feel his hand slide beneath my underwear.

I stop breathing.

I stop moving.

I feel two fingers gently graze the peak spot between my thighs, and I start.

Oh, my god.

"Are you okay?" He whispers.

I rest my forehead against his. "Yeah," I lie. I hate lying, but I don't want him to stop. I know I'm just nervous. I'm not afraid.

I'm not afraid.

My breathing increases as he slides a finger down to my opening. "Peyton?"

My eyes flutter close as I give him a single nod. And very slowly, he pushes his finger inside of me. I gasp, my fingers gripping his hair, causing him to pause. "I'm okay," I breathe.

Lex shifts his hand, and I suck in a breath as his thumb presses down on the peak spot between my thighs. He carefully slides his finger out of me, only to add another, and I cry out at the sensation.

Holy shit.

He stops moving, and cups my face in his other hand. "Is this too much?"

I look him straight in the eye. "No."

Lex drops his hand from my face, trailing his fingers down my side and around to my back, pressing his palm there.

He begins to slide his fingers in and out of me, pressing down on that spot with his thumb. He moves slow at first, and I gasp and buck my hips into him, stirring his hard on beneath me. I can feel him groan as his eyes meet mine, giving me a disapproving look. I grin and try to steel myself, allowing his fingers to do the work.

And, fuck, do they know how to work.

Every nerve in my body is alive as I kiss him feverishly. Lex's other hand comes around to cup my breast, his finger grazes over my nipple. His fingers work in and out of me, and I never knew it was possible to feel so many things all at once.

I can't believe Lex is touching me, and I'm okay with it.

And I'm okay with it.

I can't believe how good this feels.

How good *Lex* feels.

His hand continues to move, and I gasp as Lex takes my breast in his mouth. I wrap my arms around his neck, trying to steady myself, and he whispers, "Is this okay?"

All I can do is moan in reply.

I can feel his smile as he presses a kiss to my nipple and his fingers increase speed, his thumb pressing down harder, circling faster. He drags his tongue across my nipple, my back arching into him. He switches to my other breast, repeating the same motions, making me grab onto the back of the couch for support. A gleam of sweat coats my skin as Lex kisses his way up my chest, my neck, to my earlobe, his fingers moving at a steady pace inside me, his thumb pressing against that spot, and I can't help myself. I start to move my hips against his hand.

An intense sensation builds in my core, something I've never felt before. The more Lex touches me, the stronger it becomes.

"Lex, I..."

I wrap my arms around his neck as my hips move faster with him. He presses just a bit harder, moves just a bit faster, and my body stiffens on top of him, and then I'm shuddering, my hand grips his hair as my entire body explodes with plea-sure. I tremble with release as he slows his strokes as I come down until I'm limp against him. We sit there, panting, trying to catch our breaths, and neither of us move.

After a moment, he slowly removes his fingers and slides his hand out from my pants.

My arms are wrapped around his neck, and I lean against him.

Lex wraps his arms around me, nuzzling his face in my neck. "Are you okay?"

"Yeah," I manage to say, but my body continues to betray me.

"You're trembling," he says, pressing a kiss to my neck. He pushes me back so he can see my face, and I'm sure my cheeks look as hot as they feel. He brushes a stray hair behind my ear. "Are you sure I didn't hurt you?"

"No, you didn't hurt me," I reassure him with a grin, taking his hand in mine and pressing it to my cheek. "I've just... that was... I've never felt..."

I can't even find the words.

He smiles at me. "Was that your first?"

I bite my lip and look away, my cheeks getting even hotter.

"Wow," he says and kisses me. "Glad I could be of service."

"If *that's* what I've been missing this whole time, *oh, my god*," I kiss him, and I never want to stop. He smiles and looks at me with those blue-gray eyes that make me melt.

I slide my hands down his chest and try once again to reach my hand inside his pants, and just when I'm almost there, he grabs my wrist and pulls back, eyeing me. "Peyton, please."

"I don't understand. Why can't I touch you, too?"

"Because the second you start touching me there, I'm afraid I might lose control, and I don't want to do that." He presses his lips to my heart. Then he grabs me by the hips, lifts me up and pushes me carefully onto the couch. "So, I need to go take a shower before things get dangerous."

I grab his hand. "Are you sure? Because I can—"

But he stops me. "Not yet. I don't trust myself, and the last thing I want to do is hurt you or scare you. Please, trust me on this."

I nod and watch him walk into the bedroom. I find my shirt on the floor and toss it back on. I go into the bedroom and grab my phone from the charger and connect it to the WiFi so I can iMessage Sammy. She is going to *flip*.

19

"Great Indoors" // John Mayer

'So, Lex loves me, and he gave me my first Screaming O this morning. How's your weekend going?' I text Sammy.

Clean and simple, and I can't stop laughing.

Her reply is equally hilarious.

'WHO DID WHAT IN THE WHERE NOW?'

'HE LOVES YOU? OMG DID HE SAY HE LOVES YOU?'

'AWWWWW!' Hug emoji, hug emoji, red heart emoji.

Followed by a string of eggplant emojis.

Lex is still in the shower as I sit on the bed and laugh.

'I don't know what's going on with me, but the flashbacks have stopped. The nightmares are gone. All of it just stopped. I don't know how or why, but I'm not complaining.'

'Tell me how! Hands or tongue?'

Oh, god.

'Fingers and thumb.'

'Does he have magic fingers?'

'*Apparently?*' Shrug emoji. '*First time. I don't have a clue what I'm doing but he definitely does.*'

'*But no sex yet, right?*'

'*No, no sex yet.*' I type with a sigh.

'*It's all right, girl. Take it slow. One step at a time.*'

I fall back on the bed and watch the three dots on the screen that indicates she's typing.

'*Did you do anything for him?*'

I can't help but roll my eyes, '*No, he wouldn't let me.*'

'*Really? Why not?*' She asks.

I explain what Lex told me with disappointment.

'*Hmm...*'

I'm not sure what else to say about it, so I ask, '*Is my Dad doing okay?*'

I wait for her reply. '*Yup, just left your house. On my way to work now. I'll check on him later on my way home.*'

'*I love you. You're the best.*'

'*I know. Okay, got to go. I can't wait to hear about the rest of your weekend! Have fun!*'

I sit up on the bed just as Lex walks out of the bathroom with nothing but a white towel around his waist, rubbing another towel through his dripping wet hair. I stare at him as he walks toward the dresser on the opposite side of the room. The towels drop, and I let out a noise as my jaw hits the mattress.

Lex looks back at me with a smirk. "Like what you see?"

His naked ass is staring at me, and I try to look away and say something, anything, but all that comes out is, "Uh huh."

He smiles as he slips on his boxers, not turning around for me to see anything else.

I frown as he turns to me with a pair of sweat pants in his hands and sits next to me on the bed.

"Do you feel better?" I ask.

He looks me over, eyeing my lips, my neck, my bra-less breasts beneath my shirt. "For now."

My cheeks flush as I glance out the window to my left and watch the rain pour down on top of us. "Is it ever going to stop?"

He slides his pants on and looks outside. "Not for a while."

"So, what do we do now?"

He leans forward, resting his elbows on his knees. "We can watch movies? I've got a Roku hooked up to the TV out there. Or we can read if you want. I see you've brought some books."

"I think I'd be a bit too distracted to read," I admit.

He leans over and kisses me. "Yeah?"

"Yeah. Way too distracted." I kiss him before he pulls away and stands. He walks over to the dresser to grab a shirt out of the middle drawer.

"I'm sorry," he says as he pulls it over his head. "I should have planned for rain. I didn't even think about it. We can go home early if you want."

I slink back into the bed. "What?"

"I just feel bad, there isn't much to do up here that isn't outdoors."

My face falls as I look at my hands. "Is that what you want?"

"No, but I understand—"

"Lex, no." I cut him off. "I don't want to go home." I get up and wrap my arms around his waist. "I really don't mind just staying here and hanging out with you. Believe it or not, I like hanging out with you. Having you all to myself in a cozy cabin with a fireplace and Netflix is actually very appealing."

He hugs me back. "Are you sure?"

"One hundred percent," I say as I look up and kiss him.

I TAKE A SHOWER, PUT ON A PAIR OF CLEAN BLACK SWEAT PANTS and a t-shirt with a cat in outer space on the front, then brush my long wet hair up into a cute, albeit messy, bun.

I make my way out into the living room to see Lex reading one of the books I brought with me, perusing the page I had bookmarked, and my cheeks flush.

He looks up at me with a cocky grin and wide eyes. "Damn, Peyton. I didn't realize you were into such dirty literature."

I practically jump on the couch to grab the book from him, but he holds it up higher than I can reach. I slink back on the sofa on my knees and glare at him. "First of all, that's the second book in the series."

I run back in the bedroom and rifle through my bag. I hold up the bright red book in my hand and hold it out to him. "This is the first one. Now, it does have maybe two love scenes in it, but it's nothing compared to book two. Secondly, if you're going to read Sarah J. Maas, you have to read them in order, and not mock me for them. These are my favorite books in the world, besides Harry Potter, but it's Harry-freaking-Potter. So, you give me back the blue book, and I'll give you the red book and," I take a deep breath. "I will let you borrow it."

"Wow, this is really hard for you."

"I've read these books five times."

His eyes go wider at that. "You've read a book series *five times?*"

"Yes, and I swear to every single deity ever invented by humanity, if you damage or lose it, I will murder you in your sleep."

He laughs and pauses. "Wait, let me just finish this one part. It's excellent. They're all covered in paint and—"

I grab the book from his hand. "You can't read the blue book first! You will be so confused when you read the red one."

He sighs. "Fine."

I grin. "It was good, right?"

He lets out a breath. "I don't think I've ever *read* porn before."

I playfully punch him in the arm and set both books onto the coffee table. "So, what do you want to do?"

He knits his brows together. "You said you love Harry Potter?"

"I do."

"You know, I've never read the books or seen any of the movies."

My face falls in shock. "You've never seen the Harry Potter movies?"

"Nope."

"You go make popcorn. I'll sign into my Amazon account on the Roku. I own them all. We're having a marathon!"

He kisses me on the nose as he gets up, heading for the kitchen.

I queue up the first movie as Lex sits down with two sodas in one hand and a giant bowl of popcorn in the other. I snuggle up against him and press play.

~

WE FINISH THE FIRST TWO MOVIES, AND LEX LOOKS AT ME WIDE-eyed. "Whoa," he says as the credits roll. "I can't believe I've never seen these before. And they get better from here?"

"Just you wait."

"Which one is your favorite?" He asks.

"Oh, god," I say, and I stand up, desperately needing to pee. "I like them all. It's hard to choose. I guess I'd say the last one is my favorite. Well, the last two. They broke up the seventh book into two movies, and it's epic. You're going to love it!" I say as I make my way to the bathroom.

When I walk back out, I see Lex standing in the kitchen. "What are you doing?"

"I figured we could use some real food to eat while we watch the third movie if you're hungry."

"I'm starving. What do we have?"

"I bought steaks to grill," he says as he looks out the window at the rain that is still pouring down on us.

"Damn."

"Luckily, I have a stove top grill," he says as he pulls out a rectangular cast iron grill and sets it on top of two burners.

"Can I please help this time?"

He considers for a moment before saying, "I guess. There are vegetables in the fridge for a salad, if you'd be so kind."

I smile and pull out what I need. Lex shows me where the chopping board and knives are, and I begin to chop as he heats up the grill. "Careful, though. Those knives are sharp."

I glare at him. "I cook for my Dad all the time. He's not really the cooking type."

"How's your Dad doing?"

"He seems okay right now. I texted Sammy earlier, and she said he's fine. Thank you, by the way. For having her check up on him for me."

He smiles. "No problem. So, no more relapses, then?"

I shake my head. "Nope. I think I might have finally gotten through to him."

Fuck, I hope I got through to him.

I finish preparing the salad and set it aside, and I watch Lex set the steaks on the grill top. I'm not sure why, but watching him cook is so incredibly hot, it's hard for me not to push him against a wall and rip his shirt off.

I pull out my phone, and Lex smiles. "Are you going to play me more music?"

I smile. "Do you want me to?"

He shrugs. "Sure. The speakers are on Bluetooth," he says as he points to the speakers in each corner of the cabin that I didn't notice before.

This is going to be fun.

I slide through my playlist and smile wickedly.

I select a song I think he might have heard, but probably not the band.

It's a cover of *Every Little Thing She Does Is Magic* by Sleeping At Last.

I set my phone down on the counter and take his hand, pulling him away from the stove.

He eyes me suspiciously. "Peyton," his tone is curious, but he's smiling.

"Dance with me," I say as I twirl. He wraps an arm around my waist, and I put mine around his neck. "We've got a few minutes."

He pulls me closer as we dance in the middle of the cabin. His hands roaming across the small of my back, around to my hips, his forehead resting on mine. He bites his lip. "I like this song," he whispers.

"Me, too."

He kisses me as we dance slowly to the song, along with the sound of the storm outside. Lex takes my hand and spins me, then pulls me back into him. He wraps one arm around me, placing his hand on my back and kisses me again, long and hard and eager.

For a moment, we've forgotten about the steaks.

Maybe being cooped up in this cabin with him is dangerous.

We dance until the song ends, but he doesn't move. We stand there in the center of the cabin, his mouth on mine, his hands exploring my body again, and I force myself to pull away.

"Lex, the steaks."

He turns. "Shit." He dashes over to the stoves and flips them over before they overcook and turns back to me.

I bite back a smile as I approach him. "Sorry, I didn't mean to distract you."

He eyes me sidelong. "Yes, you did."

I snort. "Not like that."

He shakes his head and sighs. "Okay, no more music until the food is done."

"Promise."

I don't say another word until Lex is finished cooking, and we serve the steaks and salads. We eat in the living room tonight and watch the third Harry Potter movie, Lex, on the edge of his seat.

"There's a werewolf?"

"No spoilers," I say.

He pours us each some wine, and I can't help but laugh at his reactions as the plot of the movie unfolds. I set my glass down on the table and start cleaning up as the movie gets closer to the end.

"Hey? What are you doing? It's not over."

"Yeah, but I've seen it a hundred times. I'll be right back," I say.

I take our plates to the sink and smile, happy that I get to share this with him. As I rinse off the dishes and load them in the dishwasher, I wonder what things Lex loves that he wants to share with me. Besides the plans he had for the weekend. He's clearly an outdoorsy person—that kind of surprises me— and it isn't something I've ever been. I don't mind hiking the waterfall trails in Genesee Falls, but actual mountain hiking is a bit beyond my capabilities. But I'm willing to give it a shot for him.

Shit, I'd walk the entire Pacific Crest Trail if he asked me to.

I pull out my phone and text Sammy.

'It's been pouring all day here, so instead of Lex's plans of hiking and taking me out on his boat, we've been binge-watching Harry Potter movies. He's never seen them, and he loves them. Almost done with number three.'

She doesn't reply right away, so I stick my phone back in my pocket and crawl back onto the couch with Lex.

When the movie ends, Lex is eager to watch number four, so we pour some more wine and start it up. I feel my phone buzz in my pocket and see a text from Sammy.

'He's never seen HP? Poor, secluded, rich boy. He's lucky to have found you.'

I smile as I watch Lex watch the movie, glad we've found something new to bond over.

20

"Delicate" // Taylor Swift

When we finish with the fifth Harry Potter movie, the storm outside seems to be getting worse, not better. Lex opens the weather app on his iPad.

"Oh," he starts and I glance up at him. "Apparently, a second storm is on us now, and this one is even worse." He shows me the radar map, and we're right in the red zone. It's just past midnight now, and before I even get the chance to queue up the sixth movie, a crack of lightning echoes so loud, the power in the cabin goes out.

And it's very dark—minus the fireplace.

"Uh, oh," I say.

Lex gets up and walks over to a small closet in the corner of the room to the left of the fireplace on the far wall. Inside is a box with circuit breakers. He clicks them on and off a few times before closing it. "The storm must have knocked the power out."

"I guess we'll have to wait it out."

He looks defeated as he closes the closet door and walks back over to the couch. "It'll probably be a while. Being in the middle of nowhere means there aren't many people in the area so, we're not really a top priority."

I smile as I snuggle up close to him. "Whatever will we do?"

He puts his arm around me. "I don't know. The two of us alone in the dark with nothing but a fireplace to keep us warm during a thunderstorm."

"Wait," I say, and sit up to look at him. "I swear, I've seen this movie."

He laughs and scoots me aside. "I'm going to pull the candles out and light them around the room."

"I'll help."

In the same closet with the circuit breaker box are two small boxes filled with white pillar candles. He brings them out onto the kitchen table, and we arrange the candles all around the room, lighting each one as we go.

By the time we're done, it's like Tinkerbell threw up in here.

I'm standing in the middle of the cabin, and it's absolutely fucking beautiful.

Lex comes up behind me, putting his hands on my hips, admiring our work. "Wow, it's all romantic, and I wasn't even trying."

Mm-hmm.

I turn and smirk. "You know there's only one thing missing, right?"

I take a few steps back toward the coffee table and grab my phone.

He eyes me suspiciously with a grin. "Oh, boy."

I unlock my phone and scroll through my music. "What song should I play now?"

Lex watches me nervously as I go through the music on my

phone. My fingers dance between two songs. One love song, and one sexy song. My stomach clenches; maybe I'll play them back to back.

I click on *Chasing Cars*. Originally by Snow Patrol, but this beautiful cover is by Sleeping At Last, and set my phone on the table.

I take Lex's hand, and he spins me around. He pulls me into him, and we dance in the center of the cabin.

He smiles. "You always pick the perfect songs. I don't know how you do it."

I shrug. "I'm really good with music. It's kind of my thing."

I wrap my arms around his neck, and his arms tighten around my back, and we dance slowly in a circle. He kisses me gently as his hands move up and down my back and sides. We move together, his face buried in my neck, my head resting on his shoulder until the song ends.

And now my insides are twisting.

I take a deep breath, and Lex pulls away from me. "What is it?"

I bite my lip. "There's one more song."

As soon as *Love Me Like You Do* by Ellie Goulding starts playing, my stomach turns into butterflies, but I don't let go of Lex. I keep my arms around his shoulders and pull him into me and kiss him feverishly.

He kisses me back, but as soon as he hears the lyrics, he pulls back. "Peyton," he whispers.

I shake my head. "Don't," I say. "Just kiss me."

And he does. He kisses me deeply, and the next thing I know, he's lifting me up and pressing me against the wall again, kissing a trail up my neck, nipping my ear. My legs wrap around him and I can feel that sound emit from deep in his chest as he pushes himself into me.

His fingers dance along my hips until he grips them, his

mouth on mine again. I bite on his lower lip, and he comes undone. He lifts me up again and carries me into the bedroom, lying me down on the bed.

My insides have officially liquefied and I'm afraid might I implode.

His hands explore under my shirt, and I let them. I grab the hem of his shirt and pull it over his head. I'm so caught up in the moment, I have no idea where it lands. Lex lifts up my shirt and kisses my stomach, starting at my navel and moving up toward my breasts. He pushes it up and over my head. I never put a bra on after I got out of the shower earlier; I figured I didn't need one.

I guess I was right.

Lex's mouth is on my breast, and his hands are on the hem of my sweat pants.

My heart skips a beat.

Lightning flashes outside and the roar of thunder follows, causing me to jump. I glance out the window to my left for just a second, and before I have the chance to say anything, Lex has my sweat pants off, and his lips are on me again. My stomach, my chest.

But he doesn't touch my thighs.

Fuck.

I scoot back onto the bed a bit, and Lex crawls over me. My entire body is trembling as I look up at him. His eyes are ravenous as he looks down at me, and I'm pretty sure I look absolutely terrified.

But he doesn't say a word.

And I wonder if he really has lost control.

His hands roam down the sides of my body. His fingers slide under the seam of my underwear, and I panic.

I legit fucking panic.

"Lex, wait. Don't."

His fingers stop, but he doesn't move them.

"Please, I'm sorry. This is too much. I can't—" I push on his chest, and he doesn't move at first. I watch him for the longest second of my life as he closes his eyes and lets out a long breath before he moves his hand and rolls over next to me, laying on his back to my right. I grab the sheet and cover myself up, fighting the burning in my eyes.

Lex doesn't say a word. He just shoots up from the bed and walks into the bathroom, shutting the door behind him. I hear the shower turn on. I get up and grab my clothes and get dressed as quickly as I can.

I feel horrible.

I feel sick.

I hate this.

What is wrong with me?

Did I really think I was ready for this?

I grab all my things and toss them in my bag. I pack the rest of my clothes, my books, my charger. I don't even care about the blankets in the back of Lex's truck. I just need to get out of here. I need to fucking *breathe*.

Lex isn't in the shower very long. He walks out, wearing the same pants as before and looks at me, surprised. "Peyton?"

I'm crying and can't meet his gaze. "I'm sorry. I didn't mean for it to go that far."

"What are you doing?" His tone is calm, almost worried.

I grab my bag and bring it into the living room and grab the few things I have out there. He follows me, pulling a shirt over his head.

"I need to go home," I say.

Lex looks at me like I just punched him in the heart. "Why?"

I slam my bags onto the table. "None of this is fair to you, Lex!" I grab my phone and stuff it in my purse.

"Peyton, please."

"I can't keep doing this to you!"

"Just try to calm down," his tone is so fucking calm, I want to throw a book at his head.

"Are you fucking serious right now?"

"Look outside. You can't drive back to Genesee Falls in this storm. You've also had wine. I'm not trying to force you to stay. I just don't think it's safe for you to be driving right now." He approaches me, and I back away, covering my mouth with the sleeve of my hoodie. "Please, Peyton. At least wait until the morning. I'll sleep on the couch. You can have the bed. Please, I just want you to be safe."

I know he's right, as much as I hate to admit it. It's pouring outside, and lightning is going off every few minutes. I know if I get in my car and try to drive home, I'd probably be killed by a fallen tree or telephone pole. But I'm so ashamed of myself.

"I'm sorry. I'm so sorry." I sob.

Slowly, Lex takes my hand and shushes me, carefully pulling me into him until his arms are around me, and I'm crying into his chest. "You have nothing to be sorry for," he whispers. He holds me tight against him. "I lost control. I got caught up in the moment and I'm sorry. I should have stopped it. I should have asked if you were okay but I kept going when I shouldn't have." I can hear his voice straining. "*I'm* sorry, Peyton."

I'm suddenly so tired. Leaning onto Lex is the only thing keeping me standing. Lex carefully puts an arm under my legs and lifts me up and carries me into the bedroom. He lays me down on the bed and covers me with the blanket, before grabbing a pillow and making his way into the living room.

He closes the double doors to the bedroom, and I cry into my pillow. I can't keep doing this to him. But is this my fault, or his? Or is it both?

He's right, though, he should have asked me if I was okay. I know he saw my face and didn't say anything, but even so, I should have said something.

Fuck, I don't even know anymore.

How much of this is me not telling him to stop, or him not asking for consent? Everyone keeps saying not saying no doesn't mean yes.

I reach in my hoodie pocket to pull out my phone, only to remember I tossed it into my purse that's on the kitchen table. *Fuck*, I could really use some advice from Sammy right about now. Then I remember the WiFi went out with the power, and with the limited cell service, I probably couldn't get a message to her if I tried. I roll over and toss the blanket over my head, fighting the urge to scream into my pillow.

I LIE IN BED FOR WHAT SEEMS LIKE FOREVER BUT IS PROBABLY only an hour, maybe two, and I can't sleep. I take a breath, toss the covers aside and tiptoe over to the double doors, carefully pulling them open. I can't tell if Lex is sleeping or not. So, I stand in the doorway for a long moment before I hear him tossing on the couch and let out a long, frustrated sigh.

"Lex?" I whisper.

He sits up and looks at me. I walk up to him, and I can see his eyes are bloodshot, and there are tear stains on his face. "Are you okay?" He asks.

I shake my head. "Not really. I can't sleep."

"Me, either."

I stand there for a minute before I finally say, "I don't want you to sleep on the couch."

He looks away from me, ashamed. "Peyton—"

"Please. I won't be able to sleep tonight without you next to me. I'm not mad at you. I promise."

It takes him a minute before he kicks off the blanket, grabs his pillow, and follows me back into the bedroom. We climb into bed, and I turn onto my left side and wait for him to get comfortable. I scoot over a little, so my back is touching his front, and he sighs and wraps me in his arms.

"Peyton?" Lex whispers.

"Yeah?"

"I really am sorry."

"Me, too."

21

"Everything Has Changed" // Taylor Swift & Ed Sheeran

The next morning, I wake up to Lex asleep next to me, his arms still around me, and the storm has finally cleared. The sun is shining through the window, and it takes my eyes a few minutes to adjust to the brightness. I don't want to move from where I lie next to him. I shift and Lex's arms tighten around me, and I smile.

Last night was such a cluster fuck, and all I hope is we're able to move past it. I'm not angry with him—truly, I'm not. Both of us got carried away and let things go too far. I think we're equally to blame.

I should have said something.

He should have said something.

But neither of us did because deep down, even though I was afraid, I wanted him.

And then I panicked.

When I get home, I'm going to make an appointment with

Dr. Young. I need to figure out what is going on with me lately. Why am I fine one minute, and totally freaking out the next? I know money is tight right now with my Dad's latest hospital stint, but I need this. I need to figure out how to have a normal relationship with Lex—if it's even possible.

I lie in his arms for a while before deciding to wake him up. Slowly, I turn to face him, and plant a kiss on his forehead, his nose, his lips. Hoping maybe some of the ice will melt. I kiss him until I feel his lips smile against mine. "Morning," he says.

"Morning."

He doesn't pull away from me. He just looks at me, eyes filled with sadness and regret. He glances out the window, then back at me. "Do you still want to leave?"

I slide my arm across his waist. "No."

"Are you sure? I won't be upset if you do."

I scoot closer to him. "I don't want to leave. I didn't really want to leave last night, I just overreacted. I got scared and panicked."

He pulls me tighter to his chest. "I know. I'm sorry."

I can tell he's struggling, and I can feel the guilt radiating off him. "I don't blame you for what happened. Both of us got carried away," I place my hand on his cheek. "I think we just need to take some time to figure out how this is going to work. I thought after what happened, I was ready for more, and maybe I'm ready for a little, but clearly, I'm not ready for everything yet."

"I understand. And I don't ever want to pressure you. I'm sorry I did that."

I kiss him again. "And I'm sorry I let it go so far."

He blinks hard. "Peyton, I told you I never wanted you to be sorry again."

"Well, too bad. Because I'm not perfect, and there are going to be times when I fuck up, so, get over it."

He chuckles. "Okay, okay. We're both sorry. And we're both forgiven?"

"We're both forgiven."

He kisses me, sweetly, lovingly. Lex finally pulls away from me and climbs out of bed. "I'm going to take a shower. I don't think today will be any better for my plans. I'm pretty sure all the hiking trails are nothing but mud, and the lake will be too high to go out on the boat."

"Do we have power?"

He goes to the light switch and flicks it on and off. "Nope. Cold shower it is."

I rifle through my bag for some clean clothes to change into, at least.

When Lex is clean and dressed, we start packing our things up and close down the cabin. He helps me pack up my car and brings the blankets from his truck to my back seat.

"I'll have to bring you back up here another time. Maybe this summer. There's more to do, and I promise I will check the weather forecast before we come."

I smile. "It was fun."

"I'll meet you back in the Falls and take you out to eat."

"Okay. I'm going to shower and change first, though," I say and kiss him goodbye.

"Peyton," he calls to me before I get in my car.

"Yeah?"

"Be careful driving back down. There might be some trees and power lines down from last night."

I nod. "I will. I'll see you in a bit."

I get in my car, pull out of the driveway and head back out onto the road.

Lex wasn't joking. The roads are pretty clear, but all along the sides are branches and huge parts of trees. I drive the first thirty minutes way too slowly, luckily the only other person on the road apart from me is Lex.

Once I hit the highway, everything is smooth sailing.

I'm so relieved to pull into my driveway. I grab my bags and run up the porch and into the house. My Dad isn't home, and I remember he's on first shift today.

I run upstairs, plug my phone in, strip off my clothes, and take the longest, hottest shower I possibly can.

Once I'm finished, I get dressed and brush out my hair. I pick up my phone and see I have a few missed texts from Sammy.

'Checked on your Dad. Everything's good. I just wanted to let you know.'

'Hope you kids have fun watching Harry Potter. Party hardly!'

I text her back. 'Hey are you working? I really need to talk. I'm home. Last night was bad. Let me know when you're free.'

Relief fills my insides when my phone dings back almost instantly with her reply. 'I'm not due at work for another hour. I'm on my way over now. Are you okay?'

'Yes, and no. I'll explain everything when you get here.'

SAMMY ARRIVES JUST IN TIME. SHE THROWS OPEN MY DOOR, NOT bothering to knock because my house is basically her second home, and I run down the stairs and hug her so tight, she starts to panic.

"What's wrong? What happened? Why are you back so early? What did he do?"

"It's not that," I say as I pull away and lead her into the living room and we sit down on the couch. "The rainstorm knocked out the power last night, and it was still out when we woke up this morning, so we decided to leave early, but... that's not the problem..."

So, I tell her everything.

I tell her about dancing in the cabin.

About him pinning me up against the wall.

That how I finally told him everything that happened with Steve in the limo.

More dancing, more wall pinning, and how he lied me down on the bed with him and stripped me to nothing but my underwear... and how I finally freaked out.

Cold showers. Packing my shit. Me wanting to leave, but I couldn't drive in the crazy-ass thunderstorm.

I lay everything out on the table for her.

Sammy looks at me, wide-eyed, her mouth agape. "Holy shit, Peyton. That's a lot for one day."

"No shit."

"Are you guys fighting?"

I shake my head. "No. We talked a bit. He slept on the couch, but I couldn't sleep, so I went out there and asked him to come to bed. He did, and then when we woke up, I told him I didn't blame him."

"Peyton."

"It was *both* of our faults. Neither one of us stopped it. I should have said no sooner, and he should have been like, '*Is this okay?*' But neither of us did because *both* of us got caught up in the moment. I just can't figure it out."

"What can't you figure out?"

"I was okay Friday night and Saturday morning. When he was touching me, that was okay. I was nervous, but I didn't panic, and I liked it. But then a few hours later, I'm freaking out again? It doesn't make any sense."

"You're just moving too fast. The bed of a pickup truck doesn't really scream 'Let's get it on!' does it? And what happened Saturday morning was different, right?"

I tug on the sleeve of my hoodie. "I don't know?"

"Well, where were you? On the bed?"

"No, on the couch."

"Okay, the couch is in the living room. A neutral space. Not a space where sexual things are expected to happen. Then he pinned you against the wall in the...?"

"It's kind of a space in the middle of the cabin before you get to the bedroom doors."

"Again, another neutral area. Then all of a sudden, he throws you onto a bed. A bed where people might feel expected to have sex. Maybe that triggered your freak out. Maybe you felt like you *had* to have sex with him."

"I guess I never thought of it like that."

Sammy leans back onto the couch, resting her head on her hand. "Peyton, you of all people know that anxiety and PTSD don't always make sense. Sometimes it's something small like a location or a smell or a color that can trigger it."

"Yeah. I think I'm going to call Dr. Young and set up an appointment."

Sammy eyes me concerned. "Is it that serious?"

I look down at my sleeve and twist a stray black thread around my finger. "No, I just think I could use some professional advice. Maybe she can give me insight on how to make this work."

Sammy nods. "That's actually an excellent idea. Why didn't I think of it?"

I hit her in the arm with a pillow. "You don't have *all* the good ideas, Samantha Clarke."

"No, just most of them," she says with a wink.

～

SAMMY LEAVES FOR WORK, JUST AS MY PHONE BUZZES ON THE coffee table. It's a text from Lex.

'Hey, I can't make it for lunch today. I got a bunch of missed calls

*from my Dad and work that I have to take care of before tomorrow.
I'm sorry, I owe you one, XXX'*

I flop down on the couch with a sigh and reply, *'It's okay. See
you tomorrow.'* Red heart emoji.

Dr. Young and I have a special relationship. I was one of the
few patients she gave her personal cell phone number to. Even
after I left, she told me that if I ever needed her services again,
I should feel free to contact her anytime.

So, that's what I do. I slide down my list of contacts and call
her number.

The line rings three times before she answers. "Well, Peyton
Katz, as I live and breathe," she says.

"Hey, Doc, how are you?" I ask.

"I'm doing well, thank you. I'm guessing you're not doing so
good? Hence the call?"

"Well, I'm doing okay, for the most part, but I could use
some advice. And I was wondering if you had any appoint-
ments open this week?"

"For you, of course, I do! Let me just check my book," she
says, and I can hear her shuffling around some papers,
mumbling to herself. "Ah, okay, let's see. I've got at one o'clock
tomorrow?"

"I have to work tomorrow."

"Okay, how about eleven on Tuesday?"

"That's perfect."

"All right, I've got you written down, Peyton. I'm excited to
see you."

"Yeah, well, I've got a lot to tell you. I hope you're not busy
at noon."

She laughs. "For you, I've got all the time in the world."

"Thank you, Dr. Young. I'll see you on Tuesday."

"Goodbye, Sweetheart."

I hang up the phone, feeling the slightest bit better.

Until I remember that Dr. Young's office is directly across the street from the pharmacy.

Fuck me.

~

I PARK MY CAR DOWN A SIDE STREET AND WALK DOWN THE BLOCK to Dr. Maggie Young's office wearing sunglasses and my hood over my head.

Like I could be anymore inconspicuous.

I open the door to her office and pull off my hood and sunglasses. Her secretary, Cindy, waves at me. "Hey, Peyton! It's so nice to see you!"

"Hey, Cindy. I have an appointment with Maggie at eleven."

"Yup! It will just be a few minutes. She's finishing up with another patient."

"Okay, thanks," I smile and take a seat against the wall next to a table with magazines. There's a silent TV on the wall in the upper left corner with the subtitles on. Some news anchorwoman talking about politics, so I don't pay attention.

I sit there, the only person in the room besides Cindy, who looks to be checking her social media accounts on the computer behind the desk, and I snort. I pull out my phone and shoot Sammy a message.

'I just got to Dr. Young's office. In the waiting room. I don't know why I'm nervous, but I feel nervous.'

I know Sammy can't text me back since she's working behind the pharmacy counter at the moment. Still, I keep texting her anyway, knowing she'll read them eventually.

'Please don't tell Lex I'm here. I figured I'll talk to him about it later, depending on whether or not this helps me at all. I mean, it should. It probably will. I don't know.'

God, what is wrong with me?

I click my phone on vibrate just as Dr. Young opens the

door to her office, leading out an older gentleman, wiping away tears from his eyes. I try not to look at him because I have no idea what he could be crying about, but I instantly feel sorry for the poor guy.

"Cindy will schedule you for your next appointment. Next week, all right?"

The man nods, and Cindy pulls up a chart on the computer.

"Peyton!" Dr. Young calls me, and I look at her. "Come on in!"

I stand and make my way into her office. It's a decent size room with a desk, a large sofa, and two armchairs. Dr. Young is in her mid-fifties, wears big round black plastic glasses, is maybe an inch or two shorter than me, but super slender. In the warmer months, she's always wearing sundresses or pretty skirts with cute tops, with open-toed sandals. Her salt and pepper hair is always swept up into a neat bun on the back of her head.

"So, Peyton," she says as she sits down in one of the big armchairs, "what brings you in today?"

I sit down on the couch across from her, setting my purse next to me, and pull off my hoodie. It's way too hot for one, and I was only wearing it to hide from *Kingston's*. "Well, it's kind of a long story..."

So, I tell her everything.

It takes me a while, getting it all out. Trying to remember all the details of the past few weeks, about my Dad's relapse, about the store remodel, about school ending, and of course, everything about Lex.

"And that's why I'm here. I can't figure it out. I don't understand why sometimes I'm okay, and other times I'm not. I know he can't touch my thighs, and he knows that part, too. And once I told him, he's never tried or anything. I just can't seem to figure out where the line is. And how am I ever going to be in a normal relationship if he can't even touch me?"

Dr. Young smiles kindly at me, tapping her pen back and forth between her fingers. "Well, this is the first relationship you've been in since the incident with Steve. And you've only been dating for, what, three weeks?"

I look down at my hands on my lap. "Yeah."

"I think you're putting too much pressure on yourself. It hasn't been that long at all, and I understand you're worried because he's older and more experienced than you. But right now, you guys are in what's called the new relationship stage. Everything you're feeling is heightened, enhanced, because it's new and exciting and different. And that's totally normal. But you've got to put the brakes on. Your mental health is more important than his sexual angst. And if this guy cares about you like he says he does, he'll understand that."

"I know. He does understand. I'm just torn because I want to be with him, and I don't want to be afraid. I want to be ready."

"But you can't force yourself, Peyton. These things take time. I do have one suggestion for you, that you may find a little silly at first, but I've found it to be very helpful in these types of situations."

"All right," I say, my interests piqued.

"Have you ever heard of a safe word?"

I snort. "You mean like *Fifty Shades* kind of safe word?"

She chuckles. "Not exactly. Yes, a lot of people associate safe words with things like BDSM. Still, psychologists and psychiatrists have found that safe words work in many other areas in life. Like for people who struggle with dealing with confrontation. If you're arguing with a parent or spouse and need a break, you can use a safe word as a way to take a time out and come back to the discussion later. But with you," she says as she gets up from her chair and heads over to her desk. "I think I have a paper here somewhere..." She shuffles around her desk, that's nothing but a mess of scattered papers and books.

"Shoot. I'll email you the link to the article," she comes around and sits back down. "For survivors of trauma, especially sexual trauma, whether it's rape or assault or molestation, it's generally incredibly difficult to get back out there. Every situation is different. Some people can overcome it in a few months, others can take years."

Years?

"I think with everything that's happened, you're doing really well. I don't think it's going to take you years, but it is going to take some time. And I think the use of a safe word could be beneficial in your situation."

"Okay. How?"

"Safe words have crystal clear intent, and avoid a strong emotional response, like you having a panic attack. When you hear the word, you disengage without question, but you don't have to stop completely. He just needs to stop whatever he's doing that made you say the safe word. Like if his hand moves up to your thigh, you say "peanut butter," and he moves his hand back. You guys don't have to stop fooling around completely, he just needs to not touch your thigh. And that way, you don't have a panic attack."

"Okay."

"And the more you guys use the safe word, and the more Lex listens to it, the more you begin to trust him. And over time, you won't need the safe word anymore because you'll trust him enough to know that he won't ever hurt you. That he's *not* Steve. And one day, you'll be able to have a normal sex life."

I knit my brows together. "I feel like that's almost too easy."

She scribbles something down on her notepad and smiles. "Well, it's not a guarantee. This is one of those experiments that I personally think might work for you, just because I know you. And based on everything you've told me so far, it seems like the best route to take for now, if this is what you want. You say you love this man, or you care very deeply for him. If you want to have a 'normal' relationship with him," she says with air quotes around the word *normal*. "You've got to try different strategies. Talk to Lex about this, see if he's willing to try. If he cares about you like you says he does, I think he'd be willing. I also think he'd be willing to wait until you're ready, no matter how long that might be."

I pull a piece of lint off my jeans. "Yeah, I know."

"You shouldn't feel guilty about any of this, Peyton. None of it is your fault."

"I know that, too. I still fucking hate Steve, though."

She grins at me. "I hate that fucker, too."

I smile. *God, I love Dr. Young.*

"How else are you doing? How's your anxiety?"

"On a scale of one to ten? Somewhere between a sinking ship and a plane crashing."

She reaches over for her prescription pad. "It's been a while, but I'm going to write you a prescription for Xanax. Just a month's supply. You don't have to take it, but I think maybe you could use it a little."

"Maybe, just a little," I admit. Actually, that sounds really fucking awesome right about now.

She rips off the paper and hands it to me. "Only use it when you need it, and I know you won't use it a lot. But I'd rather you'd have it than not."

I take it from her. "Thanks." It's the same as my old prescription. Half a milligram up to twice a day, quantity sixty.

This is going to last me forever. But it's nice to have it, just in case.

I thank Dr. Young again before I leave the office. "Promise to call if you need another appointment?"

"I promise," I say and smile as I head out into the waiting room. "Can I still pay you online?"

"Yes, right on the website."

"Okay, thanks," I say, not looking forward to that bill.

I swear, all these bills are going to kill me one day.

She pats me on the shoulder. "Good luck, sweetheart."

"Thanks," I say as I wave Cindy goodbye, and head across the street to drop off my prescription, hoping Lex is in the office when I walk in.

22

"A Beautiful Mess" // Jason Mraz

I walk into the pharmacy and see Sammy behind the counter, hanging up prescription bags. I manage to get her attention, but I put a finger to my lips. I mouth, *'Where's Lex?'*

She shrugs and points with her thumb. "In the back."

I blow out a relieved sigh and approach the pharmacy as quick as I can. "Here, give that to Lisa, and tell her to keep it on the *DL*."

Sammy rolls her eyes at me. "Like Lisa would ever tell anyone." She looks down at the script and up at me. "Are you okay?"

I arrange the small display of allergy medicine on the corner of the counter, making them neatly aligned. "I'm fine. Dr. Young gave it to me. Just in case."

Sammy watches me with a raised brow, then goes back and hands the paper to Lisa, whispering in her ear. Lisa looks at me and gives me a simple nod. "Give me about fifteen minutes."

"Thanks," I say.

Sammy comes back and leans against the counter. "So, how'd it go?"

"Well," I start, my face a mask of uncertainty. "It was interesting."

"Did she give you anything helpful?"

"Possibly?"

Sammy eyes me impatiently. "What did she say?"

I shake my head. "Not here. I'll tell you later."

She takes the hint. "All right. But I'm on the edge of my seat."

I play with the pamphlets on the opposite corner—little booklets about diabetes and high blood pressure and the dangers of opioid addiction. "I promise I'll fill you in on everything."

"Fill her in on what?"

That sexy, familiar voice comes from behind me, and a part of me sinks, and the rest of me jumps ten feet. "Lex," I say.

He approaches me, resting his hand on the small of my back. "You don't work here on Tuesdays," he smiles, and leans down to kiss me.

"All right, enough, you two. This is a place of business," Sammy jokes as she pretends to break us up.

"Are you interrupting my best employee?" Lex asks.

"Excuse me?"

Sammy grins wickedly. "That's right, Miss Katz. And no, she's not interrupting me. She's here on business."

I eye her hard, and she presses her lips together.

Lex looks at me. "What's up?"

I look around for something else to organize, but there's nothing left on the counter for me to straighten. "Just dropping off a prescription," I admit, avoiding his gaze.

"Is everything okay?"

"Yeah, everything's fine." Not a lie, but not the truth either.

"It's for her Dad," Sammy lies, and now I want to kick her in the face. *Why did she have to lie? She knows how much I hate lying!* I just smile, neither confirming nor denying the truth of it.

"All right, well, I need to get back. I think Sydney is about to have a meltdown about the new freezer section being installed this week."

"Fun stuff," I say.

"Tons," he kisses me again. "I'll see you later?"

"Definitely."

"Okay." And he swaggers back toward the break room, his ass really working in those pants.

As soon as he's gone, I pinch Sammy on the arm. "Dude, what the fuck?"

"I'm sorry, I panicked!"

"But you don't lie! You *never* lie, not about this! I'm going to tell him about the prescription, I just didn't want to do it in the store!"

"I'm sorry!"

Before I can say anything more, a customer approaches the counter, so I sit down in one of the blue chairs in the tiny pharmacy waiting area.

Fuck, Sammy!

I love her, I love her, I love her, I remind myself.

I decide to stay in the chair and play on my phone until Sammy calls me up. "Peyton, it's ready."

I approach the counter as she scans the bottle. I keep looking to my right at the double doors that lead to the break room, praying Lex doesn't make another appearance before I get this and get the hell out of here.

"It's generic, so it's only a three-dollar co-pay."

"Okay," I say as I dig through my purse and pull out the cash.

Sammy hands me my receipt and medicine, and I take the pharmacy bag with my pills and stuff them into my purse. "Peyton, I really am sorry."

I look at her, with those big brown, puppy dog eyes. How can I be mad at her? "Yeah, I know. It's all right."

"Are we okay?"

I let out a breath. "Of course we are. You're my best friend. What would I do without you?"

She smiles. "Crawl into a dark hole and die?"

"Exactly," I say as I back away and wave goodbye.

"Don't forget! On the edge of my seat here!" She calls out to me as I open the pharmacy doors.

"Call me!" I shout, and make my way down to my car parked around the block.

WHEN I GET HOME, I FIND MY DAD AND COSMO HANGING OUT in the living room, watching more fishing shows on TV. "You know, we have this thing here called a lake you should check out. You could take Cosmo and some fishing poles, and, you know, *go fishing.*"

My Dad looks down at Cosmo, who eyes him excitedly, and my Dad shrugs. "This is less work. And I don't need a license for this."

I shake my head and sigh. "You need to get out more. Go do something. Call up Uncle Jack and do whatever men your age do."

My father raises an eyebrow. "And what exactly do you think *men my age do?*"

I point to the television. "That!"

But Harry Katz is set in his ways. "Peyton, I work twelve-hour shifts five days a week. I don't have the energy to do things *other guys do.*"

I blow out a breath. "Don't you ever get lonely?" I ask as I sit down on the couch next to his chair, setting my purse next to me.

He looks down and pets Cosmo. "I've got my dog, I've got my daughter. What more do I need?"

"I don't know. A special lady friend?"

My father almost chokes, he laughs so hard. "Peyton, you worry about your own love life. Stay out of mine."

"Dad, you do know that one day, I'm going to move out."

"I know."

"I mean, not any time soon."

"I know that, too."

"But, eventually I won't live here forever."

He smiles at me. "And I'll be happy for you."

"And you're going to be all alone in this house. Just you and Cosmo."

"Peyton, please—"

"Dad, I can't help it. I worry about you."

"Well, you can stop. I'm a grown man. I took care of you all by myself after your Mom died. I promise, I can take care of myself when you leave."

Only he didn't.

His two best friends helped him out when I was little. But I can't even remember the last time I saw them.

"We should invite Uncle Jack and Aunt Michelle over soon. For a cookout or something. They can bring the kids."

"Ugh, those kids drive me crazy."

I roll my eyes. "They drive me nuts, too, but he's your best friend."

"You'll invite Sammy and Lex?"

"Yeah, we'll make a day of it. We've got some new people starting at the pharmacy soon, so maybe once they're trained, I'll see if all three of us can manage to get a day off."

"All right, well, let me know, and I'll call Jack."

I reach out and grab his hand, giving it a squeeze. "It's a plan."

23

"Umbrella" // Rihanna

Around five-thirty, I hear Sammy downstairs talking to my Dad then running up the stairs. I'm sitting at my desk, paying the bill for Dr. Young's visit today as Sammy enters my room and plops onto my bed.

"What, you don't knock anymore?" I ask sarcastically.

"Why would I have to knock to come into my own house?" She counters.

I smile. "I know, I'm just fucking with you."

I click the pay now button on the computer, and the payment sends.

"Okay. Spill."

"Give me a second," I say. "Is Lex still at the store?"

"Yeah, I think Sydney is going to keep him there for a bit longer. She's really freaking out over the new freezer section," Sammy says with an eye roll.

"Maybe I should slip her one of my Xanax," I joke.

"Oh, my god, yes! Please, bring one tomorrow and just

crush it into her coffee!"

I laugh. "They taste like shit. She'd notice."

"Damn!"

I close out the browser, shut my laptop, and climb onto the bed with Sammy, sitting up against the wall, bringing my pillow around to hug. Sammy turns and eyes me expectantly. "Dish, woman!"

"Have you ever heard of a safe word?"

And I tell her everything Dr. Young told me.

At first, Sammy laughs, but once I explain the concept the way Dr. Young did, Sammy's face changes from humor to understanding.

"I guess I've never heard of them being used that way before, but it does make sense," she says. "It could work."

"Now, I just have to convince Lex to be open-minded enough to try it without laughing."

"He's going to laugh. But once he thinks about it, he might be okay with it."

I shake my head and fall into the pillow, mumbling words I know Sammy can't understand.

"What?" She asks.

"I said, am I crazy for even trying this?"

"No, I think this is a step in the right direction. You want to have a normal relationship with Lex, and you had this horrible, traumatic thing happen to you that's getting in the way of it. So, you have to try things that may seem weird to get to that point of normalcy. But, it's trial and error. This might work, or it won't. And if it doesn't, you try something else. But, Peyton, I really do think this could work. It's like a trust-building exercise."

"That's exactly what it is," I say. "And I do trust him."

"I know you do, but your mind and body are still in this weird place, and they're kind of fighting with each other about your comfort level. I think you want to trust him, but you can't force yourself to trust him overnight. It takes time. It's only been, like, a month."

"Three weeks, but it feels like a lot longer," I admit.

"Tell me about it. Everything's happened so fast with the store and you and Lex and your Dad. And me and Shane. I never got the chance to tell you about my parents showing up on Sunday."

"What? Samantha? Oh, my god!"

"It wasn't a big deal. They didn't stay long."

"Why did they come? What happened?"

"I guess they 'lost' my phone number, but got my address from someone, I don't even know who. And I got home from work, and they were waiting there for me, with Shane just sitting there, and I was like, 'Um, hi?'"

"Oh, my god."

"Yeah, I guess my Grandma died—not the nice one, the old, evil one from Utah who hates me—and they wanted to let me know that she died, and the funeral is this weekend. But it's in fucking Utah, and if I want to go, I have to get there myself. I was like, I don't have the money for a plane ticket or a car that would make it to Utah and back, so thanks for telling me but I don't think I can go. And then they left."

"And that was all they said?"

"Yup."

"They were really that cold?"

"I'm telling you, it was like a freaking arctic habitat in there. A polar bear walked by and said, '*It's too cold in here!*' And left."

"I'm so sorry."

Sammy idly traces the pattern of my comforter with her finger. "It's fine. I've been over my parents not accepting me for a long time."

I crawl over and give her a hug. "You know my Dad is your Dad, too, right?"

She smiles. "Yes, I know. Harry Katz will always be my

Dad."

"Forever."

"And ever, and ever."

"Peyton!"

We both laugh. "Speaking of which..." Sammy says.

"Yeah?" I shout.

"Your boyfriend's here!"

"Oh, my god," I mumble. "So, send him up!"

I can hear my father say something to Lex, but I can't make out the words.

"Um, is this the first time they're meeting?" Sammy checks.

"Oh, shit!" I realize.

I jump off the bed and run downstairs, slipping on the broken tread but catch myself from falling just in time, only to find Lex standing in the hallway with my father and Cosmo next to him, growling.

"Cosmo!" I get to the end of the stairs and pull Cosmo back into the living room. "Go lie down!" He whines but listens to my command. "Sorry," I say. I look at the two most important men in my life and say, "Dad, this is Lex. Lex, this is my Dad, Harry."

"We've spoken on the phone before, when he left the enve-lope for me to give you," my Dad says. "It's nice to finally meet you, Lex." He eyes him up and down, Lex still wearing his work clothes.

Lex smiles. "It's nice to meet you too, sir."

My Dad laughs. "Please, call me Harry."

Sammy makes her way downstairs and bites back a smile as she watches the three of us standing there, awkwardly. "I think I'm going to get going. I'll see you later, Peyton. Dad," she says to my Dad, and I smile.

"Goodbye, other daughter," my father says, and my heart explodes, I love him so much.

Sammy opens the door and leaves us standing there.

Awkward and silent.

"So, Lex?"

"Right, I was wondering if you were free for dinner?"

"She's free," my Dad answers for me. "You kids have fun." My Dad makes his way back into the living room and sits in his chair, watching whatever is on the television.

I smile at Lex, biting back a laugh. "Yeah, let me just go change." I signal with my head for him to follow me upstairs.

We get into my bedroom and shut the door behind me. Lex scoops me into his arms and kisses me. "Hi."

"Hi."

"So, where are we going?" I ask as he sets me down.

"Anywhere you want," he answers.

I open my closet. "Well, I need to dress accordingly," I say as I start to undress in front of him, pulling off my shirt. He watches as I toss my t-shirt onto the floor and begin to undo my jeans. I glance over my shoulder, his hands in the pockets of his black dress pants as he eyes me. I shimmy out of my jeans and kick them to the side. "So, what am I wearing?"

"What you're in now is perfectly fine with me," he says with a cocky grin.

I laugh. "Most places have a no pants, no service policy."

I can tell he's fighting the urge to approach me and toss me down onto the bed right here and now, but my father is downstairs. He lets out a breath and bites his lip. "I'd like to eat you for dinner."

My cheeks flush, and I smile. "Sorry, I'm not on the menu." I sigh and start looking for something, anything to put on before he loses it again. I pick out a cute knee-high, V-neck red dress I got on the clearance rack for four dollars, and toss it on. "Does this work?"

He licks his lips and eyes me up and down. "Peyton, you make anything look good."

"Okay," I slide on my red flats. "Now, where are we going?"

24

"Lifestyles of the Rich & Famous" // Good Charlotte

W e get in Lex's car, and I connect my phone to his Bluetooth. I slide through my phone and decide tonight is Billie Eilish night, and play *bad guy*. I can't help but smile as I see Lex tapping his thumb to the beat.

We're driving toward Octavia when Lex says, "Do you mind if we swing by my apartment first? I'd like to change out of my work clothes if that's all right with you."

"Yeah, sure."

He smiles and takes my left hand. "Thanks. It's been a long day, and I feel kind of gross."

I glance at him and watch him drive. He looks exhausted but happy, and I can't help but wonder which one of those I am the cause of.

We get into downtown Octavia, and Lex pulls into a parking garage, and into a space marked *reserved* with the number 2800 on the wall in front of us. We get out and enter the building through a door to the left and walk down a long hallway where an elevator sits at the end. To the left is a lobby with a concierge. An older gentleman wearing a crimson uniform stands behind the desk. He glances up at us with a smile and waves. "Hello, Mr. Kingston!"

"Evening, Willis," he says with a wave.

The elevator doors open for us, and we get in. Lex pulls out a key and pushes it into a slot in the elevator and presses the button for the top floor, and the elevator lurches upward making my stomach drop.

We go up for what seems like forever, until the doors open up into his apartment.

Into his apartment.

His fucking penthouse apartment.

Because I stand there for a split second, wondering where the hallway is until he pulls on my hand, and I'm standing in his foyer.

In front of me is the living room with a dark gray sectional couch with a chaise, a square oak coffee table in the center, and a chair on the other side. Mounted on the wall above the fireplace must be the largest fucking television in the entire world.

To my right is a hallway where I assume leads to the bedrooms and bathrooms, not sure how many are in here but probably more than one of each.

Straight ahead, passed the living room, I see a set of floor to ceiling glass doors that lead to a terrace. Chairs and potted plants fill the area with probably the most beautiful view of Octavia there is to see.

To my left is a kitchen and dining area with a rectangular oak table and four chairs. Lex empties his pockets onto the island in the kitchen, then leads me down the long hallway. I pass a small bedroom on my left, across from which is a small bathroom on my right and straight ahead is the master bedroom. I swear to every star in the sky, it's as big as the entire downstairs living space of my house.

His bed is the biggest bed I've ever seen and sits way too high off the ground. "How the hell..." I start.

"What?" He asks me from the attached bathroom.

I turn to him as he's unbuttoning his shirt. His bed comes up to my waist. "How do you get into this bed? Is it on stilts or something?" I ask as I bend down to look underneath.

He laughs. "Magic."

I shake my head and walk into the bathroom. "Oh, my god."

"What now?"

"Have you seen this bathroom?"

"No, I haven't. First time I've ever been in here. Oh, my god, is that a toilet?"

I glare at him. "Dude, there's a freaking bidet!"

He looks down and knits his eyebrows. "Hmm. Is that what that is?"

I scoff. "Shut up. Why is there a bidet in here? Are we in Italy?"

"Hey, I just rent the place," he admits.

He pulls off his shirt and turns to me, taking my hand. "Would you mind, terribly, if I showered first? Today was brutal."

I glance around the bathroom one last time. "No, that's fine."

He kisses me. "You're welcome to join me."

I smirk. "I'll just go wait in the living room. Where it's safe."

He starts to unbutton his pants as he walks over to the shower. "I won't take long."

I make my way back out into the main room and toss my purse onto the coffee table. I walk toward the terrace and open the double doors that lead outside. The view of Octavia really is beautiful from up here. I stand at the edge and lean against the railing, the wind blowing through my hair.

"*Lifestyles of the rich and famous...*" I say to myself and sigh. I can only imagine what this apartment costs a month. Not that it matters. It doesn't. It shouldn't. It's crazy for me to even be thinking about it.

But goddamn it, I'm worried about paying a fifty dollar doctor bill.

I breathe and rub my face with my hands.

We just come from two different worlds. His is a world of freedom to do whatever he wants, whenever he wants, at whatever cost. He never has to check his bank account because the money is always there. He never has to make a late payment on a bill, or beg the gas company not to shut him off if he promises to pay them on Friday. He never has to pray to find enough loose change in the couch cushions to put gas in his car, or live on Instant Ramen noodles for three days because that's all the food he can afford. He never has to worry about what his health insurance will or won't cover because he can afford to pay the difference. Lex has never had to worry about money, and a small part of me is starting to resent him for it.

And I know it's not entirely fair. It's not his fault he was born into wealth, and I wasn't. I just wish it was a little bit easier, a little more balanced.

That we didn't have to struggle *so* much.

I don't even hear Lex come up behind me. "It's nice, isn't it?"

I jump, startled. "Shit! You showered fast."

"I promised I'd be quick." He wraps his arms around me and kisses my cheek.

"I think, if this was my apartment, I'd live right here on this terrace. Even in January, I'd sleep on that chaise all year round."

He tightens his arms around my waist. "You be pretty cold."

"I'd be freezing, but it'd be worth it for this view."

"So, where do you want to eat?"

I think for a minute. "Actually, do you think we could stay here and order in?"

He smiles against my neck. "That sounds perfect."

Lex heads back inside, and I let out a breath. This lets me talk to him about my session with Dr. Young today and explain everything she told me.

I'm just glad I kept my Xanax in my purse.

"There's actually a restaurant downstairs that does a room service type of thing. It's not exactly like a hotel, but more like *Postmates*. The restaurant just happens to be in the same building, so they have one of the waiters bring it up."

I follow him into the living room and sit next to him on the sofa, kicking off my shoes, pulling my feet up under me. "Okay, that sounds good."

"I've got a menu here," he says and opens the drawer of the coffee table. Pulling out a folded brown menu, we peruse it until we each pick out a dish. He uses the landline to place the order, so they know what room to bring it to, and when he's done, he tosses the menu back in the drawer.

"Would you like some wine?"

"Sure," I say, hoping that will make this easier.

"There's actually something I need to talk to you about," he says, and I'm a bit thrown.

"Okay." *Shit, does he already know about the prescription?*

"I got a phone call from my father today."

Lovely.

"There's a charity event this weekend down in Manhattan, and he expects me to attend, as all Kingston's are expected to be there."

"There's more than the two of you?"

"No, which is why I'm expected to be there," he says as he sits down, handing me a glass. "I was wondering if you'd like to go with me?"

I look at him, my face frozen. "Lex, I don't know." Meeting his Dad? Going to a fancy charity event with a bunch of rich people?

"It's boring, I know. But there will be an open bar, and they never ID anyone at those things."

"No, it's not that. It's just... I had last weekend off, and I'm just not sure if Sydney will let me have two weekends off in a row."

"Don't worry about that. We've got two new people starting tomorrow."

I look at him, surprised. "We do?"

"Yeah, Sydney and I officially hired—oh, what are their names—Arjun Khatri, and Madison Brooks. Sydney and I will be doing most of their training, but you and Sammy will do some of it when we've got manager stuff to do in the back."

"Well, that's great." *Less hours for me.*

"And I know we can have them both working this weekend to cover for you," Lex says.

"It's not so much that," I admit.

"What is it?"

I take a drink of wine. "I need the money, Lex," I say, my tone slightly irritated. He really doesn't understand why people work. He works because his father told him he had to, not for a paycheck. Does he even get a paycheck? I breathe, and take another drink of my wine. "I have to talk to you about something, too."

He sets his glass down on the table, eyeing me worriedly. "All right. Is everything okay?"

I stare down at my hands holding my glass, my one leg bouncing up and down beneath me. "Look, I'm sorry, but Sammy lied to you today. I didn't tell her to. She just panicked when you came out of the office."

"Lied to me about what?"

"The prescription I dropped off wasn't for my Dad. It was for me. I had a doctor's appointment this morning."

"Oh," he looks surprised. "Are you okay?"

I nod. "Yeah, everything's fine. I'm fine. It's just..." I pause and take another sip of wine. "I told you I used to go to therapy, right?"

He's thoughtful for a moment. "I don't remember."

Shit.

"Okay, well, after what happened with Steve last year, I started seeing a therapist to help deal with my anxiety and PTSD. Things were pretty bad in the beginning. I couldn't even hug my Dad." Lex is silent but raises his eyebrows in surprise. "I saw Dr. Young once or twice a week for about nine months, but I had to stop seeing her a few months ago because I couldn't afford it anymore with all my Dad's medical bills. But after this past weekend, I thought I could use some professional advice. About this, about us."

"But, you're okay."

"Yeah, I'm okay."

"So, what was the prescription for?"

I take in a breath. "Xanax. For anxiety. She used to give it to me before, and she thought, just in case I needed it again. I may not even need it. But with everything happening lately, and not just with us, but with my Dad, and school, and the store, and me hopefully starting the PT job in August—she just wanted me to have it. Just in case."

"Okay." He takes my hand in his and kisses it. "So, did she give you any good advice?"

And here we go.

"I think, maybe, yeah. But I need something from you first."

Before he can say anything, there's a knock at the door. "Hold that thought," he says and holds up a finger as he gets up to answer the door. I take another drink of my wine as Lex tips the waiter and wheels over the food cart.

"Do you want to eat here, or over at the table?"

"It doesn't matter," I admit with a shrug. I am way too nervous to eat right now, anyway. Lex smiles and sets the covered plates on the coffee table in front of us and comes back to sit next to me. I don't pick up my fork.

"Do you want to finish talking first?"

I eye him. "Is that okay with you?"

He picks up his wine glass and sits back on the couch. "Of course. Go ahead. What do you need from me?"

"I need you to keep an open mind and not laugh."

His eyes narrow. "Why would I laugh?"

"Because I laughed at first until Dr. Young explained it to me. And Sammy almost fell on the floor. "

He chuckles. "You told Sammy?"

"Of course I did. I tell her everything."

He looks at me. "Everything?"

"*Everything.*"

His face flushes. "I wish you hadn't told me that."

"I don't keep secrets, and I don't lie. I hate lies. And I hate secrets. And Sammy is my best friend in the entire world."

He smiles. "I've noticed that about you."

"Not telling you everything about me was really hard for me, and I didn't like doing it. I only did it because I was afraid—"

"Peyton, you don't have to explain that to me. I understand. Just tell me about Dr. Young. Explain that to me." He sits back on the couch, wine in one hand, his other draped across the back of the sofa, one leg resting upon his knee.

"I'm assuming since you have experience with this stuff, that you've heard of a safe word?"

He smiles, and presses his lips together. "Yes, I've heard of safe words."

"Okay, seriously, don't laugh."

"I'm not laughing." But his mouth is twitching so hard.

I blink and take another drink of wine before I continue. "Dr. Young explained that safe words can be used for more than just BDSM. They can also be used as a sort of trust exercise."

His eyebrows knit together and he looks at me curiously. "I never thought of that."

"Me, either. She said that instead of us just fooling around until I freak out and push you away, we should come up with a safe word. It can literally be any word in the world. And when we're kissing, and you touch me, if I want you to stop, all I have to do is say that word, and you move your hand away. It means we don't have to completely stop, we just switch gears. She even said you can keep trying, because the more I say the safe word and the more you listen to the safe word, the more I grow to trust you. And the more I trust you, the more I let my guard down. Which, in turn, means the more stuff we can do without me having a panic attack."

Lex is thoughtful for a long moment before a grin tugs at the corner of his lips. "So, what's the safe word?"

I stare at him blankly for a second, the words getting caught in my throat. "I don't know, I hadn't thought that far ahead."

"How far ahead have you thought?"

My cheeks flush. "Honestly, I was just waiting to see if you'd be open to the idea."

"I'll try anything if it makes you more comfortable, but you know I'm not in a rush."

I look away and take another drink of my wine, finishing the glass. "I'm not either. I'm just trying to make it easier on both of us. So you're not worried about scaring me, and I'm not worried about having a panic attack."

He sets his glass down and takes my hand again. "Peyton, I'll do anything for you. I know this weekend..." He pauses and leans forward, turning to me. "Everything got messed up between us."

"No, Lex—"

"Yes, it did. It made you go back to therapy. *I* made you go back to therapy."

"It was just one session. I only went to try to figure things out."

"I know, but if I didn't behave the way I did, you never would have gone."

"And then I never would have learned how to fix this. Lex, please, you didn't push me back into therapy. That's not what I meant at all. I knew when I started a new relationship, I'd have to go back. She told me months ago, if I ever got into a new relationship, I'd have to go back, eventually."

I can see on his face Lex is fighting with himself, over whether or not I'm right. But I am, and he knows it.

"If I ever want to have a normal relationship with you, we have to learn how to do it. Because unfortunately, I'm a little broken, and it's going to take some time to repair the damage. And none of it is your fault, or mine. But we need to learn how to put the pieces back together."

Lex nods. "Okay, I get it," he pulls me into him and kisses me. "We'll figure it out." He smiles and hands me my fork. "We should probably eat before it gets cold."

I take the fork, and he removes the metal covers. We eat in silence for a while before he asks, "So, is that a no on Manhattan?"

I slink back in my seat, my face a mask of uncertainty.

"If you want, I'll talk to Sydney tomorrow about giving you more hours next week, if you're really worried about the money."

That could work. And I want to go with him. I want to support him. I want to be there for him while he has to deal with his asshole father, so I relax my shoulders a bit. "I don't have a dress nice enough for an event like that."

He quirks an eyebrow at me. "Would you let me buy you one?"

I groan and eye him sidelong. "I guess if it's not too much."

His face lights up. "Have you ever been to Manhattan before?"

I shake my head as I take a bite of my chicken. "No."

His smile widens. "You're going to love it."

I give him half a smile, suddenly very grateful for my Xanax prescription.

25

"Thrift Shop" // Macklemore & Ryan Lewis, Feat. Wanz

Lex talks to Sydney about my schedule and she doesn't mind me taking another weekend off, and gives me hours the following Tuesday and Thursday to make up for missing the weekend. I'm relieved to have at least one good paycheck this month, and I thank Sydney for being so understanding.

I have to work this Friday morning, and then Lex has a private plane that will fly us down into the city.

His own private plane. Well, it's *Kingston's* plane, but I don't really understand the difference.

When I go into work on Wednesday, I meet Arjun and Madison. They're our two new customer service associates, who will mostly be working on registers in the back and in the pharmacy.

Sydney takes Arjun in the back of the store to get him started, and Lex and I start training Madison on the pharmacy counter.

She's a cute, tiny girl, with shoulder-length blonde hair and green eyes.

"Number one rule," I start. "No one is allowed behind the door unless you're a pharmacist or a pharmacy technician. Hopefully, in August, I will be a pharmacy tech," I say, and cross my fingers. "This one here," I say as I point to Ben, and he looks up and smiles. "Is leaving us for out of state college, so someone has to take over for him."

A few customers come in, and I walk her through the steps of ringing out prescriptions. Madison seems like a nice girl and picks up the register pretty quickly.

Lex looks at the two of us. "Well, it looks like you've got this handled," he eyes me for confirmation.

"Yeah, I'm good. I'll call you if I need any help."

He smiles and kisses me on the cheek, then heads back to the office.

Madison's eyebrows knit together. "Is he that friendly with everyone or...?"

I laugh. "No. He's my boyfriend."

Her mouth falls open. "Your boyfriend is Lex Kingston?"

I nod, and can't help but smile. "Yup."

"Oh, my god, you're lucky. He is so hot."

My smile fades quickly, and I eye her. "Yeah, I've noticed. Kind of why he's *my* boyfriend."

She puts her hands up defensively. "I was just making an observation."

I chuckle. "I'm just messing with you. You should see him with his shirt off," I say, and she relaxes. "In a little while, you'll get to meet my favorite person, and my best friend, Sammy Clarke. She works twelve to nine, and she's the best. She'll also help train you on here for a bit. Usually, once she gets here, I go out on the floor and stock. I know the store is still a bit of a mess, but Lex has really improved it over the past few weeks. I think it's going to look really good once it's done."

"And he said something about everyone getting a raise?"

"Yeah, but not for a few months."

"That sucks."

The morning drags on as I impatiently wait for Sammy to arrive so I can discuss this Manhattan trip with her. I never got the chance to text her last night after Lex dropped me off. After we ate dinner, we watched a movie, and I fell asleep on his couch. He woke me up after eleven to bring me home, and I didn't want to wake her up.

I show Madison how to hang the prescriptions, which I mean, a monkey could do, so it literally takes three minutes. And by the time Sammy arrives, I'm practically jumping out of my skin.

"Sammy!"

She stops and looks at me. "Peyton!"

"Madison, this is Sammy. Sammy, this is Madison. You're going to help train her today, but she's excellent so far. Um, Madison, will you be okay by yourself for like five minutes?"

She shrugs. "Yeah, sure."

"If you need any help, just pick up the phone and press the intercom button and say 'Peyton to the pharmacy,' okay?"

"Okay."

"Thanks! You're aces! We'll be right back!" I say as I grab Sammy's arm and pull her into the break room.

"Dude, what is up?" Sammy asks as we enter, and I glance over at the office door and see it's closed.

Finally, I catch a freaking break.

"I need to talk to you," I say, and take a deep breath. "So, I asked Lex about the safe word, and he's totally open to the idea, and we're going to try it as soon as we think of one."

"Oh my god, that's great!"

"Yeah, yeah, it's amazing, I'm so excited. But that's not what I need to talk to you about."

"Peyton, breathe."

"So, last night, Lex also wanted to talk to me about something," my voice is low because I know the office door is not soundproof. "There's a charity event down in Manhattan on Saturday night and Lex asked me if I'd go with him—" Her mouth drops, but I stop her from speaking. "I'm not done!" I say as I hold up a finger. "And at first I was like, *'Lex I already had last weekend off, and now you want me to take another weekend in a row?'* And I was sure Sydney would say no, but," I say, and point out toward the store, "we have two new people starting today who are both on the schedule for this weekend, so I guess no one needs me to work."

"Peyton."

"So, that's no longer a problem. But holy shit, Sammy, this is a fucking charity event with not only Lex, but *his father*. And all these rich socialites and their ten thousand dollar Birkin bags, and the little yip dogs they carry around inside them, and their Aston Martins and Rolls-Royces, and half plastic body parts and their jokes about firing the maid because *'she was a clomper'*—"

"Okay, you're watching way too much *Gilmore girls*. And I'm pretty sure Birkin bags are more like twenty thousand."

"I do not fit into that world. I'm nothing to those people. I'm the kind of person they should start a charity for! If my Dad would let me, I'd start a *Go Fund Me* page!"

Sammy looks thoughtful for a second. "You should start a *Go Fund Me* page."

"That's not the point, Samantha!"

"Okay, okay," she pulls me to one of the new chairs and sits me down. "Do you need a Xanax?"

"Probably, but I can't take it at work. It will make me all sleepy, and Lex would know. You can tell when I've taken one."

She sits in the chair next to me but turns to face me, taking my hands in hers. "Lex wants to bring you into his world. He wants to show you off to all the people at this place because he thinks you *do* fit into it in your own way. Maybe he thinks you're better than they are. Not in a snobby, mean way. Just in a 'this person is genuine and kind and loving and beautiful.' He wants you to meet his father, that means something."

"First, Lex hates his father. They do not get along. Second, he's leaving, remember? He's leaving in three weeks. I don't understand why he wants all of this when he's not even going to be here in a month."

"Well, maybe he wants to introduce you to his father, not giving a single fuck what his father thinks, and, what if he's *not* leaving?"

"But what if he is? I've been trying so hard not to think about it. I've just been putting it out of my mind, but the closer it gets, the more I think about it."

"So, ask him."

I groan. "This still puts a lot of pressure on me. And he's buying me a dress for this thing."

Sammy squeals and I shush her. "Oh, my god. It has to sparkle! Make sure it sparkles and shines the fuck out of that room!"

"Yeah, okay. Because I want to be the center of attention," I say sarcastically.

"Honey, on Lex's arm, you will be the center of attention. So, drink some wine and pack your Xanax, because you're going to need it."

Fuck me.

"I don't even know what this charity is for."

Sammy laughs. "I doubt anyone at that charity will know what the charity is for. It's just a thing rich people do to feel less guilty about spending money on useless garbage they don't need."

I snort. "I should probably ask Lex if he knows."

"He might be the only one who actually does," she says with

a shrug. "We really should get back out there and save Madison."

"Shit!"

"It's okay, I got it. Go take your lunch, and I'll clock in. I think I'm already late."

I sigh. "God, I'm sorry."

She shrugs. "It's fine. I can spare an extra five minutes for my best friend."

We stand, and I hug her, and she goes to clock in and heads back out to the pharmacy.

~

I DON'T HAVE LONG BEFORE MY SUMMER CLASSES START. SO ON Thursday, I take the day to just *breathe*.

I wake up at quarter to six in the morning, and cannot turn my brain off. A million thoughts race around like gerbils running in metal wheels about everything from the store, to school, my Dad, the medical bills, paying for my summer classes, paying for Dr. Young again if I need to go back, and Lex.

Beautiful, incredible, amazing, sexy as fuck Lex.

And then I start thinking about the stupid charity event.

My anxiety about this weekend is making me crazy, so, reluctantly, I take a Xanax, and after twenty minutes, I fall back to sleep.

I wake up again just before noon, feeling better.

Well, *a little* better.

I pull my phone from my nightstand and see I have a few messages waiting for me. They're from Lex.

'Are you busy today? I found a few dress shops in Buffalo that have gowns perfect for the charity.'

I groan and sigh and make a face I know he can't see—but kind of wish he could—so he knew how much I did not want to fucking do this. But all relationships require compromises and sacrifice and doing things for the other person we don't want to do.

Fuck that shit. Goddamn it.

I love him, I love him, I love him.

I breathe, and reply, *'I'm free all day.'*

~

WHEN I OPEN THE FRONT DOOR, I EXPECT TO SEE LEX STANDING there in his fancy black dress pants and blue shirt, waiting for me with his hands in his pockets, his hair a sexy tousled mess. But instead, I see a tiny girl with short turquoise hair and a smile, holding a black credit card out in front of her.

"Get in bitch, we're going shopping!"

I look at her and shake my head. "It's *'get in loser',*" I correct.

"Whatever! Lex handed me his fucking black credit card, told me the names of three dress shops in Buffalo, and said, *'Go take Peyton dress shopping!'* She squeals.

"Oh, my god," I groan. It's the American Express Black card. I fight back the pang in my gut as I grab my keys and purse, and head out the door. "Do you want to drive, or should I?"

"My car is newer and safer."

"Your car is one year newer than mine, Sammy."

"Still newer."

"And have I mentioned how much I don't want to do this?" I say as I get in the passenger side.

"Yes, but we're doing it anyway!" Sammy says as she starts up the car.

"Well, I'm picking the music," I say with an evil laugh, and she groans.

"God, please, no Taylor Swift!"

I give her an evil smile as I sing *Shake It Off* loud.

Sammy rolls her eyes as she pulls out into the street. "Yeah,

I know you got nothing in your brain." She laughs as I keep singing, but I know how much she hates this, and it makes me feel just a little bit better.

Once the song ends, Sammy grabs my phone. "Please, Peyton, anything but Swifty."

"Fine. What do you want me to play?"

"I don't know. Tell me how you're feeling with a song."

I eye her. "All right, John Mayer, it is," I say.

"God, really?" She sounds concerned.

"I could always play *Under Pressure?* I mean, it's accurate."

"Now Bowie and Queen? I should definitely be worried about you."

"I'm an emotional mess right now, Sammy. Maybe I need some mood stabilizers."

"Is there a song for that?"

"Probably. *Broken* by lovelytheband? *Anxiety* by Julia Michaels? *Control* by Halsey?"

Sammy let's out a breath. "System of a Down?"

"Yes! *Aerials! Chop Suey!* My meditation music!"

We both laugh, and I'm suddenly very grateful that Lex let Sammy take me shopping instead of himself. "I'm so glad you're here," I say.

"I know," she says with a smile. "We are going to pick you the perfect dress, and Lex is going to plotz!"

❧

SAMMY FOLLOWS THE DIRECTIONS THE GPS TELLS HER, AND WE pull into the small parking lot of a store called *little black dress.*

"This doesn't look too bad," I admit.

She shrugs. "It looks like a dress store."

I instantly regret what I said as soon as we enter the place. It has every kind of gown you can imagine; prom, evening, wedding, cocktail, and I'm not sure which one is right for a charity event. Long or short? Black or white? Silk or chiffon?

Does it even matter?

A tall woman with short-cropped black hair and bangs approaches us, eyeing both of us suspiciously like we're clearly too poor to be in this store. "Can I help you?" She asks, but it sounds more like she wanted to ask, '*Are you lost?*'

Sammy and I look at each other, and I'm about to say something, but Sammy beats me to it. "Yes, actually. My friend here is looking for a dress for a charity event this weekend down in Manhattan, and her boyfriend, Lex Kingston, told us—"

"You must be Peyton!" The woman's demeanor instantly changes at the sound of Lex's name. "It's so nice to meet you. My name is Wendy. Mr. Kingston and I spoke on the phone earlier. He explained everything. I think we have exactly what you need. Follow me, please," she says and turns around.

I look at Sammy and grab her hand as we follow Wendy through the store. Through rows and rows of chiffon and tulle and silk until we reach a half-circle of changing rooms, and to my left is a rack of dresses with a sign that says '*reserved.*'

"I've picked out these six dresses for you to try on for now. If none of these work, just let me know and we can find you something."

"Wait, what? You've already picked out dresses for me?"

"Mr. Kingston was very specific. He let me know exactly what he was looking for; something blue. And he gave me an idea of your size," she says as she looks me up and down. "And he seems to be right."

I look at Sammy, and she shrugs.

"Take your time, and if you need any help, just let me know," she says as she hands me the first dress before walking away.

I eye Sammy, who sits down on a cushioned bench in the

center of the room and crosses her legs. "Go try it on! I want to see it! I hope it's sparkly!"

I moan and head into the dressing room behind me.

I unzip the black bag and carefully pull it out. It's a pretty sapphire blue with, of course, sparkles. It's long with a v-neck-line, and I'm worried, even with heels, I might trip over it.

But I strip down to my underwear and put it on. "Can you come zip me up?"

Sammy pushes the curtain aside and zips up the back of the dress. It fits me perfectly, and when I look in the mirror, I feel slightly dizzy.

"Holy shit," Sammy says. "You look like a movie star. You're going to walk the red carpet!"

"I don't know if I like the mermaid style."

"All right, let's try on another one." She unzips me and lets me get undressed. I hand her this one through the curtain, and she gives me the second dress.

I slip it on, but it's a two-piece and short with way too much tulle and poof. "Sammy?" I slide the curtain open, and the look on her face says everything.

"God, no! Get it off! Burn it!"

"Yup!"

I strip down again and hand it to her, and she hands me the third dress.

Growing up poor, I never enjoyed shopping for clothes. When you spend your time focusing on the price tag over the look, shopping tends to become more of a chore than an extracurricular activity. That's thrift shopping, though.

"Sammy, I need a zip."

She slips in the dressing room and zips me up, and we both look at me in the mirror at the same time. My eyes go wide.

"Holy shit," she says.

I eye myself up and down. It takes me a second to gather

my thoughts. I turn to see my back and the rest of me. "Holy shit." I echo Sammy and look at her.

Sammy's mouth is agape as she stares at me, then I stare at myself in disbelief.

"Well, I think we found the dress," I say.

26

"The Middle" // Jimmy Eat World

I go to work on Friday and give Lex back his credit card. He smiles at me as he tucks it away in his wallet. "So, did you and Sammy have fun?"

I lean against the desk. "I wouldn't call it fun. Entertaining? Maybe."

His brows knit together. "Did you find a dress?"

"Yes, and I'm sorry."

"Why are you sorry?"

"I'm pretty sure it cost more than your car," I say, not hiding the guilty expression on my face. "But you're going to love it."

He laughs. "That's why I gave you the good credit card." I bite my lip and look down at my feet, fighting the urge to make a snide comment. "Did you guys get anything else?"

I eye him. "With your card? No."

"Really?"

I furrow my brows. "Lex, come on. I wouldn't do that."

"You could have."

Now I'm starting to get annoyed. "No, I couldn't have. You gave me the card for a dress, and I got a dress. What? Did you think I was going to buy myself a new car?"

"No, but, you could have gone out to eat."

"We did, but we paid for it *ourselves*." I push back from the desk and cross my arms. "Not everyone is going to take advantage of a piece of plastic that doesn't belong to them."

Lex looks at me and leans back in the office chair, "Okay. I'm sorry." He starts. I look down at my feet, wishing I hadn't yelled.

"I have to get out there before the manager catches me back here and fires someone," I say.

He smiles just a little. "Sydney would never fire you."

"But she might fire you," I say and turn on my heels toward the store.

"Ouch." He says, but he doesn't follow me, and I'm grateful.

I make my way out to the store to find Arjun standing behind the pharmacy counter and Emily standing behind him with beet-red cheeks and fighting the urge to smile.

Someone's got a crush on the new boy.

And I can see why. Arjun is good looking. He has olive skin with brown hair and eyes, and from what I can tell from his biceps in his *Kingston's* polo, he definitely works out. He's tall, at least as tall as Lex. When I approach the pharmacy counter, he smiles at me, and his eyes roam over me, and my lips form a tight line.

"Arjun, I'm Peyton."

"Peyton Katz. I've heard a lot about you," he says.

I knit my brows together. *I do not need this today.* "I doubt that. I'll be training you here today. Have you met Emily Martinez, our Pharmacy Tech?"

He glances behind us and looks at her. "Hey," he says.

She blushes and smiles. "Hey."

"And our head pharmacist, Lisa Wu."

He turns again and nods in Lisa's direction, and Lisa lifts a hand in greeting.

I can already tell this is going to be a long day—and I'm leaving early.

I give him the rundown of the rules, show him how to hang the bags, how to ring out prescriptions. He's not as smart as Madison, or as quick to catch on, but I don't think he will be in the pharmacy much. If what Lex told me is right, Arjun will mostly be in the back register with the Dave's and stocking shelves, and Madison will be in the pharmacy with Sammy and me.

Thank the fucking stars.

We get through the morning with only a few problems. Arjun is easily confused by the touch screen, clearly never having used a smart phone in his life, but I have the patience of a saint. Not sure where it came from, though.

My patience is slowly dying when Sammy arrives at one, instead of noon, Lex and I are off for the weekend.

"Okay, Arjun, I'm leaving, but Sammy is going to take over for the rest of your shift. Good luck," I say and pat him on the shoulder. I eye Emily and mouth, *'Talk to him,'* before I head into the break room.

I clock out and grab my things out of my locker just as Sammy comes up behind me. "How are you feeling?"

"Normal things. Irritated. Terrified. A little dizzy. My fingers are a bit tingly." I close my locker and turn to face her. Her hair is bluer than it was yesterday. "Did you dye your hair again?"

"It needed a fresh coat," she says and hugs me.

I snort. "A fresh coat of *hair dye?*"

"Yes, that is the correct terminology."

"I really wish you were coming with me."

"I'm just a phone call away, a FaceTime, a text message."

"I know. It's still not the same as a Samantha Clarke hug."

"Nothing ever is." She pulls away and looks at me. "Please remember to have fun. You're going to Manhattan with Lex! You're going to a rich people party! Oh, my god, the jokes you're going to make!"

I smile. "I'll text you,"

"You will text me pictures for context!"

I laugh. "I will definitely try. And you're sure you're okay with checking on my Dad again?"

"Don't you mean *our* Dad?"

I pull her into a hug again. "Yes, *our* Dad."

She pulls away. "Yes, Peyton. I will make sure Dad is okay. I'll check the house when he leaves for work. I remember all of his hiding spots."

"Thank you," I say.

Lex appears behind me. "Are you ready?"

I look at Sammy one more time and shake my head.

But she answers for me. "She's ready."

I PULL MY CAR INTO THE DRIVEWAY, ALL THE WAY INTO THE BACK yard, so it's not in my Dad's way while I'm gone. Lex pulls up behind me, but parks at the end. I grab everything I need and get out of my car, and we both head inside.

The dress is hanging on the back of my bedroom door in a black zipper bag, so Lex can't see it when he walks in.

He takes it down and holds it out. "Are you going to show me?"

"No! Not until right before the ball."

He laughs. "The *ball*?"

"If we're going to this thing, I'm going like fucking Cinderella and making you wait until the last minute to see me."

He cocks his head to one side. "You are evil, Peyton Katz. The suspense is killing me."

I smirk. "Good."

I'd packed most everything last night, except for the few things I needed today. "What time is the flight?" I ask.

"Anytime we want."

"How does that work?"

"It's a private plane. *Kingston's* owns it."

I eye him perplexed for a second. "And private planes don't keep schedules?"

"Not really."

"So, no one else needs it?"

"Well, it's mostly just my Dad and me. Sometimes, some of the higher-ups borrow it with my Dad's permission. But this weekend, it's mine."

"So, you *do* own a plane?"

Lex walks up to me and sets the dress bag on the bed. "I don't own a plane. I do own a small boat, but not a plane."

"But your Dad does?"

"The company owns it."

I shake my head. "This is giving me a headache. I need to finish packing."

"Can I help?" He asks as he walks over to my underwear drawer and starts to peruse.

"Hey!"

"These would look very nice." Lex holds up a pair of red underwear, but I snatch them out of his hands and close the drawer.

"I'm good, thanks."

He smiles and takes my hands. "We don't have to rush." He kisses me, and I feel myself relax. "Is your Dad working?"

"Yes."

The corner of his lip curls up, and I back away. "We should really get going. Don't we have to stop by your place, too?"

He groans. "Yes, I have to grab my things."

"Do you have a place in Manhattan?" I ask as I grab my bag of toiletries and toss them in my travel bag.

"No, and I had absolutely no desire to stay with my father, so I booked us a room at the Four Seasons."

Holy shit balls. I look at Lex, my eyes so wide, I swear they're about to pop out of my head.

"I see you've heard of it."

"Yeah, anyone who has ever watched television has heard of it."

"They have an amazing spa, and I thought if you were up for it, maybe, either before or after the charity, we could have a couples massage. You even have the option of them coming to your room if that makes you more comfortable."

I cringe a little. "I don't know. I've never had some random person touch me before."

"Or I could give you a massage," he says mischievously.

"I think I'd like that better," I admit, with a smile. I shake myself out of it, breaking eye contact.

I finish packing, and we grab all my things. I double, triple check that I have everything I need before I run downstairs and feed Cosmo as Lex starts packing up the car.

I grab my purse and look around the house one more time before I walk out, closing the door behind me.

As we pull out of my driveway, Lex asks, "So, what's on Peyton's playlist today?"

I smile as I pull out my phone and connect to his Bluetooth.

"Hmm, what are you in the mood for?" I ask.

"I've learned from our first date to always let Peyton pick the music, whether I like it or not."

I beam with pride. "I've taught you well, young Padawan."

He looks at me, almost in shock. "You know Star Wars?"

I roll my eyes. "Hello? Raised by a single father here," I say as I point to myself. "Of course I do. I was taught young, too."

Lex stares out into the distance, but I know he wants to look at me. "I didn't think it was possible to love you any more than I already do, but, fuck Peyton. Will you marry me?"

I laugh so hard, I'm glad I wasn't drinking anything because it'd be all over his dashboard. "You know I'm a giant nerd, right?"

He shrugs. "No?"

"Lex, I read like crazy. Well, I haven't been lately because *someone's* been distracting me," I say as I gesture at him. "But I love all things nerdy. Star Wars, Star Trek, Harry Potter, Marvel movies, Lord of the Rings. I love almost everything, fantasy, and science fiction. Right now, I'm really into all things Fae."

"Fae?"

"Yeah, like fairies."

"Like those books with all the porn in them."

I elbow him playfully in the arm. I'm looking through my songs, trying to find something to play, but I'm having a hard time deciding. "You really can't give me any ideas for music?"

He thinks for a minute. "Well, Sammy says sometimes you tell people how you feel through music. So, tell me how you're feeling right now with a song."

Fuck.

I bite my lip. "Okay." I click on *Anxiety* by Julia Michaels. I wait for Lex to say something, but he doesn't. I guess he already knows I'm feeling anxious about this weekend.

We pull into the parking garage of his apartment building and make our way to his penthouse to get his things. I stand in the doorway of his bedroom and watch him finish gathering his things and place them in his suitcase. "Can I help?"

He smiles at me. "Sure. Top drawer. Pick out some sexy underwear for me?"

I glare at him. "You think you're so funny." I approach him just as he zips up his suitcase and places it on the floor.

"I've been known to be pretty freaking hilarious." He wraps an arm around my waist and kisses me. I feel like it's been so long since he's kissed me like this, even though it's barely been a few days. But then he lifts me up and sets me onto the bed. It sits so high, my legs meet his waist at his belly button.

"This bed is insane," I say.

"Yeah, it is ridiculous. I should probably have someone come lower it a bit."

He kisses me again, and a part of me wants to fall backward and pull him on top of me, but we still haven't decided on a safe word.

He pulls away and looks at me, his eyes filled with concern. "Are you really that worried about this weekend?"

"What do you mean?"

"You've just been a bit off over the past few days. You've been a bit irritable, and the song in the car about anxiety. I wasn't sure if it's about flying or the charity? Or me?"

I hate lying. Even omitting information, so I tell him. "I'm honestly not really afraid to fly. But the charity. Yeah, I'm a bit terrified of that."

He brushes a stray hair behind my ear. "Why?"

I blow out a breath, slightly frustrated that he still doesn't get it. "Lex, I don't come from that world. I'm not rich, and I'm going to be surrounded by a bunch of millionaires who toss out thousands of dollars like it's pocket change. I'm just afraid I won't fit in with that part of your world."

"But they don't know who you are," Lex retorts.

"So, what are you going to tell them? When they ask you who I am?"

"I'm going to say, *this is my girlfriend, Peyton.*"

"And when they ask, '*Where did you two meet?*'"

Lex pauses for a second. "I'll say we met at work."

"*She works for Kingston's? Is she a corporate businesswoman? A lawyer? No, she's too young to be any of those.*" Lex doesn't say anything. "Are you going to tell them I work at a pharmacy, and go to community college?"

He shakes his head. "None of that matters."

I blink hard and press my lips together. "I know it doesn't, and you know it doesn't, but to them, and to *your father*, it does. I'm nothing to those people, Lex. I'm one of the little people they pay every week who demand fifteen dollars an hour, which they refuse to pay. I'm the 98% who demand affordable health insurance, but wait, I'm not full time, so I don't even qualify for health insurance."

Lex pulls away and gathers his things. "Let's just get this stuff down to the car, okay?"

"You asked me, Lex. I'm sorry if you don't like my answer."

He doesn't say anything. He just grabs his bags and walks out of the bedroom.

I jump down from the bed, and follow after him.

27

"Welcome To New York" // Taylor Swift

W e drive to Octavia's tiny airport in silence, and it's making my stomach twist. Part of me wants to cry because I feel like I started the argument back at the apartment. Still, him being silent isn't helping the situation, either.

Lex drives up to the hanger where a small airplane is waiting for us, and a few men in black suits with earpieces and sunglasses stand nearby. Lex gets out and hands his keys to one of the men, while another gets our luggage and brings it onto the plane.

I follow Lex with my purse over my shoulder, and we walk up the stairs. The plane is small, it can maybe carry eight to ten passengers at most. But this trip is only us and apparently two security guards? The seats are large and comfortable. One side is set up more like a couch, but Lex and I sit in the chairs.

It doesn't take long before the doors close, and the captain's voice comes on through the intercom, telling us to put on our seat belts and turn off our phones. We have one flight attendant showing us all the emergency exits and how to use the oxygen masks in case we need them.

And then we start to move.

Lex still hasn't said a word to me.

And there are too many people on this plane for me to start crying now.

Once we're in the air, we get the signal to take off our seat belts and turn our phones back on. I pull out my iPhone in an attempt to text Sammy, but I hear Lex say, "Do you guys mind giving us a few minutes?" To his security and the flight attendant.

The two men get up and walk into the back of the plane, and the woman, whose name tag I now see says "*Kristen*" leaves us with two bottles of water and follows the security guards. I look at Lex expectantly, turning in my seat a little, but he's quiet.

I wait for him to say something, but I don't think he can find the words. "Lex?"

"Do you think I'm ashamed of you?"

I frown. "What?"

"Do you think I'm ashamed of you?" He repeats.

I think for a moment and shake my head. "No."

"Then why would you say that? Why would you think I'm embarrassed by what you do and where you go to school?"

"I don't think *you're* ashamed of me, but aren't you the least bit worried the people at this charity, or your father, might be?"

The corner of his lips curl up into the slightest smile. "Fuck them."

I sigh. "Lex, be serious."

"I am serious. Fuck them. I don't care what my father thinks at all. And I really don't care what a bunch of random people at a charity think."

"But aren't some of these people your friends? Friends from school or with your family? Or business partners?"

"Yes, and it's none of their goddamn business where you came from or what you do. It matters who you are. You are Peyton Katz, you are kind and loving and caring. You are the girl who puts her father's needs before her own. The girl who would take a bullet for her best friend. The girl who never lies no matter how hard it is, and the girl I love. That's what matters. And that's *all* that matters."

I take his hand in mine and nod. "You're right. I'm sorry. I'm just nervous about this whole thing."

"You don't need to be nervous. I'll be right there with you the whole time."

I sink back in my seat as he kisses my hand, and I relax a little.

The flight to Manhattan is only an hour and a half, and just as I look out my window and see it for the first time, I pull out my phone and play a song. Mostly as a joke, but also because it's true; *Welcome to New York* by Taylor Swift.

I start singing along as we're flying over skyscrapers and parks and rivers and bridges, and Lex is laughing at me. Then the captain comes back on the intercom telling us to please fasten our seat belts and turn off all cellphones.

When we get off the plane, a car is waiting for us. It's a fancy black SUV with a driver and more security guards. One of the men opens the door for me, and Lex helps me inside. Once we're in and start driving, I look at Lex. "So, what's with all the men in black, Jay Z?"

He snorts as he clicks his seat belt on. "It's just protocol. My father is—what's the word? *Insane.* Whenever I come into the city, he sends them. I tell him I'll accept one, two at the most, and he sends me ten. It's ridiculous."

"Yeah, I can't wait to meet him," I say sarcastically.

Lex puts an arm around my shoulder. "Don't worry about

him. I know what he's going to say. He's going to be an ass to you for absolutely no reason, but don't take it personally. I'll handle him."

I lean into him and take a deep breath. He smells like musk and cedar and mint. "How far is the hotel?" I ask.

He chuckles. "Well, it's not far, but it's going to take a while."

"Right. Traffic here is—"

"Ridiculous."

So, the car starts to move, and we drive, and we stop. And we drive, and we stop. And this happens a lot, before I ask, "Would it be faster to walk?"

Lex laughs. "No, we're almost there."

Almost clearly means something different in my world than it does in his. We're driving five miles an hour and stuck in traffic for another thirty minutes before we pull up to a curb and park.

"We're here, sir," the driver says.

"Thank you," Lex says, and I start to open my door, but he stops me. "Wait, he'll get it."

I look at Lex and fold my hands in my lap. "This is how it's going to be all weekend, isn't it?"

He looks at me with those blue-gray eyes and lifts one shoulder. "I'm afraid so. You might as well get used to it now."

I bite my lip and let out a breath. "Okay."

I can do this. It's only for a weekend.

The door opens, and the guard holds a hand out for me. I smile politely and take it. I look up at the building before me, craning my neck, but it's so tall, I can't see the top. The streets are packed with cars and people and tourists and the doors to the Four Seasons open by two doormen wearing uniforms. A woman wearing a white dress that probably cost more than my car walks out carrying a small black clutch purse and sunglasses, and a diamond necklace so fucking big, it makes my star look like cheap costume jewelry. My hand instinctively

256

reaches for it, and I eye the woman as she turns and walks down the street, completely ignoring my existence, as though my ripped jeans and black tank top are somehow beneath her.

Lex nudges me, placing a hand on the small of my back. "Are you ready?"

I look at him and back at the hotel. "I don't know. Will they let me in or should I change really quick in the car?" I say as I motion to my outfit.

"You're beautiful. And those jeans are sexy as fuck." He kisses me and takes my hand and leads me inside the Four Seasons.

We walk into a beautiful lobby with vaulted ceilings and pillars and three sets of stairs before we get to the check-in counter. The floors are different-colored marble in shapes that form together to create some fancy art deco Spirograph. I let Lex speak to the woman at the desk while I stare in awe of the place. On one side there is a bar and maybe a restaurant, and on the other side is the spa he was telling me about, but I'm not totally sure. This place is massive.

Lex gets the key cards to our room, thanks the woman, and we make our way toward the elevators. Lex's bodyguards follow closely behind, carrying our luggage in tow. We get into the elevator, and Lex pushes the button for the eighth floor. I'm honestly surprised we aren't higher up, but then again, this is a fancy hotel. I'm sure every room here is extravagant.

The doors open up, and we go to the right, and we stop in front of room 827. Lex looks at me. "Are you ready?"

"I guess."

He slides the key card inside, and the door clicks open. The first thing I see when we walk in is the bathroom. Straight ahead from the doors, on one side is a deep soaking tub, with a separate glass-enclosed shower, and on the other side is a pair of sinks with a gorgeous marble countertop and mirror, and TV. There's a freaking TV in the bathroom.

"Wow," I breathe as I walk around the room. Next to the bathroom is a walk-in closet that has more room than anyone could ever possibly need, and next to that is the main room.

A king-size bed sits to my right with two small tables and a lamp on each side. In the far right is a white couch with a coffee table in front of it. On the opposite wall is a giant TV hung on the wall. Next to that in the left corner is a small desk.

And straight ahead are the glass doors that open out onto our own private terrace.

The men in black bring our things inside, and Lex helps them put everything in the closet. I set my purse down on the desk and open the terrace doors and step outside. We're only on the eighth floor, but the view is still amazing. I can only imagine what it would be like if we were higher up. It's starting to get dark now, after a long day of working, then packing, and traveling, and finally getting here. I walk back into the room to text Sammy.

'Hey, how's everything back home? We just got to the hotel. Holy shit, this place is fucking insane.'

I'm surprised when I get a response right away since she's working at the pharmacy until close.

'Everything's good. I'll text you later after I check on your Dad. Take pictures!'

So, I do. I take a picture of the terrace, and three of the living/bedroom area, a few in the bathroom and closet, and everywhere I can think. Even the TV in the bathroom because I know that will make her laugh, and send them all her way.

28

"Angst In My Pants" // Sparks

The men in black are gone now, but one is stationed outside of the door at all times.

"Seriously, what is up with the security?" I ask Lex.

Lex smiles as he unpacks his suitcase in the dresser under the television. "I'm just my father's pet."

"Wait, is this for your protection, or for your Dad to keep tabs on you?" Lex cocks his head to the side and raises his brows at me as if to say *now you're catching on.* "I see."

"He hasn't seen me in a few months, and now that I'm in his city again."

"His city?" I ask.

"He likes to think so."

I shake my head as I jump up onto the bed and fall backward. "Oh, my god, this bed."

Lex comes over and jumps up next to me, and I almost fall off. I laugh, but he catches me, wrapping his arms around my waist. "I was going to ask if you were hungry."

I eye him seductively. "I'm starving," I say and kiss him.

We're lying on the bed, side by side, and Lex's hands are on the small of my back. He pulls me closer to him and breaks the kiss. "So, should I order room service?"

"Definitely." I kiss him again, wrapping my arms around him, sliding one arm under his side so he can't escape. I lift my right leg up and hook it around him, and that deep, sexy moan vibrates through his chest.

"Peyton," he says in warning.

But my lips meet his, hard and eager. My mouth opens for him, and he slides his tongue in, his hands now sliding down from my back to my ass, down my leg, and I pause for a second, but he doesn't touch my thigh.

Then I remember and pull back. "We never decided on a safe word."

"I know, that's why I was being careful," he admits.

"Do you have any ideas?" I ask.

He bites back a smile. "I do have one, but it's silly."

"That's good. They're supposed to be. The article Dr. Young gave me said the more nonsensical the word, the better."

"Well, it's not nonsensical. We just might feel dumb saying it."

"I'm pretty sure that's how everyone feels at first. What is it?" I bite my lip, thankful he actually came up with an idea, so I don't have to.

He takes a deep breath and says, "Well, I was just thinking, with all the music you like to play for me, and you've introduced me to a lot of music—"

"God, please not 'Taylor Swift,' or 'Swifty' or any variation of her name or songs—"

He bursts out laughing. "No! That would be a horrible safe word. Unless you *are* Taylor Swift, and she's into that sort of thing. But no, that's *not* what I was thinking."

"Thank the freaking stars."

"I thought about that, too, actually. I thought about 'Cosmo', but I figured since that's your dog's name, that would be weird."

"Yes, it would be. So, please tell me what you picked because I'm dying here."

He pauses and says. "Playlist."

I think for a second. "Playlist?"

"Yeah, it's generic, it's simple, and it's you."

I nod and say it aloud again. "Playlist." I laugh a little. "Yeah, that will take some time getting used to. But I think it works."

Lex smiles. "Good. So, it's official. 'Playlist' is the safe word?"

I take a deep breath. "Yes, 'playlist' is the safe word."

"Okay, now that that's settled." His lips meet mine, his hand on the back of my leg, pulling me closer to him. "Am I ordering that food or...?"

I laugh and shake my head, pulling him closer. I am starving, but I want him more. I want *this* more. Lex is so fast, I'm not sure how he does it, but he manages to pull me on top of him and sit up, grabbing my legs so I'm straddling him. My arms fly around his neck and I'm holding on to him, so I don't fall off the bed. "You're quick," I say.

He smiles, inches from my face. "Well, I've had experience," he admits, his eyes lit with an inner glow of mischief. "And you're so light. So easy to pick up and toss anywhere I want."

My cheeks turn hot. "Yeah? How do you want me?"

That noise in his chest rumbles again. "Just like this." And his lips are on mine, hard and fast and impatient. His hands are on my hips, squeezing, and my hands make their way into his tousled hair.

And in this moment, right here, right now, all my fears melt away as I give myself to him. I feel my heart lighten, and it feels so wonderful, I almost want to cry. I bring my hands down to his chest and start unbuttoning his shirt. Lex pulls away for a second to look at me, and I can see the worry in his eyes.

He lets me remove his shirt, and my hands reach for the hem of my tank top, but he puts his hands on mine and shakes his head. "Playlist," he says.

He says it first, and I want to ask him why, but I know we're not supposed to question it.

I don't take my shirt off.

My hands slide up his chest and around his neck, and I want to know what he's thinking. I pull myself closer to him, as close as I possibly can, and his hands wrap around me, holding me there. I kiss him gently, our eyes still locked on to each other. My eyes are filled with questions, and his are filled with concern.

I pull back and slide down from his lap. "What's wrong?"

"You're not supposed to question the safe word."

"I'm not. It's fine if you want me to keep my shirt on. It's the look in your eyes I'm worried about."

He pauses for a second before sighing, and says, "I'm just worried now that we have this solution, you're going to jump in the deep end, thinking you're ready when you've only had one swim lesson."

I quirk an eyebrow. "Was that a metaphor?"

"A bad one, yes. Sorry. It's just because we have this one idea that *might* work, doesn't mean we have to dive right in. We can still take things slow."

I take his hand and twine our fingers together. "I know. I'm not trying to push us to move faster, I just want to test out the water."

Lex snorts, "Was *that* a metaphor?"

I roll my eyes, "Yes," I say and I crush my lips to his. "I mean, ever since that morning in the cabin, I haven't been able to stop thinking about your magic fingers."

He chuckles, his cheeks turning red. "If you think my

fingers are magic, you should see what I can do with my tongue."

My face burns. "Really?"

"And I am starving."

I bite my lip, trying not to laugh, but my body betrays me. *Oh, my god.*

Lex looks at me expectantly as his hands trail down my waist to the button of my jeans. "What do you think? Are you ready to give third base a shot?"

"That's third base?" I ask.

He nods. "Yeah. It's okay if you don't want to."

I kiss him, hard, desperate, even though my stomach is made entirely out of butterflies. I pull back. "Okay."

"Just say the word."

"I know."

He undoes the button of my jeans and my stomach clenches. Lex carefully lifts me off of his lap and sets me down on the bed, our eyes never leaving each other. My breathing increases as his hands reach under me, and he pulls my jeans down, tossing them onto the floor.

My entire body is shaking.

Fuck. Breathe, Peyton.

Lex is sitting back on his knees, and he looks at me, waiting for me to say it.

I don't.

I bite my lip as he crawls over me, hovering above me. He kisses me lovingly as his hand slides up under my tank, lifting it as he does. He pulls away and takes my shirt in both hands and lifts it up and over my head.

I'm lying before him in my black lacy bra and underwear—both of them new, along with the few other new pairs I bought with Sammy the other day while we were out shopping for dresses. Lex hovers above me and looks over me like he wants to eat me alive. He looks up at me again, waiting for me to say the word, but I don't.

He nips at my earlobe, making my back arch into him, and I can feel his wicked grin as he makes a trail of kisses down my neck to my chest, placing one kiss on each breast, but he doesn't remove my bra. He continues his way down, kissing me everywhere, my stomach clenches with each kiss and the closer he gets to my underwear, the more nervous I get.

Breathe.

I let my head fall back onto the bed and close my eyes.

"Peyton?"

I look down at him, and he's looking at me, his eyes asking me a silent question.

"I'm okay," I reassure him.

His fingers slip under the hem of my black underwear, and I lift my butt up from the bed just a little, and they slide right off.

Holy shit.

He places a hand on each of my knees, his eyes still locked on mine, waiting for me to say it.

But I don't.

He finally looks down at me, and I know he's looking at my scars.

I forgot about them for a second.

I look down and think I might panic, but Lex says. "I won't touch them."

I meet his gaze and nod.

I'm okay.

Lex slowly and carefully grips me by the waist and pulls me down to the edge of the bed. He bends down onto his knees and hooks my legs over his shoulders.

Whoa.

First, I feel him kiss my inner thigh so gently, and I bite back a laugh.

Yeah, that kind of tickles.

He kisses me more, a few on each leg, and it takes everything in me not to start laughing or squeeze my legs together.

Holy shit, it fucking tickles.

And I let a small laugh escape my lips, and my cheeks flush. Lex looks up at me, and I cover my face with my hands.

"Are you laughing?"

Yes, I am. I'm fucking laughing because this is incredibly awkward and slightly hilarious, and it fucking tickles. "Sorry, sorry," I say as I try to calm myself down. I take a deep breath and move my hands from my face. I look at Lex, and he's looking at me with a quirked brow. "It tickles."

Now he's laughing, and I start laughing again. "It tickles?" He asks. "When you kiss me, yeah, it tickles," I say through my laughs.

"You mean like this?" He kisses my inner thigh again.

"Yes!" I shout through a fit of laughter.

Lex looks at me, his lips curled in a wicked smile. "I guess I'm being too gentle with you."

I bite my lip as Lex scrapes his teeth along the inside of my thigh, not enough to hurt, but it definitely doesn't tickle.

My laughter stops, and my insides knot together. When he kisses me this time, he presses down hard, and it sends a jolt of nerves up into the pit of my stomach.

I can feel my legs trembling as they lie across his shoulders, but Lex puts a hand on my stomach, and my breathing hitches the first time I feel his tongue slide down my center. His tongue moves against me, making my back arch into him.

Oh, my god.

He stops and looks up at me. "Does *that* tickle?"

I shake my head, and he lowers his mouth back onto me, taking me in long, unending strokes. It's a strange sensation at first, but every time his tongue hits that spot of nerves, I want more. All I can think about is how much more I want of him.

My left hand reaches above my head, fists into the sheets, and my right hand reaches lower, grabbing onto his hair. He moans in approval and moves faster, and I feel his fingers at my opening. He slides one inside of me and my back arches again, my hips begin to move in pace with him.

Lex slides a second finger inside of me, and I know I'm close. The combination of his fingers pushing in and out of me, while his tongue moves against the spot, that intense sensation is building in my core again. Every nerve in my body is on fire as he moves his fingers inside of me, faster and faster. His tongue working with fervor as my moans get louder and louder until my body explodes with release.

Lex slows down his motions but doesn't stop until I tell him to. I lie there panting, gleaming with sweat, and a dumb smile plastered on my face. Lex hovers above and kisses me, and I can taste myself on his mouth, but it doesn't bother me. His hand roams up my side, the other one supporting himself, and I can feel how hard he is through his pants.

I know what he's thinking, but we both know we shouldn't. Maybe he'll let me help him in another way this time? I let my hands slide down his chest, and I reach for the button of his pants. I expect him to pull away and say the safe word, but he doesn't.

Instead, he breaks the kiss and looks down at my hands and watches me undo the zipper. His eyes meet mine as I slowly slide my fingers under the seam of his boxers, and slip my hand inside.

My heart is pounding because I honestly have no idea what the fuck I am doing. I've never touched a man before. I mean, it doesn't seem that *difficult*. So, I wrap my hand around him, squeezing gently, and begin to stroke.

I can't believe he's letting me do this.

Lex looks up and meets my gaze, his eyes ravenous, and he kisses me, hard, and desperate, and wanting, so I move faster, and he moans against my mouth. His hand reaches up for my breast, and I'm sure he wishes he took my bra off now.

He breaks the kiss and looks down again. "Fuck," he says.

And the next thing I know, he's standing. My hand is free and his pants are now on the floor.

I look up at him, questioningly. "What's wrong?"

He doesn't answer me. He bends over me and grabs me by the waist and tosses me up higher on the bed, and suddenly, I think I know where this is going, and my insides turn to jello.

"Was I doing it wrong?" I ask naively.

He shakes his head. "No, of course not."

He hovers above me and kisses me again. My entire body is shaking, and I break the kiss. "Then why did you stop me?"

He rests his head on my forehead and closes his eyes. He kisses me again, and with his knee, he starts to nudge my legs apart, and I think I might throw up.

"Playlist," I say.

Lex breathes out a sigh of relief, or maybe disappointment, I honestly can't tell, and he rolls off me. He lies next to me on the bed, and I turn to face him. "Can't I just keep doing what I was doing?"

Lex lets out a long breath and turns to me, his lips curled into half a smile. He kisses me sweetly. "I'm going to take a shower." He gets up off the bed and heads into the bathroom, and I lie there feeling satisfied and frustrated at the same time.

29

"Girls Just Want to Have Fun" // STRFKR

The next day, I awake to an empty bed and a note on the pillow next to me.

Have a few meetings this morning. You have an appointment at the spa at one o'clock. I booked you for a 'mani/pedi', and hair and makeup afterward. I left you a tray of breakfast. I'll meet you later before the Conserve Wildlife Foundation Charity. XXX Lex.

So, *that's* what the charity is for.

I sit up in bed and notice the cart and covered tray, and I can smell the bacon. I crawl over the bed and uncover the tray and find scrambled eggs, french toast, bacon, and coffee waiting for me. I grab the TV remote off of the nightstand and flip through the channels as I eat, wishing Lex had told me this before.

When I'm finished eating, I get up and grab my phone off the desk, thankful it's not entirely dead, but I grab my charger from my bag to plug it in. I have a message from Sammy.

'Hey, just checked Dad. Everything's good. I searched around the

house a bit, didn't find bourbon or anything else. I hope you guys are having fun!'

I reply, *'Thanks. Lex is in meetings this morning, so I get to go get my nails, hair, and makeup done in the spa downstairs later.'* With a few added emojis showing just how excited I am about it.

She's going to laugh at that.

I've never had a mani-pedi in my life, and now I get to go and do it alone.

My phone goes off in my hand. *'Oo, la, la! Lucky girl! They better make you look hot and you better send me pictures!'*

I chuckle. *'I will.'*

I set my phone down on the bedside table and jump in the shower. I watch TV and impatiently wait around the room until twelve forty-five rolls around. I'm not entirely sure what to wear, so I just dress in my regular clothes, a pair of dark non-ripped jeans and a t-shirt, but don't put on my sneakers. Instead, I slip on a pair of hotel flip flops. I slide my phone and some cash in my back pocket and make my way down.

When the elevator doors open, I follow the signs that lead to the spa. A woman wearing a black polo with the words *L. Raphael Spa* written in a fancy script on the right side, and a name tag on the other greets me.

"Hi, I have an appointment at one, but I'm not sure what name he put it under?"

"Okay, what's the room number?"

"827," I tell her.

"Okay, yes. I have you right here. You're Peyton?"

"Yes, that's me," I smile.

"We've got you booked for a pedicure and a manicure. If you go over to that wall, you can pick which colors you want, or if you want the same color for both," she explains.

"Thanks," I say and head to my left and look at the giant wall of all the different colors. I look and bite my lip, wondering which one will look best with my dress. I pick a dark blue called *Chopstix and Stones* and decide it's good enough for both my fingers and toes.

"Peyton?" The woman calls. "We're ready for you."

And off I go.

~

I'M STANDING IN THE BATHROOM OF OUR HOTEL ROOM, STARING at myself. My hair done half up and curled in bobby pins and pulled to my left side. I'm wearing the necklace Lex gave me, and a pair of fake earrings Sammy found that kind of match, and I'm fighting with this zipper. I finally get it up and lean against the sink as I pull on the ankle strap platform blue heels Sammy helped me pick out that match my dress.

I look in the mirror again and feel like they put way too much makeup on me. Part of me wants to take some of it off, but I know I won't be able to fix it before I meet Lex down-stairs. My phone buzzes on the counter. It's from Lex.

'I'm here.'

I take a breath, grab my little blue clutch with my anxiety medicine already inside, toss in my phone, and make my way down to the lobby to meet him.

He's standing in the lobby wearing a very sexy tuxedo, black tie, and shoes, and I walk down the stairs. He looks up at me, his eyes widen, and his mouth opens slightly as his lips curl into a smile. My dress is that sapphire blue he wanted, and a strapless chiffon Aline gown with a crystal beaded bodice.

I hold on to the railing, so I don't fall and ruin my entrance. I get to the bottom step, and he stands before me, eye level.

"Peyton," he says, a little breathy.

I bite my lip and smile. "Lex."

"You're right."

"I am?"

He nods. "That dress *did* cost more than my car." I chuckle, and he kisses me. "You are breathtaking."

I blush, and he holds out a hand to me. I take it and step down the final stair, and we make our way out of the hotel door.

Outside waiting for us is a black limo. All of the color drains from my face. "Seriously?"

"*Kingston's* orders I'm afraid."

I let out a breath, and crawl into the back.

As soon as I sit down, my skin feels sticky. I roll down the window to my left, praying the fresh air will help calm me down, but my stomach is starting to churn.

"Peyton?" Lex looks at me, and realization dawns on his face. "Oh, shit," he says.

"How long does it take to get there?" I ask. I squeeze my eyes shut, trying not to look, praying I don't get a flashback of that night a year ago.

We start moving, and I know I'm stuck inside of this limo until we arrive.

Lex takes my hand. "Peyton, look at me." I'm fighting with myself, but Lex gently puts his fingers on my chin and turns my head toward him. "Peyton, it's okay. You're safe." I take in a deep breath and force myself not to cry. I *cannot* ruin my makeup and walk into this event with mascara running down my cheeks and fake eyelashes falling off.

I open my eyes, and Lex pulls my phone out of my purse and connects it to the Bluetooth of the limo. "What song should I play?" He asks.

I look at him, confused. "What?"

"What's your go-to happy song? What song always makes you feel better?" I can't help but chuckle. "It can be a Taylor Swift song. I won't judge."

I laugh and take my phone from his hand. I slide through my playlist and click on a cover of *Girls Just Want To Have Fun* by STRFKR. Lex turns the volume up all the way and starts dancing in the back of the limo.

He looks at me with wide eyes. "Hey, I know this song!"

My jaw drops. "What?"

Lex gets on his knees and shimmies in front of me as he sings along. And I burst out laughing. I can't believe he's doing this. This is the first song I've ever played that he actually knows.

"How? How do you know this song?"

But he doesn't answer. Instead, he keeps on singing, albeit badly, and I sing along with him. He's swaying his hips and flipping his hair, and he takes my hand, and I start dancing, too, and I can't help but fall in love with him even more.

We sing and dance along until the song ends, and another one starts. He stays with me the entire time, distracting me from my own memories, my own thoughts, the whole limo ride.

We pull to a stop when we arrive at Goldman Sachs. Lex clicks my phone off and puts it back in my purse. I wrap my arms around him so tight because I am so grateful to him at this moment, there are no words.

He pulls away, his lips curled up in that sexy smile, and he looks down at me, lovingly. "I'm sorry. I didn't even think—"

"It's okay. You just made it better."

The limo door opens. Lex gets out first, and I follow after him. The outside of the building is lit up in a light blue, and people are approaching from every direction. "Are you ready?" He asks.

I shake my head. "No, but I don't think I will ever be."

He takes my hand and squeezes. "Me either. But at least we've got each other."

I smile as we make our way into the building.

30

"Royals" // Lorde

We walk into the building and into the most beautiful ballroom I've ever seen. The ceiling is four stories high, with chandeliers hanging everywhere. Tables are set around the room, and there's a dance floor in the middle, but no one is dancing. Right now, most people are getting drinks at the bar and walking around, mingling.

I take a breath. "So, do we mingle, or do we drink?"

"We're going to need a drink first."

"Thank the stars," I say.

"You stay here, and I'll get you something."

I look at him, my face filled with panic, my eyes screaming at him, *do not leave me alone!*

He kisses me gently. "I'll be quick, I promise." And off he goes to the bar, and I'm left standing in the middle of the room with a bunch of snooty rich people I don't know. A couple of people look at me, and I smile, trying to be friendly, but they wrinkle their noses and turn away from me.

"Well, fuck you, too," I mutter under my breath.

I walk around the room and notice there are placement cards at each table, and a name on every plate, and I can't help but wonder which table Lex and I are assigned.

He returns, holding two glasses of champagne, and hands one of them to me.

"Thank you," I say.

"You're welcome. You're going to need it," he says and takes a sip.

"So, where's our table?"

He turns to the other side of the room and points to a table next to a window. "Over there somewhere, I'm sure. My father usually gets one of the 'good' tables."

I narrow my eyes. "There are good tables and bad tables?"

"Yeah, you do not want to be caught at the slosh table."

"What's a slosh table? Wait, that's a real thing?"

Lex laughs as he pulls me over toward the windows, looking for our names, or his name at least, on a card. He finds it, and next to him is not my name, but the word 'Guest'.

"I'm assuming that's me?"

His expression changes to annoyance and groans. "My father didn't even bother asking your name when I told him I was bringing someone."

"How thoughtful," I say as I look around the room. "Well, no one is sitting yet."

"I'd say we should find my father, but he'll find me first."

We walk around the room, and Lex points out a few people to me. Some people his father works with, a few parents of kids he went to school with, when a man's voice booms from behind us, giving me goosebumps up my arms.

"Lex!"

"See? Told you he'd find me," he whispers in my ear.

We turn, and a man Lex's height wearing almost the same

suit, stands before us, with short white hair and a groomed white beard.

The white beard Lex still hasn't managed to grow.

A small smile forms on my lips at the memory as we approach him. "Dad," Lex says.

His father reaches out his hand to Lex, and my mouth falls open.

Is he shaking his own son's hand?

Lex takes it, and they shake. *Wow.*

"I've heard things are going well with the pharmacy," he says indifferently.

Lex nods. "Very well. Much better than anticipated." I can tell Lex wants to go into further detail, but his father couldn't be anymore uninterested.

His father takes a drink of his cocktail, a faint smile forming at his lips as his eyes roam over me. "Who's your friend?"

"This is my girlfriend, Peyton Katz. Peyton, this is my father, Thomas Kingston."

I reach out my hand to him, and he takes it. "It's nice to meet you, Peyton."

Liar.

"So, where did you two meet?" Thomas asks, either one of us really, but Lex answers.

"In Genesee Falls. She works at the pharmacy."

Thomas looks me over, and his lips purse into a tight line. "Well, you know what they say about small town charm. But it will only get you so far."

"Dad," Lex says through gritted teeth. "Don't speak to Peyton like that."

Thomas finally looks back at Lex. "You're right, son. Tonight isn't about her, or anyone else you decide to bring home. It's a charity," he smiles. "So let's go donate some money and help some defenseless people we've never met."

"This charity is for a wildlife reserve," Lex points out.

"Even better," Thomas takes another sip of his drink.

"Aren't you wondering how the pharmacy is *really* doing? Don't you want to know what I've done with it?"

"Of course, son. Do tell," Thomas says, as he looks around the room, clearly bored.

"Since I took over, profits have doubled. We have more customers, not just in the pharmacy, but in the store itself. We have to hire another pharmacist because we can't keep up with the demand. We've already hired more employees and will be hiring even more soon. I ripped that store apart, built a brand new one and gave it the Kingston name. You should really go and see it sometime, Dad. Seeing as it's *your* store."

His father smiles. "That's wonderful to hear, son. Maybe you're ready to take on a real part of the company now."

I can feel the anger radiating off Lex, and I squeeze his hand, reminding him I'm here. That I'm *always* here.

Lex takes a breath and steps back, smiling. "I appreciate the opportunity, Dad. But I already have some business dealings of my own. You see, I've invested in a few start-up companies in Buffalo and Syracuse, and a few substantial businesses that you never would." Lex looks around the room and points a finger to a man in the far corner with brown hair and a mustache, speaking to a woman with short blonde hair wearing a long black dress. "Reginald Wexner and Natasha Darrington have been asking me to work with them since I turned twenty-one. I decided it was finally time I said yes."

Thomas wrinkles his nose in disgust.

Lex points behind him to another woman with brown skin and beautiful, curly hair wearing a dress similar to the color of mine. "Estelle and Chase Walker started calling me the minute I was out of this city and in Octavia. It took me a few days to consider their offer, but I did. It was an outstanding offer, Dad. I think you'd be proud if you read the papers."

Thomas' face is red as he eyes the two of us, and I just stand there, watching the two of them, praying no one throws a punch.

"If you think you've got anything at twenty-four years old, you're lying to yourself, Lex," Thomas starts. "These people don't care about you. They only care about the Kingston name."

"Actually, Dad, I don't think they do," Lex replies as he pulls out a business card and hands it to his father.

"What is the meaning of this?"

"It's the name of *my* company."

I look at Lex, my mouth gaping.

My company? *Lex started his own company? Holy shit.*

His father pushes the card into Lex's chest. "You have some nerve—" He starts.

But Lex stops him. He grabs his father's hand and pulls the card out from it and pushes his father's hand down. "No, I really don't. I just wanted to branch out on my own. Be my own person. See who I could be without Thomas Kingston. Turns out, I'm better off without you."

Thomas lets out a huff of air and storms off toward the bar, leaving Lex and I standing there, a wide smile spread across his face.

I look at him, smiling. "Lex, oh, my god!" In all the time I've known him, I've never seen his face light up like this—like he just won the battle he's been fighting his entire life. No matter where he went or what he did, Thomas Kingston would no longer be standing in his way, threatening to hurt him, or holding a fist to his face.

Lex just conquered his father with nothing more than a few words, and a few people by his side.

He finally looks down at me and laughs. "I've been waiting for weeks to do that, Peyton. *Weeks!*" Lex says. "That felt so good."

"Why didn't you tell me?" He looks at me, confused. "You started your own company?"

"Oh, that," Lex pulls out the business card and hands it to me, and it doesn't say *Kingston's*.

It says, *Lily Peyton Enterprises*.

I look at Lex, confused. "Sorry, I stole your name. I just have no desire to use my father's name anymore. So, I combined my mother's name with yours. I hope it's okay with you."

I look down at the card again, and back up at him, at an utter loss of words. "I don't know what to say."

He leans down and kisses me. "You don't have to say anything."

He takes the card and slips it back in his jacket pocket. "I'm sorry he was such a dick to you."

"I expected it," I say.

"That still doesn't make it okay."

I brush a piece of lint off his shoulder. "It also doesn't make it your fault."

"I know, but I don't like it when my father hurts the people I care about."

I place my hand on his cheek and kiss him. "Well, this is some party," I admit.

"And it's only the beginning."

"And the music is horrible," I say as I turn toward the horrible muzak being played on a sound system next to the bar.

"If only they had your playlists," Lex jokes.

I smile and nudge him with my elbow. Lex takes my hand, and we wander around some more, and I sip on my champagne.

Suddenly, he spins and looks at me wide-eyed. "Two o'clock, keep your guard up. She bites," he says, and he turns back around, pulling me closer to his side. A tall, dark-haired woman stands before us, wearing a long red dress with a giant square diamond on her left ring finger. I look up at Lex and see he's noticed it, too. But he squeezes my hand and smiles. "Victoria," he says.

Victoria? As in *Victoria Locke*, his ex-girlfriend who broke his heart?

Well, this night just keeps getting better and better.

She looks up at him, and a small smile appears on her face as if remembering a fond memory from her childhood. "Lex," she says, and he leans down to kiss her cheek.

I want to glare at him, but I don't because kissing cheeks is apparently the proper way to greet rich women. Or at least, it's how they all do it here.

She looks at me, and her smile starts to fade as she eyes me up and down. "Who's your friend?"

Excuse me, bitch?

Lex introduces us. She gives me a small smile and extends her hand. "It's nice to meet you," I say politely even though it's not true.

"Likewise," she replies as she holds a cocktail to her mouth and takes a drink.

Victoria is incredibly slender, to the point where you can see her collar bones poking out through her skin. I wonder if this is intentional, or maybe she's sick, when a man comes around and takes the drink out of her hands.

"Darling, you shouldn't drink that. You wouldn't want to gain any weight before the wedding. You just had the dress fitting last week," he says in a thick southern accent, and her cheeks flush red. A waiter carrying a tray of vegetables passes by, and the man picks up a celery stick. "Here, have one of these instead."

Well, that answers my question.

Karma sure is a bitch, isn't she?

Victoria takes the celery stick from his hand with a look of disdain on her face. Her fiancé finally looks at us and smiles. "Hello, I'm Thurston Price."

Lex smiles. "Lex Kingston," he says, and they shake hands. "This is my girlfriend, Peyton."

Thurston glances at me and nods, barely noticing I exist, because why would he?

"Kingston, huh? Wow, I finally get to meet the famous Lex Kingston. It's a pleasure, I'm sure. How are things in, oh, where are you now? Some small town upstate, is that right?"

"That's right. My father let me take over one of the smaller company holdings as a start-up."

Thurston smiles, as though it's some small victory for him. "Well, wasn't that nice of him. I'm running for governor of West Virginia."

Lex nods. "I wish you luck in the races."

"Thank you, Lex. It's been a pleasure," he says as he takes Victoria by the arm and pulls her away, probably to go speak to someone better than us.

I look up at Lex in disbelief. "Holy shit," I say in a low voice. And I see that triumphant smile plastered across his face.

I pinch him on the arm. "Ow!"

"You look *way* too happy."

He lifts his hands up in a defensive manner. "I am happy. Victoria finally got all that she wanted, and everything she deserves."

I shake my head, but can't control my smile. "And what about you, Lex? Did you get everything you wanted?"

He looks down at me and wraps an arm around my waist. "And then some."

31

"I Don't Care" (Acoustic Version) // Ed Sheeran

After an hour and a half of mingling, Lex is exhausted from all the introductions, and I'm exhausted from trying to remember all of these names.

I mean, who the hell names their kid Bibsy?

Some of these people will be working with Lex and are essential to the new *Lily Peyton Enterprises*. Still, most of them are just snooty, old rich people that Lex has an obligation to be nice to because it's "proper etiquette" and we wouldn't want to make Lex's father look bad.

He does that to himself already.

We're wandering around the beautiful banquet hall when I ask, "How long do these things normally last?"

"Three or four hours."

My eyes widen. "Are you freaking kidding me?"

"Nope."

"When do they serve dinner?"

He looks at his watch. "Soon. Within the next hour."

"Oh, my god," I mumble to myself. I've already had four glasses of champagne and I told Lex to cut me off before I start dancing on top of a table. "Do you have to make a donation?"

"Already done. My father made one for *Kingston's*, so I made one for *Lily Peyton*."

I smile at him, pride beaming from my cheeks. "So do we really have to stay?"

"I mean, we're supposed to. It's—"

"*Proper etiquette*, I know. But you showed up. You made a donation. You talked to everyone you need to talk to. What more is there to do? Eat? Dance? We can do that anywhere."

Lex wraps an arm around my shoulder and pulls me into him. "I promise it won't be much longer."

"You look exhausted," I argue.

"I am because I can't stand most of these people, but it's all about keeping up appearances."

I sigh exasperated because I'm exhausted too and a little tipsy from the champagne.

And on top of everything else, this music is driving me fucking crazy. I glance over at the soundboard and realize there *is* a person in charge after all.

And now I have a very, very bad idea.

I look back at Lex. "I'll be right back." And leave before he has a chance to protest.

I walk up to the man behind the sound system. He isn't much taller than me, with dark brown hair and groomed facial hair that was obviously done professionally. He's wearing an all-black suit and tie and I can see small bits of tattoos poking through the bottom of the long sleeves of his shirt. He's staring at the screen of his computer when I approach. "Excuse me?" I say and he looks up. "Are we allowed to make requests?" I ask.

The DJ looks up at me in surprise. "Um, I guess. Most people never do at these things, but sure. What do you want me to play?"

I tell him the name of the song, and he eyes me nervously. "I'm not sure about that."

"You see that man over there?" I ask as I point to Lex. "That's my boyfriend. He is having a terrible night and I just want to cheer him up. Could you maybe make an exception? Just this once?" I give him my most prominent puppy dog eyes. "Everyone else will hate it." And my wickedest smile.

The DJ laughs at me and shakes his head. "Okay, miss, but if I get into trouble."

"You can blame me! Thank you!" I beam.

He nods and stops the song that is currently playing.

I walk up to Lex, take his hand and pull him out onto the dance floor.

"What did you do?"

I place his arms around my waist and wrap my arms around his neck as the song begins to play.

"Requested a song for us."

I Don't Care (Acoustic Version) by Ed Sheeran.

His face lights up as we start to dance. The people around become quiet and turn and look at us. Lex eyes me long and hard and kisses me right there in front of everyone.

I kiss him back.

"This is so our song," I laugh as the music plays for us, and only us.

Lex rests his forehead against mine. "It really is." He pulls me closer as we sway along the dance floor. We're the only ones out here.

"I love you so fucking much," he says.

I look into those big blue-gray eyes, and my stomach drops. "I know."

"How did you get the DJ to play this song?" He asks.

I smile wide. "Honestly, I think he liked the idea. He must be an Ed Sheeran fan."

Lex shakes his head. "You're an evil genius."

I nod. "I really am." I glance around the room and I notice all eyes are on us. It makes the knot in my stomach tighten. "Everyone is staring," I whisper.

He shrugs. "Let them."

I look around the room and Thomas appears from the double doors that lead outside and he watches us on the dance floor, and I grin as I look back at Lex. And in this moment, right here and right now, I couldn't give a single fuck what Lex's father or ex-girlfriend or any of these hoity-toity people think about me or us together. Because in the end, they don't matter. The knot in my stomach loosens. This party, this charity event, is just one night out of hundreds that I get to spend with Lex and I'll probably never see most of these people again. So, I pull Lex as close to me as humanly possible and pretend that just for a minute, we're the only two people in the room. In the city. In the whole world.

When the song ends, I snap out of my trance and realize that everyone is watching us, whispering among themselves, eyeing us both suspiciously.

For the first time in a long time, I don't care. And I have to admit, it's a damn good feeling.

"Not a song more accurate," I say to Lex.

He looks down at me with eyes full of admiration and love. I don't think he's ever looked at me like this before. "Do you want to get out of here now?" He asks.

"More than anything."

He grips my hand and we make our way through the crowd, and without a word to his father, we leave Goldman Sachs.

32

"Dress" // Taylor Swift

L ex doesn't bother getting the limo back. Instead, he pulls me along as we run down West Street, and he waves down a taxi. I breathe a sigh of relief. One stops just in front of us, and we get in, laughing as I pull my dress out of his way, so he doesn't trip on it.

"Four Seasons hotel in Manhattan, please," he tells the driver.

The driver nods, and Lex pulls me close to him, my purse falling from my lap onto the seat between us. "I can't believe you played that song back there."

I shrug. "You know me, Lex," I say as I brush back his tousled hair with my fingers. "I don't like to lie."

Lex snakes an arm around my back, lifting me onto his lap and kisses me. My other hand goes to his face, resting on his cheek as I open for him, and his tongue slides in. He wraps his other arm around me, pulling me closer.

I break the kiss. "Thank you."

"For what?"

"For getting a taxi."

He frowns. "I never should have agreed to that limo. I'm so sorry. I never meant to—"

But I kiss him before he can finish his sentence. "It's okay. I know it was an accident."

I wrap my arms around him, as Lex's hands explore my body, moving down my back and around my hips. We kiss deeply, passionately, and all I want to do is rip his goddamn shirt off right here in this cab. I let my hand slide down from his neck, down his chest and up under his jacket, and Lex bites my bottom lip lightly in approval. My other hand reaches up and fists his hair, and I can feel that deep moan coming from his chest.

I love this dress, and even though it cost as much as his car, I want nothing more than for him to rip it off.

I lean my head to the side, giving him room to kiss my neck as my hand tugs on his button-down shirt. I try to pull it out from his pants, wanting desperately to slide my hand up and under, to feel his skin on mine, and I know Lex wants the same. He slips a hand under the skirt of my dress and slowly glides his fingers up my leg. My stomach twists the higher they go, but he stops just above my knee and places his palm down.

Lex nips on my earlobe, and my back arches into him, and his hand, very carefully, slides up my center. He pushes my legs apart just enough, and I look at him, my cheeks flush. "Lex," I whisper. My eyes are wide, but I smile as I feel a finger graze down my center.

I glance back at the taxi driver who is listening to a talk radio station, and I don't think he is paying us any attention. However, I still feel very strange doing this in the back of a cab.

He presses two fingers down on that spot between my

thighs, and it takes everything in me not to gasp. I bring my lips to his ear. "You're mean."

He grins at me wickedly. "I'm just getting started."

And then he tugs at the seam of my underwear, trying to slip a finger where I know he should not be slipping a finger right now, and my anxiety wins. "Playlist," I say.

Lex looks at me with a semi-cocky grin, but pulls his hand out and back down, resting it on my knee.

I remain on his lap, and we kiss until the cab pulls up in front of the Four Seasons. Lex pays the man, tipping him generously, and we make our way inside. Lex is practically pulling me to the elevators. As soon as the doors close, his mouth finds mine again until the doors open on the eighth floor. We run down the hall to our room, and Lex pushes the key card into the slot, and we almost fall on the floor as we enter.

Lex catches me by my waist and spins me around, kicking the door shut with his foot. I grab his jacket and undo the buttons as our mouths are a clash of tongues and teeth and lips. His hands desperately search for the zipper of my dress. I pull his black jacket off and guide his hand to my left side, letting his fingers feel for the metal piece.

And he pulls it down, and I let my dress fall.

I pull down on his black tie, trying to loosen it, but it gets stuck as I try to pull it over his head, and we both laugh.

"Hold on," he says as he pulls the knot down and tosses the tie across the room. I take his white shirt in my hands and start to unbutton as he rests his forehead on mine. "Peyton," he says my name like he's desperate for air, and I kiss him.

I push his shirt off as he guides me to the bed. He lifts me in one swift movement, and I'm lying on my back, and he's hovering above me, my heart pounding, my stomach in knots.

But I don't want him to stop.

Lex kisses me as my hands trail down his chest, down his

torso, and I unbutton his pants. He breaks the kiss and looks down at me. "Peyton." And I can hear the desperation in his voice.

Please, stop doing this to me. He doesn't actually say it, but he doesn't need to.

And I'm suddenly overcome with guilt. I let go of his pants and reach up to touch his face. "Lex," I say, my voice cracking. I pull his face down to kiss me.

My fingers find their way into his hair as a single tear rolls down the side of my face. Lex breaks the kiss and looks at me. "Peyton?"

I look into those blue-gray eyes, those eyes that have shown me nothing but love and kindness and goodness and concern, and say, "I love you."

He smiles and kisses my tears away. "I know." He makes a trail of kisses down my neck to my chest and back up before he finds my lips again.

And as much as I don't want to, as much as I want to try to keep going, I know I need to stop before things go too far. Before we have a repeat of last night.

"Playlist," I say.

Lex simply smiles and kisses my face.

I expect him to go get in the shower, but he doesn't. He rolls to my left and lies next to me, wrapping his arms around me, pulling me into his chest. We lie like that for hours, neither one of us saying a word, and I don't remember when I fall asleep. But I remember feeling safe and happy and content in his arms before I do.

33

"Fix You" // Coldplay

We arrive at the airport early the next morning where, surprisingly, *Kingston's* plane is waiting for us. "I'm surprised your Dad didn't pull your privileges of using the company plane."

"Well, I do still technically work for the company, as long as I'm working at the pharmacy. That and I'm sure my Dad's probably too hungover from last night to bother making the call."

Last night, we managed to escape the guards, the men in black with guns and sunglasses and earpieces. But, this morning, they were posted right outside our hotel room door again, waiting to take us to the airport in a private black SUV.

At least it wasn't a limo.

The men carry our bags onto the plane, and I follow Lex up the steps, and we sit in the same seats we sat in on Friday. I check my phone quickly and have no new messages, before turning it off. The flight isn't that long, so Sammy should be all right, checking on my Dad this morning before I get home.

I toss my phone back in my purse and look over at Lex. The plane starts moving, and I can tell by the look on his face, something is brewing in that head of his. I nudge him with my elbow. "What's up?"

He looks over at me with a smirk. "I just wasn't expecting last night to go the way it went."

"Which part?"

He chuckles. "All of it. My Dad. Victoria. You."

"Me?" I laugh.

He smiles at me. "You were brave, playing that song for all those stuck up rich people. It was hot."

My cheeks flush. "You standing up to your Dad was hot."

He nods. "It felt so good. As soon as I'm done at the pharmacy, I'm done with him. I can be my own person. I can run *my* companies the way I want to run them. And I won't be stuck under his thumb, and it just feels so..."

"Freeing?"

He takes my hand and entwines our fingers. "I hope someday, you'll know what this feels like. Being free from everything that's holding you back. I hope you'll let me help you get there if I can."

I smile and kiss him, and turn to look out the window to watch the city below us disappear beneath the clouds.

When we land, and I get in Lex's car, I pull my phone out of my purse and turn it on.

My heart stops when I see I have 20 missed calls and 12 texts, all from Sammy.

'*Call me ASAP.*'

'Are you back yet?'
'Where are you??'
'OMG, Peyton!'
'Seriously??'
'You need to answer your fucking phone!'
'I've tried Lex, too!'
'Hello?'
'Peyton! Please!'
'Are you in the air?'
'WHERE THE FUCK ARE YOU?'
'Your Dad had a stroke! Come to Octavia Memorial ASAP. As soon as you land. NOW!'

My heart stops beating. I swear, I can't feel it anymore.

It's like that one time I fell off the swings at the playground and landed flat on my chest, and all the wind was knocked right out of me, and I literally couldn't take in any air.

Lex looks over at me. "Hey, are you okay? You're white."

"Drive to Octavia Memorial now. Drive now!"

He doesn't question me, he just starts the car and peels out of the parking lot of the airport.

The drive to the hospital feels like we're going in slow motion. I'm holding my phone in my hands, and I keep reading Sammy's last text over and over again. *'Your Dad had a stroke!'*

'Your Dad had a stroke!'

My Dad had a stroke.

I try to reply to Sammy's message, but I can't focus on the letters, and I can't find the words, so my message ends up looking like, *'On uor ywa. BEe erthe oosn'*

Yeah, that's not English, Peyton.

Lex is speaking to me, but I can't hear him.

"What?"

He speaks again, but his words are muffled, or my ears are stuffed with cotton balls. "What?" I ask again.

"Peyton!" He shouts. I snap out of my trance and look at him. "What's going on?"

I want to answer him, but I can't say the words out loud. He pulls up to a stoplight, and I show him the text from Sammy.

I can see the expression on his face change as he reads it. "Holy shit." He looks back at me, and he knows I'm not okay. "It's going to be all right. We're almost there. I'll drop you off in front and go park in the garage. You go find Sammy, and text me where you are, okay?"

I nod, hoping I can remember everything he just said.

The light turns green, and he guns it, slamming his foot on the gas.

We make it to the hospital, and I get out of the car, holding my phone in one hand and purse in the other. "Go find Sammy," Lex tells me. I turn to him and nod and close the car door. He peels out of the loop and heads for the parking garage, and I walk in the double doors.

I text Sammy again, *'Where are you?'* This message is much more coherent as I walk into the hospital. On the walls are different colored lines: red, blue, orange, and green—each one going in a different direction. And I have no idea which one I am supposed to follow.

So, I stand in the middle of an intersection, waiting for Sammy to reply. But she doesn't. The hospital has shit reception, so I don't even know if she got my message.

"Can I help you?" A plump woman with curly brown hair sitting behind the front desk asks me, and I stare at her blankly. "Are you all right, miss? Are you looking for someone?"

I nod. "Yes. My father. Harry Katz. He had a stroke."

He had a stroke...

She types in his name in the computer system as I approach her desk. "You said he's your father?"

I nod again. "Yes. My name is Peyton Katz."

"Okay, Peyton," she pulls out a visitor sticker and writes my name on it. "Stick this on your chest. Your father is in the ICU, so it's family only. I see your sister, Samantha, is with him now. Is that correct?"

I smile slightly and try not to cry. "Yes, that's correct. She's my sister."

And that is not a fucking lie.

"You're going to follow the blue line to the silver elevators up to the fourth floor. Once you get up there, continue to follow the blue line to room number 4110."

"Thank you," I panic for a second, worried about Lex. I pull out my phone to try to text him.

But before I get the chance, he's running down the hall toward me. "Hey, did you find out where he is?"

I look up at him and nod. I look at the lady then back at Lex and say, "Excuse me, but my husband needs a name tag, too. His name is Lex." Lex looks at me, confused, but I eye him long and hard, and he doesn't say a word.

The woman hands him a name tag, and we make our way down the hall to our right to the silver elevators. Once we're inside, I hit the button for the fourth floor.

"I'm sorry," I say, "My Dad is in the ICU, and she said it's family only, and I knew they wouldn't let you come in unless I told them you were my husband."

Lex pulls me into him. "I had a feeling it was something like that. A lot of hospitals have a family only policy."

I let out a sigh of relief.

"I mean, you could have said I was your brother."

I am going to kick you so hard.

I glare at him. "But then if I kissed you in front of a nurse, they'd think weird shit about our family. And it's bad enough Sammy already said she was my sister. But that's not even a lie, so I don't care about that."

Lex nods. "Is she here?"

The elevator doors open. "Yeah, she should be in the room with him."

I pull him out, and I follow the blue lines again until I reach room 4110. I see his name written below the number, and my heart starts to dance erratically in my chest. Lex squeezes my hand as we slowly walk into the room. At first, I see Sammy, fast asleep in a green pull-out sleeper chair, and behind the curtain is my father.

My hand flies over my mouth, and tears burn behind my eyes. More tubes and wires are sticking out of my father than I've ever seen before, and this time, he has a tube down his throat with a breathing machine attached. The entire left side of his face is drooping.

Why is he on a ventilator?

I'm just standing there staring at him, unable to speak or move or even think straight when a nurse walks in the room. She gives me a sympathetic smile. "Hello, sweetheart. I'm Kate, your Dad's nurse today," she says as she checks all the machines, and reads the numbers. "Is there anything I can help you with?"

I blink hard and steel myself. "Why does he need the ventilator?"

"After your father had the stroke, he was having a difficult time breathing on his own, so the doctors made the decision to put him on the machine."

"Is he sedated?"

"Yes, he was very agitated when he was brought in, so we didn't have much of a choice," she explains, and I can tell by the look on her face she must have seen that shit show.

"Did you do blood tests on him when he got here?"

"Yes, it's standard procedure."

"Was there alcohol in his system?"

Nurse Kate picks up his chart and flips back a few pages.

She lets out a breath and looks up at me. "His blood alcohol level was .21. I'm sorry, honey."

If Lex weren't there to catch me, I would have collapsed onto the floor. But he lifts me into his arms and sets me down into the blue plastic chair next to Sammy.

"I'll bring in another chair for you guys," Kate says.

I'm crying so hard, I can't even thank her, so Lex does it for me.

He grabs a small box of tissues and wipes my face clean. But I can't stop.

I'm so fucking angry.

"What am I going to do? He can't work anymore. We're going to lose his insurance, we're going to lose our house," I say through a fit of sobs.

The nurse appears with another green pull-out sleeper chair, and Lex thanks her again and sits down, pulling me onto his lap, wrapping his arms around me. "Well, I mean, we are married."

"You're never going to let me live that down, are you?"

He kisses my forehead. "No."

I shake my head and cover my face with my hands.

Once I'm able to steel myself, I turn to Sammy and shake her awake. She opens her eyes and straightens. "Peyton!" She's so relieved I'm finally here, she jumps up and hugs both of us. "I went to go check on your Dad, and he wasn't feeling well, and all of a sudden, he just fell and started convulsing."

"God, Sammy, I'm so sorry."

This is the second time in a month she was the one to find my Dad. All because I was too busy philandering my time away with my boyfriend to take care of him.

"It's not your fault, Peyton. I was just scared, and I knew you'd be pissed. Once the paramedics got there, I saw the bourbon bottles."

Bottles? Plural?

I blink hard and bite back the tears.

"The doctor told me a lot of things, but I don't remember it all. He said something about how liver damage can cause your liver to stop making things that help in the clotting of blood, so it can increase the risk of stroke. Something about plasma proteins and coagulation? I don't know, I figured since you're a nursing major, you'd understand it better than I do."

"I've only finished one year of Bio. I mean, it sounds familiar, but my head isn't exactly clear right now."

"They're worried. His liver is worse, and I guess he's got some other things going on, too. His blood pressure was super high when the paramedics took it, and the doctors are worried about his kidneys. He's been having abnormal heart rhythms, something called 'atrial fibrillation,' they said."

I shake my head and cover my face again, and let the tears fall. "Why can't he just stop? Why am I not enough to make him stop drinking?"

Lex and Sammy wrap me in their arms and hold me while I cry, tears of anger and frustration and sadness.

"You are enough, Peyton. You are so much more than enough," Lex says, and I can hear his voice breaking. "But you can't force an alcoholic to stop drinking. They have to want it."

"Lex is right," Sammy cuts in. "It's not about you."

Somewhere in the back of my mind, I know they're right, but it doesn't feel that way. I've spent my entire life taking care of my father when he should have been taking care of me, but I don't hate him for it. I don't even resent him. I understood him. I understood he was just too sad after my Mom died. I was sad, too.

We were sad together.

I sit up straight and grab my phone. "I have to make a phone call. I'll be right back."

I get up from Lex's lap and go out into the hallway,

scrolling through my phone until I find his name. I press down on it and bring it to my ear, praying it fucking works in this damn hospital.

It rings three times before he answers. "Uncle Jack? It's Peyton."

34

"Time After Time" // Cyndi Lauper

Two hours later, Jack and Michelle appear in the doorway, both wearing name tags of their own. I stand from the chair as Uncle Jack holds his arms out to me. I hug him, gratefully. "Thank you for coming."

He holds me tight. "I only wish you'd called us sooner."

I let go, and Michelle pulls me into her. "We would have gotten here faster, but I had to wait for my sister. She's watching the kids."

"It's fine. I'm just glad you're here now." Lex stands up behind me, and I introduce them. They smirk when I use the air quotes around the word 'husband.'

They both look at my Dad with shock and concern, and I fill them in on everything the doctors have told me so far.

Sammy went home to shower, change, and eat, so Michelle takes a seat in the green chair next to my Dad.

"I'm going to go get some coffee and food," Lex starts. "I'll grab you something, okay?" He offers.

I give him a half smile. "Yeah, thanks."

He squeezes my hand before leaving the room, and Jack sits in the blue chair, leaving me the last green one.

They exchange a glance before looking at me. "Peyton, we're so sorry," Jack starts.

I knit my brow. "About what?"

"We haven't been there for you at all over the past few years. We never should have stopped checking in. But ever since Michelle had Jackson four years ago, we've been busy, and we've kept our distance, and it's my fault. I didn't want my kids to be around that, as much as I love Harry, I didn't want him to ever see that, and I'm sorry."

I pull my knees up to my chin as I watch my father's chest rise and fall with the air being pumped into him. "It's not your fault. Harry isn't your responsibility."

Michelle reaches over and takes my hand. "He isn't yours either."

I shake my head. "Yes, he is. He's my father. Someone has to take care of him."

Jack lets out a breath. "Peyton, you're just a kid. It's not fair that all of this is put on you. Harry should be taking care of himself. He should be taking care of *you*. Not the other way around."

"I stopped being a kid a long time ago," I say.

Jack turns to face me. "You were probably too young to remember any of this, but right after your Mom died is when your Dad started drinking. At first, it was just a little, and we knew he was just dealing with the loss of his wife, so we didn't think anything of it. But then a few weeks went by, and he just kept getting worse. And one day, we went over to check on you guys, and Harry was passed out on the living room floor, and you were sitting on the couch crying because you were hungry, and he hadn't fed you. You hadn't eaten anything at all that day. So, we took you home and got you something to eat, and that's when you started staying with us.

"That was when the lies started. Your Dad wasn't always working overnights. Sometimes, it was true. But seventy-five percent of the time, he was just too drunk to take care of you. And we didn't want you to get hurt, or go to bed hungry."

I feel like I should be more shocked by this, but I'm not.

"How come you never called anyone?" Jack knits his brows together. "Like child protective services, or the police? Why was he never reported?"

"Because he loved you, Peyton, and he just lost the love of his life to cancer. I knew if you were taken away from him too, he probably would have killed himself, and I couldn't bear the thought of my best friend dying and you losing both your parents. I just couldn't do it. So instead, we'd go over there every night and see if he was drunk, or needed to work, and either way, we'd bring you over and keep you safe and fed and well-rested for school, and that was all that mattered."

"Then, you got older." Michelle cut in. "You were, what, thirteen, fourteen, and you were really good at taking care of yourself. You taught yourself how to cook, and you cleaned and did your own laundry. You grew up faster than you should have, but you were a smart, good kid. And you did okay. You started taking care of your Dad. And we understood. He was the only parent you had left, and you never gave up on him."

"But we should have kept the invitation open for you, and we didn't. And for that, we're sorry, Peyton. We never should have left you alone with this. It wasn't fair to you."

I avert my eyes because I don't want them to see me cry. I was never angry with them for leaving me alone with my Dad. I understood they had their own family, their own lives, their own problems to deal with. They didn't need to deal with my alcoholic father on top of it.

So, I shake my head. "It's okay. We did okay for a while."

Because he stopped drinking for a while, or at least, he hid it well enough to where I couldn't see it. I never saw him drink, and I never saw him drunk.

But that's the magic of a functioning alcoholic. They make sure you never see them drunk.

I'm not sure if he was drinking at work, or while I was at school, or, anywhere I couldn't see.

Not that it matters anymore. Because my Dad has officially drunk himself into a hole so deep, he may never fully recover. He'll need months of rehab, physical therapy, speech therapy, and I have to figure out a way to pay for it all because he's going to lose his job.

Lex walks back into the room with four cups of coffee and a variety of snacks from the cafeteria. I glance up at him and smile slightly in thanks.

Jack and Michelle thank him for the coffee, and Lex sets down a paper bag filled with creamers and sugars. "I wasn't sure how everyone took their coffee, so I just grabbed a bag and threw some stuff in."

Jack looks at the two of us and back at me. "Hey, why don't you guys get out of here. Go get some rest for a while. I can stay the night with Harry."

I shake my head. "No, no, I'll stay—"

But before I can finish, Jack cuts me off. "Peyton, you've done enough. Let me do this."

I want to argue with him, but I sigh and nod. "All right."

We all stand, and I hug them both goodbye, before approaching my father carefully, not to mess with any of the wires, and kiss him on the cheek. "Love you, Dad."

I can't take my eyes off of him as Lex takes my hand and we walk out of the room. I don't look away until we're out in the hall, and I'm left with this empty, hollow feeling in the pit of my stomach.

35

"Soon You'll Get Better" // Taylor Swift, feat. the Chicks

I crash at Lex's apartment that night, not wanting to go back to the house all by myself, and I have Sammy take care of Cosmo. I feel bad enough, knowing I should be home, but I can't walk into that house knowing my father may never step foot inside of it again.

I push the thought aside for now, as I look at Lex's bed, that's way too high up off the ground, and kick off my shoes and pull off my jeans.

"So, do I make a running start and just jump?"

Lex laughs and pulls out a small set of steps at the end of the bed.

Who the fuck needs stairs to get into bed?

I shake my head and step up, crawling into the bed and collapse. Lex follows behind in nothing but a pair of thin sleep pants and pulls me in close to him, spooning me. His fingers trace my hairline around my ear, tucking it behind, and I feel him maneuver even closer. "Peyton," he starts, and I can only *hmm* a reply. "Are you okay?"

"I'm fine," I say.

"I don't mean right now, I mean with everything. I haven't had a chance to ask you how you're handling it. I know this must be hard."

I close my eyes, and all I can see is my father lying in that hospital bed, an empty shell of himself.

"I think I'm handling it the way any daughter would," I admit.

He holds me tighter. "I'm here for you. Whatever you need. No matter what it is, to talk, to cry, to distract you. Just tell me what you need, and I'll give it to you."

I don't think I can possibly cry any more than I already have today because I'm exhausted, and there's nothing left in me. So, I take his arm and wrap it around me even more. "Just hold me," I say.

And he does.

~

THE NEXT MORNING, LEX PULLS UP IN FRONT OF THE HOSPITAL to drop me off. "If you need me to come and get you, or if you just want me to be here, text me. I've already talked to Sydney about everything."

"I should be going to work, Lex," I say, as I struggle with this internal fight. I'm so angry with my father for putting me in this position. Not only will I not have money to pay his medical bills, but if I keep missing work, I won't be able to pay the necessary household bills. Then the shut off notices will start rolling in. I won't even be able to buy Ramen noodles.

Lex takes my hand. "You should be with your Dad right now. You're not going to get fired. Sydney loves you. She'd never do that."

"It's not about getting fired, it's about not getting paid for all the work I'm missing," I say.

Lex kisses the back of my hand. "It's going to be okay."

I look over at him, and I want to scream because he has no idea what it's like to struggle. He has no fucking clue what any of this is like to deal with financially. His bank account has never-ending zeros, while mine is pretty damn close to zero, and he just doesn't get it. "No, it's not," I say, and I get out of the car and make my way inside the hospital.

I grab another name tag and follow the same route I took yesterday to my father's room. When I get there, Uncle Jack is sitting in one of the green chairs drinking a cup of coffee, playing on his phone.

"Hey," I say.

He looks up and puts his phone in his pocket. "Hey." He stands and hugs me.

"How was he last night?" I ask.

"The same. The nurses came in a few times and checked on him, but he has remained stable for now. There's nothing new since you left last night."

I smile and nod. "Thanks for staying with him."

"Of course. Anything you need, Michelle and I are here for you, okay?"

I give him a half smile. I'm not used to having adults I can rely on.

How sad is that?

"Look, I have to get home. I have to be at work soon."

"Of course."

"But Michelle is going to come by this afternoon. She just needed to get someone to watch the kids. We've been able to work something out between daycare, my parents, and hers, so at least one of us can be here, and one of us can still work."

I knit my brows together. "You guys really don't need to go through all the trouble—"

Uncle Jack puts a hand on my shoulder. "Yes, we do." His tone is firm, and I almost feel like I'm in trouble. "If you need anything, don't be afraid to text me."

"Okay."

"Michelle will be by later." He pulls me into his chest, giving me a very fatherly hug. "I'll see you, kid," he says and makes his way out of the room.

I sit down in the green chair and take my Dad's hand. "Hey, Daddy," I say, not entirely sure he can hear me. I'm sure he's probably dreaming about my Mom or fishing or Cosmo or maybe all of them together. "I just want you to know that I'm here. And Uncle Jack was here, too. And Aunt Michelle."

Part of me hopes I'll get a response from him—maybe he'll squeeze my hand—but nothing happens. So, I pull my knees into my chest. I watch his chest rise and fall with the breathing machine, listen to his heart rate on the monitor, relieved to know that at least he's still alive.

I slink back in the chair and stick my earbuds in my ears. When I hit the shuffle button on my playlist, it's like my phone can read my mind. Or maybe smart phones really can hear what's going on because the saddest, most accurate song starts playing in my ears, and I fight back the tears. But they win, like they always do.

And Taylor Swift has done it again.

36

"Say Something" // A Great Big World & Christina Aguilera

I spend most of the day reading and listening to music on my phone when Michelle walks in the room around four. I smile at the coffee she's carrying, and something in a Tupperware container with a fork on top.

"I brought you something to eat," she says.

I set my book and phone down on the table and take it gratefully. "Thank you."

"It's leftover lasagna from the other night. I remember when you were a kid, you used to love my lasagna."

I open the container and smile. "Oh, my god, I remember this."

She smiles. "I'm glad." She sits down next to me in the other green chair. "How's he doing?"

I swallow the bite in my mouth before I answer. "Same as yesterday," I say, my tone filled with disappointment.

"That's what Jack said." Michelle looks at my father as if she's looking into the past, as if she can see him in some distant memory in her mind. As if she can see the man he once was but no longer is.

She's quiet while I finish eating the lasagna and when I'm done, I clean my face on the paper towel she brought. "It tastes just how I remember it, too." I put the lid back on the container and smile slightly, taking a sip of coffee. "Thank you."

"You're welcome," she says. "So, how are *you* doing?"

I play with the strings of my hoodie. "I'm doing okay. I mean, as good as anyone would be doing, I guess."

She eyes me warily. "It's a tough situation."

"Yeah. I'm feeling so many things at once, I'm not sure which one I'm supposed to be feeling," I admit.

"So, *all the feels*."

I snort as I twist the string around my finger. "Yeah, pretty much."

"My kids taught me that, you know."

"Your four year old and two year old know the phrase '*all the feels*'?"

She shakes her head. "Daycare, man. Those teachers are like twenty, and teach my kids some weird shit." I chuckle and take another sip of coffee. "So, I hear you're working almost full time at the pharmacy, going to school for nursing, getting your pharmacy technician certificate, *and* dating Lex Kingston?"

I smile sheepishly and nod.

"And on top of all of those things, you're taking care of your sick father all by yourself."

"That's not entirely true. I have Sammy."

"Sammy?"

"She's my best friend, slash adopted sister. She lived with us for a while after she came out to her parents and they kicked her out. She helps me take care of Dad sometimes. Like, when I went away with Lex this weekend, and last weekend." And I can feel the guilt creeping back in, making the lasagna rise in my stomach.

But Michelle puts a hand on mine. "Peyton, don't feel bad for having a life. You're nineteen. You're supposed to be doing those things."

Then why do I always feel guilty?

Michelle leans back in the chair and sips her coffee. "You know your Mom and I were friends, right?"

"No. I mean, I knew all four of you guys were friends, but I didn't know how close you were."

"Lizzy and I were best friends for awhile back then."

It feels like a knife goes straight through my heart. I turn and look at my father. *Why didn't you tell me?*

"What has he told you about Lizzy?" She asks as she motions her head toward my Dad.

"Not much. He doesn't like to talk about her. It hurts too much. And anytime I bring her up, he starts drinking again."

Michelle blinks hard and shakes her head. "Honey, I'm sorry."

"It's not your fault."

"No, but you should know about your Mom."

"I know she was a photographer. I know she loved taking pictures, especially of me."

Michelle laughs. "She really did."

"I know she had jobs at weddings and parties and stuff."

"Your Mom wanted to remember everything. And she thought a picture could capture a memory, a single moment in time, forever. That was what she wanted."

I can picture it, too. From all of the pictures I have of my mother, I can imagine her as clear as day, holding a camera in her hands and snapping photos of everything. Of me doing my makeup in the mirror; of my Dad cooking bacon in the kitchen; of me writing a paper for school.

Mundane, ordinary things that to ordinary people would seem meaningless, but to Liz Katz, would mean the world.

"Lizzy had so many things planned for you, Peyton. When

you turned eighteen, she wanted to bring you to Paris and Madrid and all over Europe, to every single museum and art gallery on the continent. And there are a lot of them." I smile and see it in my mind. "She wanted to take you to the Museum of Modern Art and the Metropolitan Museum of Art in New York. She didn't even know if you'd be interested in any of it. She just wanted to share that part of her life with you. Lizzy was going to take you everywhere, and take pictures of you everywhere you went together. Harry said he'd stay home and let you girls have fun together, just the two of you."

Of course, he did. Harry Katz isn't exactly a man of travel.

I didn't know my Mom was either, until now. I glance over at him again, his body completely still save for his chest rising and falling with the ventilator. I want him to wake up. I just want him to wake up and *say something*.

"What else was she like?" I ask Michelle. Now, it's all I want to know, and I can't ask my Dad.

"She was smart, and sarcastic, and had a wicked sense of humor, even after she got sick. She didn't want to be remembered as sickly and sad. Lizzy was always cracking jokes at every doctor's appointment, every chemotherapy, even at the very end. She sang to you every night, do you remember that?"

I think back, trying to remember, but I don't. "What did she sing?"

"She sang you a lot of music; the Cure, Modern English, David Bowie, Peter Gabriel, Cyndi Lauper, Tears for Fears. I mean, she was *really* big into 80's music. But I think one of her favorite songs to sing to you was *Take on Me* by Aha."

And now, I'm crying. Literally bawling my eyes out because I had no idea we shared the same taste in music, and I can't help but wonder if she would have liked Taylor Swift.

Michelle takes my hand. "Do you remember that at all?"

I shake my head. "No," I say as I pull out my phone and show her my playlist. "But I think we have a lot in common."

Michelle scrolls through my music and smiles. "Wow. You really had no idea?"

I shake my head and wipe my face and nose with a tissue.

Michelle hands me back my phone. "I'm not sure if she would share your love of *modern* pop music," she says, and I laugh. She turns and looks over at my Dad, still sedated and unconscious. "I knew your Mom for a long time, and I know this," she says as she points to my father, "is not the life she would have wanted for you.

"If Lizzy knew you stayed in Genesee Falls to take care of Harry, never went away to college, never lived your dreams because you felt like you had to stay here and take care of him, she would be livid. And not at you, but at him. For making you feel that way. For making you feel like you had no other choice. You've spent your entire life taking care of him when he should have been taking care of you, and that needs to stop."

I pull my knees into my chest and blink, letting the tears fall.

"Honey, we both know this needs to stop. You've held this burden on your shoulders for too long, and it's time to let it go. It's time for Peyton to start living for Peyton. What does Peyton want in life? What does Peyton want to do? Want to be? Want to become? Where does Peyton want to live? Who does she want to live with?"

She's asking me all of the questions I've never been able to ask myself because I knew they were never an option for me. Even if I did have answers to them, I could never go and do them because I have to stay here to take care of my Dad.

"Honey, it's time for you to live your own life. It's what your Mom wanted for you. And I know it's what your Dad wants, too. He doesn't want to be the thing standing in the way of your dreams. No matter how sick he may be."

I look at her. "I wouldn't even know where to start," I admit.

She wraps an arm around my shoulder. "That's okay. You've got time to think about it."

Up until I met Lex, I wasn't really living. I'd spent my entire life just existing. Just going through the motions, doing what I thought I had to do to survive.

Keeping my father alive was one of those things.

Michelle looks over at me. "Hey, why don't you get out of here? Go see Lex or Sammy for a bit. I've got this."

"Are you sure?" She eyes me, and I put my hands up defensively. "Okay, I'm going." I get up, kiss my father on the forehead and whisper, "I love you, Dad." And I make my way out of the hospital.

I pull out my phone and text Lex, *'Can you come pick me up?'*

'Of course. Be there as soon as I can,' he replies.

37

"Wonderwall" (Acoustic Version) // Katy McAllister (Cover)

I'm waiting outside on a bench when I see Lex's car pull into the loop. I get in and he hands me a plastic bag. "It's from Sammy. She stopped by your house and grabbed you some more clothes. I figured you probably didn't pack enough to last you, and I wasn't sure if you wanted to go home or if you still wanted to stay with me."

I smile, setting the bag in between my feet on the floor and take his face in my hands. "Thank you," and I kiss him.

I should go home, but I need to stay close to my Dad.

I pull away and take my phone out of my purse to text Sammy, *'You are the best best friend in the entire universe. I love you so much, Thank you.'*

Lex makes his way out of the loop, and we head toward his apartment.

"How's your Dad?" He asks.

"Same as yesterday."

He takes my hand and laces our fingers together. "He's going to be okay, Peyton."

I want to believe him, but I don't.

Sammy replies, '*Love you, too. I've got everything covered here. Cosmo is taken care of, just take care of Dad. Let me know if you need anything else.*'

When we get to his apartment, I smell like hospital disinfectant, and all I want to do is scrub it off. I carry the bag into Lex's bedroom and go through the clothes in my suitcase to see if I have anything left that's clean, but find nothing.

"I do have a washing machine if you need to do laundry. And a dryer."

I look at him. "Wow. Mr. Fancy McBig Bucks sure knows how to win a girls heart."

He chuckles as I stand and toss a pair of black yoga pants, clean underwear, and a t-shirt onto his bed from the bag Sammy packed for me. He takes my chin in his fingers. "It's nice to see you still have a sense of humor."

I shake my head. "It's more like a defense mechanism. I took one of those *Buzzfeed* quizzes on my phone and I got '*You are Chandler from Friends!*' all three times."

He snorts. "Are you hungry?"

"Not really. Michelle brought me some lasagna. But I'm going to take a shower if that's okay."

"Of course," he says. "I'll leave you to it."

"Thanks."

I carry my clothes into the bathroom and set them on the counter next to the sink. This bathroom is so huge, it's almost the size of my bedroom at home. I turn on the shower to get the water hot and undress.

Once I get in and close the glass door, I look around and notice there are three different shower heads.

Who the hell needs three fucking shower heads?

I stick my head under the hot water and let it rinse away

the day. I stand there for a long time, allowing Michelle's words replay in my mind over and over again.

What does Peyton want in life?

This isn't the life your Mom wanted for you.

Who does Peyton want to be?

I finally collapse onto the floor, sobbing into my hands. Because I don't know what I want. The idea of me having a life outside of Harry Katz was never an option for me, so I never gave it any thought.

And how am I supposed to do it now?

My Dad is going to need more help than ever. I can't just abandon him.

But what if I had help? What if Jack and Michelle really do stick around and help me so I'm not in this alone?

I know Lex would help me if I asked him to. Lex would do anything for me, even if that meant paying a nurse to be with my Dad twenty-four hours a day. But I can't ask him for that. It's too much. And I would never be able to live with that guilt.

I look down at my legs, at the scars on my thighs, and trace over them with my fingers. I can't help but wonder what my Mom would have done, if she'd been alive when Steve assaulted me?

I wonder if my Mom had been alive, would I have even dated Steve White at all?

That prick took so much away from me. He took so much of my time and energy and joy, and Lex has given it all back.

I continue to trace the scars with my fingers. I close my eyes, pretending it's Lex touching them, that it's his fingers tracing over the thick, jagged lines.

My stomach jolts and my eyes fly open. I take a breath, and do it again. I picture Lex's fingers moving along them, and my stomach pangs and my heart skips a beat. But I keep picturing it. Over and over and over again, and I don't stop until the panic stops. Until my breathing evens. Until my heart slows. Until I'm not afraid anymore.

Because Lex would never hurt me. He's proven that time and time again.

It takes me a while to get there. I remain in the shower until the water goes cold.

I think back to what Michelle asked me. *"What does Peyton want?"*

And all I can think is *Lex.*

38

"Such Great Heights" // Iron & Wine (Cover)

I stare at myself in the bathroom mirror. I'm wearing the comfortable clothes Sammy picked out for me, my hair is still wet from the shower, and I realize I desperately need a haircut. It's hanging far passed my elbows now, but once it dries, the natural wave will make it look shorter.

I lift up my shirt a little and look at my stomach, at my belly button, at my waistline, at parts of me I've never really thought much about. I've never had low self-esteem, but I never thought I was better looking than anyone else. I always thought of myself as a regular girl, just as pretty as the next. But I guess it's different when you're with a guy. You start to question yourself, even if it's just a little. Does he think I'm pretty? Or does he think she's prettier?

I don't know if that's weird or if we all get a little insecure sometimes.

And it's not like Lex hasn't already seen me naked.

I know what I want, even if every part of me is made out of

butterflies. I'm ready to take control of my body back. And I have never wanted anything more than I want Lex.

He walks into the bedroom and smiles at me. He's still in his work uniform, and he pulls off his light blue button-down. "You feel better now?" He asks.

I don't even wait. I walk up to him and kiss him, wrapping my arms around his neck.

He smiles and pulls away. "What's up?" I grab my shirt by the hem and pull it over my head, tossing it on the floor. He looks at me, his expression changed from amused to confused. "Peyton?"

This time I jump into his arms, wrapping myself around him, and he catches me, falling backward onto the bed.

I kiss him, deeply, opening for him, letting his tongue brush against mine. He spins and sets me down on the bed, breaking the kiss. "What's going on?"

I slide back on the bed a bit, giving him room to join me. I signal him with my finger, and he crawls up onto the bed, but he doesn't hover above me. Instead, he kneels next to me, waiting for me to answer him.

So, I sit up straight, placing my hand on his cheek. "I love you. I love you so fucking much that I didn't even know it was possible to love another person like this. And maybe you could say that I had an epiphany, or something akin to one. But today, I realized what *I* want. And I want you."

And my mouth is on his.

He opens for me, letting my tongue brush against his, but I can tell he's hesitating. I pull back and eye him, questioningly. "Are you sure you're not just upset about everything?" He asks.

"No. I feel like I finally see things clearly. I know what I want in my life. And it's you. It's been you since the day we met, and I don't want to miss another second of it."

This is something more—a decision to take control and make my body my own again. For the first time in a year, *I'm* calling the shots, and it feels incredible. No anxiety, no panic attacks, no worries about flashbacks. I am entirely focused on Lex and me and us together.

Lex brushes my hair behind my ear and looks at me with those beautiful blue-gray eyes and says, "Are you sure?"

"I've never been more sure about anything."

He kisses me gently. "If you get scared—"

"I'll say it. I promise."

But I know I won't need to.

He looks down at my legs and says. "What about—"

"It's okay," I start and slide my yoga pants off. "I'm not afraid of you touching them anymore." His eyes go wide as he looks down at my scars and back up at my face. "It's okay," I say. "Go ahead."

He hesitates at first, so I take his hand and guide his fingers slowly up my leg until he reaches them, and I don't panic. My stomach doesn't even flinch. He's watching my face the entire time, and he smiles. "Wow. That's some serious growth."

I smile back. "I know."

I let go and allow his hands to explore my body, let him roam anywhere he wants to. They slide up to my back as he unclasps my bra and slides it down my arms, letting it fall somewhere off the bed.

He pushes me onto my back and hovers above me, then leans down, making a trail of kisses from my earlobe, down my neck, over my breasts. He takes my nipple in his mouth as he trails down my abdomen until he reaches my underwear. He slides a finger under the hem and pulls and off them one swift movement. He leans back on his knees, taking me in.

I sit up and unbutton his pants, and I'm starting to think he's more nervous about this than I am.

He puts his hands on mine. "We don't have to rush. We can still go slow."

And I look up at him. "I think we've taken things slow enough."

He bites his lip and lets me pull down his pants, and he stands for a second to get them off. I can see how hard he is through his boxers. I reach out to take them off, but he pushes me back down onto the bed and kisses me everywhere his lips want to touch. He slides his hands down my torso until they reach my center, and his fingers slide inside, his thumb grazing that spot between my thighs, and I gasp at the contact.

And as amazing as his fingers feel inside of me, it's not what I want. I want to feel *him* inside of me.

"Lex," I say, gripping his shoulders, my tone practically begging, but he only increases his speed. His lips moving to my breasts, taking one in his mouth. My moans only make him go faster and faster until I feel the heat building in my core, and pleasure explodes throughout as release finds me. Lex slows his fingers until I've come down completely. He slides his fingers out of me and moves his hands up my sides.

Lex comes back up to kiss me, sweat gleaming on my face, my cheeks red with heat as he looks down on me one last time. "Are you sure?"

I look at him reassuringly, and push his boxers down. His forehead rests on mine as kicks them all the way off. He remains hovering above me, and my insides are starting to dance, and my breathing becomes a bit uneven. I grip his biceps with unsteady fingers and he kisses me so tenderly that I think I might melt into his bed.

Lex takes an uneven breath and pushes my trembling legs apart with his knees. "Just say the word."

I nod.

My legs continue to shake and my stomach clenches as he starts to slide inside. It's okay at first, and I try to stay relaxed. But Lex pushes himself deeper inside of me, and I make a noise that sounds more like a whimper than anything else. I blink hard, and my fingernails dig into his back.

He stops moving. "Are you okay?"

I open my eyes, and smile. "I'm fine."

Lex rests his forehead on mine as he starts to move again. He's so gentle and slow, I honestly have no idea how he's able to compose himself after weeks of constant teasing.

The more he moves inside me, the better it begins to feel. Lex buries his face in my neck and his hand grip the sheets. I turn and nip on his ear lobe. He pulls back and looks down at me, smiles on both of our faces. He kisses me, and one hand moves to cup my breast.

My legs are no longer trembling, but are wrapped around him. We start to move together, and not once, not even for a second, do I even consider saying the safe word.

Because I don't need it anymore.

With each thrust, I can't help but wonder why I was so afraid of this in the first place?

He kisses me long and hard, moving a little bit faster, pushing a little deeper, and every nerve in my body has come alive, and they're all focusing on one thing. Where Lex and I are connected, and all I can think is how amazing this feels and how I wish we could stay like this forever.

But I sense he's starting to lose control. "Oh, fuck."

He crushes me into the bed, but I don't mind. His lips meet that spot between my neck and shoulder blade. His hand roams down to my hip, and he grips it tight, and with one final loud moan, he comes undone, collapsing on top of me.

We lie there, trying to catch our breaths. As soon as he composes himself, he looks up at me. "Are you okay?"

I smile and shake my head. "I'm fine," I kiss him gently, running my fingers through his messy hair.

"I love you," he says.

I smile. "I know."

His lips quirk into a smile, and he carefully slides out and rolls next to me, but pulls me into his arms, kissing my shoulder. "You're sure I didn't hurt you?"

I shake my head. "You worry too much."

And he laughs as he turns my head to face him, and crushes his lips to mine.

~

AFTERWARD, WE SHOWER TOGETHER AND LET THE WATER WASH off the stress and tension of the past few days. We get back into bed and fall asleep. A few hours wrapped in each other's arms, with nothing on my mind but the sound of Lex's heartbeat and the way his skin feels against mine.

And for the first time in what feels like forever, I am truly happy.

39

"I Grieve" // Peter Gabriel

I awake a few hours later, Lex is still asleep next to me. I get up and put my clothes back on, trying to be as quiet as I can so I don't wake him. A smile still plastered across my face.

I lie on the bed and watch Lex sleep for a while, thinking about my future. Do I want to stay in Genesee Falls? Or even here in Octavia? Do I want to go back to *Genesee Valley Community College*? Do I really want to be a nurse? The main reason I picked nursing as a major was so I could be more helpful to my Dad when he got sick, so I knew what to do if something like this ever happened—it just happened too soon.

I get up and go over to the dresser where my purse is and pull out my phone.

I freeze.

I have eight missed calls from Michelle and Jack. And the hospital.

I call Michelle back, and she answers on the first ring. "Peyton, you need to get back down here, now."

~

Everything is going by in slow motion. Lex parks in the emergency parking lot, and we run. We run passed the woman at the front desk, and to the elevators. As soon as the doors open on the fourth floor, I run toward my father's room. But before I can get inside, I see Uncle Jack, Michelle, and Sammy standing outside in the hallway, looking in. Lex never lets go of my hand as I run to them.

Michelle is crying in Jack's arms, and Sammy's fingers are running through her turquoise hair.

I reach Sammy's side and turn to look in my father's room, and my stomach drops.

Inside, there are doctors and nurses, and the machine that monitors my father's heart has flatlined, the sound growing louder and louder in my ears as the rest of the world fades out around me.

I blink hard and breathe.

When I open my eyes again, the world comes back into focus. I watch as the doctor picks up the defibrillators and place them on his chest. "Clear!"

Shock.

No response.

"Clear!"

Shock.

Still nothing.

And I'm just standing there, watching the doctor shock him over and over and over again, unable to do anything to fix this. My fingers touch my lips as if they could somehow steady them, but my hands are shaking too hard. My entire body trembles as I watch my worst fear come true.

The doctor keeps trying to revive my father as Lex holds me in his arms, his lips whispering distorted words in my ear.

When nurse Kate eyes the doctor with a look I can't even

name, and give him a nod so small I'm surprised he even saw it, the doctor stops and sets the defibrillators down.

Wait, what are you doing?

He looks up at the clock on the wall, and calls time of death.

"What?"

No. No, they can't!

And a scream escapes me so loud, everyone turns and stares. Tears stream down my face as I try to run to him, but Lex holds me back, gripping me around my waist. I'm kicking and screaming and squirming, trying to break free of his grasp, but his hold is firm.

And I know I'm saying words, but I don't know what I'm saying.

Then Sammy's arms are around me as she cries with me.

My father just died.

My father just died.

The next thing I know, my knees hit the cold white tiles of the hospital floor. My stomach clenches so hard, I think I might throw up. Lex is on one side of me, and Sammy is on the other, and I look up at my father's body, lying empty and lifeless on the hospital bed.

Tears cloud my vision as a man in a white coat comes out to speak to us, but I can't hear a word he says. Michelle lets go of Jack and gets down on the floor with me, wrapping me in her arms as we all cry together.

I don't know how long I'm down there. I don't know how long they all hold me.

And I don't know what I want anymore.

What am I going to do now?

40

"Hold On" // Sarah McLachlan

The next few days go by in a blur. I spend my time lying in Lex's bed, crying, or sleeping. But mostly crying.

And I can't go home.

I don't even care about work anymore.

Because what does any of it matter? I was doing all of it for my Dad. Working all those hours, getting my pharmacy technician certificate to make more money, becoming a nurse. Everything I've ever done in my life has been for my Dad.

So, what am I supposed to do with my life now?

Sammy shows up at Lex's apartment and crawls into the bed with me, holding me as I cry into my pillow. I don't even know what day it is.

"Why is this bed so high up off the floor?" She asks, and I know she's trying to make a dumb joke to make me feel better, but I don't say anything.

"You should see the store now. The remodel is finished, and we've got another new employee who works the back registers. Sydney is looking to hire an assistant supervisor, but I think she might be promoting one of us. I heard a rumor, from Lex, that she's considering me. Which would be awesome because it's full time and it comes with benefits."

I want to be happy for her. I want to turn around and hug her and jump up and down on this ridiculous bed, but I just don't care.

So, instead, she keeps talking to me, and I listen even though I don't respond.

Everyone has a shift. I'm never left alone in the apartment at any given time, even though all I want is to be left the fuck alone.

When Lex is at work, Michelle comes by, then Jack, then Sammy, and they all take turns babysitting me like I'm a fucking four-year-old.

Michelle tries to get me to eat, every single goddamn day, but I'm not hungry. I'm not thirsty.

I'm not anything. *Am I even alive?*

After a few days pass, Lex forces me to drink some water. "Peyton, you're going to get dehydrated, then I'm going to bring you to the hospital, and they'll give you an IV and put a goddamn tube in your stomach. So, drink this, or I'm carrying you downstairs myself."

I take the bottle and sit up for the first time, and my head spins from the sudden movement. But I drink it.

It actually tastes good and makes my throat feel better from all the crying.

Lex sits down on the bed next to me and sighs. "I know this is hard for you. But you can't just give up. Your Dad wouldn't want that. Neither of your parents would."

I slam the bottle down on the nightstand and turn my back to him.

Fuck him. He doesn't know what my parents would have wanted.

I fall on to the bed and I sob into the pillows.

~

JACK, MICHELLE, AND LEX GOT TOGETHER TO ARRANGE A service for my father on Friday. I didn't ask them to, they just did it. Because they knew I couldn't. Michelle and Sammy went shopping together to buy me a dress to wear, and by the time Friday rolls around, I'm dreading getting out of this bed.

They walk into the bedroom and throw open the curtains. Sammy sets the bag down on the bed, and Michelle turns to me. "It's time to get up now, Peyton."

I blink away the bright sun and try to cover my eyes with my hands, but Michelle grabs my arms and pulls me up. "Let's get you in the shower."

I haven't showered in four days, and I smell ripe.

Sammy comes over and helps Michelle pull my shirt off and makes a face. "Damn girl, when was the last time you changed?"

I think back. "Monday." *The day my Dad died.*

She lets out a breath. "You can tell. Come on, we need to get you cleaned up."

The tears form in my eyes again. "I don't think I can do this."

Michelle looks me straight in the eyes. "I know, sweetheart. But you have to. We *all* have to do this." She gently takes my face in her hands. "I know you're suffering the most from this, Peyton, but you're not the only one who lost Harry."

I blink and let the tears fall, because I know she's right. Uncle Jack and Harry had been best friends since they were six years old.

But he was my father.

I look up at Sammy, and I'm trying to figure out how she's able to keep it all together because he was her father, too. Not biologically, but he was the one who took her in when her own parents disowned her. He accepted her, loved her, gave her a sister who would do anything for her...

And now I realize she's keeping it together for me.

They have to half carry me into the bathroom because I'm so weak, I can hardly stand. Michelle turns on the water, and Sammy strips down to underwear and gets in with me so I don't fall.

I hold on to her shoulders as she washes my hair, and she smiles at me. "What?"

Her smile is cunning. "Lex is a very lucky man."

I stare at her blankly for a minute, then I burst out laughing.

For the first time in a week, I actually fucking laugh.

Michelle stayed in the bathroom with us, and I can hear her laughing with me. Next thing I know, Sammy starts laughing, too. "Oh, my god, Sammy."

And then I start to cry.

Not because I'm sad, but because I'm so grateful to have a best friend willing to get in the shower with me when I'm too weak to do it by myself, and make a dumb ass joke about it. "Thank you," I say, and I hug her.

"You're getting shampoo in my eyes."

"Shit, sorry," I say and hand her a washcloth.

But she just laughs and wipes off her face. She takes down one of the shower heads and rinses my hair.

"How did you figure that out?"

"Lex showed me how to use this crazy-ass shower. I mean, who the fuck needs three shower heads?"

"Right?" I reply.

Sammy lets me clean myself, but keeps me balanced so I don't fall over, and we get out. Michelle hands us each a towel and then wraps my hair up in a third.

They show me the dress they picked out for the service. It's a simple black, knee-length skirt with a v-neckline. It's your basic funeral attire, nothing fancy about it.

Michelle closes the bedroom door as soon as we hear male voices out in the living room. Lex and Uncle Jack must be out there.

Michelle smiles at me. "Jack likes him," she says.

My lip curls up the tiniest bit. "Really?"

"Yeah, they've been talking a lot while you've been out of commission."

I shake my head, and my lips pull back just a little more. "Dad liked him, too, I think. I mean, he didn't really say much. He was just like, 'you kids have fun.'"

Michelle chuckles. "That sounds like something Harry would say."

I pull on the memory in my mind—the time when Lex and my Dad first officially met, and my Dad just stood there like, "*Okay.*"

A total Harry Katz move.

Once I get the dress on, Michelle zips me up and pulls the towel out of my hair. I look at myself in the mirror above Lex's dresser, and I look hollow. Like all the life has been drained out of me, and all that's left is an empty shell of who I used to be.

I sit down on a stool and let Michelle and Sammy brush out my hair. I'm not really paying attention to what they're doing when there's a knock on the door.

"You may enter," Michelle says.

Lex pokes his head inside, and when he sees me, he smiles. "Well, look at that. Peyton Katz is finally back."

A part of me wants to respond with some snarky comment, and the rest of me wants to tell him to fuck off and crawl back into bed. So, I don't say anything. I just stare at my hands.

He holds out a cup to me, and I take it, scowling at its contents.

"It's a smoothie. It's got a lot of stuff in it, but I promise it tastes like strawberries."

"It's green," I say as I eye him.

"Just try it." So, I do. And he's right. It does taste like strawberries. "Drink it. It will give you energy today." I finish the smoothie and give him back the cup. "See? That wasn't so hard."

Michelle and Sammy finish my hair and slide over a pair of black flats for me to slip on.

"You guys ready?" Lex asks.

Michelle and Sammy nod and I stand, knowing I'll never be ready for this.

~

THE GENESEE FALLS FUNERAL HOME IS A TINY PLACE IN THE center of town, just down the street from the pharmacy. As we walk inside, I see a picture of my father from a few years ago, before he got sick, sitting on the porch next to Cosmo. Next to that is the urn with his ashes.

Cremation is way cheaper than a burial, so that's the road we took. It was the same with my mother. And that was the last time I was in this place.

A few days ago, when I was able to temporarily think straight, Lex sat down next to me on the bed and explained what had happened. "Your Dad suffered from cardiac arrest because there wasn't enough blood flow to his vital organs due to the stroke, and one of those organs was his heart."

I lay on the bed, thinking about how the human body works, and all I could think was, *this happened to my father just because he couldn't stop drinking?*

Lex closes the pharmacy Friday morning, because everyone in town knows who died.

Almost everyone from the pharmacy shows up, a bunch of

people from the factory my father was friends with, and even some people who only talked to him once or twice.

Cosmo sits next to me on the floor, and I'm honestly surprised they even let a dog in the funeral home. He keeps looking up at me and whimpering. Every time someone walks in the door, he perks up, expecting my father to walk in and my heart breaks. How does a dog understand the death of their human? It takes us a while, but between Sammy, Jack, and myself, we get Cosmo to lie down at my feet and stay there.

The service is short. Uncle Jack gets up and gives the eulogy for my Dad, even though I should be the one up there, but I'm just not ready.

"Harry Katz was a good man, a devoted husband to his late wife, Lizzy, and a loving father to his daughter, Peyton. He was also my best friend."

Tears swell in my eyes as he speaks, and just being here again, I get a flash of a memory of me sitting on my father's lap as my mother's picture sits up there next to her urn.

Jack's voice fades out of focus as he tells a story about the two of them as kids, and I sit here and realize for the first time that I don't have parents anymore.

I'm alone in the world, with nothing but a mound of debt and a dog I can't even take care of.

Lex takes my hand as he sees the tears stream down my face. And all I want to do is crawl back into bed and sleep for another week.

WHEN THE SERVICE IS OVER, THE FUNERAL DIRECTOR TRIES TO hand me the urn. I just stare at him. *What the hell am I supposed to do with that?*

Michelle comes up next to me and takes it. "I've got it." I let out a shaky, but grateful, breath. "Okay, let's get you home."

My eyes go wide as I look at them. "No. I can't. I can't go back to the house."

Jack and Michelle exchange a look. "Okay, honey. You go back to the apartment with Lex. We'll get Cosmo home."

But Sammy steps in. "I've got him," she says as she bends down and scratches him behind the ears. "We've become good friends lately, huh, buddy?"

"Thank you, guys," I say. "For everything. For doing this. Thank you."

I hug them goodbye, and Lex and I head back to Octavia. As I sit in the car, staring blankly out of the window, he takes my hand. "Are you doing okay?"

I think for a second, and answer him honestly. "No, not really."

"You will be."

And I find it very hard to believe.

WHEN WE GET BACK TO HIS APARTMENT, I GO RIGHT INTO THE bathroom and tear off my dress, ripping it in the process. I don't mean to, but I'm just so fucking angry.

Lex runs into the bathroom after me and watches me as I throw it across the room. I start picking up anything I can find, and throw it as hard as I can; a toothbrush, a bar of soap, my hairbrush. He walks in the bathroom and grabs my arms and holds them down, shushing me and pulls me into his chest as I cry. He lifts me into his arms and carries me to the bed, and I grab a fist full of blankets wanting to rip them apart. But Lex lies next to me, wrapping me tightly in his arms, and lets me cry until there's nothing left.

41

"Be Still" // The Fray

A few days later, I'm lying on the bed, staring at the perfectly painted ceiling, wondering how whoever painted this was able to do it without making a single mistake, when I feel a dip in the bed. I look to my left and see Lex sitting on the edge. I try to give him a smile as he lies down next to me, but my lips feel frozen, immovable, as if I'll never be able to smile again.

"Hey," he starts. "How was your day?"

"Fine." I'm getting used to lying about how I'm feeling these days because it's a lot easier than having to explain to everyone that every day sucks. I keep forgetting that my father is gone.

My father is gone.

"Michelle said you broke your phone?"

I growl as I eye it on the nightstand and pick it up. "It's not broken. I just cracked the screen." I hold it in my hands. The lock screen is a picture of Sammy and me goofing around in the break room at *Kingston's*—she's sticking out her tongue, I'm

337

flipping off the camera. Lex holds out his hand, and I give it to him.

He slides it unlocked and plays with it a bit. "You *shattered* the screen. You're lucky the touch sensor still works."

I fold my arms across my chest. "It doesn't matter. It's just a phone."

"You want to tell me what happened?"

"Not really," I admit.

Lex lets out a breath and hands me my phone back. "You tried to call him."

Tears sting my eyes as I take the phone and toss it on the bed. "I said I didn't want to talk about it."

"I know. But I do. Because I did the same thing when my Mom died."

I blink hard and turn away from him. "You broke your phone?"

"No, I tried to call her because I forgot for a minute that she was gone and I couldn't call her anymore."

"Oh." My voice is quiet and hoarse, and I'm fighting the pang in my stomach.

"You were only five when your Mom died, so you probably don't remember it the same. It didn't feel as strongly as this does."

I shake my head, my fingers touch my quivering mouth as if they could steady my lips. "I only remember bits and pieces. I remember feeling sad. My Dad was... not just sad, but *devastated*. He was a mess after she died, and I was just a spectator. I don't even remember him comforting me. I remember Michelle hugging me and picking me up, and Uncle Jack and Dad were in the living room, but I don't know what they were saying."

Lex turns onto his side and slides his hand over mine. "My mother has been gone for half of my life, and I still grieve for her." I eye him with a furrowed brow. "Everyone grieves differently, but it never truly goes away. It gets better over time, it gets easier. Every day is one step in that direction, but you have to let yourself heal. You have to let yourself grieve. You have to let yourself feel. And in time, things will get easier.

"You'll have good days when you'll think of your Dad, and the memories will make you happy. And then you'll have bad days when you'll miss him, and it hurts. Or you're angry at him for leaving you, and it'll hurt even more. I wish I could promise you that in exactly five months, two weeks, six days, fourteen hours, and twelve minutes, you will be completely healed and no longer in any pain. But it doesn't work like that. Losing people we love—especially a parent—is one of the hardest things we have to live through. But it's what we do. We need to keep on living. Otherwise, what the hell are we even here for?"

My cheeks are wet as I blink away more tears. I turn to Lex and bury my face in his chest. He takes me in his arms, kisses my head, my face, anywhere his lips can reach, just to comfort me, and lets me cry into him.

"I didn't feel this bad when my Mom died. I didn't feel so lost."

"You were only five, Peyton. And you still had your Dad."

Now I have no one.

"What am I going to do? My whole life was Harry Katz. Every part of me. Everything I did, my whole existence was for him. I don't know who I am without him."

Lex pulls me in closer, wrapping his arm around my back. "I don't believe that's true."

"But it is! Everything I've ever done in my life has been for him! I majored in nursing so I could help him! So I could be *his* nurse when he needed one! I never moved out of the house, never went away to school so I could be there for him. I could have left, you know!" Lex doesn't interrupt my diatribe. "I could have gone to a four-year SUNY school with financial aid and student loans. It would've sucked because I would have walked out with more debt than the United States Government, but I *could* have done it. I *chose* to stay with my Dad. I stayed to keep him from drinking, to keep him alive. *And he fucking died anyway!* Everything I've done my entire life has been for nothing!"

Lex holds me tight and shushes me.

"I've been fighting for fourteen years to keep him alive, and it's all been for nothing." I pull away from Lex and wipe my face on my shirt. "And now I'm alone. I have no family left. I have no one."

Lex grabs the box of tissues from the nightstand and hands it to me. He gives me a minute to clean myself up. Then he takes my face in his hand. "Peyton, you are *not* alone. You've never been alone. You will always have me and Sammy and Michelle and Jack, and everyone at *Kingston's.* I know we're not your blood family. But I don't have any blood relatives either, except my Florida Grandma. Peyton," he pauses and takes both of my hands in his. "Sometimes, family isn't the people you're born into, it's the people you choose. *You* are my family now. And I'm not going anywhere."

"Neither am I," I look behind Lex and see Sammy standing in the doorway with bloodshot eyes and tissues in her hand. She walks around the bed and climbs up, lying down behind me, wrapping an arm around me. I squeeze my eyes shut as my body convulses.

I remember the moment in the hospital when the doctor called time of death. The moment when I actually felt my heart break. The moment my father was officially, medically, verifiably gone.

And now as I lie in this bed, squeezed in between the two people I love most in this world, the two people who are alive with beating hearts and breathing lungs and blood pumping through their veins, the two people who love me, I think maybe—just maybe—one of those pieces might be starting to heal.

∾

THE NEXT DAY, I WAKE UP FEELING HUNGRY FOR THE FIRST TIME in days. So, I get out of bed, put some clothes on, and head out of the bedroom. Lex is standing in the kitchen, drinking a cup of coffee when he looks up surprised, and smiles. "Hey."

"Hey," I say. I walk up and sit on the stool in front of the island. "You have anything to eat?"

His smile widens. "You want some eggs? I've got toast and bacon, or a bagel?"

I smile a little. "Eggs and toast sound good."

He turns to me as he pulls the carton of eggs out of the fridge. "And how would you like your eggs, milady?"

I chuckle and roll my eyes. "Scrambled, please."

I watch him cook for me, and I get up and pour myself a cup of coffee. He glances over at me as I lean against the counter. "You seem to be doing a bit better?"

"I'm hungry, so it's a start, I guess."

"How else are you feeling?"

"Well, I read somewhere that there are seven stages of grief, but I don't think I'm going through them in the right order."

"Everyone grieves differently, Peyton," he repeats part of what he said last night.

I sit back down on the stool and sip my coffee. "I know he's gone. I just don't want to believe it. That's why I'm afraid to go back to the house," I admit.

Lex puts a plate of eggs and toast in front of me and leans against the island. "You can stay here as long as you want." He pauses, and bites his lip. "But just keep in mind, the longer you wait, the harder it's going to be."

I know he's right, but avoidance is all I have right now. I pick up my fork and start to eat, fighting the urge to cry again.

All I've been doing is crying. *When is it finally going to stop?*

"Thank you for letting me stay," I say.

"You're welcome." He sets his coffee cup in the sink. "I have to get ready. Sydney needs me at the store today, but I'll only be a few hours. You're more than welcome to come if you want. You don't have to work, but if you wanted to hang out. Get out of the apartment for a little while."

The last thing I want right now is to be surrounded by people who feel sorry for me. "No, thanks," I say, but I can see the worry on his face. "I'll be fine here. I promise. Look, see? I'm out of bed. I'm dressed. I'm even eating."

He eyes me with concern, and I know what he's thinking but doesn't say. "Just promise you'll text me, or Sammy, or Michelle."

"I will. I promise."

He walks around the island and kisses the top of my head before making his way toward the bedroom.

And I sit there, pushing my eggs around with my fork, wondering where my home is now.

Where do I even belong?

42

"Welcome Home" // Joy Williams

I spend the next week at Lex's apartment, not sleeping, and trying not to cry—at least not when there are people around. I was supposed to start my summer classes this week, but I've decided that's not going to happen. I never got around to pay for them so it's not like I lost any money.

Why am I even going to Community College? Do I really want to be a pharmacy technician? Do I want to be a nurse? All of these questions keep running through my mind, and I have to make them stop. So, I distract myself.

I try to keep busy, and drive Lex insane in the process. I organize his bookshelf, his medicine cabinet, his cupboards, his closets, and when he gets home, he reaches for a glass and pulls out a plate.

"Peyton?" Lex says, leaning against the door frame.

"Yeah?"

"What are you doing?" he asks as I sit on his bedroom floor, organizing his dresser.

"Keeping busy. Organizing. I like to organize things when I can't do anything else."

"Okay. Well, thank you. That's very thoughtful. But I don't know where anything is."

"I made a sheet," I say as I stand up and grab it off of the bed.

His eyes widen. "You made a sheet?" He takes it from me and glances at it.

"Yeah, it tells you which drawer I put your pants in, and what shelf the linens are on and... yeah, I'm sorry."

He sets the sheet down on the dresser. "It's okay. But it's been a while now, and you've been washing and wearing the same four outfits."

"I thought you liked these jeans."

"I do," he says with a smirk. "But don't you think maybe it's time you went back to the house?"

I look down, avoiding his gaze. "You want me to leave."

"No, Peyton."

I tug at the hem of my shirt because I know I can't stay here forever. I have to go back. I have bills to pay and cleaning to do, and I have to go back to work. My bank account is almost empty. "No, it's fine. You're right. I need to go home. It's where I live. It's where all my stuff is. It's where my poor dog is all alone most of the time now."

Lex closes the distance between us and takes my hand. "Sammy and Jack have been taking care of Cosmo. He's fine, I promise. You can always stay here. I just think the longer you wait..." he trails off.

I blink hard and sigh, because as much as I don't want to, I know he's right. "Okay." I bend down and put the rest of his clothes away. "Let me just get my stuff together." My voice is broken and hollow, and I wonder if I'll ever sound like me again.

"We don't have to go right now. I can drop you off in the morning."

I shake my head. "No. If I stay here tonight knowing I'm going back in the morning, I won't be able to sleep."

He brushes his thumb across my cheek. "Okay."

Lex helps me pack up all my stuff from the New York trip and everything Sammy sent over, and we head down to the car.

The drive back to Genesee Falls takes longer than usual, or it feels that way. Maybe because the sense of impending doom lingers over me, and no matter how much Xanax I take, it won't go away.

I have been trying not to take it, but when Dad first died, I was taking it to help me sleep away the pain.

Dr. Young is not going to be happy about that.

I haven't told anyone, either. Not even Lex. And I hate it. I feel like I'm lying, and I fucking hate lying. Lying and hiding and sneaking is what killed my father.

When we pull into my driveway, Lex helps carry everything onto my porch, and I set my bags down next to me.

He looks at me with raised eyebrows. "Are you going in or are you sleeping on the swing?"

I look up at Lex and close the distance between us. "I think I need to do this part alone."

He shakes his head. "Peyton, no—"

"Please. I need to go in there. I need to take care of my dog. I need to figure out how I'm going to do all of this without my Dad. But I won't be able to do that if you're here," I say as tears sting in my eyes.

Lex pulls me into him, holding me tight. "I really don't want to leave you alone right now."

I inhale his musky scent, savoring it. "I have to do this, Lex. It's the only way." He kisses the top of my head, and I pull back. I touch his face, brushing my thumb along his cheek, and kiss him. "I love you, and I'm so grateful for everything you've done for me."

He kisses my forehead. "Promise you'll call me, or Sammy, or Jack or Michelle if you change your mind?"

"I promise. If I go in there and realize I can't be alone, I'll call you."

He kisses me one last time before turning away and heading down the porch steps. "You're sure—"

"Lex!"

He puts his hands up defensively and gets in his car. I watch him drive away before I turn back to the front door of the house and pull my keys out of my purse.

Well, it's now or never.

I open the screen door and slide my key into the deadbolt and turn. The lock clicks, and I turn the knob and push the door open just a jar. I grab two of my bags and nudge the door open with my elbow, and step inside.

I stand in the hallway for a second and breathe.

I set my bags on the steps going upstairs, and grab the rest of my things off the porch and repeat the process, and shut the door behind me.

I lean my back against the door. The only thing separating me from the living room now is a small wall about five feet long, where we hang our coats and keys.

So, I hang my keys on the old brass hook and take it one step at a time.

Tears stream down my face because there is still a tiny ball of hope in the pit of my stomach that I'm going to walk into the living room, and he's going to be sitting in his recliner with Cosmo lying next to him, watching fishing shows on television. But just as I round the corner, I look up, and all I see is Cosmo lying in Dad's recliner, alone.

I fall to my knees and let the tears fall with me. Cosmo jumps down from the chair and whimpers, licking the tears from my face, and I look up at my poor dog and say, "I'm sorry, Buddy. But he's gone. And he's not coming back."

Being back in this house makes it even more real. My father will never sit in this room again. He will never pet our dog again. He will never watch his shows again. He will never hug me again. He will never ask me how my day was again. He will never get annoyed at me for taking care of him again. He will never tell me he loves me again. He will never drink bourbon again.

And I have to figure out how to live without him.

I SIT IN THE RECLINER FOR A WHILE WITH COSMO, CURLED UP IN a ball with my Dad's red checkered fleece blanket he always used on cold nights. It smells like him, and every time I smell it, I get a flash of him. A memory of a time when things were different.

All of the things Jack and Michelle told me in the hospital were true, but those aren't *my* memories of my father. I remember the time we sat here in this chair and watched *The Goonies* and ate Cookie Dough ice cream for dinner. I remember the time we built a fort in the living room out of pillows and blankets. We got flashlights and gathered all of my favorite books and he read them with me. I remember my eighth birthday when we baked a three-layer chocolate cake together, and he let me put on as much pink frosting as I wanted.

It was the first time I'd ever cooked.

My father was a broken man, but I know he loved me.

I curl closer to Cosmo and close my eyes until sleep takes me.

43

"Daughters" // John Mayer

I awake to someone on top of me, hugging both Cosmo and me in the chair. I blink and look at them. "Sammy?"

"Hey," she says. "You're home."

"Lex convinced me it was time." I look out and see it's morning. "Shit, what time is it?"

"Eight-thirty."

"Damn, I must have slept here all night," I say as she gets up, and I try to move, but my neck and back and legs are stiff from being in an awkward position all night.

"I'm glad you're home," Sammy says.

I rub my neck with my left hand. "Yeah, well, I couldn't run away forever."

Sammy's holding a stack of envelopes and tosses them on the coffee table in front of the couch. "I got your mail."

"Thanks," I say as I stare at the pile. I look down, and I see FINAL NOTICE written in big red letters.

Great.

I push through the stack and see a bill from the hospital. I pick it up, and dread fills my insides. "So, how much do you think this is going to be?"

Sammy eyes me sympathetically. "Well, at least now you can start a *Go Fund Me* page."

I rip open the bill. I take a deep breath as I pull it out and unfold the letter.

My eyes furrow as I look down at the outstanding balance.

It says *zero*. I stand from the chair and shake my head. "Uh, what the fuck?"

"What is it? Is it that bad?" She asks, concerned.

I show her the bill, that looks more like a receipt, and she looks up at me, confused. "How is that even possible?"

"This must be an error with the billing department. Those stupid asshats," I say as I reach inside my purse, pull out my phone and dial the number on the upper right corner. "Yes, hi, I'm calling about an invoice I just received. I think there's an error because it says the outstanding balance is zero, but that's impossible. Is there any way you can check on that for me please?"

I hear the door open, and I see Lex walk inside. He looks over at me and smiles, and I hold up a finger and mouth, *'Just a sec.'*

He nods and waits with his hands in his pockets as Sammy sits down on the couch.

"Yeah, the patient's name is Harry Katz. The account number is 10892872."

I notice Sammy and Lex exchange a look, but the woman on the phone is still speaking.

"What do you mean the account has been paid in full? That bill was over one hundred thousand dollars. That's not—"

And then I look at Lex, and he looks at me with a sheepish smile.

I stare at him in disbelief.

The woman on the phone keeps talking, but I drop my phone—literally, *drop* my phone—and look at Lex. "You paid his medical bills?" I breathe.

Lex shrugs. "Yeah."

My entire body is shaking. "Why? I didn't ask you to do that, Lex. Why would you do that?"

He approaches me, but I put my hands up, telling him to keep his distance. "I just wanted to help you."

Guilt consumes me. "I can't believe you did this without even asking me."

"Peyton, please."

"No, this is not okay. Just because you have all the money in the world and have *never* known what it's like to struggle doesn't mean you can just go around paying peoples bills without their permission." It sounds stupid the moment it comes out of my mouth, but it's not right. It's not fair. Lex stares at me with furrowed brows. Tears swell in my eyes. "You will never understand, Lex. You've had everything handed to you on a silver platter! You've never had to work for anything! You don't even fucking work at *Kingston's*! It's not a paycheck to you. It's not how you survive on a weekly basis. It's just a way to prove to your Daddy you're an adult now and can handle a *real* business."

"Peyton," Both Lex and Sammy say at the same time.

"And who the fuck has over a hundred grand just lying around like pocket change? What normal person has the ability to do what you did? No one, Lex! That's who!"

My hands fly over my face, and I wipe the tears away. Lex is just standing there, his hands in his pockets, staring at me like I've just ripped his heart out with my bare hands.

"I think you should go," I say, and I head toward the kitchen.

Sammy stands and grabs my arm. "He was just trying to help you."

I pull my arm free and shake my head. "He should have asked me first," I say and walk away.

I lean against the kitchen sink, and can't control the tears. Part of me believes I shouldn't be mad at him for this, but how can I not be? This is too much. And I can never pay him back.

How could he do this?

I hear him and Sammy talking out in the hallway, but I can't make out the words. Then the door closes.

Sammy appears by my side and puts a hand on my shoulder. "Hey," she says, sympathetically. "You okay?"

"He didn't even ask me," I say as the tears stream down my face.

She wraps her arms around me. "If he had, would you've let him?"

"Of course, not! It was over one hundred thousand dollars!"

"That's probably why he did it. All he wanted to do was help you. He loves you."

"I can't pay him back!"

"I don't think he wants you to. You're focusing on the wrong thing. I get it. Both of us grew up poor and still are, but it's not about the money, it's the gesture. Lex would do anything for you, no matter the cost, because he loves you."

"But I don't want his money."

"You're in a relationship with a multimillionaire, Peyton. It's kind of a package deal."

Goddamn it, why are you always fucking right, Samantha Clarke?

Sammy hugs me for a long time until I've calmed down and then steps back, holding me by my shoulders. "So, what did you have planned for the day? Before Mr. Big Bucks decided to shower you with money?"

I ignore her quip for the time being. "I have to go to the bank and get my father's money out so I can pay bills and nothing gets shut off. I have his death certificate in my bags somewhere. I should probably unpack all my shit. Shower, put some clean clothes on, start acting like a person again."

"Well, one step at a time, okay?"

"Yeah, one step at a time."

~

SAMMY IS OFF WORK TODAY, AND I'M GRATEFUL. JUST HAVING her with me to do all of these things makes it easier.

And I'm lucky my father was lazy and had all of his accounts through the same bank. His savings, his mortgage, his car, his credit card.

When we walk inside, I show them his death certificate, and they explain how the process works. Luckily, I'm already listed as his beneficiary, so making the transfer isn't difficult.

When I get home, I have money in my account again, so I get right on my computer and pay the bills that have shut off notices and past due dates.

Sammy is sitting on the couch, flipping through the cable channels, when someone rings the doorbell, making Cosmo growl and bark.

"Cosmo, relax," I say as I set my laptop down on the coffee table and get up to answer the door.

An older man in a gray suit and tie stands before me with a briefcase. "Hello. Can I help you?" I ask.

"Hi! Are you Peyton Katz?"

I knit my brows, thinking he's about to serve me court papers. "Yes," I say, but it sounds more like a question.

"Then, yes, you can help me. My name is John Anderson, I'm a lawyer with ACore Electric."

"Oh," I say, still confused.

"Would it be okay if I came in so we could talk?"

"Sure, I guess," I say and open the screen door, stepping aside to let him in.

We walk into the living room, and Sammy looks up at us in wonder. "This is my non-biological sister, Sammy."

"Hello," he says and reaches out his hand to her.

She shakes it. "Hi."

"Do you mind if I sit?" He asks.

"No, not at all," Sammy says, and she moves down to the other end of the couch so Mr. Anderson can sit next to me by the recliner. Cosmo growls as he walks by, and I repeat his name. He cowers and lies back down.

I sit in the recliner. "Sorry about the mess," I say, referring to the coffee table. "Everything's just been piling up since Dad passed."

"It's no problem, Peyton. I understand. That's actually why I'm here. On behalf of everyone at ACore, we're deeply sorry for your loss. We know this must be a tough time for you."

"Thank you," I say. "But I still don't understand why you're here?"

"It's regarding your father's life insurance policy."

My heart stops dead in my chest. "His what?"

"His life insurance policy."

I shake my head and look over at Sammy, whose mouth is gaping. "I didn't realize he had one."

"Harry took it out years ago, not long after your mother passed away. I actually knew your Dad pretty well. He was well liked at the factory. We all knew he struggled with things after Lizzy passed away, but he was a nice guy." He opens up his briefcase and pulls out some papers. "Yes, this policy was taken out in January of 2006."

Just a few months after my mother passed away. "He never told me." *Like so many other things.*

"That's actually pretty common. He took the policy out before he got sick, and once you take it out, you're not required to go through any type of medical checks afterward.

If he'd waited until after his diagnosis, he wouldn't have been able to get this. You're a lucky girl."

And now I want to punch this asshole in the throat. "I don't think *lucky* is the right word."

His face pales. "I apologize, I didn't mean it like that. I just meant with him being able to get the life insurance for you."

He goes through a stack of papers and pulls one out. "All I need you to do is sign your name right here and date here. All this states is that you are, indeed, Peyton Katz, the beneficiary of this policy and that I gave you this check."

"I get a check today?"

"We were able to expedite the process for you. So, as long as you sign this, yes."

I take the paper in my hand and glance over it. He hands me a pen and a clipboard, and I sign my name on the line.

"All right, and here is your check."

He hands me a check, and I almost fall out of the recliner.

"Are you... is this... is this a joke?" I ask.

Mr. Anderson shakes his head. "It is not a joke. That is a real check. It might take a few days to clear, banks are a little finicky about that, but yes. That is now yours."

My mouth is on the floor. Sammy shoots up from her seat and sits on the arm of the chair next to me. "Holy. Mother. Fucking. Shit balls."

Mr. Anderson laughs. "You'd be surprised how often I hear that." He closes his briefcase and gets up from the couch. "Well, it was very nice to meet you, Peyton. Your father always said such wonderful things about his daughter. And his adopted daughter, Samantha."

I look up at Sammy and see the tears forming in her eyes.

I stand up and shake his hand. "Yes, thank you. Thank you very much."

"I'll see myself out. You girls have a good day. And don't spend it all in one place, huh?"

I force myself not to roll my eyes.

I smile slightly, and wave him off, and he closes the door behind him.

As soon as he's gone, Sammy and I stare at the check, stunned into silence.

Two Hundred Fifty Thousand Dollars.

I get Two Hundred Fifty Thousand Dollars?

I can pay Lex back.

I can pay off every bill I've ever had. I can go to school anywhere I want. I can give some to Sammy.

I fall back into the recliner and stare at the check with my name on it in thick, black letters.

"Peyton Katz. $250,000."

I stare at this piece of paper in my hands in disbelief. Never in my entire life have I ever imagined having this much money. At least, not that I could call my own. Not even if I saved every single penny I earned. Even if I did become a nurse.

I close my eyes as silent tears stream down my cheeks as I think about my father.

I'd spent my whole life taking care of him, but in death, he's finally taking care of me. And I know I would give every cent of this money back in a heartbeat if it meant I could have my Dad back.

But he's not coming back.

And *this* is what he left me.

44

"Good Old Days" // Macklemore (featuring Kesha)

S ammy and I go right back to the bank to deposit the
check. The teller explains it will take about five business
days for it to clear, and I'm okay with that.

When we get back to the house, Sammy helps me unpack
all my stuff. "We should celebrate," she says.

I eye her, "Celebrate what? The fact that I have no parents
left?"

She walks out of my closet and glares at me, "You know
that's not what I meant. And I have no parents either, in case
you forgot."

I fold the jeans on my lap and eye her sympathetically, "At
least they're still alive."

"What difference does that make? My family has shunned
me because I'm a lesbian. They won't see me, talk to me, or
even acknowledge my existence. So what's the difference? I'm
dead to them."

I put my jeans in the drawer and bite my lip. She's right.

There isn't one. "I guess I hadn't thought about it like that. I'm sorry, Sammy."

"Well, I guess there is *one* difference."

"What?"

"Your Dad loved you."

I blink hard as I stand, and guilt radiates through me as I go to her, flinging my arms around her neck. "He loved you, too." Tears sting both of our eyes now as we think about him, and I pull away.

"We need to get you out of this," she starts. "It's been weeks, and I miss my best friend. I really need her to come back now. I know how hard this is. I miss him, too. But I *really* miss my Peyton."

"I'm standing right here," I say, and try to give her a smile.

She smiles back, "Okay, then let's celebrate that in a few days, you're going to have a shit ton of money for the first time in your entire life. We don't have to go crazy, but we should... I don't know, order a pizza without a coupon!"

I laugh, pulling my phone out of my back pocket and hand it to her.

As she orders, I walk into the hallway. To my right is the bathroom, to my left is the linen closet, and straight ahead is my father's bedroom.

I stand in the doorway and flip on the light.

It's the way it's always looked. A typical single man's bedroom. Clothes in piles, his laundry basket overflowing, since I was the one who did his laundry. I guess the two weekends I was gone, he never thought to do it himself.

His bed is never made. His dresser is dusty and covered with deodorant and aftershave and cologne, and most of them are empty.

I sit down on his bed, and everything in the room smells like him. He always smelled like aftershave and pine. I close my eyes and picture him. He's standing in front of the small mirror attached to the dresser, slapping a little aftershave on his cheeks, glancing back at me, asking, "So, how do I look?"

And I'd smile and say, "Like you're ready to take on a museum that comes to life at night."

That was one of our favorite movies.

Tears stream down my face as I lift his blanket to my nose. An overwhelming feeling of desolation fills my chest and rises in my throat as I fall onto his bed and weep into his sheets. I can hear Sammy down the hall on the phone with Genesee Falls pizza, ordering way more food than we normally do, and all I can think of is how I wish Lex was here. I wish he was lying behind me, holding me as I mourn for my father. But I was so horrible to him earlier. I don't even know where we stand. I don't know if he'll forgive me for the terrible things I said.

I pull myself up to sit and wipe my face off on my shirt. I'm about to stand when my foot kicks something under the bed. I look down and see a rectangular hat box I've never seen before. I get down on my hands and knees and look under his bed.

It's hard to tell without a light, but I think there is more than one.

"Sammy? Can you bring me my phone?"

I pull out the one box I can reach and slide it in front of me. I flip open the lid, and inside are pictures.

Pictures of my Mom.

Pictures of my Dad.

Pictures I've never seen before.

Sammy appears, and hands me my phone. "Pizza is ordered, along with the cheesy bread we always want but never get, and I threw in a dozen hot wings, too, because why the hell not!"

I don't respond. I turn on my flashlight and shine it under the bed. "Holy shit."

"What is it?"

"My Dad had a lot of secrets, Sammy," I say, wiping a stray tear on my shirt.

She bends down and looks. "Whoa."

Under the bed are four more boxes. I'm not sure what's in them, but Sammy and I manage to get all of them out.

I go through one at a time, each one different from the last. I look at the first box and realize something. "Sammy, look," I say as I point to the front of the box. "They're all dated."

H+L - 1999.

H+L+P- 2000.

H+L+P - 2001.

H+L+P - 2002.

All except for the last box.

I open the last box and realize these are pictures of my mother's last year, the last few months before she died. And inside this box is a camera.

"But what about 2003 and 2004?" Sammy asks.

I shake my head. "I'm not sure. Maybe they're in the closet? Or hidden away somewhere else? I don't think he could fit anymore boxes under his bed."

I pick up the camera and look around the box. All the pieces seem to be here; the battery, the charger, the zoom lens attachment, the external flash.

"Peyton, look," she says. "There has to be fifty SD cards in here."

"Maybe that's where 2003 and 2004 are?" I suggest.

"Maybe? If your Mom never got around to printing them."

"You know what this means, right?"

"We're going to get all of these printed, aren't we?"

I look down at all the SD cards. "Yeah. We are."

45

"Out of the Woods" // Taylor Swift

I walk into the pharmacy the next day, not because I have to work, but because I need to speak to Sydney. I look around the store in awe.

Everything is finished. The walls are painted, the new frozen section is up and running, the floors have been waxed, the back of the store looks brand new. I can't believe how much work Lex put into this tiny, small-town pharmacy.

I wave to Emily and Lisa and they smile at me sympathetically. "Hey, Peyton," Emily says.

Madison is leaning against the counter staring at her nails and looks at me, quickly straightening. "Hey, Peyton," she starts, seemingly nervous. "I heard about your Dad. I'm sorry."

I give her a small smile, "Thanks."

"How's everything going?" Emily asks as I hear her pour pills into a bottle.

I shrug, "It's hard. But life goes on. I'm still trying to figure out how." I admit.

Emily sets a bottle of tablets down on the counter, leaves the pharmacy and crashes into me with a hug I wasn't expecting. I hug her back. "If you need anything, we're all here for you."

"Thank you."

We break apart and with one final glance, she goes back to work and I head into the break room.

I'm half expecting to see Lex, but I'm relieved when I don't. I'm not quite ready to face him yet. Sydney is sitting in the office chair, working on the computer. "Peyton! Girl, we've missed you!"

She stands up and hugs me. "I know. I'm sorry I've been MIA lately."

"Honey, don't you worry about that. I've got your job waiting for you when you're ready to come back."

"I came here to ask you for a favor."

"Of course, sweetheart. Anything."

"Are there any empty boxes I could have? There's a lot of stuff I've got to pack up at the house."

"We've always got boxes. You know where they are. Take as many as you need."

I smile. "Thanks, Sydney."

She looks at me. "Do you know when you're planning on coming back? I could put you down on the schedule anytime you want."

I take a deep breath. "Actually, I need to talk to you about that, too."

I'M STANDING OUTSIDE OF THE ELEVATOR TO LEX'S APARTMENT, trying to figure out how the hell I'm supposed to get up there without a key. I approach the front desk, and the doorman smiles at me. "Hello, Miss. How can I help you?"

"I'm trying to get up to my boyfriend's apartment. Lex Kingston. But I don't have a key."

"That's all right. I've seen you two together before. I've got a key right here," he says, and he waves me over to the elevator. He opens the door and puts his key in the slot and presses the button, but steps out before the doors close.

"Thank you!"

And he smiles at me.

My insides are twisting together. I haven't talked to him since yesterday morning when he showed up at my house and I said the most awful things to him.

And I feel horrible.

The elevator opens, and I step into his apartment. "Lex?"

His apartment is eerily quiet as I walk out into the living room. I see him standing out on the terrace, talking on the phone. I make my way out there and stand in the doorway and knock on the glass door.

He turns, surprised, and looks at me. "Hey Reggie, I'm going to have to call you back, okay? Yeah, I'll talk to you soon. Okay. Bye."

He hangs up the phone and looks at me, his expression seemingly shocked. He slides his phone in his pocket along with his hands and stares down at his feet.

And I think he's about to cry.

"Hi," I say.

"Hi," he replies.

I stand in the doorway, both of us silent for a long moment before I take in a breath. "I'm sorry," I start, tears already clouding my vision.

Stupid fucking tears! Will you ever end?

I breathe and start again, "I didn't mean what I said. I was just shocked and grieving and angry at my Dad for leaving me and I took it out on you, and I'm sorry."

Lex finally looks up at me with bloodshot eyes. "But that

came from somewhere, Peyton. People don't just say the things you said."

I look down at my hands, playing with the sleeve of my hoodie, "I don't know how to fix this. Please, just tell me how to fix this because I cannot lose you and my Dad at the same time. I will not survive that, Lex. My heart will stop beating if I lose you, too. Please. I'm sorry. I love you," I say through a fit of sobs because now, I'm officially terrified.

He blinks hard then closes the distance between us, taking me in his arms, crushing me into his chest. And I feel like I can finally breathe again. He shushes me as I cry against his chest, kissing the top of my head. "I love you, too. That's why I did what I did." We break apart, his hands sliding down my arms and slipping into mine. "I get that money is a big deal to you when you don't have it. I understand you've struggled most of your life, but I don't want to see you struggle. I don't want the person I love most in this world to suffer when I have the ability to ease that suffering. I don't think of it as a hand out or charity. I think of it as taking care of the people you love. You took care of your Dad and Sammy when they needed you the only way you could," he brushes a loose hair behind my ear. "So, I decided it was time someone finally take care of you."

I lean my cheek against his hand and my eyes flutter closed. "Well, you aren't the only one who's finally taking care of me," I say, and open my eyes to meet his gaze.

Lex quirks an eyebrow, "What do you mean?"

"Well, before I get into that," I start and take a breath. "I've decided to take some time off from *Kingston's*."

His eyes grow wide as his hand drops from my face. "Seriously?"

"Yeah. Not forever. I talked to Sydney and she's given me a six-month leave of absence, but I also have to run it by you."

Lex looks confused, but doesn't argue. "If that's what you need to do, I won't stop you. And I'll make sure your job will be waiting for you when you get back. If you decide you still want it."

"Thank you. That's not the only thing," I start, twisting the sleeve of my hoodie between my fingers. "I've decided I'm not going back to GVCC next year."

His brows knit together as he looks at me very confused. "Okay, I'm officially lost. What's happened in the last twenty-four hours that I'm missing?"

"A few hours after you left yesterday, a lawyer from ACore Electric showed up at my house with a life insurance policy my Dad left me that I didn't know about."

"Wow."

"Yeah. Two hundred and fifty grand."

"Holy shit, Peyton."

I look at him with as much confidence as I can muster. "Lex, I want to pay you back for the medical bills."

Lex puts his hands up, shaking his head. "No. Absolutely not."

"But I don't need you to do that for me anymore. I have the money—"

"I didn't pay that for you because I wanted you to pay me back. I did it because I love you, and at the time, you needed it. Please, keep the money. Use it for school. Use it to travel. Go see the world. Do whatever you want with it. Just don't think you owe me anything."

I let out a breath. "I had a feeling you were going to say that."

Lex takes my hand. "Well, they don't call you 'Community College Girl' for nothing."

I roll my eyes at his little nickname for me. "Well, I'm not Community College Girl anymore."

"So, what are you going to be?"

"I don't know, but *Mrs. Peyton Kingston* has a nice ring to it, don't you think?"

Lex drops my hand, and for the first time in a long time, he bellows out a laugh so hard, I think he might choke. His face turns bright red as he struggles to take in air, and his laughter is so infectious, I start laughing with him. "You're getting a bit ahead of yourself," he manages to say.

"That's what you get for calling me 'Community College Girl'."

Lex shakes his head at me, coughing, "And it was well deserved."

I give him a minute to catch his breath before I say, "I'm also going to put the house up for sale."

He looks at me, surprised. "Really?"

"It's just not the same without him there. It's too hard to be there alone, and I need somewhere to start over, start new," I say, and take a breath. "And if it's okay with you, I'd like that place to be with you."

Lex takes my face in his hands. "It's definitely okay with me." His lips are on mine, soft and sweet. He pulls away, and I can already feel my heart starting to heal.

46

"Where We Come Alive" // Ruelle

Four Weeks Later

Over the past few weeks, Uncle Jack and Michelle, along with Lex and Sammy, have helped me pack up the house. I let Jack take anything he wanted of my Dads, which Michelle wasn't too happy with me about, once we opened the garage and saw what a shit show that was.

Most of my things are in Lex's spare bedroom. Even though we share his room, he wanted me to have space for my things, for all of the pictures I now own and refuse to get rid of.

Sammy and I were able to get every single picture printed from the SD cards we found under my Dad's bed. Michelle, Sammy, and I took all of the pictures from my father's boxes, and made a collage that took up the whole right wall of the bedroom, from floor to ceiling. Over a thousand pictures of my parents, some of them together, some of them alone, and some of them with the three of us.

Every time I step back and look at it, a song plays in my head, a song neither of my parents would know, but I know my Mom would understand.

Where We Come Alive by Ruelle.

Because this is where I come alive.

Ever since I found my mother's camera, I've been playing with it. Taking pictures of random things, of Sammy and Lex and Michelle and Jack and Cosmo and clouds and flowers. It's different from just using my iPhone.

I don't know if I'm any good at photography. But it makes me feel closer to my mother.

I never got to know my Mom. But maybe with these pictures, maybe with her camera, I'll be able to see the world through her eyes. Maybe I'll get a better idea of who my parents were, of who my father was before alcohol took over his life. Of who my mother was before she was diagnosed with cancer. Of who I was when I had two living, breathing parents.

WE'RE STANDING OUTSIDE OF THE HOUSE WITH THE U-HAUL packed. I take the For Sale sign and stick it into the grass in front of the house.

Jack and Michelle hold Cosmo by the leash as he whimpers at me. I bend down on my knees and scratch him behind the ears. "You be a good boy for Uncle Jack, okay?"

"Are you sure you want us to take him?" Michelle asks.

I stand and nod. "Cosmo needs a real home with a real family. And he's really good with little kids, he's very protective. And with all the traveling Lex and I are doing, I can't just leave him in the apartment for two months."

"And we're not allowed to have pets in our apartment," Sammy says, disappointed.

"Okay. We'll keep an eye on the house for you while you're gone," Michelle says.

"Thanks. I told the real estate agent I'd be out of the country for a few months. I gave her your number, in case there are any offers," I say as I turn to Lex, who's leaning against the Mercedes, hands in his pockets.

I was so happy when he told me he took time off from his new businesses to travel around Europe with me. He'll have to work remotely via video chat, but he promised me it would only be for emergencies.

And even after all the traveling, I'll still have enough money left to transfer to a four-year university. It will last me through a master's degree if I want one.

I'm still not sure what I want to do yet, but everyone keeps telling me I've got time to figure it out.

I look up at the house one last time before turning to Jack and hugging him. "Thank you," I say. Then I turn to Michelle. "For everything."

I pull away, and they both smile at me. "You're more than welcome, Peyton. We love you, kiddo."

"I love you, too."

And then I turn to Sammy, who is crying, like hardcore, legit balling her eyes out. "I'll be back in two months. I'm not leaving forever." I say and pull her into my arms. "Then things will go back to semi-normal. I'll be living in Octavia with Lex. It's not that far away."

"What am I going to do for two whole months without my best friend?"

"You're going to be fine. You can text and call me all you want. I have an international calling plan now. And we can FaceTime."

"I'm going to miss you, and all your crazy music."

I smirk at her. "Don't worry," I say, and hand Sammy her

phone. "I made you a playlist to remember me by." Sammy smiles with tears in her eyes, and hugs me again.

"Guys, I hate to break this up but, we've got a flight to catch," Lex reminds me.

"Okay, I've got to go. Love you, sister."

"Love you, too."

I slowly back away toward Lex's car and wave everyone goodbye.

Lex and I get in the car, and I pull out my brand new iPhone, connecting it to his Bluetooth.

"What song should I play?" I ask.

He looks at me and scoffs, "I learned a long time ago not to get in the middle of Peyton and her playlists."

"But what's a good traveling-to-the-airport song?"

"How should I know? You're the music aficionado."

"Fine," I sigh and scroll through my songs. I think of my parents, of all the pictures I'd discovered and put up on the wall of our apartment, of the memories they made together, that *we* made together, and I remember the songs Michelle told me my mother loved. I look down at my phone and press on the screen, and *I Melt With You* by Modern English comes blaring through the speakers.

And I smile.

Around my neck is my mother's old digital camera that I've been playing with for the past few weeks. I bought new SD cards with bigger storage space, so I can take all the pictures my mother had planned. All the cities and art galleries and museums she wanted to take me to. Lex and I are going together.

And I couldn't be happier.

"Have you figured that thing out yet?" Lex asks as he pulls out onto the road.

"I think so," I say, and I turn the camera on Lex, and snap his photo.

THE END.

ACKNOWLEDGMENTS

Bitter Sweet Symphony // The Verve

I keep asking myself if this is real. Did I really write a book? Did I, after all these years of writing and having ideas and starting stories, finally finish a whole book? Well, it only took fourteen years.

The basic bones of this story have been inside my head ever since I was eighteen years old, back when I worked at *Eckerd Drugs*—a pharmacy that is not around anymore. It was a small store in a small town and I *didn't* work in the pharmacy, but in the front of the store, where you buy all the other products like drinks and snacks and make-up.

So, if you're wondering where the inspiration for this story came from—there you go. But only the part about a girl who works at a drug store. The rest of *Peyton's Playlist* came from totally different parts of my life and my imagination.

I'd like to thank my Mom, Linda, for being the first person to read the first draft in two days, and telling me it's "fantastic," and for promising me you're not being biased.

My friend, Yehudit, for being the second person to read the entire book, reassuring me over and over again that it doesn't suck, and telling me, "No, do not delete that scene!" Even though I really wanted to delete that scene. I'm glad I didn't.

To my son, Dylan, thank you for existing. Thank you for being the sweetest, funniest, most generous teenager in the entire world. Thank you for always believing in me, especially when I didn't believe in myself. Thank you for being my number one fan. I love you more than anything, *ever*.

To my best friend—my soul sister—Katie. You saw things in my book that I didn't. You were the first person who actually helped me make this book better. *Peyton's Playlist* would not be what it is today if it were not for you. Thank you for being my person.

To the only other human being in this world that I love as much as I love Dylan—my Siddha Bean—thank you for posing as the model for the cover of this book. It's perfect. I had this weird little vision in my head and you helped bring it to life. No one else could have made it better. I love you so much, Bubby.

To the man I call my husband, Matt, thank you for all of the support you've given me over the years. I know contemporary romance isn't your genre. If we're being honest, it's not even really mine. But sometimes as a writer, and a person, we need to step outside of our comfort zone and try something new. You've been patient with me for a decade, but it's finally happened. I wrote a book. It's a thing. I'm a big kid now!

To all the BETA readers, whether you're an old friend, a co-worker of my husband, an editor I found on Twitter, or someone from Fiverr, you have no idea how much you've helped me. Just by reading the book and giving me feedback of any kind. Thank you.

And finally, to every single person who has read, or is planning on reading this book—thank you. From the bottom of my heart, *thank you.* Creating art is wonderful and fun and exciting. Sharing it with the world is terrifying and nerve-wrecking. I don't know if I'm alone in this—I think it's a bit presumptuous to assume so—but I spent a lot of time worrying about what was going to happen once this book is released into the world.

Will people like it? Will people even read it? Can I write a book? What if I say the wrong thing? Am I doing this right? Am I doing this wrong? Am I doing everything wrong? Do I belong here? What am I even doing here?

I don't know if I'm doing it all right. But what I do know is that I need to stop beating myself up over it, and realize that *I wrote a book.* I did something I've been dreaming of doing since I was twenty-two years old and now it's out in the world. And that's a win. So, I'm going to celebrate that win.

We should all celebrate our wins. Each and every one of us, no matter what our anxiety tells us. Because if I've learned anything from this, it's that your anxiety is lying to you. So, tell your impostor syndrome to kindly fuck off, and enjoy life! Because as far as we know, we only get one.

ABOUT THE AUTHOR

Jessica L Russell has a deep love of young adult fantasy novels and has been writing stories since the fifth grade. She has an associate's degree from Broome Community College. She lives in Upstate New York with her husband, two teenage boys, and three cats.

You can follow her on Twitter @authorJLR and on Instagram @authorJLR.